Post-Adolescence

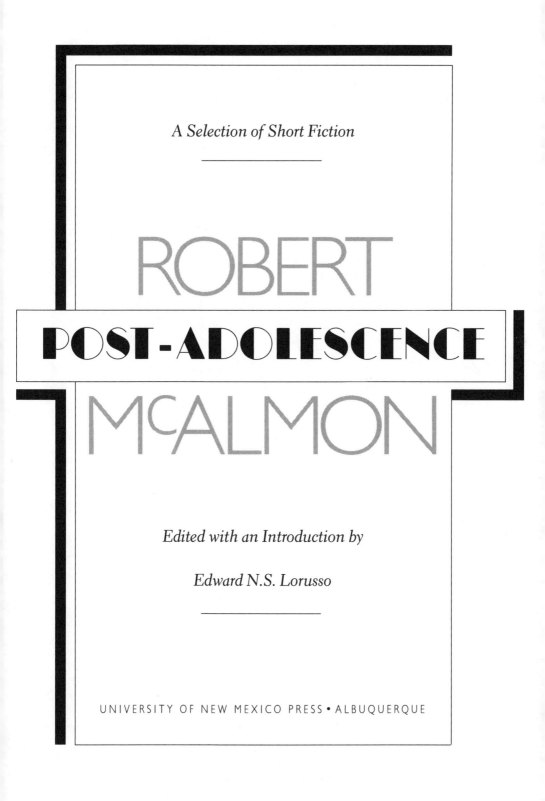

A Selection of Short Fiction

ROBERT

POST-ADOLESCENCE

McALMON

Edited with an Introduction by

Edward N.S. Lorusso

UNIVERSITY OF NEW MEXICO PRESS • ALBUQUERQUE

Library of Congress Cataloging-in-Publication Data

McAlmon, Robert, 1896–1956.
   Post-adolescence : a selection of short fiction / by Robert
McAlmon ; edited, with an introduction, by Edward N.S. Lorusso.
     p. cm.
   ISBN 0-8263-1310-8
   I. Lorusso, Edward N. S. II. Title.
PS3525.A1143A6 1991
813'.52—dc20   91-18987
                                          CIP

SC
MCALMON

CONTENTS

ACKNOWLEDGMENTS

For the publication of this book I am much indebted to several people for their interest, encouragement, and prodding. Beth Hadas of the University of New Mexico Press was always available to listen to my tales of woe as I tried to gather stories for this collection; my close friends, Phil Perkins and Gayle Creighton, never hesitated to offer advice, both positive and negative, whether or not I asked for it. To all, thanks.

This book is dedicated to

P H I L   A N D   G A Y L E

Introduction

f ROBERT MCALMON had written only 'A Boy's Discovery' and 'A Vacation's Job,'" says Kay Boyle in her afterword to *A Hasty Bunch*, "he would be more than worth remembering." The point that Boyle is making is that McAlmon has not been remembered, either by critics or readers.

Despite (or perhaps because of) the fact that he could not get an American publisher during the 1920s and 1930s, McAlmon did write more than the above-mentioned short stories; he wrote lots of short stories and novels and poems and essays and memoirs. But during his lifetime (1896–1956), Robert McAlmon saw few of his works published, and most of what was published he printed through his own Contact Publishing Company.

Of course the simple act of writing has never equaled the fact of publication. There are probably countless drawers and closets and garages throughout the world bulging with unpubishable works. The aspect of quality needs to be considered. The question then, in the case at hand, is, Was McAlmon's stuff any good? The answer is a qualified "yes." Although McAlmon had his backers in literary figures like Boyle, Ezra Pound, and William Carlos Williams, there has always been the nagging problem of McAlmon's own sloppiness (exacerbated by his self-publishing) regarding such matters as punctuation, spelling, and consistency.

It is sometimes difficult to wade through his writing because of his sloppiness, for there are instances of names changing, unidentified dialogue, and the abrupt endings that do just that—end. But these matters could have been adjusted by any good editor. So the modern reader must look beyond the cosmetics of McAlmon's writing in order to judge its merits. And I believe that the sought-for quality is there.

If the old adage about writing about what one knows has any credence, McAlmon certainly seems to have been a believer. He generally wrote about himself. This does not mean that his fiction is limited in scope or subject. While he did not write about wars or history or bullfighting, he did write about life, death, birth, sex, and the wonderment of existence.

In nearly all his short fiction, McAlmon questions something. His concerns are the same as the cares and worries of the people he grew up with in the American Midwest as well as those of the sophisticates of Greenwich Village and Paris. The realization that the twentieth century was vastly different from the preceding century haunts McAlmon's fiction. Like many of the other expatriates who lived and worked in 1920s Paris, he saw new forces at work in the twentieth-century universe, forces that compelled humanity to redirect itself, to break with the old traditions.

In "A Vacation's Job," David states: "The only ambition I have is to understand, to be able to accept reality instead of try to re-create the universe. . . . the whole process of life is a miserably futile one." To combat this fatalism, McAlmon believed simply in living. Memoirs and biographies about the expatriates (including McAlmon's excellent *Being Geniuses Together*) abound in examples of McAlmon's taking his own advice: he lived. Perhaps he even lived up to fellow expatriate Natalie Barney's often quoted phrase about getting more out of life than is in it.

In "The Psychoanalyzed Girl," the narrator asks the title character, Dania, "Why stand on the threshold of 'experience' eternally saying that you don't live, but merely exist?" This question is wasted on Dania because she is attempting to discover some inward truth instead of just living her life. She is one of McAlmon's victims and one of his reproaches to an American society that blindly follows worn-out ideals to the grave.

Robert McAlmon dropped out of college in California and headed east to learn about life firsthand. Like David in "A Vacation's Job," McAlmon believed that college could teach nothing relevant, that a life fully lived was a successful life. McAlmon knocked around Greenwich Village in the early 1920s and met his future wife, the British heiress and poet Bryher.

In fairy-tale fashion, she proposed marriage to him and they sailed away to honeymoon in Europe on an ocean liner owned by her father. But the fairy tale did not have a particularly happy ending for McAlmon. Bryher was a lesbian, then having an affair with the American poet Hilda Doolittle (known as H.D.), who accompanied the newlyweds on their honeymoon. As grotesque as this sounds, it proved to be a quick education in the ways of the world, and McAlmon was an apt pupil.

Bryher gave McAlmon a large allowance and, upon their eventual divorce, an even larger settlement. The wags about Paris quickly dubbed him "McAlimony." But being a pragmatist, McAlmon set out to publish his books and the books of other promising writers then in Paris. He started Contact Publishing Company and in rapid succession published Ernest Hemingway's *Three Stories and Ten Poems*, Gertrude Stein's *The Making of Americans*, and his own *Village*. McAlmon quickly became the leading publisher of the avant garde and the unknown.

During the decade of the 1920s, McAlmon would publish books by Bryher, William Carlos Williams, Djuna Barnes, Mina

Loy, H.D., and Marsden Hartley. He would also self-publish *A Hasty Bunch, Post-Adolescence,* and *Portrait of a Generation.*

Because of the content of many of these books, American authorities quickly banned any publications bearing the Contact imprint. Of course many of the writers McAlmon published in Paris found publishers and audiences elsewhere, but McAlmon himself did not. The history of his inability to find an American publisher is as fascinating as it is frustrating.

During his lifetime, McAlmon saw only one volume of poetry (*Not Alone Lost*) published in his native land. After his death in 1956, a few reprints appeared. *Distinguished Air* appeared as *There Was a Rustle of Black Silk Stockings,* a cheap attempt to cash in on the sexual content of McAlmon's stories. It is long out of print. *A Hasty Bunch* surfaced in the early 1970s as part of the "lost fiction" series from Southern Illinois University Press, but it too is out of print. It was not until 1990 that *Village,* written in 1924, made its American debut. Kay Boyle wrote alternating chapters to a heavily edited reprint of McAlmon's memoirs, *Being Geniuses Together;* it remains one of the best portraits of the Paris crowd in the 1920s. Robert Knoll used several of McAlmon's short stories and excerpts from the novels to create a "self-portrait" of the writer. The present volume includes the American debuts of some of the stories originally published in *The Indefinite Huntress* as well as the first American publication of *Post-Adolescence,* McAlmon's first novel.

Why? This question has been asked by modern critics as well as by McAlmon's contemporaries, which list would be lengthy. Sanford Smoller, who wrote McAlmon's biography, only touches on the stories and events that surround the mystery of McAlmon's inability to find an American publisher. Perhaps the reason rests with his enemies—and he had many; perhaps the homophobia that was rampant in the America of the 1920s and 1930s is another. Ultimately, it does not matter.

McAlmon's novels and short fiction are being published now. Reviewers have been quick to note the keen eye, the caustic wit, and the spare prose of Robert McAlmon. James R. Mellow, in *The New York Times Book Review,* noted that "*Village* is, structurally, a tour de force: a long, remarkably sustained fugue on the theme of village life, an extended epic of the lives, queer alliances and frail family bonds of plain people. . . ." The review also proclaims that the novel is "startlingly fresh for its time and, for that matter, any time." The novel compares favorably with Sherwood Anderson's *Winesburg, Ohio* and Sinclair Lewis's *Main Street.*

But this posthumous acclaim is half a century too late. When he died in Desert Hot Springs in February 1956, he was a long-forgotten literary figure. Starting from his return to this country at the outbreak of World War II, his health was in a steady decline. From the boulevards of Paris and the beaches of the Mediterranean, McAlmon spent his last years in the American Southwest, slowly dying of tuberculosis and alcoholism.

*　*　*

The fiction in this collection has appeared in several different collections and editions. Rather than reprint any one existing collection, I have sought to show the diversity of Robert McAlmon's writing by picking and choosing from the various available books. The key word here is "available." I sought in vain for a copy of *Distinguished Air*; it was not to be had. The ongoing inaccessibility of McAlmon's writings continues to plague those of us interested in reevaluating his work, and, in turn, continues the cycle of McAlmon's oblivion. The current collection, including the short novel *Post-Adolescence,* represents work published by McAlmon from approximately 1920 to 1932, his entire working life.

Post-Adolescence is a short autobiographical piece written just after McAlmon's Greenwich Village period. Ford Madox Ford called it a "journal in time"; it's really more of a portrait of the artist as a young man. McAlmon fictionalizes the literary and artistic figures he met in New York and relates a story about a young man's obsession with his awakening sexual desires and his musings on the relevance of existence.

Although it was written in 1920 and not published until 1923, *Post-Adolescence* is admirably frank in its treatment of sex. In the novel's opening section, Peter, who is McAlmon, has a wet dream:

> *He dozed. He was caressing somebody who did not resist, and he was apathetic, with no attitude in his mind at all, no will—drifting—he was yielding—was being buoyed to sensation—gradually an effusion of nervous reaction—gratification?—then his mind was black of imagination, though there had been no dream. He awoke, uncomfortable. O the devil! He moved to the other side of the bed....*

Although the scene is not graphic by today's standards, it may be the first description of a wet dream in American fiction. Throughout the novel, Peter grapples with his own desires as he attempts to make some sense out of life in New York and life in general. The modern reader may need a score card in order to discover who is who in *Post-Adolescence*.

Peter is Robert McAlmon

Jim Boyle is William Carlos Williams

Nellie is Florence Williams

Brander Ogden is Marsden Hartley

Gusta Rolph is Mina Loy

Vere St. Vitus is Edna St. Vincent Millay

Martha Wallus is Marianne Moore

Dora is Lola Ridge

Reginald is Alfred Kreymbourg

O'Brian is Kenneth Burke

The only missing person here is Djuna Barnes. For whatever reason, McAlmon, who met Barnes during the Greenwich Village days and remained a friend and associate, saw fit to omit

her from the above catalog. There is also no mention of his
meeting Bryher and H.D. But this is not unusual; McAlmon
remained tight-lipped about his relationship with Bryher. Indeed, he broke off his friendship with William Carlos Williams
when the latter wrote in his autobiography about McAlmon's
being duped by the lesbians.

Much of the "action" in *Post-Adolescence* is interior mono-
logue, perhaps a foreshadowing of some of *Ulysses*, as Peter
tries to unlock the universal mysteries. Much of Peter's mind
is revealed through his attempts at writing poetry. In a coffee
house, Peter writes:

> *May not some day the ocean waves*
> *Keep rolling so the earth will too*
> *Rise into waves and hurl us under*
> *And let the tide recoiling suck us back*
> *And down, down, down*
> *Down to depths never to be excavated*
> *Never to be reported on any page of history.*
> > *What does one do?*
> > *What does one do?*
> *Will the cold clear sky erect before us*
> *Break like thin glass and crash us under....*

The young poet in the novel pushes aside the poem; he is in too
good a mood to continue it.

McAlmon drew freely from his New York experiences in the
writing of *Post-Adolescence*. He describes the rounds of parties,
the lack of money, and his work as an artists' model. In another
remarkable section, McAlmon reveals his own self-love:

> *He sat on the model stand.... Nice lines he had after all,*
> *there around the belly particularly. It was nice being slen-*
> *der.... He ran his lips along his arms, his hands up and*
> *down his legs. Legs are graceful things; slender, deer-like, and*
> *how fine the skin is on the side of the foot, frogbelly fine*

with ethereal tiny pores and pearly white. That's the nicest skin on the body. He wondered if he could touch it with his mouth, and strained to do so. . . .

Even as a very young writer, McAlmon was keenly aware of and interested in his own body. In several stories, a young boy, a version of McAlmon, is described as a beautiful and desirable sex object, usually lusted after by a burly older man. In "Green Grow the Grasses," Antoine, an older man who drives an oil wagon, gives a ride to the young narrator of the story. The boy notices that Antoine is "the most beautiful person I had ever seen" and notes "his dark eyes, and their beauty." Of course, in the best fantasy fashion, Antoine reciprocates: "You're a nice looking kid. How old are you?" Also, "You have the prettiest eyes I ever saw. . . ." This is a love affair as imagined by an innocent boy. As they ride along, the man puts his hand on the boy's leg and says, "You're a well set up kid." The boy repeats this phrase several times during the story. McAlmon is wise enough to know (or remember) that this kind of encounter would whirl in a boy's mind. The retelling of this incident may also reveal something about McAlmon's personality.

Boys are not the only ones scrutinized in McAlmon's short fiction. In stories like "The Little Ninny," "The Psychoanalyzed Girl," and "The Fast Girl," McAlmon takes a look at the flapper, that fast-living creature of the twenties. The little ninny of the title is Goldie, the party girl who has gone through all the men in town. Goldie faces a dilemma: she has such a bad reputation that no one of any social standing will marry her. She may have eyes for Tom, the local high school athlete who has gone away to college, but she settles for Tim, a local nobody. Even though Goldie must marry beneath her, she has the last laugh: Tom dies; Goldie has a successful marriage and several children.

"The Fast Girl" is Louise Dutton. The town is divided on her: "One party said that Louise rouged, screwed like a mink, and only got away with it because she was clever; the other side said that her color was naturally vivid. . . ." But like Goldie,

xviii

Louise is nobody's fool. She lives fast and hard. Louise makes arrangements for a rendezvous in Minneapolis with a man who slips her ten $20 bills. A few weeks later, the man returns from the city. "He had not seen Louise Dutton. . . . Neither Jerry nor the town ever saw her again."

"The Psychoanalyzed Girl" predates by several decades all of Woody Allen's slightly paranoid heroines. Dania is a beautiful girl and she knows it. She cannot enjoy life because she is always analyzing it and herself. She flirts with a particular Frenchman who wears a red scarf around his neck, but cannot do anything.

Not one of these girls is what she at first appears to be. They all use their sexuality, but it doesn't necessarily gain them happiness. Dania is sexually dysfunctional; Louise is gang raped; Goldie never forgets her true love. True to McAlmon's universe, life is made up of futility.

McAlmon's autobiographical boys' tales are among his best stories. In "Green Grow the Grasses," the young narrator matures to discover that his homosexual love for Antoine was just a phase. Through adult's eyes, the narrator sees Antoine as a failed, seedy character, but this appraisal is necessary in order for the boy to commence with his life and not pine for his idealized love. "Potato Picking" was one of McAlmon's most praised stories. It was included in *Best Short Stories of 1929.* "A Boy's Discovery" is an excellent story about sexual initiation among a group of prepubescent children. It is difficult to say which boy makes what discovery. Arguments could be made for Harry Wright, who dies of lockjaw; Harold Morris, who teaches Harry about life; or Tuffy Thomas, who thinks he knows all about sex. The story's ending is ambiguous, but the tone it captures when describing the boys' bartering with Ruthie and Hazel for their ten-year-old wares is brilliant.

All in all, the group of boys' stories must rank with the best American short fiction. McAlmon is able to recapture perfectly the tone of childish innocence and the cadence of the prairie. In no story does he do this better than in "The Jack Rabbit Drive."

This is a wonderfully complex story about two children who sneak behind their parents' backs to resell beer bottles to a local bar-keep. Horace and Sally comb the alleys of their prairie town in search of returnable beer bottles in order to buy candy. McAlmon once again captures the fears and false bravado of children. When Horace and Sally emerge from the saloon, gun shots are being fired and crowds of enraged people are rushing toward them. But it is only the jack rabbit drive. McAlmon quickly turns the tale from one of childhood pranks and whimsy to one of horror as thousands of rabbits are slaughtered in the bloody stampede. In one stroke, little Horace learns all about life.

Paralleling *Post-Adolescence* are two stories about young manhood. "New York Harbor" recounts the author's life on a barge. As this story describes, he was a virtual prisoner. Although the city was only a mile away, says the narrator, "the captain wouldn't let me lower the boat. He said it leaked." So, while trapped on the barge, the young man fights bed bugs, trades insults with the captain's slatternly wife, and examines the strange passersby—corpses as well as condoms floating downstream.

McAlmon does some of his best writing in "A Vacation's Job," the story of a young man who drops out of college to learn about life. While working on a dam project somewhere in the Southwest, David meets an assortment of societal misfits. There's Old Man Woods, an engineer who was happy to be blasting—it didn't matter where; a cook, a "horribly dirty Mexican with a screw fastened into a wood stump serving as one arm"; Charlie Ling, "in the same Chinese slippers, and black slipover shirt that he'd worn two years before." But what David really learns in this long story is that there is no escape from the facade of intellectualism; he has debates with Old Man Woods and another man about politics, religion, philosophy, and sex.

Another story that deals with McAlmon's migratory ways is "Mexican Interval." This long account of the culture and people and cantinas of Mexico, notable for its unique locale, mirrors McAlmon's dissatisfaction with life outside of Paris. Although there are scenic wonders in Mexico and in the American Southwest (there is a long reverie about the desert landscape in "A Vacation's Job"), what McAlmon craved was "life and lots of it."

Four stories revolve around the worldly McAlmon, that blasé denizen of the Parisian demimonde. In "Light Woven into Wavespray," the narrator sums up McAlmon's philosophy about a rootless existence: "Fearsome inaction is a bitterer experience than any other." This warning is similar to that given to the psychoanalyzed girl—live! Any sort of experience is better than no experience. Kay Boyle says that in this story, "McAlmon comes closer than anyone who has written of him . . . to a definition of his predicament as writer and as man."

And if anyone "lives" in McAlmon's fiction, it is certainly Toodles Dawson of "Evening on the Riviera." Toodles is a completely self-centered older woman who throws parties for herself, inviting young gigolos. Although she apparently lives off the generosity of another couple, Toodles never relents in her hedonistic lifestyle of booze and young men. "Toodles bore no one ill will, except at moments when they stood in the way of her desire to bubble on. . . ." Toodles is a woman who has never learned that there is an end to everything. As the story reaches its conclusion, another couple overhears Toodles begging one of the gigolos to stay with her. It seems that the private Toodles is a different woman from the public one.

On the opposite end of the scale is Miss Forbes, the elderly English lady who has never heard a phonograph before. In "Machine-Age Romance," the narrator, who describes himself as a "modern," befriends Miss Forbes on an ocean crossing. The "romance" is of course platonic; each person appears to have something the other lacks. In many ways, it is McAlmon's sweetest romance. The world-weary narrator frets about the English lady, who is going to Vancouver, but realizes that he, as a representative of the modern age, and she, a symbol of the past century, must part. The peripheral characters are unsavory types. There is a gaggle of old maids, one of whom is a man; another man is referred to as an "English lily"; also aboard is a boorish couple, the Brisbanes. If these people represent McAlmon's view of contemporary society, one can readily see why he is drawn to Miss Forbes and her nineteenth-century naïveté.

The only story set in Paris, "The Highly Prized Pajamas," is a cynical tale about the Parisienne prostitutes (*poules*) who inhabit the Latin Quarter. This is a subject McAlmon knows well. Yoland, the focus of the story, is a wild woman. We see her in a series of relationships in which she is in turn the abused and the abuser. She sharpens her fingernails into claws. Somehow, Yoland always comes out ahead. But then she meets Mr. Stout and her world turns upside down. She allows Stout to buy her clothes and jewelry and to give her money. When he finally goes back to Canada, Yoland and her pig-faced friend, Andra, howl about how they took Stout for everything he was worth—except a magnificent pair of blue pajamas.

It can only be hoped that this collection of Robert McAlmon's short fiction, along with the recent success of *Village*, will help find him his proper place in American letters. Several of these stories are true gems; others have memorable sections. McAlmon's writing is never free of flaws; he can still produce a sentence like, "Paul separated and joined David" (from "A Vacation's Job"). Looking behind these stylistic oddities, however, one will find a unique American experience and an often comic and sometimes cynical vision of life—his life—one that was lived and described to the fullest.

Edward N.S. Lorusso

Although McAlmon's books were plagued by poor typesetting and careless proofreading, which resulted in books with far too many typographical errors, the editing of this collection has been kept to a minimum in order to maintain, as much as possible, the original flavor of McAlmon's writing. Obvious misspellings and typos have been corrected; some punctuation has been standardized; and only in a few places have I eliminated superfluous punctuation in order to make a passage read more clearly.

Ed Lorusso
Albuquerque
January 1991

Explorations. London: The Egoist Press, 1921

A Hasty Bunch. Paris: Contact, 1922

A Companion Volume. Paris: Contact, 1923

Post-Adolescence. Paris: Contact, 1923

Village. Paris: Contact, 1924

Distinguished Air. Paris: Three Mountain Press, 1925

The Portrait of a Generation. Paris: Contact, 1926

North America, Continent of Conjecture. Paris:
    Contact, 1929

The Indefinite Huntress and Other Stories. Paris:
    Crosby Continental Editions, 1932

Not Alone Lost. Norfolk, Conn.: New Directions,
    1937

Being Geniuses Together. London: Secker and
    Warburg, 1938

McAlmon and the Lost Generation. ed. Robert E.
    Knoll. Lincoln: University of Nebraska Press,
    1962

There Was a Rustle of Black Silk Stockings. New York:
    Belmont, 1963

Being Geniuses Together. Revised by Kay Boyle.
    Garden City: Doubleday & Co., 1968

BOOKS PUBLISHED BY CONTACT PUBLISHING:

1 9 2 2

A Hasty Bunch by Robert McAlmon

1 9 2 3

A Companion Volume by Robert McAlmon
Post-Adolescence by Robert McAlmon
Two Selves by Bryher
Three Stories and Ten Poems by Ernest Hemingway
Twenty-five Poems by Marsden Hartley
Spring and All by William Carlos Williams

1 9 2 4

Village by Robert McAlmon

1 9 2 5

Contact Edition of Contemporary Writers
Ashe of Rings by Mary Butts
My First Thirty Years by Gertrude Beasley
A Hurried Man by Emanuel Carnevali
The Making of Americans by Gertrude Stein

1 9 2 6

Palimpsest by H.D.
The Portrait of a Generation by Robert McAlmon
The Eater of Darkness by Robert M. Coates
Ladies Almanack by Djuna Barnes

1 9 2 9

North America, Continent of Conjecture by Robert McAlmon
Sailors Don't Care by Edwin Lanham
Quaint Tales of the Samurai by Saikaku Ibara, tr. Ken Sato

1 9 3 1

The Dream Life of Balso Snell by Nathanael West

Post-Adolescence

SHE LAUGHED AND RUSHED on speaking, loosemouthedly, always accidentally spitting bubbles of saliva into a listener's face in her vivacity overgushing. Peter wished—O well, have to take her as she was—too bad there wasn't somebody else to go out with nights to dance. Her talk about making the best of her married life tired him, as did her "queer little emotions when he speaks of his newest love." A husband would get tired of her effusion of loose embraces. He himself would have to evade somehow her coming and departing kiss. He'd dance with her; drink with her—to help a heavy head.

She shook her bobbed hair, and running a comb through it the wrong way, tossed it back over her head with a flinging gesture. "I thought when I was married and had a child I'd feel quieter about things" she commented, "but I'm just as wild for life as ever. I can't ask Fred to take me out nights either, not only because he's working sometimes, but because he may want to take out some other woman. I've always hated tied up marriages."

"Yes, I know" Peter answered, and waited for the music to start. The wine was going to his head so that he was feeling the devil may care now, limbs detached, body tending to float, mind naive with curiosity at the state of being. The music started rollickingly, "oui, oui, Marie—and you do *this* for me, and I'll do *that* for you." At once the rhythm swooped into his body's pulsations, so that abandon had him.

"Let's dance" he commanded joyously. His feet were lilting his body, flowing into the music—syncopation, joynoise—ja, da da la la, umphoty umph—to hell with worry or weariness— shuffle feet, squirm body, electricity in the limbs from the wine, her body, her limbs following his as they danced; her body, any body to dance with, to touch, to feel the form of life moving. This was one of the self-unconscious conscious moments of life with no purpose or reason; a questionless answered moment. How voluptuous and clearly gratifying. If things would only always keep moving rhythmically, wildly, but free from obstruction, in the ethers of rhythm forgetfulness with the consciousness all ducked under, swimming in joy sensuality, life would be great. She was a dancer, curling her movements into the cadences of his. He could forget her dandruff-tossing, eye-glistening semitic vivacity, and swing with her warm wine golden glowing movements into dance. He would drink wine.

So time passed and she did all the talking while he felt the wine deliciously itching through his blood, over his ribs. He ran his hand over his thigh, liking the feel of flesh on himself. His brain was in an aura of wine and jazz music. Jazz! Not poorly translated Wagner like Tristan at the opera last night—heavy German singers, shouting "Say what thou willst," slaveminded translators—the one thing to remember, the trailing of moss green draperies over deep lilac, rippling upon gray cobblestone stairways in the stage noonlight, while the sky paled to green slowly.

He pressed her hand and arm when she thrust them upon

2

them, as he always did out of reticence to deny but now because of desiring emotion in him. She was flesh. Silly too; she wouldn't let him go home with her; she'd talk of freedom and say at the last minute she didn't know why but she was afraid. Training and Jewish blood within her perhaps, she'd think, because she knew her mind was anything but a chaste one. Well, to hell with it, he didn't want her anyway. It'd be better perhaps not to start an affair there as he didn't actually like her.

Later he was not unwilling to kiss her, and let her teeth, tongue tip, and lips mouth his. He didn't usually like that with her, but now he was too intoxicated to resent the surface-passionateness of her moist embrace. But he broke away feeling an irritation in him, and stumbled from her, calling back goodnight. Half forming thoughts played through his muddled brain; he didn't want to think, feeling too alive and carefree. He'd sleep with a tang; cool sheets; his body was humming, his blood was ocean undercurrent with singdancing—young health—so foolish to fret about either tedium of attainment. Dance! Sleep! He felt flying.

He was in bed, but he could not sleep for his blood was tingling and itching irritably within him. Grayly sleep came on drowsily to dangle cobwebs of unconsciousness over his mind. Down on the streets those damned cats were screeching their everlasting serenades of torment and success in love. To the devil with them. The quilts were knotting and tangling themselves about his limbs so that drafts came in upon the middle of his back where they did not cover. He couldn't make them stay on him in all his squirmings—why the devil weren't quilts made larger, and the damnable absurdity of having to squirm with unquenched desire. The will was made to express, you'd suppose, rather than to suppress. To hell! There should be somebody in bed with him. Where could the will to progress come from if one used up all one's energy fighting a damn fool thing like sex desire. The orchid forms of young girls swayed toward him in his half sleeping inebriated mind. He could sense their scented flesh and their facile lovely yielding of their bodies to his, and then they evaded him. He could almost lean over

3

and simply take them, but he did not, dreading to find them not there. His discomfiture awoke him completely. By God, he'd take up with Mayme again in spite of their quarrel and not have to take chances on what he could pick up on Fourteenth Street. He'd lie to her now, and pretend he was in love with her. What a damn fool he'd been to try and explain the condition of his emotions regarding her, but he'd thought she'd understand. That wouldn't be the only hypocrisy life forced him to. Ridiculous affair, life. He could hardly believe it actually *was* at moments; and sex—how completely grotesque and absurd. Was it really so? It was so little and so much, and all unreal, except that it was burning him out for the moment with the carnal craving it put within him.

He dozed. He was caressing somebody who did not resist, and he was apathetic, with no attitude in his mind at all, no will—drifting—he was yielding—was being buoyed to sensation—gradually an effusion of nervous reaction—gratification?—then his mind was black of imagination, though there had been no dream. He awoke, uncomfortable. O the devil! He moved to the other side of the bed, tossed about a bit, and dropped off again to sleep, dreamless and blank now. Sleep, so vacuous and so complete a solution.

II

Morning! The alarm. Hell's bell. Get up? No—just five minutes more, just a tossover—wonder, could he pretend sick today, no, it'd be him who'd lose the money—well, a few minutes more. . . What! eight thirty, Christ! He jumped out of bed. Have to get up when the alarm rang after this—getting a habit—have to quit smoking so many cigarettes—have to quit drinking so much coffee at night and eating at irregular hours —o to hell with it all—he wouldn't have to quit anything; all oughts and musts and can'ts in existence anyway—who makes an ought that ought to be, who's so damn good at judging as all that if nature or some supposed God doesn't let us know in our impulses. Too many conventions in the world. . . Morning's a

4

heavy time. He needed to get outdoors. He washed in the cold running water. Nice tasting toothpaste, cold vital touch of water on face, over sticky sleepy eyes, fine on a leady head. Now for the cold outdoors. Too damned little ventilation in the room.

He went out and had hot milk and oatmeal with coffee; a delicious warm downflowing liquid that, coffee—everything made up of little warm or little cold sensations—or big hot, or cold ones. Huh! the exalted, the sublime—glad he was past the days of metaphysical yearnings in college, when he was worried about not being able to think beginning or end, or to discover decent purpose in nature. Bally college rot, that. It's enough to dig into the possibilities of oneself, and of today without a past or future. The time! . . . well, he didn't mind being late anyway.

There were no students yet at the studio when he arrived, but he undressed anyway, and took some exercise on the rings, chinning himself and trying to do a giant swing. That tired him. He wasn't feeling alert yet; takes a couple of hours after waking up to feel lively. He sat on the model stand. The looking glass faced him, reflecting his body. What was he posing for? None of the students would ever sketch or sculpture him well enough for it to matter. Nice lines he had after all, there around the belly particularly. It was nice being slender, but his belly might be getting a little too paunchy. He'd have to stand straighter, draw it up, take some exercises. Hated a paunchy belly. He ran his lips along his arms, his hands up and down his legs. Legs are graceful things; slender, deer-like, and how fine the skin is on the side of the foot, frogbelly fine with ethereal tiny pores and pearly white. That's the nicest skin on the body. He wondered if he could touch it with his mouth, and strained to do so, but was unsuccessful. He supposed a contortionist could. Wished there was a young girl in here with him, and undressed, but she'd have to be young and slender. He was tired of older women, too sophisticated, and not buoyant enough; wanted one with exuberance, not shy but capricious—what to hell anyway; why was his mind always dwelling on stuff like that, always looking forward to a climax, a change, a progression. Are these things? The mind grows in its ability to experience—experi-

5

ence what—not much that isn't tiresome—maybe his short-coming not to have gone beyond that, but who has that's to be respected—persons dogmatizing their hopes into a faith—didn't matter though, whatever is or isn't one goes on somehow even if one is questioning and rebelling all the time.

Students began to come in. There was red-faced, shiny-eyed, overserious Green, with his dogged habit of plugging away every possible minute at his clay and doing the poorest sculpturing of them all. Not a flicker of light in his derived talk about "discipline of the will," "hard workers," and "big conceptions." Perhaps, though, his trained-to-acceptance attitudes were no worse than trained-to-rebellion ones. Both attitudes are full of mistakes, and boring. What does anyone know, and why should anyone pretend to know beyond the point where simple confronting facts assert their being. He was tired of people who try proving things.

Louie slouched in and fumbled about the room with his long arms dangling from his slumping shoulders that sank down towards his fat stomach. He said he'd make a new start on his figure. Who in the devil ever made him think he wanted to be a sculptor? His lazy good nature and weak amiability were amusing though. Pozbick there too, painstakingly imitating the Jewish painter he most admired. What is sculpturing? What is an art? Lovely lines, reeds whistling form melody in the wind, swaying; a field of lilies breezebending, pistiline flowers gesturing to the moon or to the sun; many longstalked gracile bodies in a marsh. (Damn those puttering students. He was tired holding his ankle on one knee, posing for them to putter and dabble away, and the best of them mattered how much?) Is sculpturing important then? If so maybe they mattered. The human body, wonderful alive, but in clay as they handled it—what could he think—why not sculpture water falls, the conception. Falling, surge-rushing, breathtaking madness of water, burbling, boiling, seething, cold granite swirling of green or blue or purple ocean water, and its wills on dark and highly colored days. What's the will of water, and what's its form.

He liked the idea of what he could conceive as sculptured

better than anything any one of them could sculpture, or than what he could dabble with himself. Singing concepts. Polished stone, tinted, enameled pale blue, faint pink, shiny as a sun-basking snake's belly, polished slender stone, or gleaming pigeonblood stone, fireglowing, passionately kissable stone, warm red, lyric bright, with a song going upwards fluidly, tinctured with brilliant tragic ecstacy. Say, the diamond on the platinum hoofs of an ivory antelope in the sunlight glistening have clangored on tuned steel and a note soars high into the pitch of hypnotic silence. Sculpture that. Not the colour; not the tone; the motion, colour ringing, motion singing in space; domination of relationship inexplicably lovely. Body, of antelopes, of waterfalls, of people?—No, not body, creation! The impulse to break away, to annihilate, to create, to be free. The contour in mass, the potential germ to emerge matured, the grace out of protoplasm groping gelatinously.

He wished he sculptured, in stone, cold, freezing with the inhibition of conceptions. Life is a prison of yearnings, joy, and anguish that physical motion or intellectual will cannot attain expression of. He wanted lyric bronze that lilted upward jubilantly, meaning nothing and everything. What do men's bodies, or women's bodies, say of all the blood wishes, the soul craves, the mind thinks or strives to think. How are bodies sculptured in dead stone, white duplicates of pulp flesh, and where is the blush of madness, of shyness, the sensitive eye-twitching or nervous muscle-on-legs jerking from impatience to be off accomplishing some desire, and when accomplished what is accomplished? Ach? These people here sculpturing "his" body. O hell. What did they know of what he was thinking and feeling. But if people think they want to, then they do want to, but why. Why not abstract, stone music, frozen, imperishable, of iced movement, a floe of rigid inarticulate sound and line of beauty riding the wavecrests of relativity:—a golden bird with agate eyes whistling a dirge; a long legged bird with silver white throat, vermilion blood life-forceful beneath the glittering white feathers; agate eyes towards the sun, singing, graceful voice song-praying to the sun in colour, so undulant,

7

gracious, hard and cold, dentlessly flowing before and forever into infinite space. Mysticism submerged in conscious intellect; a pillar tip pointed signifying there is no end, diminishing gradually into the immeasurable and ascending therefore into the irrational, and sole abiding beauty.

Green spoke, interrupting Peter's rhapsodizing reveries that beneath his present-thinking mind he was doubting. "I don't like most of the pictures at the Granger exhibition. Too many cheap subjects."

"There isn't any such thing as a cheap subject. Things are. If the pictures are cheap the painters' minds made them so," Peter said, disgustedly, feeling antagonistic because his body was cramped with posing.

"I guess you're right," Green responded, "but . . ."

"No use talking to our model. He won't stand for anything not modern, Green," Louie joked.

"Balls on you!" Peter exploded. "You don't know what I'll stand, and I won't try to tell you. Your mind and your clay are confused enough, I'd judge. One has a right to some selection though, even if you don't think so."

"Is that so?" said Louie, throwing a small piece of clay at Peter. "If you'd sit still a few minutes . . ."

"You would feel the need of smoking another cigarette. Don't kid the goldfish, old top. You're about as intent on your work as a streetcleaner. Tell me though, did you manage to make a date with that girl who's posing for you afternoons?"

"Not yet, but maybe I'll get to it. She acts willing enough but how's one going to see her alone with this bunch of roughnecks hanging around all the time, I'm asking you? Green's the only one who works while she's posing."

"She wants too much attention. She talks almost as much as our present model," Poznick said curtly.

Peter felt anger at Poznick bilge up in him. Damned Seventh Street Jew, he thought. "Well, probably what both she and the present model say in talking will count as much as any work that's turned out of this classroom," he grunted, and after a pause when his irritation had subsided he chuckled and said in an aside to Louie, "Every once and a while my little trick of conversing to get extra rest is met with distrust and suspicion. Temperamentally I wasn't exactly meant for a model, I'd judge."

"Say, boy, me neither. What do you do it for—going to school somewhere?"

"No, I'm through that. It's just less binding than a day-in and day-out job at some office or on a newspaper. Some days I don't pose at all; and some days I don't eat, too; but between not eating now and then and doing eight hours' work a day, I'll take the former."

The talk stopped. Peter wondered if he was being square trying to keep from posing. Suppose there was some one of the students who was wanting to work, and was a good workman. He'd have to be open-minded, as long as he was pretending to pose. He didn't think much of any of them, but it takes a few thousand to find a good one; perhaps this class was of value. Oh, to the dickens with them all. What's valuable? His own emotions were as valuable as anything in this room; he'd bet more on himself than on any one of them, and that was as far from being lost regarding any sense of value as he could get. Is it best to try and stay all open-minded? One can go wild with the chaos of that attempt, and in trying to discover a basis. What is a basis, when one's own emotions and one's own mind do not respond. He'd have to stop thinking so much, but how, his mind would run on if only on futility, and bafflement. But still—things would come about as they would come about.

He couldn't solve anything at this moment but this moment.

III

In the afternoon Peter had an appointment to meet Jim Boyle. He sauntered about the streets to pass away time. Wondered how Jim would be today, harried as usual, and tired out, or maybe the clear spring weather had let him get more rested than usual as so many people wouldn't be ailing as had been the slushy days a week or so back. Funny mixture Jim was, Italian, Irish, Welsh, Yankee, and he thought there was a little Jewish blood in him too. No wonder he was up in the air most of the time, with a feminine will and intuition thrown in upon his impulses, if. . . well, yes, maybe. There was no doubt anyway that Jim's wife, Nellie, was the stronger of the two if it was only because being feminine and maternal made her narrower so that she wasn't so easy a victim to confusion.

Strolling about he encountered Brander Ogden who was as leisurely as he at the moment. "How glad I am to have a few words with you, Peter," Brander assured him. "I haven't been out of my rooms except to go to the bakery for almost a week. It just seemed as if I'd had enough of all kinds of social contact New York had to offer me, so I went into seclusion, but today I thought I'd venture out and look them over again."

"I'm meeting Jim Boyle in a little while, and would say for you to come with me, but we're up to a great scheme for re-arranging the universe that we want to talk over alone together," Peter responded.

"Such a new wardrobe as I've been looking over, if I ever get enough money that I feel I can put out," Brander said, for the moment preoccupied with his own needs. "My god, there are so many exquisite little sensations in life. The ties. The hand-kerchiefs. The perfumes. The last word. You must walk down Fifth Avenue with me someday soon while I look over the shop windows. Too delightful, some of them." As he walked he strolled along with deliberate eagle-like dignity, his great cold blue eyes staring about him. Peter felt amused at what some-one had called his dowager gestures, and noted his high beak-like nose, and his face with its fierce grandmother's profile.

"O Brander, it's certainly damned good to see you again. I've wondered if something I'd said hadn't got back to you and upset you when I didn't see you around for a month or more. I've been pent up and disgusted with everything all winter, or I'd come around to look you up."

"Indeed not, I've heard nothing that upset me. New York in the winter just drives me into my hole to hibernate. Don't you fear, I understand you and your rantings. I've never had any doubt about you from the first. You'll land on your feet all right, and what you say. . . you understand me too. Great lads, you and Jim. Tell him we must see each other soon, now that I'm about again."

"He was asking about you last week."

"Is he the same old goat?" Brander chuckled. "He just never will know to handle the many different qualities and personalities within himself. My, I ceased long back ever asking what he thinks about anything, because that puts him in a panic, so he has to run home immediately to try and think out what he does think, and that means another seige of trying to calm him down for Nellie. There is so much wild imagination, audacity, and timidity mixed up in him indiscriminately that nobody can ever know where he is, least of all himself."

"I don't know about that. I think Nellie's pretty hep about how to handle him. He just gets ideas, he's becoming too settled and that terrifies him now and then, but now too he's wanting too many "final solutions" to things to actually break any tethers."

Brander and Peter separated after a few minutes and Peter turned for a moment to watch Brander proceeding down the street like a whole caravan to himself going in orderly procession, that surely had need of a crown and a train. Turning on his heel to go towards the clinic hospital at which he was to pick up Jim, a feeling of aversion to entering the charity ward came to him. Already the dusk was beginning to come upon the city so that it forced consciousness of the smoke in the air, and brought upon him a feeling of depression. There'd be all those screeching youngsters at the clinic, as though their bones were being pulled from them, and their dull, soggy-eyed mothers, Jewesses at the period in life of fruition and opulence of fecundity—ugh—the new generation. Why should life go on to present such diseased, dull, and poverty-stricken aspects? Why should life go on? Does anyone like it?

Jim met him at the entrance to the hospital informing him that his work had finished sooner than he'd expected this afternoon. His brown oval face lighted up for the moment of greeting, so Peter judged that tiredness had not made him apathetic towards everything today as often.

11

"After being up almost every night for three weeks I began to get a rest the beginning of this week," Jim commented. "Maybe I'll get a chance to do some of the things I want to, rather than treating kids for belly aches, or old ladies for colds, or men for clap. Let's go and have some tea, or something."

"I have some ideas in my head about getting writers and painters together. It's got to be done in this country; nobody else will help them if they don't help each other. . . but I don't know; a few minutes' talk with most of them and there's no agreement anyway, but we'll have to start something somehow."

"I don't get this modern art at all, but I can't find the terms with which to condemn it either. Tradition doesn't satisfy. We haven't any base at all."

"Rats, modern art, bunk. Which is modern and which isn't, and what's derived, and what's real? I don't know anything about such class terms. I know only individuals and what they do, and if it doesn't matter, to the devil with it. We haven't a religion any more; we don't accept scholastic, or esthetic standards, or the old ideas of morality any longer, so we must recognize individual qualities more."

"That's too little; I want something inclusive."

"Anything individual, and really so, is inclusive and simply one of many possible variations. Any other kind of individualism is a stunt and that's about as old and cheap a trick as there is in time."

"Somebody said that if a fact is a fact why say anything more about it, since talk doesn't create new facts."

"Maybe it rediscovers them or emphasizes them in a new way though. Besides it isn't the facts that matter; it's what can we do in the midst of them that's worth doing. Dance, sing, paint, copulate, eat, sleep, and finally die, and if that isn't all there is to it, — show me — I'm looking."

"That damned woman who's been sending me love letters and obscene photographs of herself has taken to coming out to the house in the country and leaving big packages of notes and photographs on my steps. Nellie says she'll call in the cops someday. She doesn't give a tinker's damn, except that it's a nuisance."

12

"Ah, don't let that old dame worry you. She likes to think of herself as a rampant adventuring conquering super-woman. Take her as a joke. You're too inclined to let little episodes like that frighten you. Have you answered any of her letters?"

"I wrote her two, letting her know I thought she was an old hag, and now she's threatening to blackmail me by showing them at the clinic hospital if I don't come and sleep with her."

Peter laughed. "O hell, she won't do that. It's only a bluff, and if she did show them what could they do? You don't depend on them. You just let your imagination run away with you when you thought you admired her for her reckless vagabondage a few months back. A look at her should have told you she was a complete nut."

"I don't know. It bothers me, and I don't know what I'll do this summer, whether I can get a month's vacation in or not. By Christ, I should never have been a family doctor, but it was some idea about duty I had when I was a kid. I'd like to chuck it and go to Europe for a year."

"Why don't you? You've money enough put aside, haven't you?"

"Yes, but there's the youngsters at school. They're too young to put in a boarding school yet, and then—I don't know— maybe I have freedom now, and always have had it, and don't know how to take it. It's in the mind anyway. I want to feel definitely free."

"God Jim, am I ten years younger than you, or you ten years younger than I? Anyway, I lost the idea of definite freedom at least a year back, in the way you mean it. I don't think one can insure it anyway. You just have to take a leap and if you slip and bang your ass in the mudpuddle, tra la, c'est la vie."

A cat scurried past them with a dog in pursuit. Suddenly the cat whirled, as though to say "to hell with running away," and stood baleful-eyed, hair-erectedly terrifying before the dog. He barked yappingly, but did not go too near the green eyes, alternately yellow with ire-flame. Suddenly a claw reached out and dug into his nose, so that he rushed off yelping with his tail definitely down in retreat. The cat, the cold fighter, sauntered away in dignified contemptuous victory.

"That's the answer" Peter commented. "Run like hell. Fight like hell when you have to. There's the cat with nine lives to protect and madam cat takes the protection of them upon herself and doesn't leave too much to nature. Maybe that's definite freedom."

Jimmy, having promised Nellie to be home for dinner, had to depart, without their having discussed plans that seemed to have become too impractical for Peter to suggest when he was confronted with Jim's temperament and situation. He walked away, wondering, as Jimmy went down into the tubes to ride home. Home, and is it a place for the spirit, or a place of bodily security? Well, a situation that, and what does one do with situations? Use them, or search continually for new situations that are doubtfully more valuable. What did he himself want, finally, knowingly? It was too damnable that every time he and Jimmy got together Jimmy's occupation made him go back home, or on a sick call, before they could have a decent conversation. But that's how things were.

IV

"She is commonly what is known as brilliant, isn't she Rollie?" Beryl Marks asked sarcastically, opening her handbag to take out a lipstick and deliberately apply a straight heavy splash of bright rouge across her crooked mouth.

"People don't grasp her meanings; naturally they think she's intellectual. She has a romantic soul underneath sophistication, which is painful to herself, I suspect," Rollie Walters answered, and continued to sit apathetically slunk in his chair, looking ahead at nothing with his burnt-out grey eyes.

"Well, for God's sake, all I have to say is I wish she'd show up then. I've got to have a bright flash in my life soon."

"She's been down on her luck lately, and feeling miserable; unhappy about a dead husband, or lover, or some such thing."

"Ah that; who in hell is happy anyway; there's too much said about that. Does she write anything worth looking at?"

"Her ideas and style are unique, unusual to her. She writes

brittly about ideas, insistent in her ideas on irony. Maybe that's second rate. Something alive in her work though. The last time I talked to her she spoke, with a touch of reality in her remark, of turning the gas on in her room and finishing it all, but I don't suppose she believes enough in anything to do that. Her attempt to believe in her own writing is too obvious a sham for her own wit, but in some way she seems to still expect adventure or romance—after what she's seen."

"She doesn't sound like a hell of a lot different from the rest of us, except I suppose she's more of a lady than I am. I'm so lacking in culture, they all tell me. What is it, and where do you get it so I can qualify."

"You'd better keep rough Beryl, so at least there's someone around to express a sort of protest. This generation! This civilization!"

Two spirals of smoke veered and wabbled into each other and at last submerged their gray undulating lines into the paler gray of restaurant atmosphere. Coffee was autocrat of odors; white slabbed tables littered the restaurant and were in turn littered with foodstuck dishes. The warble of conversation fought feebly with the clatter of the elevated and tramcar rattle outside the door on Sixth Street, and broke frequently on the pitch of weariness and boredom.

She, Gusta Rolph, came through the door past the pastry counter. Windgusts yowled through the doorcracks like wolves in a hungerpack, it occurred to her senses vaguely, as she went down the aisle. The splotch of two heads—one Rollie's—did not please her. She was not wanting to see anybody, but she joined them, acknowledging her introduction to Beryl disinterestedly.

"I intended going out this afternoon to see if I couldn't get some fashion design work to do, but my will seems paralyzed for the time being. What's the use of any kind of movement," she said hardly. "Don't mind me, Miss Marks; I'm just not up to being anything but wearing upon your nerves at the moment until I get a cup of coffee within me. My mind will keep wondering about that husband of mine—whether he's really

15

drowned or not. If it had only been my first husband so he couldn't pester me about the children."

"You have children—and in the plural—were they accidents?" Beryl asked.

"No, not quite. The third, who is only two, I wanted because I liked her father so much. The other two I rather wanted because I detested their father so much, and thought they'd keep me from reflecting on that all the time. I married so young that it took me some years to have sense enough to break away, and we lived in a horrible conventional English environment in Florence. One got to thinking there might be nothing else in the world."

"My children ain't. I took well care to see that they weren't, though one operation nearly did me in," Beryl commented, and laughed raucously. "And there's some tell me I'm all mother and should have seventeen, but who'd keep them? I, like a poor boob, have spent most of my young life supporting men, brothers, one husband, and lovers through some periods. I've no luck at all."

"We'll have to form a union of women to show the men up, and make ourselves exhibits A and B of horrible examples."

"The poor cusses," Rollie said attempting a droll grimace, "but I don't think they're really the seat of the trouble with the world."

"What then?"

"Say sex; it's an answer; or morality; or capital; or the weather. . ."

"What people we are; what a party we are," Gusta exclaimed in irritated tiredness. "To change the awful trend of thought tell me, how does one make a living? Of course, though, that's the worst possible question."

Droll suggestions were made, that drugged her unexpectant hopes. Conversation went on dragging its tedium-soiled links over the old pulverized-to-dust grounds. Gusta's mind retreated, and she listened dimly, her thoughts fluttering weakly among ideas and falling away from them. Apathy battled with a slight fear. She had only 15 cents; couldn't eat on that. What was she going on for, and towards? She was talented, as talent goes, but what would it bring her in this country, or elsewhere? Change, rest here, motion there. But she mustn't become help-less before experience, but this awful inaction of fate. God damn the inevitability of existence. She would not have life so much dull and coercive. There must be some way out, but no—one fights universal forces, one's own cravings, mass stupidities and desires.

The futility of aimless thought surged into vapour that rolled over her mind, muffling it, so that she felt as if her conscious-ness was being smothered to fainting. Baffled her mind came back to thought and fought on.

"I must go back to England" she asserted, not purposing an intention, simply to make a remark.

"O no, you must not. Everyone likes you so well here," Beryl assured her with warmth.

"Yes, people never quite dislike a person when she is fin-ished," Gusta brooded, and her emotions and thoughts played around memory of her husband. She saw his white body, as it perhaps looked, drowned, a white bulk bloated with water. A woman's reason for being is her relation to a man, it occurred to her. She'd have to stop thinking; so abject a process that. Somedays by a not-to-be-analyzed magnetism of a person, an object, an element, because of the freshness of a breeze, sun on limbs, wind cutting, she enjoyed being. She wished to scream inwardly at the futility of everything to her now, but sophisti-cation submerged the scream with apathy.

"Have you seen . . ." Rollie started to ask her.

"Don't please ask me what I've seen. I'm bored to death with seeing, and with the necessity of being interested in anything: plays, music, books, painting, what not. Really I'm not fit to talk tonight. Don't be courteous and stay to talk to me, for I'm going to simply sit here hours. Please go; I know neither of you can want to talk with me as I am now. Another time," Gusta said in a stream, too aware that none of them had anything to say to each other at the moment, and resistant of frustrated half-attempts to make conversation. As they departed she called

17

after them, "Good night. Don't let my bad humour annoy you."

"Hell, I've just begun to like you because you showed real emotion in wanting us to go to the devil for boring you. We'll see each other again. I'm not always so down and out as I am tonight; I've had a run of hellish luck myself" Beryl told her from the doorway.

"Coffee again," Gusta called to the waiter, and listened around her.

"Like vinegar it is, and you can't ask when you're buying it because the bootleggers lie," she heard. She needed something to intoxicate her senses so she'd forget for a time. Three street women talked at the table across the aisle.

"God gave me my two hands to save a black eye, not to give one. I didn't lay out to knock him cold but he was deaddrunk and got rough and tried to sock me on the jaw. He hadn't given me no money either and I ain't in the business for nothing," a woman spoke, leering at the gaslight, and swaying, doped with rotgut liquor. The two with her looked solicitatious amongst the men in the place. A blond woman of preserved middle-aged appearance at another table was telling her old gent friend, "I was married for twelve years before I got wise to myself and what I was missing. Now when I likes a person—I does what I wants to, that's me." Her manner attempted to be that of a good fellow, as she smiled at him smirkingly with a reassuringly encouraging air.

Choosing to live rather than to talk or think about life, Gusta reflected but found herself unable to judge which mode was best, the positive or negative; not much in either way; but suppose she had to go to the street for money—no, she couldn't. Too many men disgusted her. Something must happen to see her through.

An obscenity floated to her. Humour assailed her at the "Sh" of the waiter, who looked at her meaningly. Why did her presence command such inevitable respect from servants? Was she austere to look at, and her mind so unmoral, or was it, or only futile, incapable of evaluating things clearly. She thought of the obscenity in relation to her dead lover, somehow reluctant to

18

have her mind come to that, but it was not unclean, surely; it was only erotically desiring with frustration crushing her. There was pain in her remembering her eagerness for him to have all there was of her. It wasn't mentally they had agreed; only in their indifference to mental attitudes. If she hadn't been told he was dead perhaps she wouldn't feel finished now. She gasped with a longing to have his body to caress, caressing hers, and to forget all that she could not have in the sensuous tenderness of that moment. That was so much everything; and so much nothing with a man she did not want.

—the futility of remembrance. The weakness. She planned to make plans to go on.

"You sit looking at your cup as if you hadn't eaten yet" a voice said in her ear. She looked up in relief to have her self-tormenting reverie interrupted, and feeling too that the remark meant perhaps its speaker would offer her dinner. Peter, she saw it was.

"O yes, I've eaten."

He did not believe her. She was hungry gazing into her coffee cup. Outwardly he accepted her shy pretense. "Have a chop or something with me. It won't flounder you, and I like company when I'm eating so you won't watch my jaws going and make me self-conscious. Bad for the digestion, that."

"May I have lamb chops?"

"Sure, anything you want. I'm flush tonight, with almost two dollars on me, and the prospect of getting a few more tomorrow. That's wealth in this neighborhood."

"How do you survive and make money? Employers always treat me with much respect and think the position I'm after not quite big enough for me."

"I do it irregularly, and at about eighty different kinds of work. They don't treat me too respectfully, but I don't them either. It's do and get paid. I've done a five-day hunger siege once, but one gets a little panicky after the first three days, and loses all ideas of romantic suicide. The hunger protest condemns one to life and battle. God, I wonder sometimes why such a thing as personality or will exists, when a little need

19

shoves it all aside at the command of the brute impulse of self-preservation."

His mind wondered over her state, dumfounded with a be-wilderment of life. He could pay for this meal for her, but . . . Oh well, she'd come through somehow. Contrary to experi-ence's teachings his mood rejected morbidity. . . . He noticed that the air of tired despondency lifted from her somewhat as she ate, and more colour came into her face. Was she beautiful, as everybody said she was, or did everybody just accept the statement once it'd gotten around. He scanned her face at moments when their gazes did not meet, as the only two times they'd met before had been in a dimly lighted den. Her straight Greek profile, sharp chin, and fine nose were nice, and with the large firm mouth, tremendously long eyelashes—made up he guessed—and arched eyebrows—plucked he guessed—yes, she must have been wonderfully beautiful a few years back, but pallor and nervous tiredness had taken away the flush and bloom of young loveliness. But that young type of beauty could be so easily seen; any show girl might have it.

"You're looking at me as if I had too much rouge on, or too little, or badly put on," Gusta said.

"No, not that. I've never had a good look at you because the first night we met I was misty, and the second we talked for two hours more in that smokey dark den," he answered. "You could do however with a little more rouge though, or lip colouring, unless you want to go in for interesting pallor."

"Yes, I'm inclined to be careless about my toilet these days."

"It doesn't matter, except people who can be pictures might as well be successful as possible. There's too many faces one gets tired of seeing."

"You're feeling dull tonight too, Peter. Don't."

"Let's go somewhere; do something; hear some music, or see a show. We need to have our imaginations livened up a bit."

"Tuts, what are you suggesting to me; that I lack imagination. That's an awful crime these days. Your implication is unbeara-ble, and I with a vengeful nature."

"I said we. To the divil with your vengeful nature. Let's snap

20

out of it and get out on the street anyway, or we'll be talking about art, or life, before we know it, and I'm not up to that. At any rate we can look up some place to have a whisky, and in that illicit naughtiness find solace."

V

They were on the subway, not attempting conversation. Peter's eyes surveyed the conglomeration of human faces, mainly Semitic, and smokily dark or swarthy. His eyes took to wandering in their gaze at the ankles down the aisle, picking the slender ones, in wool socks, silk stockings, cotton socks, or stockings. Wool stockings look well on trim ankles, he reflected, as his gaze met that of a girl's who looked ready to become acquainted. He wondered; should he contrive to know her? Getting out at Forty-Second Street, he commented to Gusta.

"Gad, we are punished by our own desires, aren't we? Is there an acceptable solution, one not cheap, or not mere lack of action because that saves trouble?"

"Men have it easy. It's a woman who can't play the game whether she cares about others' opinions or not. Tradition functions inwardly on her, or circumstances catch her."

"Um, yes—what's to be said?"

They were on the streets bumping along with the crowd. Glimpsed flake faces hurried by, bits of eyeflashes, blond and dark heads, chic hats, drab hats, sear-eyed men, boys, broad and narrow shoulders in well-made and in sloppy-fitting garments. The personality of the crowd was hard to get, and so definitely New York, tired-bodied, worn-faced, mind-evasively New York, each individual apparently alone and looking for something that he wouldn't find, and knew he wouldn't find in spite of his fever.

Coming to a concert hall, Peter went to stand in line to get tickets, and watched the incoming crowd done up in opera cloaks, shirt fronts, and business clothes. The convention of coming at this set hour to listen for one hour and a half to music, with appreciation donned with evening clothes, struck

21

his senses as absurd. He heard snatches of conversation. "Mrs. Ray meet Mrs. Bzzz—zzz of Seattle," and caught the eye once-overs exchanged. "O yes, charming, you must take tea with us and meet her," "adorable music," "just too wonderful," "you must go by all means." How much sincere desire of some sort there is back of all the hypocritical social mannerisms in the world, he reflected, and also how little sincere any attitude is.

"I have a feeling we won't stay long at this concert,"Gusta commented as they went up to the balcony to be seated. There the swizzle, swizzle, zu, zu, zu hum of the audience chattering all through the house sounded to them, undervoiced, churning like a whirling dynamo increasing its speed at every moment, but never becoming increased.

"It'd be terrifying to have all this potential volume of impulses directed at one in a hiss, wouldn't it?" Peter asked. "One can be thankful I suppose that mobs are seldom one-intentioned or very sure of any conviction."

The conductor came upon the stage, and soon the orchestra was playing. Music? What is music? Emotional effects of sound charted into a composition. He doubted the reality of the appreciation by most people in the audience, and watched their faces, till he turned to look at Gusta.

She seemed rapt, in memory or thought, rather than in appreciation, he judged. Her poised slender body was tiredly intense. He felt a wish to touch her sympathetically, or to in some way communicate an emotion of understanding and affection to her, but he sat still.

Gusta was remembering another time when she had heard this Mozart concerto played, years back, on the piano in an Italian villa. How coolly the noise had dripped into the still evening air at that tranquil moment. She had stood on a balcony looking out upon the ocean which moonlight had welded into the vague horizon. Across the dimlit room the black piano with its keys had seemed a part of a well-planned stage set, as all the mountains, the tall cypress trees, and the formal roundtop umbrella trees had seemed, when she turned to face them. Space was a holy thing into which plucked notes were falling devoutly, piano tones, ethereal space-hued petals clinking as they froze and fell upon the thin ringing glass of silence that gave out cold pure sound. She had been more conquering in those days, and sure of things to come that would matter to her. Too clearly she recalled the feeling of ecstasy that space, the smell of earth, and being, had made live in her at that moment. She wished now the concerto would stop, and her memory could play other music, that sent sound swaying, effortlessly gliding through her consciousness. She felt the need of gaiety, or even the pretense of gaiety about her, however grandiloquently stageset for the sake of triviality the scene might be. A horror of her mind returning in its consciousness to the drabness of her present life was in her underneath emotions.

The concerto was over, and much applause followed which seemed more to be following the tradition of carried away enthusiasm for this orchestra's performance than actual delight.

"I don't know how to judge music at all," Peter commented, "and I'm prone to doubt many others who claim to judge it. That Mozart concerto doesn't fall rightly on my senses after a New York day."

"Yes. I'm tired of the concert idea, and of public performances at which crowds gather to be entertained to order."

"Let's not stay to hear the rest then; Schuman doesn't interest me, and I've heard this Strawinsky thing is a makeshift of his."

They went out of the concert hall. "I remember nights when I was a youngster on the Dakota prairies and the wind moaned against window cracks or against eddies of itself and made me frozen up inside with some primitive emotion of fear or desolation. I'd think I heard wolves howling, or that perhaps bad men my folks scared me with were about; and perhaps the dogs would bark in the wind. I wonder what those noises would be in music; sounds that could make my spirit and blood race and coagulate in alternation, shivering with instinct and memory. Music isn't rational, but it isn't sentimental either. A strange response it evokes in one," Peter said.

23

"Yes, but not at concerts," Gusta answered, and was silent. They strolled down Fifth Avenue to look at the shop windows. In one window was a drunken-looking wax lady clad in a brilliant red Spanish gown and mantilla, before which a tittering crowd collected and dispersed. A muttering falsetoothed old lady stood near the window, tittering at moments, and murmuring maledictions upon somebody whom nobody saw but herself.

"We'll go and have some coffee and doughnuts, should we?" Peter suggested. "There are some marvelous ones down a way, frosted with cocoanut and chocolate. They are the essence of romance to me in my hard-up days."

"I feel now almost as though I were going to start being my old self again," Gusta said. "One just can't slump." She drank her coffee, and started chattering about ideas for a poem that had been coming into her mind for some time. They lingered over cigarettes, attempting to solve insolubles with their wits, but for all their mouthing of ideas the insolubles remained so; but the toothing period is never by for minds.

Gusta, explaining that a friend would put her up for the night, left Peter. He watched her sway as she walked and drifted down the street, so light footed, poised of body, yet giving such an impression of frailty. Something would have to break to take care of her. Perhaps she'd quit feeling despondent, and see it through for herself. He thought she'd been more cheerful and careless about her situation as she'd left him.

VI

Gusta walked flyingly, open to the chill wind, liking its bite, liking the feeling of strength in her limbs, of the magnetic lift of bloodsurge within her. Neither mentally nor physically did she feel tired now. Her impulses were not resistive or restive; but exhilarated completely.

Images mulled in her brain; words and ideas inverted and transposed themselves in her mind. She felt keenly cerebral, active, full of zest to play colourful and intricate games with her

24

moods, as well as with conventional and also immoral conceptions. Half realized conceptions made her eager to clarify them.
Into her came an impulse to do a satire upon a self-dramatizing
voluptuously erotic-worded author. She caught the phrases of
his she remembered with the teeth of her wit, shook their ideas
rat-terrier-like, twisted their meanings to ridicule them ironically, and was invigoratedly aware of her ability and of the hard
brilliance of her own mentality. Impatiently she rejected a
memory recalling to her some man's statement that she was
foolish to be wasting herself on cleverness. "You with your
knowledge of life and experience should not be fooling with
mere ideas; your gaze can penetrate deeper than that." The
dazzle of her own wit meant more to her; what could depth of
insight signify? Life in any of the so-called deeper aspects
wearied and baffled her. She wanted the glisten on the surface
of her stream of consciousness, where sunlight could get at it.

Making her way to the little theatre club rooms she found no
one there in the dingy barnlike room, but a half-lit gaslight
burned over a desk, and she sat herself near it, took pencil and
paper and began to jot down notes at first, and then to write
whole verses and paragraphs, trying to hear and see her sen-
tences and phrases as music, rhythmed with rest and pitch. She
liked to sense the harp in her consciousness, upon which she
willed to strike this clear tone of mockery, that cerise tinted effect, a passage of virtuosity here, and further on. Think: Across
the paleness of intangibility the black harp stands, background-
less, its strings gleaming luminously through the darkness,
punctuating space exclaimingly through the black, punctuating space exclaimingly.

Drowsiness began to come upon her, so she slumped, lead-
minded, into an easy chair and was soon asleep, too bodily tired
now of any exterior circumstance to be uncomfortable in sleep.
During the night, however, she awoke and could not get back
to sleep, so she seated herself at the table again and started writing, a long prose story, all the while smoking cigarettes feverishly. It seemed to her now that some of her old situation, the
health it let her have, and its relationships, was returning to her.

She really must act, and teach herself that she could get on well enough without the particular man she'd loved. If she couldn't manage that, her revolt against marriage, her first husband, and the binding ties of motherhood and family life would all have been a futile gesture.

VII

Peter was on the street walking leapingly, but beneath his zest, and the taste of flavourless chilly air in his mouth that his lungs drank in gulps, there was an undercurrent of storming rebellion. He flung his body into a more rapid pace, throbbing with unrest inside. "Good Christ," he swore to himself, "what's to be done with energy, with heat, with blood, with flesh?" It struck into his senses, as it had frequently before, that every impulse and thought struck and broke finally against barriers. Perhaps intelligence was the greatest barrier in life, making, when small, the narrow moralities that oppress life, and ravaging the emotions with a philosophical sense of the barrenness of life when comprehensive. Animals have their physical reactions freely, but discretion stops the human specie. He was detesting himself and life for a tolerance that was being made to grow within him because his perception saw all people the victims of nature, their own blind subsconscious yearnings making cowards, or knaves, or imbeciles of them. All any of them wanted was gratification and if they had no wisdom in their means of getting it, who could be blamed?

Going up the three flights of stairs to his skylight room, he noticed that a larger front room was empty, and the door into it was open. It occurred to him he might ask Mrs. McCarty to let him have that as it had a window and was bigger than his present room. He stepped inside to look it over but by the time he'd taken three steps he'd realized the floor had been freshly painted. A panic came over him, and he turned back quickly and went into his own room, hoping that Mrs. McCarty wouldn't know it'd been him who'd stepped on the floor she'd just painted, but he was the only lodger on that floor so she

26

surely would guess it was him. Perhaps she'd be good humoured about it, but if she had a headache . . .

He was undressed when he heard her steps on the stairways, so he quickly jumped into bed after turning out the light. He was as quiet as possible, listening in a keyed-up half-amused dread to her as she plumped around outside. Waiting, he heard her talking to herself as she frequently did. Then her voice mumbled out in a louder tone,

"Ah, the devil, some god damn fool has been walkin on me new painted floor; the bloody fool, and me workin so me back aches a paintin it."

Peter stayed as still as possible, praying that she could not hear him breathe or know he had gotten home yet, and then she might think it was some lodger from the floor below. He hoped she wouldn't knock at his door, as he'd have to answer, or she might unlock it with her key and look in on him. After a minute of muttering, however, she went on downstairs, and he felt relief as he might get out of the house before she embarrassed him with questions in the morning.

Within a few minutes after she'd gone downstairs, however, his mind was back tearing away at him with savagely brooding ideas. Why did he have expectancy, or make any kinds of demands on existence; why question all the time, analyzing, dissecting, destroying? But how could he stop his consciousness from running on; that inability in itself was a thing to rage at, that he could never know when it would buoy doubt, unbelief, and bile to its surface. Futility was all his intellectual processes could think, and how could he accept that?

Sleep finally began to pour its thick smoke upon his waking mind. He was going under like a drugged man, drowning apathetically; and apathy, it appeared, was coming to be the chief emotion in his life. But sleep, not a paleness, sleep, not a blackness, not a heaviness, not unconsciousness, not anything of quality, just sleep,—nonknowing existence for his mind, for his emotions; this sleep was upon him. He sunk, sunk, to temporary extinction.

For how long? Non knowing time, unrelated to events.

VIII

Then the nothingness of unaware being was populated. He was in the midst of people moving and talking about him, but he could not see them, or hear what they said. Gradually a feeling of impending danger numbed him with a motionless fear. Someone led him into one room, then away again, through a throng of people hurrying by unceasingly. He should call out, or break away, but his will was paralyzed. A man near him was sharpening a butcher knife. The scenes shifted without sequence but always the menacing people were there. He saw a cow butchered and its glazed-eyed head dropped into a pit. Perhaps they would drop him there and he would go sliding down in the slime. Stale terror was all through him. How absurd. He could remember that he was no longer a child. He could protest, but he did not. They took him into a dark room and he knew they were muttering about him outside. An old man (like his father) was going to put him in the stove. Then he was cold with terror. A bloody horse, it was Nellie, his old saddle pony, who'd strangled herself to death by getting her foot caught in her halter rope—was sliding down upon him, having broken away from the tree in the middle of the sidewalk to which her corpse was tied. She slid on, towards him, and his arms were pinned to his side so that he could not move. She was upon him. With a jerk he rose into the air by the nervous reaction of his horror, and was falling, falling, falling. . . . He awoke. Fear was in him yet, and a druggish utter hopelessness that weighed upon his part-dormant mind. He was recalling life of now gradually. He would go to sleep again. There was nothing to think of he wanted to face with thinking. Life or ghastly nightmares perhaps. It would come morning soon, and the routine of getting up, going through the day, to live till bedtime again, for what? Eating; meeting a few people indifferently cared for; talking talk to them; alone amongst them who were also alone, so little is real communication between people possible except at rare moments. Oh, he'd sleep. He could not let himself be possessed of his ravaging sense of futility, if he was to go on. He ran his hand over his heart and let it rest there to feel the pulse of it, and to feel flesh. Then he embraced the pillow to feel matter, and to sense again reality. In the stillness of the skylight room he could hear the alarm clock tick; through the walls of the room he could hear the clock in the next room tick. Fog horns from the bay sounded, through the solitude of space he felt stretching out all ways from him. Life, his energy, with all its virulence and violence of yearning and protest was devastating itself in the silence and darkness. What could he do, battling his own reason, as well as enmassed indifferences. He must find something to express himself on.

The thought of people came to him; his mother—what had she gotten out of life to have made it worth her while? Was she really a Christian in her beliefs expecting a hereafter? And the others, and many others—he must force himself to sleep. Sleep, sleep, sleep, sleep, and sleep did gradually blanket his consciousness, which became with repeated repetitions, sleep, heavy sleep—is it a taste of death? The mouldering of all will in the impalpable non-knowing of the mind.

Detestingly he arose in the morning, but immediately that he was up, his detached mind began to ridicule his broodings. Damnfool within himself. Were all people so sentimental in their pity of self,—oozy, sloppy, morbid, brooding self-pity, thinking thoughts of simply staying in bed and passing out of the picture, with tears inside themselves about the tragedy of it all. Bah! What to hell could it all matter? Six thousand, or six million years of the same kind of thing ought to have taught the specie to care less about their own emotions. He wasn't any more caught than millions of others; not so much caught.

Going downstairs he encountered Mrs. McCarty, and remembered with a pang his having stepped on her painted floor, which she mentioned.

"I see ye were up to tricks last night steppin on the floor in that empty room upstairs."

"O yes," he said uncomfortably. "I'm so sorry. I couldn't see that it was freshly painted in the dark and thought maybe you'd

29

let me have it since my room's so small. I'll paint it over for you if you'll let me."

"Sure and that ain't needed. I'm getting auld, and me back's aching with these damned cramps, and one gets discouraged with the likes of most lodgers. Ye're no bother though; nor was Mr. Ogden when he stayed here three years back. I like having men of parts around. There have been three writers, and a man who's become a great philosopher, and a painter on that top floor in the eight years I've been here," Mrs. McCarty conversed, holding her woolen kimono to her neck with a hand.

"Great doings amongst the Irish, aren't there; and in New York too."

"And it's a good thing that they are. Them bloody English. There should be no rest on this airth until they're all wiped out and made slaves of, like they'd have the rest of us—who are of more wit than ever they can be."

"Ah well, the Irish need their sparring partners, don't they Mrs. McCarty."

"Sure, and they can find them aisy enough without them English. Do ye know I was at a lecture the other night, and a good, sound argument it was the man made too. He said the raison the Irish were so restless a race was that they were by nature poets, and had always been forced to be agriculturists, which goes against their temperaments that crave fantasy. Think of the likes of the English..."

Peter interrupted her last sentence saying, "You know some of the Irish, like Synge, with his *Playboy of the Western World*, are a little hard on the Irish themselves."

"He should have been tarred and feathered and run out of Ireland. It's the likes of him that poisons the minds—don't ye ever think an Irish boy would be a murdering his own father and made a hero for it."

"Yes,—I'll have to rush on though or be late again this morning," Peter said, escaping with a feeling of having placated Mrs. McCarty, who followed him to the door to call out a few more temperamental ideas to him as he walked away down the street, reflecting that it was fortunate for him that Mrs. McCarty was a goodnatured old Irish woman, except when she was an aroused old Irish woman. Anyway, she'd let him stay for weeks at a time without paying his room rent.

Walking, he liked the feeling of cold air on his legs that were no longer chilled because fast walking had warmed them. He had so much vitality. What for? Too bad he couldn't pass some of it on to weary-looking individuals who passed by, on their way to work probably, and that work most of their existence—poor devils—perhaps, though, his mind over-imaged what they felt.

A dead horse was lying near the curb. Strange coincidence that, after his dream last night. A pale face went by. Death. Pale faces. Why was he recalling the still white face of his brother Lloyd as he'd looked in the coffin many years ago? Why did he connect it with calla lilies—there'd been none at that funeral, —more carnations than anything else. And he thought a myrrh-like odour. He'd never smelled myrrh. Reading. Death, Lloyd, myrrh, a Christmas tree. He'd recalled the Christmas of the year Lloyd had died when he'd sung a song at the Sunday school entertainment about "Myrrh is mine, the bitter perfume, brings a life of lingering gloom," or some such rhyming thing. There'd been a scrap between him and Lloyd because Lloyd had teased him for forgetting the lines as he was on the platform. Then Lloyd died a few weeks later, and he'd thought they would meet in a hereafter—strange sensation without emotion of grief, or fear, of only dumb wonder, he'd had looking at the pale young face shining out of the coffin. Why does sophistication overtake one? Why does one feel wearied before sentiment, or callused, or indifferent, disbelieving in the reality of all ecstasy, exaltation, and even affection. Perhaps he ought now to be doing fairy stories as he'd always told himself them in those years back, and in that case he might be able to ignore the crassness and dull tortuousness of existence. But that was an idea only, he knew. His mind was a knowing one so that it rebelled against any idealism or romanticism but that of any moment's mood. For the rest he wanted almost touchable reality to analyze, and what to hell is so irrevocable as that. One

31

makes one's own reality to a big extent. Ah well, he'd go on analyzing, diagnosing, himself and everything else about him. To
what end he couldn't know, but that was his temperament, and
that was the answer.

IX

The door bell had rung. Peter waited in the hall, listening
over the stair railing to see if it was anyone coming to see him.
Mrs. McCarty spoke his name.

"Tell whoever it is to come up," he shouted down the stairs.

"Shure, and he's younger than I am, so I will without bringing up his card to you," she called back, and within a minute
Brander Ogden came up.

"I was around the neighborhood, and thought I just must
come and have a chat with you. Things have been so deadly,
but I've concluded I must get around a bit again."

Brander sat on the bed, his steel blue eagleglaring eyes—
extended with a terror or a hatred or a suspicion of life—
persistently coldly surveying everything in the room, with an
insolent stare, as though they would vivisect any object, or rape
any person they were gazing at.

"I feel as though I've had enough—you know—of the sort
of quality about. Not bad for its kind you know. But I've had
enough of the New York quality, and must plan to get away
somewhere for the summer; must manage the economic side
of it somehow," Brander talked on as Peter puttered about the
room, hanging up garments, and putting his writing table in
order. "It's so deadly. Nothing happens. I go around, but nothing happens. Surely I remember that things were not that way
in Paris, or Germany, when I was there before the war, but these
New York people just get together and stand around dumb. At
parties I try to be ordinarily sociable, but they will just get together
and stand around. Nothing happens. The people don't know
how to play or carry on a conversation. The same people too.
They're all right, but I know them. Feel as though they have
nothing more to give me. In Europe they know how to play."

32

Peter wondered. Perhaps, in Europe. Perhaps anywhere. "Yep, they give me the gut ache too, the arty art worshippers, the moral ones, and most of the others. There ought to be laws against talking about poetry, art, or the social revolution, or any other kind of idea I think when most of them talk. Ugh! One gets fed up listening to ideas, particularly old ones."

"I don't suppose you'll want to go with me to Dora's party, then," Brander queried. "She sent me a note saying she was having a number of people at her studio in honour of—think who—that lady poetess Vere St.Vitus—the jumpy cooey little thing. O she's just too much when she gets over in the corner with some coquettish male admirer and the two of them start gurgling."

"Yes, I'll go. I've nothing else to do tonight, and I've learned to take parties like that as though I were visiting the zoo or an archeological exhibition. We'll be protection to each other too, and perhaps Jimmy will be there so we can all clear out a little later on. But lordy, if Dora gets up and starts to evangelize any of that verse of hers! Ouch! Isn't she less than could be desired, and more, when she begins swaying and spouting with a super trance look in her eyes about the perspiring moon or the hot belly of that illegitimate child of industrialism, the city? There are advantages in being a ditch digger so one doesn't feel called upon to appreciate or even comment on the beauty of the utterly urgeful affectation of sonorous agony. I hadn't ought to go to her party though, as she's aloof to me now, but I can stay under cover somewhat."

Peter started washing himself, and after shaving, did a quick manicuring process. He was conscious that Brander's eyes were on him as he stood shirtless, shaving, and thought "Gets most of his erotic satisfaction through his eyes," as he recalled a phrase Brander had used in a letter to him at one time "in my adoration of flesh." Poor, inhibited, virulently passioned Brander, with his talk of the "cold intellect." He'd continually talk of life and art as "scientific and conscious affairs," while all his own repellent force resided in his savagely repressed rhapsody of eroticism. His was a repressing circumstance and temper, since

33

he couldn't actually attract physically those he wanted. Who would want to touch skin and flesh that was so big pored and old looking?

Peter was dressed, and the two started downstairs together, Brander with his arm about Peter's shoulder. Peter could not respond and could only permit it because of some pity and a frozen antipathy that was indifference within him. He quickened his pace and slipped away from Brander's touch, and then on the street spoke, sorry for his emotion of aversion.

"Gad, Brander, I am glad you came around. I've been wanting to see and talk to you. Your mind has a stimulus, and one sees so few people about who offer anything."

"Now, now, don't start that. I get so tired of people who like me for my mind. I've thought you got other qualities in me; you've always seemed to like me, and even to understand a little."

Peter felt a desire to evade this subject, but responded, "Why certainly. What does mind mean anyway? How fundamental an affection I can have for anybody I've never had time to discover, but..."

"Yes, one shouldn't go into that too much. I so much wish I could help you solve some of your problems. If I only had money I'd ask little more of life than that I could have nice looking young people around me to take care of, and see that they never had a moment's bother about the grim side of things. There are some people who have that kind of talent, and I seem to be sought for my sympathy at times too. There's Marie Plummer—such an intellect she has. She's one of the artists of the world—and I understand she delights in giving away her stage clothes to anybody she's a bit attracted by. She just would not want anybody to have a moment's unhappiness I'm sure; not if she could help it."

"Yes, I believe she isn't supposed to care much about going in for repression of any kind."

"Completely non-moral—that's the only thing to be. If I could only get myself around to the state of feeling that as well as thinking it so decidedly as I do, I'd have much solved. But New England training is hard to escape."

34

"I know I'd do anything that I really desired to do, regardless of anybody's opinion, or any of God's commandments," Peter commented recklessly, though in his mind the immediate realization that Brander, at least, wouldn't be allowed to do many of the things he actually desired to do, because his desires generally involved people who had no corresponding desire as regarded him.

"Who could or would care, and why should they?" Brander said decisively. "Unless this fanciful god, and if he's there he doesn't seem to let anything disturb him much. The man must have frequent naps."

"Too vague a concept for my mind . . ."

"I haven't told you of a new acquaintance I've run into, a boy from upstate Maine, who used to know my family vaguely. Such a lovely boy. Such gentle soft qualities. There's nothing in his head of course, but I like him so well just for lovely human qualities he possesses, and he seems so ready to be helpful. Last week when I was staying in my room, laid up because of this damned gut of mine, he'd bring me things to eat from the delicatessen shop on the corner, and that's all I wanted to eat then. How beautiful young people can be, just as things to have about one."

They arrived at Dora's address and started up the three flights of stairs. "I get so weak from climbing stairs. My intestines drop down on me — since that accident — I have to be so careful of what I do and eat," Brander complained complacently. He didn't like making too much physical effort ever; quite apt to take to bed actually and metaphorically when life got rough, Peter reflected, mounting the stairs behind him as he ascended with slow dignity, with the calm hauteur of a camel, neck camel like, eagle eyes appraising a little camel like in their assumed ferocity.

X

In Dora's studio Brander entered at once into the conversation, deliberately gay and facetious. Peter felt ill at ease, and withdrew into a corner there to sit watching, feeling pent up and irritated at his own feelings as well as at the atmosphere. There was no one he saw he wanted to talk to, and nobody much that he knew even by sight. He saw that Dora's glance evaded his and helped her in the evasion. Darned little she and he had to say to each other; poor old thing, pretending to be revolutionary and flaming with passion when a few good meals would change all of that perhaps, except that she'd still be pathetic.

"Lackeyship to England," a phrase sounded near him, and he turned to see a middle-aged woman discoursing intensely. "We fete all these English novelists and poets, who are second rate in their own country, and not equal to our own artists, but never a fete do we fete our own worker," she was saying.

"Rats!" Peter exploded in, not bothering about an introduction, "that's the attraction of the foreign thing, and doesn't at all mean we're lackeys to England intellectually. We have the energy at the present moment, and any country is ours to learn from if there's anything to learn. What the public thinks can't matter anyway, here or anywhere else. Let the Englishmen drag some money out of it here if they can; Lord knows we won't get it anyway." Whereupon a discussion waxed hot, and ended for Peter by his settling back into himself, disgusted with argument.

The evening was not actively painful, however, until Reginald Crackye read an extract from his play "The Mummy" and became dramatic about it, much worked up apparently over his inability to keep his long hair out of his eyes and out of his fervid recitation. "Are these my eyes looking at me in the mirror. Am I then that manner of a man? No, no, away, thou phantom. Torture me not thus. I have loved; I have prayed, now this, this . . ."

Everybody applauded the reading, enthusiastic at all costs. Peter suffered from not being able to get up and walk out unto the street rapidly, and blamed himself for having presumed to expect that any variation from the usual might occur at Dora's party.

Verses were read by several ladies, and by one young man whose verses were, according to Dora, "very sensitive."

"God!" Peter ejaculated to a woman sitting near him. "Isn't

this modern poetry movement awful? Lemon water, anguish, sand and sweat. Ain't the moon gangreneous though? How do we survive this atmosphere?"

"O my, don't you like what has been read? I think it's all too wonderful. How do you clever people manage to write it. I've tried, but of course my efforts . . ."

"Um—um—yes—well," Peter commenced, eyeing her askance. Then suddenly he looked with inspiration at Brander across the room. "O I must go and talk to Brander Ogden," he declared, escaping.

"Say Brander, let's collect Jimmy and get out of here. I see he's caught up by some fervid lady. I'd like to take art and drown it in the river. Reginald Crackye! Dora! Dora! the gate."

Jimmy needed to be rescued from a woman who was sure that he'd be a greater poet if he would put more social content into his work, and make it more representative of the average person's experiences and emotions. "Certain things exist; but why should they be talked about, unless they can serve to uplift us, and give us beauty. I like to be deeply moved, and exalted, by poetry, if not by prose."

"Mr. Boyle and I have promised to be elsewhere at twelve o'clock and it's near that now, so I'll have to interrupt your conversation," Peter broke in, and soon he, Jimmy, and Brander were out on the street together.

"Ghastly!"

"Too much; just too much!"

"For Christ's sake give me a cigarette, one of you. I wish I could be a truck driver."

"Just too killing Dora is, and I used to think she had a sense of what not to do once, but—did you hear her talking to that poor English novelist she'd gotten hold of? Her reserve and irony couldn't save her from Dora. I thought she'd simply pass out when Dora actually quoted some verses she evidently wrote years back and was ashamed of."

"Yes, I don't know," Jimmy parried. "What's one to think about anything? I used to like Dora, and thought I liked some of her things. What's there to say anyway?"

They went into a coffee house to talk and smoke and there Peter sensed a reserve between Brander and Jimmy, and recalled that there'd been some break between them about a letter Jimmy had written because he'd been hearing things he didn't like about Brander, after he himself had written many unburdening letters to Brander, every time life seemed to get unbearable to him. To hell, thought Peter, why in the devil did Jimmy run at people so impulsively offering them friendship, and then break away with some disapproving terror of having them ask too much of him. One can hold people far enough away without that. But it was damnable too that Brander couldn't understand that. Jimmy's letter had simply been effusions about life, and his own ego; exuberant in a morbid way generally, but never actually at their recipients except as he or she was somebody to shout through the mail to. But Brander would have to clutch at them as signs of romantic friendship.

The conversation would not go; all three of them made starts but a group interest would not pick up, and Brander looked at Jimmy, ever attempting to keep the right degree of coldness without being pettily haughty. Jimmy was simply diffidently nervous. Peter tried flippancy, but the others did not respond, so finally he said,

"What the devil? Haven't you two patched up that scrap two months back yet? Why don't you tell each other to go kiss ass, and have it over with?"

"Well now Peter, you know yourself how little one likes personal comments," Brander said austerely.

"I know it old kid; but I like this atmosphere of refined restraint even less, and why should two old goats like you and Jim, who should be hard-boiled by now if you aren't, stand nibbling at conversation like pet rabbits, with me a bored spectator trying to be the life of the party. We'll all admit you're both damn fools, and I'm a little inclined that way. Let's take it easier."

"What's it all about?" Jimmy said, pretending unawareness.

"Well, as I said to Peter some time back, I've always liked you Jim, but after that letter I just thought, well, I can do without that friendship too."

38

"O I just had to get something off my chest," Jim defended, grinning and uncomfortable.

"Hell, sez the duchess, who up to this time had taken no part whatever in the conversation," Peter broke in. "Explanations and apologies are most incriminating and h'embarrassing. You two haven't anything agin each other. I've got to get up early in the morning so I'm going to beat it home, but let's all three have dinner together some night soon and if you're still scrappy then I'll be the referee."

XI

Alone, and feeling wakeful Peter went into another coffee house to sit for a time. The lines of a poem he had started to write the day before came into his mind:

May not some day the ocean waves
Keep rolling so the earth will too
Rise into waves and hurl us under
And let the tide recoiling suck us back
And down, down, down, Down to depths never to be
excavated
Never to be reported on any page of history.

   What does one do?
   What does one do?

Will the cold clear sky erect before us
Break like thin glass and crash us under

His mind ran on. He'd make that the motive for a long poem, but he could do nothing but jot notes now; there were too many conflicting moods to smash away from the inside of him, and too many thoughts combatting each other. His mind would ponder over solutions that he knew he would not arrive at. Jimmy's life; Brander's life; the obscurity of everything finally; where would he go, what do,

To Tahiti then, to bathe in that rich sunlight
And know the sensuous natives, childlike and simple

I do not resist a system of life.
I resist its entire process.
I resent any conceivable being as futile
On any rational basis,
But my instinct and emotions are not rational.

he read in the notebook he'd jotted his poem in. That was another thing he once started to write, intending to satirize some type of man, or of writing.

Golden sensuous hours
In which my spirit was a yellow voluptuous dandelion
Unfolding to the sun.
Its petals are preserved in the wine of my mind
And inebriate my memory.

Live as do wild animals,
The wild cat, the wolf, the moose—

No, no that didn't touch him now. Perhaps he could make a poem of it someday. He was feeling cheerful now, or at least, not too questioning and revoltful. Sticking the pencil and notebook in his pocket he walked out of the restaurant towards his room, forgetting to pay his coffee check. It was not until he'd walked a block that he remembered and then thought "only ten cents: they can stand it."

XII

Peter stood impatiently in line to buy an elevated ticket. How damnably slow the ticket seller was. Why couldn't he speed up a little. At last he was at the window, and he felt a desire to reach in and punch the man in the coop on the nose for being so meticulously slow about separating a ticket from the reel. Taking the ticket he went thought the gate into the elevated train. Crowded of course! He detested crowds. Wished to the devil the woman next him would stand still and quit shoving her elbow into his back. He'd push the man to the side of him away with a jerk if he nudged in any closer to him. Damn crowds, and people. The touch of strange bodies is irritating, if not unclean. He'd go out at the gate end and stand.

Crowded there too. At every stop, four blocks apart, the gates opened and people crowded in and out. Why in hell couldn't the car company run more cars; packing people in like this!

At one stop a bull-necked man with a foreign accent came in leading a number of peasant immigrants. "Come on! Come on," he shouted roughly, and six frightened looking men in homemade clothes hurtled into the train after him. So much like dumb animals, looking around feverish and stupified. At every stop they'd begun nervously to get out, and then fall back, afraid of displeasing the man who was directing them. So dull, and so anxious to do the right thing. They were a bunch of frightened sheep, no, more like dogs, part bold, part affectionate, partly cringing with timidity in their insistence upon handling each his own baggage, and in their reluctance to step around as the conductor ordered them when they stood in the way of opening the gate. Peter saw one of their faces as a face with personality. It was boyish, pale, with luminous brown eyes and a curly head. Quite like a sheepdog puppy wanting to be petted. He felt an impulse to touch him, or in some way tell him not to be afraid of the roughneck foreman.

Peter got off the train and walked down the street to the clinical hospital, to pick up Jimmy and have dinner with him. How suspended a process most of living is. Some moments hurtle along with satisfaction or with impatience, but most of the time it is a process of waiting. He was probably a great fool, trained all through life by his own emotions to a highly specialized expectancy, to contempts and arrogances. He was an intellectual snob, that was it. What makes superiority; what makes people and things survive; how could he judge of the innumerable things and qualities about which were the best? He wished to

41

hell he could quit having so many ideas. Ah, such futility thinking that. He hated, loved, was disgusted by, and could not conceive of not having life, and as he took it, not as somebody else
suggested it to him. Why did he feel ugliness? What is ugly?
These city streets? He looked at the shabby-looking tenement
buildings, noted the drabness and grayness of the streets, the
smokestacks in the distance. The city! Why need he think these
things ugly to the eye. The pulse of energy was beneath, but
what quality of energy? Still what makes quality? This was
retarded energy, lethargy, evidence of yearnings frustrated, but
still at this moment of feeling life vitally he wanted these around
him—simply because they were around him and he was alive
in the midst of them—more than the greenness of trees, more
than the restless solitude of oceanic expanse, more than desert
stretches,—else why wasn't he elsewhere? He wasn't sentenced
to the city. The smoky bite of the cold air invigorated him. The
winter trees, so much more bleak and lovelier than trees over-
lusciously green with summer foliage—barren lines, emacia-
tion, famishment, winter—the city. There were gesticulations
of wonder groping in the lines of the tree limbs. Bodies of grace
skeleton-thin reaching arms up and out. Skeleton bodies, foot
tied, reaching towards the sky. Trees are rooted. They stand in
one spot and their roots suck into the soil while their trunks and
limbs grow upward. If pavement is built around their roots they
evade its pressure and grow downward, or force it to crack. How
slow the growth of trees. To what end? What end do trees, or
men, or species serve? Restless, tranquil, rebellious or acquies-
cent, what end does anything serve? To express impulses, emotions, and energy, but why?

A still wonder held him.

Dimly upon his senses, objects and sounds reacted. "That's
my stumbling block" he thought. "I want answers, reasons,
and refuse them when they are offered me. Dissecting, and
rejecting."

XIII

Jimmy was still busy with patients in one of the treatment rooms but seeing Peter he said, "Come on in. I have just a case or so to attend to, and then we'll escape somewhere and have a chat."

A tiny pale girlchild was sitting on the operating table looking about her with still black brown eyes that were almost expressionless with a wonder, and fright, that had grown too patient. Taking a wooden match from a box Jimmy braised the end of it, and took the child's thin arm while he twirled the braised match end on a portion of its thin skin to inflict a bruise that broke the skin so that medicine he intended placing over it would seep into the blood. The skin did not break easily for all its delicate appearance, and the child began to whimper softly, but stopped in a breath or so.

"This baby's so patient it's uncanny," Jimmy stated. "There's something radically wrong with her. I'll have to test again for tuberculosis, though she shows none of the obvious symptoms."

"Yes, the youngster's too quiet," Peter said, turning away. "If one retained any concept of fairness in life it'd certainly seem too much for her to be made so acceptant at that age. I'd rather hear her shrieking out like some of the other poor little brats do when they're being operated on."

Jimmy simply made a grimace of weariness, and shrugged his shoulders. "Why do I keep coming here? I ought to stay at home and give the time I spend here to writing, or to resting. After a year of this what have I anyway; I'm still a family doctor to all the people out at Hungerville and they won't change to accepting me as a children's specialist. Anyway if they would I can't make myself charge them rates accordingly, so some more fashionable doctor gets all the paying patients."

"You ought to get Nellie to make out your bills, except she's as little apt to make them high as you are. . . Ah hell, if it isn't that, it's something else," Peter answered, as they went out of the building together. They walked without speaking for a time as Peter sensed too completely Jimmy's indifference come from fatigue.

43

"I saw Brander yesterday," he finally volunteered to break the silence and spiritlessness of the moment.

"He's sold a canvas and plans buying himself a magnificent wardrobe; he's just that much of a teaing and dining hound at the moment. But still he's about at the point of wanting to get away, though that's no news. He's always at or on the way to that point."

"I suppose he's still huffy at me, and would grand-manner me if we dropped around to see him now."

"Yes, I suppose so. I'm not up to facing a strained atmosphere anyway, and there wouldn't be much chance of his being in now that he's out and around again, because when he's out he's very much around. He has something on his side too, in being put out at you."

"I just had to get things straight between us."

"Yes, but one can't intrude much on anybody else's private habits; old Brander's enough of a personality, and has enough wit, to be judged for those things, if you disapprove of anything he is otherwise, but I'm no good at knowing how one can know enough about life and other people's impulses to presume to disapprove, at least until one's consulted. Not in the three years that I've known Brander has he ever impinged upon my ideas about what I will or won't have for myself; that's why I like him in spite of temporary aversions I get for him because of the awful pentup frustration he expresses at moments. He's hardly responsible for that thought, because his physical demands on life are heavy and his appearance is against his getting what he wants."

"I realize that; damn it anyway Peter, what am I! Am I a coward and afraid to face things? Somedays I think it'd be the best solution if one could go mad and have it all over with, or just jump into a puddle, head down, and wave a big toe farewell to the world, but nobody would give a damn if I did that either, I don't suppose?"

"And you wouldn't do it any more than I would. We all like playing our own little dramatic tragedies of self too well to give it up. The concept of suffering seems an utterly ridiculous one to me at moments. What in the devil difference can it make, even to one's self, what one feels inside? The show goes on, and by God there are moments when it can't play around one, with one the principal of it, hotly and quickly enough. I like it; I like it; I like it; I like it; but Jesus Christ how I hate too; all of it, sex, religion—and is there anything else?"

"Adventure? I've always retained some idea about personal freedom, and vagabondage. Some of the old hags I've doctored have made me dote on them for their filthy recklessness to everything. How calmly the tough masks of old faces express everything. I must be a coward not to break away to complete disregardlessness of even cleanness, let alone respectability; but still that kind of physical thing isn't freedom. If one could only make something happen to the mind's attitude the whole thing is solved I suppose."

Waiting at the street crossing for a heavy stream of traffic to go by, they noted a number of school children waiting there too, held back from venturing across by the commanding gesture of a good-natured traffic officer in the middle of the street. Even a dog stood waiting, sophisticatedly regarding the ways of congested city traffic, before he trotted across the street. He disregarded Peter's "here doggie" with utter nonchalance, utterly indifferent to any motive other than the one he was at the moment intent upon.

"Sensible dog that," Jimmy declared. "That's intelligence; pay attention to only what you're after. And we with our damn fool talk about sensibility, imagination, and the like, are the real boobs of the universe."

"Yes but we have imagination whether we like it or not, and how can we know the thing we're after is the thing we want after we get it; perhaps the diversion won't lead to anything more satisfactory, but I get tired of crossing the street because I've been across it, so often I know what's there, but I've stood where I was too; so help me god, what's the answer?"

"What the hell do we care, is the best answer, probably, until you believe in something you can do."

"Yes, yes, that. What the hell do we care between moments of belief."

45

Night was sifting its grey pre-darkness over the city streets. Peter knew that before long Jimmy would be saying he'd have to take the train back home, and if he'd stayed in the city for dinner he'd be restive till he did depart. He was always uneasy about departing up till the moment of departure, and then was hesitant and reluctant. But the habit of returning home had him inevitably, apparently. He could not trifle for many moments without uneasiness, but why couldn't his home wait? Home, and wife, and a few unimportant medical calls. Not once a week did a really serious sickness demand his immediate presence and when that call occurred there were other doctors in Hungerville who could be had if he weren't available. Well, he might as well be let hurry off this evening too, since neither of them were feeling vitally enough interested in anything at the moment to make the occasion stimulating. Surely enough, he spoke.

"I really ought to get home. I'm dog tired. Was there anything special about our having dinner together tonight, because if not you come out to the house Sunday, and we'll have all day together to tear around the country with the car."

"All right, jog on home then. I'd thought you might stay in town and go to a show with me, or to vaudeville, but it'd be damn boring if we ran into a poor entertainment," Peter answered, and said goodbye to Jim, observing him as he walked away, his legs a trifle bowed, his walk expressionless with worn-out protestation, his overcoat hanging shoddily upon him in his tired nonchalance. Peter wondered, was all his vitality a romantic subjective one then, so that almost none of it could show often on his exterior as personal magnetism. Perhaps he was simply using his own temperament as a weapon against himself. Had he ever actually tested the results of recklessness and audacity that he thought he so admired in the old vagabonds he talked about? What difference though? After seeking and adventuring one might come at last back to settling as the only possible audacious gesture before nature; the final signal of contempt. There was no use in raising one's hands to the sky and being hysterical with anguishings. To the devil with Jimmy

46

anyway; here he was himself. He'd have to get over his own too impressionable registering of other people's miseries. That was the hell of having an Irish temperament.

Whereupon he decided to go to a moving picture show after he'd snatched up a lunch somewhere. Seeing a quicklunch counter down the street a ways he went in and ordered hash and coffee. Sitting there, to amuse his befuddled senses he started writing in his notebook.

"I fail to understand why it is better to be sensible than to be a plain damn fool, or a decorated damn fool. There are intelligent people. Do they like themselves? No," assuming there of course that he was intelligent, and generalizing from there, and deviling about with abstractions and generalities. He nibbled at his hash, and feeling disgust at the thought of a social reformer he knew, continued writing.

"There are social ones with ideals on social reorganization; the intellectual ones, —honest, not victims of spiritual pauperism, —with spiritual hungers rooted deep in economic unrest —the biggest liars of them all. O the devil! Only the rhapsodists, the mystics, the enthusiasts, smother us worse than they with proof and disproof. The pubescently miserable ones have the thought that they will ultimately kill themselves to gloat upon. The realistic ones have nice bleak inner emotions about the devastating futility of it all."

How bloody ridiculous everybody and everything seemed to him at this moment. Who could weep tears, or laugh laughter about anything. Too much to expect. Human emotions, and the fate of men! Bah! He hadn't had any emotion but a revulsion against the mess of it yesterday when he'd seen that cab man thrown from his high seat against a lamppost when his horse tore around a corner, running away. Possibly that was disease in him, not to be able to care more, but then maybe it was a wise disease.

"Sing me a song about how you will stand off surveying the spectacle and laughing at the irony of it all," he wrote on, caught by his mood of apathetic life resentment. He'd finish this stupid thing he was writing. If he could only have liquor

47

tonight that'd relieve him somewhat, but there were other kinds of moments than this . . .

"There are incandescent moments that submerge us, but mostly we are cool—rational and calm externally—not frigid. But don't expect us—don't expect us—ah hell! let the matter drop!"

That was the answer. To the bloody hell with everything, psychology, sex, people, ethics, art, and the rest.

He finished his coffee and went out on the street, cursing within himself.

XIV

On the street, in motion, he felt somewhat quelled inside himself, but still apoplectic in his responses to impressions. A lady who had an absurd-looking Pekingese dog on a string was permitting it to squat in the middle of the sidewalk to relieve itself. He wondered why she couldn't as well have made it get over the curbing; what'd she think streets were made for? That was the trouble with people; they couldn't make a slight effort to relieve the disgusting situations.

"O Peter, what are you up to" a feminine voice asked, and he turned to greet Lillie Daniels, at first impatient at having his irritated reverie broken in upon, and glad when he saw that it was Lillie. He liked her. A lazy, utterly charming person she was. He noted her slouchy walk, and the paisley shawl she'd thrown over her faded purple broadlcoth dress. There was something heliotrope about her whole impression, so nonchalantly bizarre and colorful. It was a lovely head she had, the way her dark bobbed hair clung in at back, nestling into her neck beneath the dinky hat she wore. He'd seen actresses on the stage who could lead themselves across the stage in the same drawling manner that Lillie walked, and create a similar impression of slow charm. He'd wondered before if he and Lillie might not mean something to each other, though they'd only met a few times.

"That's a beautiful hat you have on Lil," he told her. "Where are you headed for? Have you eaten and if you haven't do you want to? Anyway what are you up to, and whatever it is take me along. I'm perishing with boredom of myself. Stick by me, for God's sake, and lead me into the bypaths of iniquity, or at least of excitement."

"I'll do anything you say, and can suggest nothing," Lillie drawled.

"Now Lil, anything, Tra la. You're going to make me use my imagination," he joked, falling into step with her, and taking her arm as he walked close to her, liking the feel of her body walking beside his. She attracted him decidely. He wished he could put his arm about her, if that was all he wished.

"My six year old daughter, Barbara, is getting another tooth," Lillie commented. "I pulled the old one last night and she's elatedly preserving it in a glass. You should have seen her dancing for me this morning. Lovely. The teacher at the school I send her to takes all the youngsters and tells them 'now listen to the music and do just what you want to. Run, jump, use your arms. Just push all of the joy in you out,' and little Ba-ba frolics around with no modesty whatever. There was no restraining her this morning, and of course I didn't want to."

"My Lord Lil, I didn't know you had a child. Does that mean a husband too?"

"Yes, but much out of it now. I don't quite know how to go about getting a divorce, but I suppose I must to make Morris know definitely that it is finished, and that I will not live with him again. He's such a softie though that I don't want to wound him too much."

"Can't you charge non-support?"

"Well—maybe—hardly though—I just don't know what I shall do."

"Yep, that good old procrastination stuff. Don't get a divorce and take to living with somebody else, and maybe he'll divorce you."

"Yes, but the men I'd live with have no money. I don't suppose it matters though. What kind of a change has one to look forward to; it costs money to get a divorce and I haven't even enough to live on."

"Have you anything you can do at all?"

"O yes, if I can make myself feel the stress of need I suppose there is. I've done newspaper work, and I do like writing articles on flowers, and weeds, the vagabond flowers. If it weren't for Ba-ba I wouldn't mind how I got on, but a youngster forces a certain standard of living."

"It's too bad papers won't use more articles of that sort. I'd like to know more than I do about botany—orchids—gad, some of them are breathlessly lovely, and a little vicious maybe. Such ones as they had the other day in a window in Fifth Avenue. About ten different kinds—lilac clusters, and tiny pink ones, and butterfly blue and yellow ones, that all seemed palpitating in vapour rather than daring to be real things at all."

"Flowers, birds, and insects, are about all I care to read about now. I'm through reading novels at any rate. Realism is too much for me as the Russians put it across, and so is the depiction of sociological situations."

"Yes, ghastly some of the stuff; self-cringing, hopeless-hopefulness, and interpretation. I thought you said you were trying to work up a flower trade once; have you dropped that?"

"Oh no, not quite. Now and then someone writes me to buy flowers for a table arrangement, or some such thing. An old man I met the other day who tried flirting with me gave me an order too to buy flowers for him daily. He suggested that I bring them to his rooms myself, but I managed to get the order and evade that. He treats me with such chivalrous respect now."

They came to Lillie's apartment, and went up, as Lillie had said she would go dancing with Peter if she could manage to get neighbors in the apartment next to her to look after Barbara should they hear her crying because she was alone.

Barbara greeted them from her cot where her father had put her, coming in from a room in the back of the big apartment building. He lingered a while, wanting to be friendly to Lillie, but she was casual to him, giving him the hint that he might as well go back to his own room. Barbara had to jump out of bed and rush in to see who the visitor was, and at once leaped upon Peter's lap and cuddled down, without ceremony. She would not sit still; tried tickling him, and pulling at his sprout mustache, assuring him that he had teeth like a dog.

"Now Ba-ba, it's time for you to go to bed," Lillie told her.

"O mother, mother, I love you so much I just can't sleep" Baba said as subterfuge to be allowed to stay up, and cuddled her wriggly bony little body into Peter, saying she must kiss him too.

"You could dispense with some of this lady's liveliness at times I'll bet," Peter said. "At that though kids aren't more of a nuisance than other people who're around all the time."

Barbara, knowing herself talked about, used this as an opportunity to stay up, and began babbling, saying obvious things that became remarkable because they were so to her. When she was not being listened to she talked to herself; listened to again she began to tell a story about angleworms. No longer listened to she babbled into incoherence, utterly vivacious and flirtatious to space, her sensitive eyebrows twitching as she made gestures and facial expressions at her imaginary characters.

"This is the sort of thing the new education does to kids, I take it."

"Not bad either; I can get Ba-ba to do what I ask her without much trouble, just by appealing to her sense of justice. Of course not always, but what system is invulnerable?"

Soon Ba-ba was back in bed, and Lillie was ready to go out again. Just outside on the street they passed Beryl Marks, who either did not speak at all, or spoke so distantly they did not notice her greeting.

"Do you know her?" Peter asked.

"I've been introduced many times, and sometimes she speaks to me, and sometimes she dosen't. She's a strange person. There's so much that is overbearing and insolent in her manner, but she certainly is a magnificent looking being, isn't she?"

'I think she covers up shyness with her insolence. I don't believe she's actually unbearably arrogant. New York's apt to make one assume a mask of bumptiousness if you have to make a living in it under some circumstances."

"Certainly anyway there's no superiority in Beryl's manner

51

of rudeness though," Lillie commented, uncritically, saying the remark as an observation.

Peter was liking Lillie much at the moment for her quiet assurance and tranquillity. It seemed as though she'd understand much without one's commenting, and beneath her calm acceptance of things there was a quality which came to him as an emanation that captured his senses.

They came to Charlie's dance club, and entered at the moment when the blind piano player was singing "Mandalay" vehemently, so that the swing and rhythm of it began at once to drunken Peter's senses to a carefree abandonment, as rhythmed music always did. He didn't mind the singer's rather raucous voice. Looking about the room he felt a slight revolt against there being so many Jewish people about. "One will never get away from the Jews in New York, and I'm wanting a vacation from them," he sputtered, and then, remembering that Lillie was Jewish he squirmed within himself for his habit-minded intolerances, and added, "the deadly commercial type I mean; what one thinks of as the obvious Jewish quality. Of course one can't fit individuals into any such generalized intolerance as that."

XV

After dancing several dances Lillie said she'd have to get back to Barbara. Damn Barbara, Peter thought, and went out of the café with her, saying "I'll come up and get you another night soon." At her place she asked him if he wanted to come upstairs for a time. He hesitated. Damn Barbara, anyway. What was the use of going up to that tiny two-adjoining room apartment with the youngster apt to be awake and listening through the curtains. He'd say no. He wondered—gad, every time he'd seen Lillie her time had been chopped into pieces by little necessary duties concerning Barbara.

"I think I won't," he told her, taking her hand to say goodnight. Holding it a moment he felt the cord in his arm twitching with its ideo-motor response to his desire to draw her to him. He felt panicky inside, afraid that she would resent it if he did, or that if she didn't resent it she might only tolerate it amusedly. Just a slight effort, and he'd know whether to expect anything. But he did not make the effort. "Goodnight, I'll see you later in the week," he said and started away, though he turned, and saw Lillie lingering a moment before starting up the stairs, and wanted to go back, but he was too nervous and diffident to create the necessary excuse, so he turned and went on. He liked Lillie, every way, mind, body—but—damn Barbara. She was all right as a youngster but why was she about all the time?

Hurtling down the street he encountered Garey O'Brien, and felt in a way glad, as it was companionship.

"Hey Garey, whatcha up to," he spoke out. "Let's fall in together and hunt up some hootch somewhere."

"Is that all you have on your mind? I'm on."

"That's good. God, I want excitement. Come along and we'll pick up Rollie Walters at the Playhouse and go on the hunt in a pack of three. I'm perishing with having led too sane and respectable a life for a long time."

They fell into step together, and strode on, the minute O'Brien puffing to keep up with Peter's long-legged stride. "I've been working like the devil the last week myself," Garey stated, "doing an article on some French writers, and trying to blast some ideas regarding subject matter in literature, which is always repetitious, and trying to locate some basis other than a pedantic one upon which to discuss form, so as to have a platform of esthetic criticism."

"Ya. I can't say I expect much of that kind of research myself. Whatever form is it's at least individual, and formulas about it aren't interesting."

"We have to build up a tradition on something."

"On Bunk, I'd say; or on stupidity; there's a traditional background for any kind of imbecility that exists, as well as for anything that stands analysis. As you say, subject matter is the same as ever, and the past has had its sentimentalities and errors upon which fervid souls will build their platforms. There probably are things that are properly permanent, but they aren't the only things retained of, or excavated from the past."

"You know I've been thinking lately that intelligence is nothing but a disease."

"I've thought life was a disease too, but where are you with thinking things like that? Why not be inclusive? You keep your nose buried in books too much."

"You'll be talking about art for life's sake at that rate in a minute; reading is one of the few decent experiences a man can have."

"Yes, but you don't take it as a satisfying experience then, because you're always trying to propagand about life because of what you've been reading. If, as you've said, there's a sheer esthetic enjoyment to be had from literature apart from subject matter and ideas, why do you always get so ideational, and set upon proving ideas you evolve from reading, mainly, rather than from actual observation?"

"My God man, you're going to be asking art to be democratic or uplifting in a moment."

"That kind of remark is about your rate. What bearing has it on what I've just said? For the love of Mike, let's stop talking ideas. You're a good enough drinking companion. I say that intelligence, if it's worth a damn, is a whole organic thing that enables the organism it resides in to cope with experience."

"That's simply saying the old 'seeing life whole' formula, and it makes travelling salesmen the ideally intelligent beings of the universe. They cope with experience."

"Like hell they do. They limit experience for themselves; I haven't said that the intelligence couldn't have imagination that explored and tried to discover, and create variations that are satisfying to one's senses. I don't know what life is; I don't know definitely what anything you can point out from where we're standing is, either, finally. You don't either. But I can sense whether a thing is authentic, and a good quality of the class of thing it is one of. Why does one need rules by which to judge things when one has alert senses with which to judge from moment to moment, and those alert senses trained somewhat in their observations by experience, and its assimilation?"

"That doesn't give a basis for judging anything, since personalities and temperaments are so different."

"However different they are if they don't discover something in common there is no basis anyway; certainly none that rules can authenticate. I don't think the scope of sensual, and emotional, experience of people is so large that there isn't a good chance of people being able to communicate to each other without formulas. By God, I think sometimes the scope is so small that I detest the way sympathy tyrannizes one's energies, and makes one feel the despair and discouragement of one's age. Even the dumb, blind, ignorant ones get one's sympathetic understanding. That's how common to everyone experience seems to me."

They came to the Playhouse, and asked at the ticket window for Rollie Walters, who appeared in a few minutes.

"O man, you have a new suit," Garey greeted Rollie. "The success of one little theatre play certainly does add to the wealth and dignity of such as create the 'artistic future' of the nation. I'll bet you've been eating regularly, and change your underwear once a month now."

Rollie smiled bravely, aware that such activity was demanded of him, and soon joined the two, so that they all set out to go to a place where they could get some sort of liquor.

"I haven't had any dinner. Do you fellows mind coming in while I have a cup of coffee and a roll?" Rollie queried, heading them towards a lunch counter.

Past the lunch counter Garey assured Peter that art is just an excrescence of the organism anyway.

"Mein gott; you'll be quoting me a Wilde, or a Whistler epigram next," Peter exploded. "At that you don't live up to the import of your own statements, with your literary mentalizing of everything, and in a way quite unrelated to what's surrounding you. You'd put peacock feathers on a moulting hen."

A wave of tiredness and aversion went over Peter, perhaps because he noticed how wearily Rollie accompanied them. O'Brien might have the sense to see how wearingly boring he was being and lay off drawing him into this arty-art discussion.

He didn't want to bother at the moment making statements he didn't feel the strength of, since his interest in ideas was completely palled for the time being. But the drone of a voice, O'Brien's, continuing beside his ear continued. Ideas filtered through the atmosphere going into and from his brain desultory as flies lazy with summer heat. He was talking without volition, almost without consciousness. As he had stepped into the restaurant a blast of coffee warm air, a humidity of vapours steeped in food odours and stale human breath, assailed him, and with this blast came another, more over-powering, of unreality, and of a nauseated indifference such as the mind will swoon into at times. Bored with whatever he, or anybody else, could think, bored with human helplessness and desire, he spoke on, wondering if awareness of unreality settled on other poeple so envelopingly as it did at times on him. An impulse within him wished to push aside O'Brien, almost to cut him down with rudeness; another impulse wanted him to reach out and to somehow make Rollie reveal himself so that there could be an easy companionship there. But he spoke instead, to O'Brien.

"Intellectual men, so-called, are the greatest naifs in the world, expecting cerebration alone to function where it is not meant to; and in evolving theories in abstraction that aren't helpful in reality. Maybe I run away too strongly from the "subjective escape," but it seems to me that it's only we subjective ones who give it to ourselves in the neck."

Then the aversion to thinking out loud what he felt overcame him. He could not talk on. He watched Rollie's face, curious, to read beneath the burnt out expression in his eyes, as he recalled the first time he'd seen Rollie, over year a back, he'd been vigorously fresh, and alive.

"We ought all go away somewhere," he spoke after a pause. "Anywhere, where people are less futilely informed than we are, with information that doesn't suit any market we can find, and cannot compete with what we think is third-rate information, that however suits the situations about us more opportunistically than does ours."

Rollie looked interested for a moment. "Yes,—I don't feel

56

like roughing it though, and I'd have to—no money. The only thing to do is to give the next generation so much of our sophistication that it rebels and vomits it up" he spoke broodingly to his reflection in the sticky shiny white of the table top before him. Peter watched him, thinking him a pathetic case, if one gave a damn about pathos. Why need he let Rollie's devitalization depress him? Why is a success so much more desirable than a failure, unless something really positively originative is attained?

"One shouldn't let oneself become extinct because of apathy though," he suggested. "One can manifest energy. Probably if you'd break away to somewhere else you'd feel more like being energetic. Anyway the chance could be taken since you haven't anything in New York you want apparently."

O'Brien came in, taking up the thread of his old antagonizing conversation with Peter. "You're between Chicago and Europe; hesitating between prairie yowling and . . ."

"No, no, no, no, let that matter drop. Wherever I am, I am, and why not? You can't prove I ought to be somewhere else if I have feeling enough about it to be where I am. After all, having life, one wants to explore if for one's self, assuming that if the process ever was worth while it's as much worth adventuring into for discovery as it ever was."

O'Brien was wounded by Peter's strongly ejaculated irritation. He felt his wit desiring to fence with and cut through the disrespect which he sensed Peter had for his perceptions, and he wished too, not to be too persistent. Condolingly he said.

"There's no esthetic sense in this country. Do you know I've thought the fact that we have no real religion in this country that signifies to the masses is largely responsible. No God acceptance is more than a mannerism here. We ought to manufacture a religion to be worshipful or blasphemous about so as to get colour and design into us some way."

"Just as you want a manifesto on other things; it's likely fortunate that such ideas can't be made to grow into the public by a foisting process. I'm glad to be free to be a complete agnostic without it being a shock to anybody! I can't conceive of a religion that would actually signify. Long ago apathy about that sort of thing rode me out of the areas where atheism, nihilism, futilism, buddhism, or agnosticism, mean anything but vague concepts of an agglomerated universe. I couldn't get any satisfaction out of being naughtily sacrilegious, or fervidly religious, either. I don't know, and I don't care, about anything but now and here, and what's to be done about this."

O'Brien, insisting that there was something wrong with his bladder, retired to the lavatory. Peter, chuckling, said to Rollie, "Poor old Garey. He cherishes a romantic notion that he will die of a twisted bladder, and uses that as proof that he is a genius since so many geniuses have had physical defects. The other day he told me that Nietzsche, de Gourmont, and Whitman had all in some way been physically or sexually incapacitated, and was sure that was the reason for their quality. Maybe that's the reason we've had so many brooding intelligences in the last generation or so. God, I don't want to hear anything more religiously or sexually ecstatic, or any more cerebral brooding, second hand. I suppose I can stand the firsthand, underived kinds."

"I'm disgusted," Rollie declared. Peter looked hopeful, believing himself too far gone for disgust, but Rollie did not add anything beyond that simple statement. O'Brien came back from the lavatory, and immediately commented,

"You know, I believe there'll be another coming of Christ soon. The world is about in the shape for it."

"Did he ever come?" Rollie questioned ironically, as they all rose to go out. A passerby in the restaurant had flicked some cigarette ashes into O'Brien's eye, and he was grumblingly trying to rub it out with his handkerchief, neurotically upset that such miserable things happen. His pale little Irish face, with its dim blue eyes, was distorted with nervous discomfort.

"Good God, a man can't leave his glasses off a minute without some damned thing happening," he declared pathetically, showing that he felt bewildered and beaten out of existence. "And if I stay out late tonight, as I'd like, and get drunk, I'll be in a hell of a shape tomorrow. I think I'll lose my job on the trade journal anyway. I can't write commercial articles, even if I have to make a living."

"Got it?" Peter asked of the cigarette ash. "All right, let's get out of here. I know a dugout where we can get some hootch that hasn't wood alcohol in it. How much money have you on you? I've only five dollars and don't want to spend it all."

XVI

The three came to a cellar with an iron barred gate. When Rollie rang the bell a woman came and stuck her head through a hole in the door, and then admitted them. The place was one that was a brothel upstairs, with a room full of tables below, where liquor was sold at high prices. As they entered Peter noticed that several men and women were about, and among them Gusta, sitting at a table with Beryl Marks.

"Someone has been telling me of a rich man who sent a writer two hundred dollars because he was going blind," Gusta remarked to Peter. "I'll have to locate that rich man and tell him I'm a writer, and losing my complexion. That's much more disastrous to a lady writer than the loss of eyesight."

"Shucks Gusta, if you want me to assure you that your skin is still ravishingly lovely, I will. That's not altogether because I'm such an easy liar either," Peter assured her, and sat at a table nearby with Rollie and O'Brien, noticing out of the corner of his eye that Gusta was feeling animated, and evidently wanted attention if her vanity was not to be piqued. He, and the others, ordered drinks, and he caught the end of a remark Garey O'Brien had just made.

"She'll be walking up and down Fourteenth Avenue picking up men some day, that's sure."

"Who's that you're speaking of?" Peter asked.

"Vera Ryder. She's a nice girl, only she doesn't use her head. She puts into practice all the freedom of action the other women around the village talk about. If she likes a man, she lets him know it at once, and lets him have her. Then he quits being interested. If she'd be a little more careful she could get herself taken care of."

"How in the devil do you know she wants that? It's too bad though she can't manage to go on the Broadway stage. She can act rather well, and looks well enough surely."

"Deuce of a nice girl, but she doesn't use her bean at all," O'Brien said, and then stopped, apparently noticing that Rollie was looking strange, and remembering that Rollie had lived with Vera for some months. Peter too, knowing this, hastily remarked,

"Let's order another round of drinks," and did so, as they all put their present drinks down in a gulp each. Before long the strong liquor was affecting them. Peter's head felt dizzy, and he was seeing vertiginously. Garey began talking more noisily about "keeping women in their place."

"The devil with it, I'll bet your wife beats you and you're the tame little husband," Peter assured him. "Why try to say where anybody's place is? Nobody ever keeps placed in the class you assign him to in a generality anyway. I'm going over and talk to Gusta for a while, before I get too glitteringly lit up."

Gusta was finishing some narration about "a charming fellow, but he doesn't learn much by experience."

"How shockingly original a being," Beryl Marks snorted.

"Who's that you're talking about? Me? It fits anyway."

"Well, it wasn't you. Do you think I think you're charming? Tush."

"Poor guy, anyway. But let's talk about thieves or murderers, or roughnecks. Or what's more important, let's have a drink."

"Yes, do order. Do you know Peter, I actually did some sketching today, for the first time in years it seems."

"Gad, do you paint too?"

"My dear, indeed yes, Gusta's her own original portrait of the artist," Beryl said huskily, and felt herself impelled to reach for her own lipstick that she never let get much rest.

"Well, I have a decided leaning towards Gusta, but this puts me to the test. Remember I pose for artists."

"She's been putting me to the test tonight too," Beryl said

with mock bitterness. "When I came in she started to tell me I was an exceptional person, and I thought she'd been reading something I'd written; but no; what she had to say was that I had a really kind heart after all. Dearie, I can tell you I've paid."

"Beryl was telling me about some of the interesting views she's had with various people as a reporter; such energy and experience as you must have, Beryl. I do envy you."

"Ho, ho, for God's sake? Me have energy? I've been dragging my hips around New York for the last five years ready to be taken away to the dump heap, and still these male editors I want to sell special articles try to feel my figure, or comment on my shape, when I go to market with my literature. You'd think they'd have learned there are mirrors in the world by now, but no, they think it's the great compliment for them to insinuate they're ready to play with you."

"Have another drink," Peter said.

"Asti spumante, dearie. Oh dearie, what asti spumante can do for one!" Beryl talked. "Sure; my gut's in a hell of a shape already, but order me some more of that firewater—what is it? I was interviewing Loraine Dale, the show girl, about her divorce yesterday, and she dearie-d me all over the map, talking about the Asti Spumante she used to get in Italy, and what a glass of it could do for her life. She got real chummy with me, and showed me 600 photographs of herself in the nude or near nude. She wanted me to understand just what it was that made her so appealing to the various husbands she's grabbed out of the rag bag. Buh-lieve me dearie, she said to me, buhlieve me, you don't mind my calling you dearie, but buhlieve me, why should I go on the stage again, when that big stiff I'm divorcing has ten cold million bucks. I ain't the kind of woman to be treated like a bauble. I make them pay, buhlieve me dearie. I do wish I had some asti spumante to offer you. . . . That's the kind of thing I have to write refined interviews from; can you see me?"

"If I begin to get incoherent from now on, be kind to me," Peter confided. "My head's swirling. But should we have another round?"

"It is strong," Gusta commented, "but I've been so excessively dull lately. Feeling finished. The war, you know, waiting three years for my husband, and coming here expecting to find him only to find that he was drowned. What's left for me?"

"What's left for anybody if you ask that enough? Don't you think you'd have tired of him someday, anyway? Maybe memory is better than actuality," Peter sympathized.

"Such a baby as you are," Beryl broke in. "I'm just wondering if I shouldn't take you home with me, and teach you— life—dearie."

"It'd better be before many more drinks then, or I won't be a very satisfactory pupil," Peter answered.

Beryl, however, departed soon, and with her went most of the expressive life in the room, since Gusta was feeling heavy headed, and disgust began to settle into Peter, morbidly. How heavy his head was—damn bootleg whisky. How oppressive the thick room, grayness, airless,—he was smothering—was there no poignancy of feeling left to protest in him . . .

Gusta was sunk in a trance of muddled abstraction. He watched her face for a moment, angry at circumstances for her, for anybody. Rebellion is a myth; apathy the only wise emotion, then. His drunkenly befogged brain was wavering on the point of unconsciousness continually, alternately blank and aware— a blind being opened and shut over his mind. He intensely resented the sound of young raucous laughter that sounded across the room at another table, and resented his own foolishness in having drunk so much. Trying to see Gusta's face as a cameo instead of a blur, he noted the dilation of her nostrils, as she blew cigarette smoke from them. A graceful spiral of smoke was going up in the air from her cigarette as she held it carelessly in her hand by her side. "Smoke comes so actually into the air, and fades away until the air is clear, or almost clear," a line said itself into his brain. "To take up speach once more; let warmth regain its reign; the unreality of thought twinge in us like a phantom pain." No, no, why did lines like that come into his mind? He wanted to stretch out his arms and emit a squack, a shout, anything to get stale air out of his lungs, his blood. Why

62

shouldn't he shriek out profanity, but why should he? He did heave a sigh, and stretched his arms back behind him, tensely across the back of his chair. He leaned his head back, and felt the blood rushing to his head, so that he seemed to be falling, fainting perhaps.

"O, are you ill?" Gusta exclaimed, and caught at his arm. He laughed, sitting upright.

"No, only stretching. Stuffy in here, isn't it?"

"Smothering."

"I think I'll go. Are you leaving soon?"

"No, I'm waiting for a woman whose apartment I'm to stay at tonight."

Peter arose, and looked down at Gusta's face as he swayed, seeing it dimly. He wanted to touch her, to lean over and put his face into her neck so as to try and shut out the heavy ache in his head, and to feel flesh, but after a moment's indecision, he stumbled away to the table where Garey and Rollie were, both drunk as he was.

"Hey, let's get out of this joint. My God, I'll choke with smoke and stinky breath in here," he jerked out at them, and saw that Vera Ryder was with them. "We can get some fresh air, and then some coffee before turning in. And then instead of turning in let's all take a train to somewhere a thousand miles away, in the country."

"That sounds good, but who has got the train fare?" Vera commented, concealing a great yawn as she drew her lithe long body taut.

"Besides, I couldn't," Rollie joined in. "I'm working on a new theory about painting. . ."

"Whoops, wait, save it," Peter halted him.

"Yes, Rollie started a picture as a geometric design, began to wind his group about a little to get a circular effect, introduced a few squares and triangles, and now he's where he started," Garey mumbled.

"How the philosophy of the eternal repetition of things will keep coming up," Peter said. "But are we going?"

At a street corner some moments later the group stood to say

63

goodnight. "I'll have to be home in time to hush the baby in her nightly yowl, that occurs at three to four in the morning," Garey said, less muddled with drink than he had been, since the cold night air had cleared his head somewhat.

"A man who devotes so much of his time to talking about the futility of existence isn't doing right by the infant to have an infant," Rollie teased him. "How is the darling?"

"Lusty. She sits right on her daddy's knee and is apt to dampen it without a moment's notice," Garey said, turning away and starting off. Rollie too said good night, and left Peter standing with Vera.

XVII

As Vera and Peter went into the night restaurant for a lunch before retiring, he commented, "Life seems to be reducing itself to drinking coffee, smoking cigarettes and waiting between times for the tenth of an appetite to do those things again."

"Yes, I tried to change the routine a little this summer by going back to my little home town in New Hampshire but that was impossible. Family."

"Didn't they approve, or have a slight understanding of you?"

"They were just oppressively familiar and personal; too far from any idea that I know or care about now."

"It's too bad to go back, but some memory, or habituary affection makes one think at moments that the family relationship might, after all, mean something."

Vera reflected a time, and said, "I almost believe I disliked my mother for her worrying affection; it was so interfering and cared so little about what I actually wanted."

"O there's no doubt that maternal attitudes are brutal in their effects at times, under the name of mother love that actually wants children to be about only so as to be some reason for their existence; something upon which the mother can express herself. It's an octopus strangle rather than love. I feel entirely confused with revolt, and desire not to wound, when my own mother's about."

Vera leaned over and patted his hand, saying "Don't look so melancholy."

He looked self-conscious. "My God, am I looking that, or only naturally gloomy?" For the first time he became really aware of Vera as a person, rather than as somebody to talk to merely.

"It's four A.M. and I have to be up at nine. Do you want to come around to my room with me?" Vera asked, and they went out together to Vera's place.

In the morning Peter awoke to see Vera smiling down at him. "Don't get up unless you want to, but I must get some breakfast and leave for rehearsal inside of half an hour." He jumped out on the floor, quickly awake. "Not going to have a heavy head, maybe," he declared, feeling relieved. "You're quite a domestic soul doing your own cooking, aren't you?"

"Forced to economically. What'll you have; eggs, and how?"

"Ever been married?"

"No, but I'm not exactly inexperienced."

"Doesn't mean too much, the concept of experience? But you don't seem to have the pestilential air of having lived, by god, that one sees about a good deal," Peter talked, and felt his eye beginning to throb. "My lord, my eye's aching. The damned thing starts that about once a week. Maybe it'll go, though, when I get out into the air."

"Why did you ask me about marriage?"

"O I wasn't going to propose to you; I was just mildly curious about your attitude. Marriage doesn't seem up to much as an institution, but then neither are any of its substitutes."

"It means as much or as little as people let it, and the letting depends on temperament, I guess. I lived with a man for over a year and felt quite wifely to him; he irritated me, but he had to be looked after and I knew rather how to manage him."

"Rollie Walters, that was, wasn't it?"

"Yes, poor Rollie."

"Why did you separate?"

"Just chance. I went to New Hampshire, and when I came back the bond between us didn't seem sufficient for us to start living together again. No novelty to inspire us."

"I don't know him well, but sometimes I get the impression that he has something worth while in him."

"He has everything, and nothing; spurts of energy that get shorter lived all the time, and now his melancholy and sentimentality seem to be conquering him."

Vera stood near Peter and reached over to give his hair a jerk. "You might comb that before you sit down to breakfast" she scolded, so he puttered away at his head a moment, and came to embrace her."

"You're a restful person, the way you don't bother to listen too much to one's ideas, or disturb one with ideas of your own. I can't decide whether you're a very wise person or not."

"Why try to?"

"I don't really, but almost as an instinct now I've taken to measuring people too much by what they possess in the way of information. That's a horrible confession, isnt' it?"

"Maybe I've gotten over that; as I got over being a social revolutionist," Vera stated. "One winter I did platform lecturing for the cause."

Peter laughed. "And the faith necessary to go on deserted you, I take it. Sometimes I feel a slight admiration for fanatics except that their convictions so seldom convince one, and are inclined to cause them to interfere with other people. Civilization, belly-pragmatized and gut-rationalized as it may be, isn't particularly helped. I get afraid of the scheme they have to release us, and think they will only bring about more cramping social moralities and conventions, too economically or religiously based. Some of them are society's subconscious I suppose, and their energy appears to be rather dirtied with the type of suppression they've gone in for that makes their conscious expressions have an unclean background of imagination. One distrusts their shame."

"Well, I'm past being ashamed, for myself, or for anybody else, whatever they do," Vera answered him, putting on her hat and coat to go out. "I'll have to be off now," she added, and soon they parted. He, on the street, watched her as she walked away, and felt, he thought, too impersonal, cold-minded, cold-hearted to her now. For a moment last night it had seemed to him that he adored her, as he wondered why more moments of tenderness such as they'd felt for each other in intercourse did not occur in life. But the passing of that kind of emotion was no new thing to him. Still he knew, he would want her again.

His head began aching vilely; and his eye. God-damn the body ailments, he stormed within himself. Was there pus in one of his sinuses or antrums? Disgusting doctors. There was no use seeing them. They didn't know how to diagnose. They'd probably have to scrape around in his head with instruments if he went to see one of them, but he couldn't have that eye aching so often. Ah, he'd let the damned thing ache; couldn't stand having his head monkeyed with — too nerve wracking. But he could taste vertiginous blood, in his eyes, so that he was dizzy, sickish. The devil with that rotgut liquor last night. He'd get Bromo-Seltzer at the druggist's and have it over with.

In the drugstore it disgusted him the sloppy way the clerk made his Bromo-Seltzer concoction. He might have been clean about it, and the stuff didn't effervesce very well either. He ought to ignore his bodily ailments as he had when he was a youngster, and stop this old maidish pampering of himself. It was too much, getting older, and cautious, as if life were worth caution, and this oncoming increase of fastidiousness, aversions, and extra sensibilities.

He drank the Bromo-Seltzer sourly, and belched, disliking the powdering foam which it left on his moustache. But he'd forget his headache now, and cut out being grumpy inside himself with self-condolence. Who'd give a damn about his ailments, and what did they matter? Soon he was out on the street, beginning to feel exuberant again, and forgetful about remembering not to be cranky about his headache.

XVIII

"Just a minute, Peter."

"Huh, Gusta, glad you've come along. If you're feeling gay you can infect me, and if you're feeling as rotten as I am there's a drugstore nearby where we can get something and die enjoying our misery mutually."

"Not me today. I'm going to the country, and wanted to see you to say goodbye. My folks in England finally sent me some money so that I feel a wealthy woman again. I'll go away and come back after I'm rested to start renting out houses, or some such thing."

"Tosh, Gusta, you a business woman?"

"I've been so miserable lately. I do hope the country air sets me up again."

"What is unhappiness anyway, or its opposite? You're doomed to confusion and misery. What does it all matter so long as there's movement of some kind?"

"Don't talk nonsense. You're such an infant. When one's unhappy one can't feel to know whether movement's about one or not."

"O, it's a type of helplessness you mean—a brooding—O I don't know. What are we talking about? Both happiness and unhappiness are types of stupidity, and what I'm saying is another kind. I'd better head for the country too."

"Who've you been seeing lately? Anybody that matters?"

"Bats, there aren't any such people if you ask me today. Well, the usual assortment. You and the others last night. Jimmy, Brander. Considered in relation they're important enough probably. My intolerations insist upon importance I guess. O Martha Wullus too—know her? I'd like to run around and say hello to her. Come along with me won't you."

"I've just met her. She's rather quaint."

"All of that. She thinks anything, disapproves of little, for other people, and is a churchgoing, cerebralizing moralist who observes sabbath day strictly, herself. I can't quite understand why with a mind like hers agnosticism hasn't eaten into her a little, but it seems not to have, or she conceals it well, for her mother's sake possibly."

"It isn't reasonable to be as rigid as that with the kind of intellect she seems to have. There's some suppression or cowardice there."

"Possibly she isn't emotionally developed much, but still there's the force of experience back of her knowledge; there must be for her to realize what she does. She needs to be seen apart from the background of her mother to be actual, though."

Going around the corner at one block they encountered Brander Ogden, surveying the street with his usual air of connoisseurship towards humanity and traffic. He greeted them gaily.

"Ha, ha, so I've run into two darlings at once. It's so natural to see you two together, though."

He joined them, to go to Martha's apartment, and chatted with deliberate facetiousness. "My word, I must tell you about the white peacocks I saw at the house of a friend in the country Sunday. They were the final thing in beauty, with their gorgeous whiteness, and the circle spots, of a different shade of white in their tails, that looked like staring blind eyes."

Peter's mind withdrew from listening but vaguely to the conversation. White peacocks. White music. White winds; white with every colour in the world in it. He'd write something about that. White and purity. What is purity? It certainly couldn't have anything to do actually with physical acts. White winds blowing, cool and fresh through the white sky. Like the days far back in North Dakota when the blizzards hurled white sleet snow across the snow-covered plains. How tired he was of apathy; how primitively clear those winds, that snow, had been; and all the while through the whiteness to the eye the winds had shrieked out a cold blue symphony. What could one say of beauty, of white peacocks, of golden pheasants? Why weren't people so colorfully beautiful. The devil with visible reality. Here, where mental and physical weariness were pursuing him, something went on storming inside him, regardless of what he said, how he acted, so that he himself or nobody else knew him.

69

From protoplasm to come, suffer the variegated impacts of experience, reaction, thinking, feeling and responding, how? — there was everything to question and nothing to understand.

"I think I'd be bored to death with Martha Wullus if it weren't that I can't get her angle," Peter broke in suddenly on Brander's and Gusta's conversation.

"Now, now, wait. I like the way this boy tells people what's what, and when, but you have to watch out for him," Brander joked looking at Peter curiously, so that Peter felt irritation come up in him because of his resentment against the look that nullified him. But the resentment passed in a flash, and he spoke up again saying, "I think I'll put an ad in the paper and try to get a job in a psychological laboratory. The kind of existence I'm leading is eating me up."

"Yes, do anything but be an artist who's interested in art. I feel myself as though I must get away and never hear the word art again."

"Hell, you'd feel as though you had to get away and never hear the word business, or education, again, if you were in circles where those terms are used frequently. Where human beings consort about ideas and trades, there's a place to want to get away from."

"I know; and of course the only possible thing to be is an artist, and enjoy the divine trivialities. Isn't it too wonderful to feel that the only thing one needs think about is a form, or a line, or a bit of colour in a design."

Arriving at Martha's place Peter rang the bell, and while waiting, Brander said: "Isn't Martha the quaint idea rather than a real human though. She's sort of a Dresden doll thing with those great contemplative Chinese eyes of hers, and that wisplike body with its thatch of carrot-coloured hair. So picturesque too in her half-boyish clothes."

"Probably it's best for her to be only an idea too, seeing that ideas is about all she'll have of life," Peter responded, and Martha was at the door inviting them in with formal hospitality that had a whimsical directness.

"O good day, and how have all of you been; you Miss Rolph,

particularly? I've so wanted to have a conversation with you because of what I've heard about your work."

"What tricks have you been up to yourself?" Brander asked Martha.

"I haven't been doing much that I want to do. My work keeps me away from—my work, the real kind I'm wanting to do."

"Bother your paid work. You observe things too uniquely to let any paid job interfere much with your writing." Gusta said rather curtly. "Though I presume you believe in self-discipline and duty more than some of us do."

"It is true that I have never expressed so far any of the things that I particularly wish to say. But I shall soon attempt to put down some of my observations; nothing absolute. To put my remarks in verse though, as I have attempted, is like trying to dance the minuet in a bathing suit, though I do have some things to say about acacias and seaweeds and serpents in plane-trees that will have to appear in fragments."

"What a person. What a person." Brander declared. "And how calm and collected you manage to remain through it all."

Martha chortled. "You must not be too sure of that. I was quite unable to control myself at the library today, and I fear I spoke curtly to the head librarian for some of her trite insistences... But I find seahorses, lizards, and such things very fascinating. Also a fox's face, the picture of which I saw recently in a magazine, haunts me like a nightmare, and contradictory as it seems, I am quite able to appreciate the 'bright beaming expression' that Xenophon talks about, on the face of the hound which was pursuing it."

Mrs. Wullus was in the sitting room when they entered, and during their stay drawled out her observations, making distinctions of her exact meaning with a too careful honesty that had its limitations, it seemed to Peter, who felt his impetuosity repelled by the older woman, who was much given to moralizing.

"While I am Irish myself I cannot approve of the way the Irish have been acting in this country." Mrs. Wullus stated. "And no more can I sympathize greatly with Mr. McSwiney in his hunger strike in Ireland."

71

"Why I wouldn't starve myself to death for any cause in the world," Martha said, and chuckled. Her mother echoed the chuckle, and laughed in a way that she must have considered immoderate.

"My, you mustn't ever make as funny a remark as that again," Mrs. Wullus declared, and went into a lengthier dissertation upon the Irish.

"Can't you get away now, and let's all go down to Solveig's and have a nice long chat over some tea, or coffee? I know you won't smoke cigarettes," Brander suggested, wanting to get Martha away from her mother, who lacked the whimsicality of Martha as a personality. Some minutes later the four of them came into Solveig's dingy little bohemian café, where several nondescript individuals were lounging about, in groups.

"Solveig's the only person about this section of town who has any reality about her," Brander asserted, after they'd seated themselves. "The first time I saw her last week after a month's absence—she must have heard that I was hard up—she told me to come here and eat whenever I needed to, and she would see me through. Isn't it fine to know that people like her, with no pretensions of any sort, actually like you for what you are? She charged upon me and shouted: Hell, Brander old dear. Where've you been keeping yourself? My God, I've wanted to see you or somebody who wasn't talking about life or art, but I didn't know your address. My nose is good, and I'm adventurous, having been a streetwalker in my day, but honestly kiddo I can't smell out where you're staying."

"Was that the truth about herself?" Peter asked curiously.

"Yes indeed. She's had experience all right, every kind. Affairs with prize fighters, policemen, sailors. I guess she doesn't even hold herself aloof from intellectuals. A wonderful girl she is. So real. Just one of the plain, dirty, outspoken, big souls of the world she is. She's one of the real women. It's so nice to encounter fine girls such as she."

Solveig came up to Brander to exchange boisterous jovialities; there were additions to their party from tables nearby as here seemed the noise center of the room, and the situation had soon resolved itself to one faltering between banal dullness and forced brilliance, punctuated by casual conversation, picked up, sustained, dropped, and again re-insisted upon. Now, sitting quietly, Peter felt tired wonder settling all through him, physically and mentally, as a reaction from his drunkenness of last night. Watching all that went about it seemed to him that he was incapable of an emotion or a conviction about anything, or any person, except an emotion of wearied bewilderment of wonder. Nothing about was in any way related to him; he could sit silly, feel burnt out, almost washed out to extinction with a day-after reaction; and no circumstance could make him to himself an actual part of it, so removed and dumfounded by all of life and by any reality was he. His eyes, looking introspectively at Martha's face, and seeing her gulp in her throat, as though seeking to drink back some inexpressible desire, or to drink of some denied gratification, found pathos in the keen sensibility of her facial expressions. "Hungry too—and for what?" he reflected, and a dully submerged wave of rebellion against his own sympathy swept over his consciousness, taking him back to bewilderment.

"Ah—er—yes, not quite desirable you know. He's rather foul, you know—hardly a decent sort," his ears heard, while his eye noted an Englishman speaking. The blur of that face attempting to express correctness angered him. What was beneath that proper exterior, with its "not quite proper" or "not quite desirable" insularities?

"Yes, well just what do you mean?" a girl asked the man, evidently wishing to tease him.

"Kitty is afraid you might mean he's an ascetic or chaste, which would be an atrocity to her," another girl broke in.

"I'll have to use that in my book on men; just another idea for showing up what a sham he is," Gusta stated, appearing animated now that many people were about. "What tricks men do play on us doting women."

"You know Gusta you like the darlings too well to do them the harsh justice they need," Brander told her.

"Don't destroy my inspiration. I must do something, even if

73

it's only trying to be clever,"Gusta said, giving the impression of the real discouragement, almost despair behind her trifling.

"For God's sake, but this is a cheerful party," Solveig said, coming to the table, to lean her mop of yolk-coloured hair upon her hand, as she leaned over Brander. "I'm getting too old to be on the qui-vee vi-vee about all the things that are talked about in my exclusive little café. I'll go into a nunnery soon, now that the war's over and I can't be a Salvation Army lassie or a nurse.

"Dear me, yes," a pallid man, near forty, spoke in. "I'm so glad every time I think of life that I'm an artist. That is the only sanctuary after all isn't it?" and Peter knew that he'd have to be leaving this atmosphere in a moment, or shriek out some profanity, or some rudeness at various people who talked.

"Put that to music, won't you," a lady answered the man.

"O Doris, do be quiet. You're so coldly intellectual and cynical. What would you have us who feel strongly do, and how should we express ourselves?" a Jewish-looking girl declared. Peter's eye caught Martha's and he began an aside conversation with her.

"This sort of atmosphere drives me wild," he said. "And one gets enough abhorring indifference to existence without staying about here."

"It's pretty bad, I admit, still it's restraining oneself in the midst of annoyances to which one is subjected that toughens the muscles. Wildness in itself is an attractive quality, but it fails to take into account the question of attrition, and attrition is inevitable," she replied.

Peter, chafing inwardly at that answered, "Yes, but I haven't your ability to take into account the inevitability of attrition so readily, or to believe it needs be accepted as much as we have to."

"I lack your swiftness, myself, or rather I have no swiftness."

". . . that places a quickly intolerant judgment upon every situation that doesn't suit your mood as my swiftness does."

"No, no, I was thinking of my writing when I said that. I find many situations as intolerable as you do, and do not hesitate, I fear, to express my distaste."

"It's bad you haven't time to write then; can't you escape some of your routine labour?"

"That wouldn't help me, I'm sure. I am telling you the truth when I say that if I had all the time in the world I should not write anything important to myself for some years. In order to work as I should have to, I should like to look into certain things and make up my mind with regard to the relevance or irrelevance of certain other things. That may be hard for you to realize but it is quite true, and I have, I think, an intuition as to how I am to succeed if I do succeed."

"Yes, that; if you can know what success is; and not feel that waiting becomes in such a scheme of things the one activity," Peter said, wavering between admiration of, and restlessness about, Martha's attitude. He could not comprehend, more than as an idea, Martha's apparent ability to weigh and balance. "Of course I don't know what there is to express except some feeling about, or perception of—should I say, and take a chance of Brander's hearing—reality."

"What's that you're saying, Peter?" Brander interrupted.

"Shucks, you would hear when I use one of the words that's your pet aversion."

"What one is that?"

"Not life, or beauty, or art, or truth—but I did try to evade being too exact in my appellations by saying reality."

"Don't, for God's sake whatever you do, use those words seriously. It simply can't be done any longer, amongst a world so full of doting ecstatics, mystics, and other chatterers. I'd like them all taken out of the language."

Martha laughed her nervously spontaneous and quickly passing chuckle, whch seemed to crumple and dry up in a moment. Brander, observing her with his eagle eyes, said sotto voce "Doesn't Martha look piquant tonight? She's a rare one. Something so keen, and diamond hard in her direct observations. She's one of the rare ones too; one of the few who come off into some actuality."

"Yes, probably. She was telling me a while ago that she and her mother lived like anchorites, and that she could work as she was situated better than anywhere else. I can't get that. Of course any situation is the best situation if one knows how to utilize it, but she must want to break away often, and refuses to admit that she's caged."

Brander was looking at Peter's face so keenly that his gaze seemed to penetrate beneath even the bony structure. Then his gaze averted and he was listening in on other conversation, so that Peter's mind reverted to its bewildering analysis and dissection of all conversation and of his own emotions. Within a moment he knew he had to leave the café, the whole atmosphere of which was stifling him with the annihilation of purpose, and the breeding of unrest within him, which it brought about. Saying good afternoon, he banged hastily out of the place, and went catapulting down the street.

XIX

For a few minutes only an oppression and depression of the spirit that had crept into him because of the conglomeration of beings collected in the café lingered in him, and then, as he walked at a rapid pace across Fifth Avenue from the park, he began feeling vital again, with a clearer chaos in his mind than had been there before. Ideas on various people, on his own past, and more, an idealess brooding, drifted rapidly through his brain, until suddenly he was aware that he was whistling, and swaying along at a tremendous pace. Not brooding; not resentful; not even a little bit unhappy; scarcely able to understand why he or anybody ever should feel anything but free, and glad of strong bodies and a strong life stream of blood. But he knew this too was only an emotion; but that did not matter either. What had bothered him back there? Why try to remember? He'd go and see if Vera was at her room. No, not that either. She might have company, and he didn't want to have to talk to anybody. Was he composing a new piece of music as he whistled to himself; couldn't recall having heard the piece he was blowing out of his lips before. It was too bad he wasn't a composer, or a painter, so as to be able to dabble around with sound and colour now and then to amuse himself. Why did he always want to put colour he liked to his lips, almost to eat it? He was always wanting some sensual realization, carnally sensual, to possess anything that pleased his senses. Damned tired of being a civilized man, if he was one; wished he were a barbarian so he could wear barbaric costumes and jewels, nose rings, earrings, anklets—wished he could go and dance somewhere with somebody who really could dance, and in a place where there was colour and music that caught him up and lived up to his desire to express his vitality of being physically. As the wind went by him, coldly stinging, he could sense that it was dancing with him, but he could not leap up and dance, whirling around, jumping, striking the wind, here in the city streets.

But he'd walk miles, walk off this spurt of energy. To the devil with any kind of care. Life would happen as it would happen, and he would not allow it to batter him into a gray mass of lethargic protoplasm; not so long as energy enough remained within him to offer an exhilarated response to life. There was nothing to know but wonder, generally, and tiny finite facts that banged him in the face, and the rest could stay open, and unsolved.

New York Harbor

HE LUMBER BARGE HAD stood in the harbor for several days and I couldn't get to shore even if it was only a mile away, because the captain wouldn't let me lower the boat. He said it leaked. There was no place to land anyway as firms owning the various storehouses and docks would not permit a boat to land on their property.

It would be hot in the city at best, with not much to do but tramp about the streets, since everybody I knew was out of town for the summer. One day had gone by with fair rapidity, because I'd taken out all my bedclothes and washed them since steersmen of the barge for years back had slept on them, from their looks, with never a thought of cleanness. The second day had gone by too, because the night before bed bugs wouldn't let me sleep, even when I'd killed a hundred of them, so I was sleepy. After having taken the mattress of my cot and ridding it of innumerable bunches of bugs, and bug's eggs, and sprinkling it with gasoline, I let it stay out in the sun all morning. Also I put newspapers on the bunk that I would put the mattress back upon. So in the afternoon, when I'd made up my bunk, I was sleepy and felt sure the bed bugs wouldn't bother me if I took a nap. They didn't either, for that nap, though they were back in numbers before long, more indefatigably persistent about annoying me than I was about getting rid of them since it meant such constant work.

The captain was a little sandy-haired Virginian of Scotch extraction, and though he said he had no education, he was rather well informed, but he didn't talk much. A quiet, ironic, little man he was, with a romantic strain in him since he read wild-west stories all day, and acted romantically gallant towards his wife, in the evening, when we all sat in back of the barge cabin. I couldn't understand his sentiment of affection for her. She was a narrow-shouldered, waspish person, given to moods and sullen temperament. Generally, she didn't accompany him on his barge trips, but this time she was doing the cooking for the three of us, and drawing salary because of that. But she refused to serve meals on time, and if he happened to have gone to town in a motor boat that came along to pick him up—we both couldn't be gone from the barge at one time—she wouldn't feed me any dinner at all. However, she wasn't cross, just crabbedly sickly perhaps, for she was as kind as could be to a little black rat terrier and her puppy that were on the barge with us. In the evenings I'd race up and down the deck having the black dog race after me, barking excitedly and snapping playfully at my heels. The puppy, a lumpy awkward ball, would do his best to follow, but he got tangled up with himself all the time, and if I should suddenly turn and bark at him, he'd turn tail and catapult back to the captain's wife, and then look at me shamefacedly out of his bead-bright eyes, once he knew all was well. So I accepted the captain's wife as a woman with not a bad heart, but so longfaced, sallow, drab, and sinewy in her skinniness was she that it was hard to understand his affection. Now and then she'd make a curtly humorous remark. So I concluded that beneath her Virginia mountain manner of silence and austerity, was whimsicality of a sort to attract him.

This night had followed an eventless day, with no flairups between the captain and his missis about her not taking enough trouble with the meals, and no kick on either of their parts because I didn't keep enough wood chopped.

After contemplating the Statue of Liberty for a time, and reflecting on the strict limitations that there are in the concept "Liberty," I sat down upon a hatch cover near the captain and his wife, a little uncomfortable because they signified nothing to me as persons, and I supposed I meant as little to them, so I thought perhaps they'd rather be alone. But the ocean seemed to have cut me off from all kinds of experience I knew anything about. There was no turbulence within it tonight, only in me the consciousness of the turbulence that was a continuing quality in New York, the habitation of turbulent masses of men and machinery.

Soon the captain got up, and walking along the side of the barge, began to see what was going by on the belly of the outgoing tide. He took the boathook, and leaned over the side of the barge to spear large pieces of wood to dry and use for fire wood. Many strange things go by on the outgoing tide, intent perhaps, as I have been intent, upon merely "getting away" to taste the solitude upon the restless loneliness of ocean expanse.

"A box of whisky or I'm a sucker," the skipper said suddenly with more excitement than I'd seen him manifest before, as he pointed at a four-fifths submerged box. "The bootleggers bring whisky in to the three-mile-limit line and throw it overboard in boxes, to be picked up by watchers in boats, and the watchers missed that one." He was jumping around, having found that by no straining could he touch the box with his boathook. It went by, well out of reach of us on the barge, and he talked about it for the next three days, declaring that he'd have jumped overboard and got it, had he been sure it was whisky.

Still, tonight, he did not let his brooding on that prevent his keeping a lookout for other valuable matter that the tide might drive past.

"I've seen as many as three dead men go by in one night!" he commented, and I listened, not skeptically or otherwise. The skipper was a great liar, but for all that there was no reason to believe that he mightn't deceive one by telling the truth occasionally, when one didn't expect it.

Dead men, I wondered. Were they generally bloated, did they float face down, where'd they come from, did their folks know they were drowned, how did their drowning come about? Any number of questions drifted through my mind giving identity to very impersonal dead men who go by on the surface of an outgoing tide.

"I haven't seen any dead men go by myself, but there are a good many of those—I suppose they're dead men potentially —which go by every night," I said after a while.

The skipper looked with wary interest where I pointed. He wasn't going to be caught napping—not he. At first he didn't believe they were what I told him, but as many more came by, and nearer the barge, he saw more distinctly. Some of them were inflated, others not, though of course they'd all served their day.

"There's lots of them used at beaches on a holiday," he said cryptically at last.

"The unrest, the wish to go to sea attacks some very early in life," I suggested.

The captain's wife had heard us talking, and her curiosity got the better of her, though she wasn't so indiscreet as to ask a question in front of me. Finally, however, standing up, looking overboard, she saw what it was we spoke of. An enigmatic expression, partly sarcastic, partly a repressed smile, some light of recognition, showed on her face. A look was exchanged by her and the captain, and she, turning away, walked into the cabin.

It was becoming dusk and hard to distinguish whether the last animal corpse that went by was a cat, a dog, a pig, or whatnot. You can't tell what salt water will do to an animal's corpse, or can't know how long these corpses are driven back and forth by incoming and outgoing tides.

Night cupped the horizon, which dimming in the darkness

was a meticulously curved arm cradling the ocean, and the opacity of distance upon unending ocean water changed into an opacity of violet gray. I stood for a time to look at the high buildings in the Wall Street district of New York, and to feel the quality of their severity, as they pointed up in the sky towards the outcoming stars. Squares, the checkerboard designs of lights, in oblongs extending upward, appeared before me as the city lights were on. Electric signboards were glimmering blue-yellow in the sky, but I could see them only as splotches of light generally, unable to discern the wordings of the lettered ones, or the illustrations of the pictorial ones. How thin, straight, and directly skyscrapers stand against dusk of early night, when there are lights inside them. Even the ones with but few lights stood out at first, but as the night deepened, they all became dim, vaporous, and unreal as a mirage.

It was useless standing by the side of the barge any longer, looking into water, all black now, and not even to be seen except that my mind remembered that it was there. Besides the skipper had advised my going to bed as I'd have to get up early and chop wood before the heat of the day, as we'd probably be picked up by a towboat tomorrow afternoon, and there'd be little time to chop wood on the way down to Norfolk.

Anyway, I knew I'd have to spend at least a half hour killing bedbugs, and putting gasoline around the bed slabs, as I'd let a night go by without doing that. Gasoline is a less offensive odor to sleep with than the oily odor of bedbugs, which itch as well as smell. I detested, also, crushing a bedbug when it was full of my own blood. So it was up to me to use gasoline in plenty.

"Your wife recognized some of those young dead men too, I noticed," I remarked to the captain as I went up the stairs of the barge cabin to my bunkroom. The captain looked a bit as though such things had not ought to be mentioned, but vouchsafed a half grin.

A *Vacation's* Job

"A TELEGRAM," HIS MOTHER said as soon as Dave came in for breakfast. "It came last night but you will stay out till all hours come what may."

He opened it with nonchalance, feverish internally only. "Come at once; flood expected," it read and was signed by his engineer friend, Paul Somerland.

"I'll have to go Garna by tonight's train; the job I've been wanting for the vacation has come through and won't wait unless I go at once."

"But college, you won't get your credits if you leave now; it's almost a month before the end of the term," she replied.

"To the devil with college. Do I get anything out of it? It isn't me that expects benefit from that damned place. College ought to be done away with. If I'd take the professors at that place for examples of what learning and education does to a person . . . God save the king. Nope. I'll leave tonight. I'll get credits for the semester too. You watch me."

His mother curled a Scotch lip into an expression betwixt resignation, irritation, and humorous toleration. She'd become that way through the years and the upbringing of her litter.

He hustled down to the depot and purchased a ticket for the seven P.M. train to Garna, then navigated himself towards the university to instruct his instructors to see that his credits came through. It was early spring, and the campus is always flooded with girls in sport coats, colored jerseys, and light frocks, in the early spring. Most of them he knew too well to be romantic about, but one doesn't want to cut off from the indifferent joy of casual campus philandering without a little farewell.

As soon as he struck the walk leading from Museum Park to the campus along came Margaret Geiss and Diana Lisbon. "My gad, Diana," he exclaimed, "I won't be able to take you to the dance Saturday night because I just received a telegram telling me to report on my summer's job at once."

Diana received the news like a Trojan. It was he who'd suffer, if either of them did, because of his not being able to take her to that dance. She didn't tilt dinky hats over her left eyebrow and swank about dressed up to the minute that was ten minutes ahead of the fashion because that was her only intention. After his airy and her airier regrets she went towards her car sitting out in front of the main college building and sat waiting for a conversation with whoever headed her way. It wasn't ten minutes later that he heard six fellows arguing with her that she ought to cut her French class and take them all for a ride around to the high school to show the infants there what grown-up students look like.

His professors in philosophy, economics, sociology, and bionomics all agreed, not with so much enthusiasm as to add too much to his conceit, that he was sufficiently brilliant to be able to miss the last month of their courses without destruction of too much potential energy, that trained rightly in time, would make for general social welfare. They assured him that they'd put in passing standings at the registrar's office, and naively suggested that if he had time he could write papers on certain themes and mail to them.

His history professor caught a habituary hiccough in his throat, gulped on his Adam's apple for a minute or so, and stated "Actually you know. . ."

David couldn't wait for him to chew his reflections, and had no time to listen to his unoriginal ideas on scholarship and thoroughness. "You shriveled up crabapple," he thought, and collected the many contempts in his nature into a manner of hauteur. "Do as you wish about my credit; I must go; I need the money from this position and it will not wait for me. If you wish to insist upon measuring information by the number of hours spent in the classroom it's not probable that our ideas on what's advantageous in education will ever meet anyway." As David left him all the distastes for scholastic mentalities, catalogued information, and tremorous erudition were belging up into the mouth of his consciousness. Going down the steps, though, he ran unto Virginia Yokes and Sally Murray, and remembered with a qualm that he was the only person—so they said—who knew they were contemplating an elopement with a couple of nineteen-year-old fellows who had jobs, itinerant he feared, with moving picture companies.

"Say Virg, for Pete's sake, I have to desert the ship and go down into the valley to watch over Mexican laborers who work on irrigation ditches. My last word of warning; for Lord's sake woman think a little bit backwards and remember that you've fallen in love with every half-respectable-looking male who's treated you gently, and postpone marriage for a year or so."

Virgie's Spanish eyes fluttered as she looked at him with side-wise contemplative coquetry. She was too dusky a rose already to blush.

"I don't know what to do, but I can't stand college another year."

"Well, if you do marry, be careful. A marriage can be wormed out of, but if you have an infant. . ."

Sally Murray lifted up her right foot to wipe dust off it on her left stocking. It was such habits of Sally's which had driven Rus-

85

sell Simpson from infatuation to rapid disapproval of Sally.
"She's a classy dresser and cute to look at, but she's too squirmy
for me," he had remarked.

"Your dad has enough money so you won't suffer anyway,"
he commented to her. "Well, what to hell, I'll come back in the
fall and find you at college whether you elope or not. You'll tire
of marriage soon, both of you. I suppose it's as interesting an
experience as any other, but you'd much better be reckless with
conventions other than with marriage laws if certain impulses
are too strong in you."

He had to hurry on, so shook hands with and kissed Sally and
Virg good bye, and ran on down the steps of the main college
building, regretting the trivial but pleasurable hours of campus
life he'd miss. At once he ran unto a group of fellows talking
about the basketball finals. Amongst them were three of his
fraternity brothers. After greeting them all, he asked his breth-
ren to walk over to the house with him because he had to
depart within a couple of hours to pack.

Burt Samuels untangled his long adolescent limbs from a
bench and casting mooning eyes towards Virg, torn between
two desires, of brotherly fellowship and of calflove, went with
him. Jack and Bernard also loitered after. When they arrived at
the house they found MacIntyre and Dr. Benjamin, respec-
tively a "Greek" poet after the Keatsian manner of that Greek
condition, and a professor of English literature who clutched
youth by living in the fraternity house where much of it abode.
Immediately verbal warfare started between Mac, the doctor,
and David. In the beginning they were defending tradition,
rhymed verse, and college education; in the end no one knew
what they were defending.

"Abstract beauty rats! Hail to thee blithe spirit, bird thou
neverwert." Dave was saying after getting well launched. "I
wish you'd leave the nightingales and roses alone for a while.
It's damned affectation; a trance throwing. No man ever thinks
or feels his emotions in that way. You (to MacIntyre), like Keats
and Shelley, think it's necessary to get upon some astral plane
of poetic emotion to write. Why can't you think and feel di-

rectly and lend all the force of your intellectual-emotional organism to perceiving rather than to the trick of fooling yourself psychologically; I know a man makes his own reality, but he can do so rationally rather than resorting to the same sort of emotional hysteria that negroes at an evangelistic meeting do."

"I can tell you I write poetry on a par with Theocritus and Homer," MacIntyre assured him.

"Who in the hell thinks so but yourself? What you do is go out and have a love affair with some blond waitress and because she lets you sleep with her, you come back and write about her immortal beauty. That'd go stronger with me if I hadn't seen some of these immortal beauties you indite your lines to; and smelled them too. It'd be all right to make love poems about these beauties, I suppose—overdone I'd say—but the point is, you romantically lie to yourself about yourself and everything in life just as you do about the females who 'inspire' your poems. Poetry is made out of the natural experience of life; you don't have to seek a particular type of experience out of which to make art, and if you do,—well that's why you're no damned good."

Doctor Benjamin hemmed, and started: "The test is the intelligence of the trained sense of the judicious."

"Yep, and the test of intelligence is intelligence, so where are we now, old top? Simply because you don't want to stir your pedagogic mind to comprehend anything written later than 1890, and claim to like all the established classics, doesn't assure me that you have a trained sense," Dave answered him, and immediately after felt sorry, seeing the hurt look across his eyes, and knowing as he knew, that consciousness of failure, by all standards, intellectual, spiritual, and popular-economic, goaded the doctor to bitterness and narrowness. During a lull in the discussion he observed the fleshy back of his yellow-haired head; his big once-athletic frame; his high forehead. He was a perverse mixture of brutishness, fine sentiency, German sentimentalism, revolting spirit, and impulse to conform to middle-class moralities.

An anxiousness to be away, and down to Garna, conversing with Paul Somerland, who had a job to fill, filled it competently, and who thought analytically rather than emotionally because of atmospheric pressure, took hold of Dave's mind. Not that he thought life remarkable, or reality at all beautiful, but a sickness of spirit possessed him on seeing the doctor, growing rapidly stolid and flabby both of body and mind, grasp so feverishly at youth by attempting to have its hilarity through indulging in its activities.

He said goodbye to all the fellows at the house, being rather distant to Mac and the doctor. For the others he felt herd companionship, simply because they had no intellect, or pretense of intellectual interest that disagreed with his own.

Of course when he got home his mother had a few words of advice to give him too, telling him that after the summer he'd better start a law course, or even a course in medicine, to have some profession upon which to fall back in making a living.

"O the devil mother, lay off, leave me alone, leave me alone won't you? I can't be a lawyer, or a doctor. Why do you insist to me so much on the common sense side of life? Who can you point out to me who has 'settled down sensibly,' as you call it, that doesn't lead such a damned, dull, animal routine of an existence, that I'd want to shoot myself if I thought that was the end," he stormed.

"I'm only trying to help you."

"Don't try to help me. You can't. I'm not a Christian, don't give a damn about economic situation, don't want the stupid respect of people whose standards you want me to acquiesce to. I'm not the kind of being you are; you're not satisfied with the life you've led yourself. . . why do you worry about me? I'll find my own way, or it won't be found, and if it isn't it doesn't matter. You can't insure your children's futures."

"Well, all right. . . but now you go to church on Sundays while in the valley. There's not so much to do down there that. . ."

"Go to church," he laughed, irritatedly. "I'll go to hell sure, mother, if I go to church. By the time I've listened to the cant that is preached in the pulpit I have enough resentment in my system to poison ten healthy souls, let alone my own."

In his bedroom he bustled around packing a grip with some rough clothes for the summer's job, disgusted with himself for not being able to take his mother humorously, and for worrying her by arguing. "Damnfool to upset her."

At seven he was at the depot and boarded the train, which pulled out within a few minutes. As the train rolled out into the country from Los Angeles so that he could see orange groves blossoming, palm trees stretching upward, a feeling of freedom came into him, and then one of melancholy. An abstract concept of the lightness, color, and young exhuberance of college life—the brightness of colored dresses worn by girls on the campus, the easy casual conversations of students strolling back and forth beneath the shade trees, cutting classes, going for auto rides; the affectionate dependent friendliness of Virg, Margaret, Diana, and of his fraternity brothers,—was in his mind, making him envious of their carefree quality. Still he realized that individually they were as little satisfied with existence as he was.

He began to look forward to seeing Paul Somerland again, telling himself that at least he'd be away from the provincialism of Californian mentalities for a time; away from the city where parents have made their money raising corn and hogs in Iowa, and from their offspring interested only in moving pictures, dress, and owning an automobile. The city of sunshine, dancing and inanity. . . He wondered if Paul looked as much "like Jesus" as he'd looked two summers before, or if he had chopped off his bronze beard, or let the desert harden the soft look of patient understanding in his gentle eyes. What if his memory had played a trick on him as it had so often done, and he found Paul heavy and prejudiced? He must earn much money this summer and get away from California, to New York, to Europe—somewhere.

He crawled into his berth and after a time went to sleep. In a half dreaming state the plot of a miraculously beautiful story that he must write at once came into his mind, but when he awoke and thought about it it seemed quite flat. So he went to sleep again. Upon awaking in the morning he looked out the

89

window across stretches of desert towards a mountain range, dun and violet, and luminously vapored with the light of the on-coming sun.

It was but five o'clock yet he arose and dressed. Leaving his baggage on the platform of the depot he walked out into desert. Aware that nobody would be up in Garna, which was about a quarter of a mile back from the sidetrack upon which the sleeping car rested, he did not go in that direction; but struck out across the sand, simply to feel the clarity and cleanliness of the desert and of its dry air, sill cool with night. An owl flew up in front of him and lighted some distance away; he walked towards it; it flew again and did this repeatedly. Many gazelle-like lizards, bronze and grey, and moss-green, ran across the sands, stopping quickly to lift a forefoot and stand alertly listening. They were impossible to catch or to hit with a stone. Ahead of him at one time he saw a rattlesnake resting stretched out on the sand. Picking up a long branch of mesquite wood he approached him. The snake rattled and jerked himself into a coil. David reached the long stick out towards him and he struck at it; and snapped back his striking head over his coil again. He struck again. At last David hit him, breaking his back, and then killed him at once, first battering his head with the stick, then grinding it into the sand with the heel of his boot.

The sun was all in view now; plainly it was going to be a very hot day, well around 110 degrees, but with a dry heat that did not disturb him.

A quality of the desert was beautiful beyond the beauty of things more sensuous and colorful: The manner in which expanse of sand followed expanse of sand; clarity of sky rested upon clarity of sky, and only the seared colors, the ascetic colors of the desert blended into the dun stretches of sand; The dim lavender of desert flowers, the dusty grey of sagebrush, seared green of mesquite branch, and rusty red of its bean—block on block of tri-dimensional extension—impalpable plane of clarity intersecting impalpable plane of clarity—the desert gave more sense of structure and of foundation than the most carefully planned metropolis.

By seven thirty, he was hungry and knew that the Chink would be serving breakfast now. When he went into the restaurant old Charlie Ling was flapping around, serving breakfast to Mexican laborers in the same Chinese slippers and black slipover shirt that he'd worn two years before, it looked to David. It seemed that for a moment a light of recognition flickered in his apathetically placid face, but Oriental contempt obliterated the light. Perhaps he remembered David, and remembered also that he'd once said so that old Ling heard, that this kitchen was so dirty it gave him indigestion to be in it.

Eating ham and eggs with his face turned toward the street window to be able to see anybody passing, he saw Paul going by and hailed him. Paul came in, and assured David that there was plenty of work for him to do, as the bi-annual flood of the Colorado River was expected any day, and he had nobody to act as foreman for one of his Mexican gangs who were piling rock along the banks of the levee to restrain the water when the flood did strike.

As they talked, several ranchers who lived near town and men who worked at the irrigation company's office came in to breakfast. Soon the restaurant was filled with the sound of voices arguing about the day of arrival for the flood, the loss of cotton crops, the price of mushmelons, the management of the water company, and the proper way of controlling the flood. Two men changed the conversation to national politics, one of them strongly defending the administration of President Wilson and his actions regarding the League of Nations. As Paul was holding forth in a condemnation of Wilson's policy, in a way that indicated clearly what school of social change journalism he followed, David reflected that he had coarsened, both in physical appearance and intellectually. He wondered if that was the inevitable attrition of an environment created by beings disturbed solely by the economic problem of life, or the settling of a naturally dogmatic organism into its mode of responding to life, once the inquisitive unrest of youth had left it.

Soon Paul and he went out on the street and down to the

levee office together, and Paul began to tell of the engineering problems, and the political problems of his position.

"They've placed a damned old fogey of an engineer on the district board, and he, partly out of ignorance, and partly to insure himself of a job as assistant engineer—who ever heard of such a thing as being an employee authorized to spend money for a county, and also on the board which gives the authority?—he insists that a channel should be blasted to form a new river bed, and thus divert a part of the river stream. Utter damnfoolishness! Millions of dollars could be spent trying to blast a river bed down to the Gulf of Mexico, some five hundred miles, and the next spring the river would resume its old course."

"What should be done," David asked.

"What we're doing, though we have to battle old Woods and his followers continually. We're blasting rock out at the various quarries along the course of the levee and piling a wall twelve feet through and fourteen feet high; and when flood waters hit that wall they won't break through."

"Old Woods! is that your competing engineer. I remember seeing that old bird when I was here two summers ago. He used to go out in the morning with helpers—that lame redheaded fellow who was drowned—and sit around in his boat somewhere in the Colorado River. Didn't give a damn where he blasted, so long as he had dynamite and blasted somewhere. Does anybody take him seriously?"

"Two-thirds of the valley think that I and my partner are young upstarts with newfangled notions who will bring destruction upon their cotton crops. All Woods wants is to secure a job for himself and his loafing friends."

They turned into the levee office and Dave picked out a canteen, threw off his coat, and soon Paul and he were on their way out to where the Mexicans were piling rock, twelve miles from town. The Ford waded bravely through sand grooved a foot deep in some places by the passing of trucks.

"You don't know how glad I am to have you here; I haven't talked to an intelligent person for six months, and don't have time to read the papers that are sent me from New York," Paul assured David.

A quality of softness and gentleness that was in him seemed to battle with mercenary lusts, and a rough irritation directed consciously at the "ignorant brutes" who made up the populace of the valley, directed subconsciously at—him, Dave felt—or at anybody who had active and current cultural interests, since all his own energies were being utilized in the politics of his engineering position. His situation was beyond Dave's ability to think through. Such work as he was doing had to be done, he couldn't hold his position and devote half-interest to its problems. Inwardly David shrugged his shoulders: either he was too fine a being to be doing such work, and somebody else would do it, or he wasn't too fine and he would do the work and gradually cease to care about development other than material, important only to such people as demand something of life other than living.

In half an hour's time, a respect and an affection that Dave cherished for him had evaporated so that he looked at and into him as much as he could, quite coldly and impersonally, noting that while the features of his profile were clean, the back of his head shot down with displeasing straightness; that beneath the first impression of a "sweet Jesus" quality was a more permanent one of harshness such as he found in Germans hospitable and kindly by tradition, rather than by nature.

It occurred to David that Paul was shocked during the course of their conversation driving out to the levee by his saying that he thought patriotism a narrow ideal. "It's simply a group-selfish ideal, is entirely economic, and quite often places a high price on insincerity and inability to think. One is born of the country to which one is native and because of that, and its environment, possesses some of the general qualities of that country. Beyond that, race indicates little when it comes to the finest expression of human energy. Why should one sentimentalize to continue a prejudice? The only ideal that is worth possessing is that of intelligence—more sentimental ideals have elements of the gross and evasive in them," he had said. Paul did not speak his disagreement.

It was evident that his attitude towards David was no longer one of personal affection, now; rather an attitude of resentment. Not that any point upon which they might disagree mattered, or that Dave's seeming to have proved a point mattered. Paul was simply aware that regardless of the correctness of David's conclusion, he was less apt now to accept judgments because they were accepted than was he himself, and he was still sentient enough to desire to arrive at his own convictions.

He started talking of literature; of the stage; of politics; David found his interest in what Paul knew of these things dead. So he asked questions about plans for the summer's work and Paul was soon talking entirely about the problem of levee construction and flood control.

"I've been wanting to put up a derrick with which to handle stone too big for men to handle alone," he declared, and drew a sketch of the derrick. "Do you think you could supervise its erection?"

"Perhaps—explain it to me a little."

It amazed and pleased David to find that he understood what Paul was saying when he did explain, because he'd been afraid that it was an involved engineering structure and that it would be necessary for him to look intelligent and say "yes, O yes" while comprehending nothing.

At last they reached a turn in the levee where some horses were tied to ropes between two poles. Paul stopped the car and they climbed out to walk down the levee together. "There's the Mexican foreman—he can't read or write well, but he had plenty of savee just the same," Paul remarked and called out:

"Harry—Oh Harry Gallego, come over here," When Harry arrived, Paul introduced him to David and in a few minutes got into the Ford saying that he must get back to town and might not be able to be out again for a couple of days.

Harry and David took to each other easily. Two minutes after Paul had departed Harry was telling Dave about his plans for being a labor contractor, and bidding for irrigation-ditch-cleaning and brush-cutting jobs, to make big money.

"They ain't nothing to being a labor contractor except a little adventuring spirit," he commented. "Me and my brother had a good start down at a mine in Arizona before the war and made sometimes as much as a thousand dollars each a month . . . Do you keep books, and write checks? Maybe you and me could get together and be partners."

"You try me kid. I can write checks and keep books all right. Start something and I'll be in with you up to my ears," David assured him.

"That's the boy. Do you drink—just a minute—keep this quiet though, don't let Mr. Somerland know I have any of this stuff on the job—try that—real fire water," he said, taking a bottle of whisky from under a pile of sacks. "And don't you ever let nobody tell you that stuff's hard to get because prohibition's on. As long as you're in this valley and stay in with me I'll see that you get all you want."

David gulped at the fire water and it tickled him down to the toes.

"Watcha doing Saturday night? They's a dance on amongst us Mexicans—that's what I am, none of this Spanish stuff for me, I ain't a highbrow—I don't dance well and my wife likes to dance. She's a nice kid, more class than I got; used to be a stenographer before she married me."

They arranged to go to the dance together Saturday night, as they walked down the levee together and Harry pointed out the laborers who were dependable workmen or who spoke English or who were "men to keep an eye on." "It's hard keeping men on this job in weather that's up to 127 in the shade."

"You can't blame them for not liking quarry work in such heat," David said.

Out across the desert for miles stretched innumerable rocky hills, from the nearer ones of which loads of stone appeared, the horses driven by Negroes or Indians or Mexicans. "We'll take the two riding ponies and do the round of gangs so you'll know where all the men are working. If you do the rounds twice a day to take the men's time and give the gang bosses any help you can, there won't be much for you to do beyond that. You can make a little extra money keeping books for me, and making out my pay checks every two weeks if you want to," Harry said, as they mounted the ponies and started out.

Up through the rocky hills they rode, Harry a round-bodied jovial moonfaced man of a horseman, a kewpyish smile on his brown face as he chattered on. On a ways they ran into his brother Ginger, whose make-up indicated a graver outlook on life and less alert precocity, but who nevertheless, perhaps due to remarks Harry made to him in Spanish, began almost at once to tell David about his private business and family affairs. The Mexican laborers in his gang surveyed David. The Indian laborers seemed less curious about the new boss. They drove on. And in about an hour's time were back at the starting point and resting on a pile of gunny sacks spred beneath a thatched roof on poles. As they half-dozed an auto drove into the stable yard and old Woods came up. He approached and began talking to Harry giving Dave a casual glance of curiosity. Dave knew that he did not know him by sight, and remained silent for a bit listening to their conversation.

"Jesus Christ, Harry, I'm getting too old to tear around on hot days like this," he exclaimed. He sat down, his broad bulky figure relaxing. For some seconds he gazed abstractedly off into space, like a dazed man trying to think what to think about. His watery-grey eyes had a dim glaze over them; his iron grey beard was clean, but nevertheless it made one feel as old men's beards generally do—that in eating, foodstuffs and liquids would cling to it, that at any time it might be spotted with tobacco juice. The curled hair on his head clung to a well-formed, round type of dome. It struck Dave that Paul was too bitter about the old man, who could be manipulated rather than credited with sufficient force to merit direct opposition.

"The county ought to fix up them roads," he said after a time. "It has left me with a pain in the loin driving out over them. Like leaving a woman half-screwed, I say it is, and that ain't considerate, is it?" the old man broke into a speech again.

"Which is that harder on, the man or the woman," Dave asked him. He turned eyes of doubt on Dave, his dignity perhaps a trifle upset to be addressed when they had not been introduced.

"Who are you?" he questioned directly.

Harry introduced them saying that Dave was a boy from college here for the summer.

"What are you taking at college?" Woods inquired.

"Not much of it takes. I have a healthy system and throw that sort of thing off readily. I've tried several things, economics under a scarecrow with a mania for statistics, sociology under a revitalized mummy with a theory that all branches of human knowledge can be card-indexed under eighty-six heads with subheads, and philosophy under an ex-Methodist minister suffering with a senile fear that he cannot justify his belief in God and the good, rationally.—O yes, I took a shot at psychology thinking that I might be a psychoanalyst until I learned what types of beings I'd have to perform upon."

Old Woods brightened up. Dave was aware at once that he might have made an error in showing him he possessed a wit, so that it would be harder to observe his specie through him in its ungarnished state. He'd concluded not to take either side in the controversy between Woods and Paul, not only because of insufficient knowledge to know the merits of their varying theories, but because Woods seemed as interesting a type as Paul, and with less intense social conscience.

"What is that stuff psychoanalysis! I've heard it mentioned and thought maybe I was getting behind the times," Woods said.

"Perhaps you'll be ahead of them by knowing nothing about it. Apart from several schools, it is the analysis of motives, subconscious, and conscious, of human organisms. You've probably been hearing about it in connection with dream-analysis, which aims to discover the type of desires suppressed, and impulses in, any subject analyzed, through their dreams . . . Not unnaturally the desires are generally found to tie up in some way with sex . . ."

"That thing sex is important, isn't it," he chuckled.

"Yes, and about one-tenth understood. It's rather too bad

that psychoanalysis should have become a subject for popular discussion since the average being can't think of sexual desire except in terms of the physically voluptuous. The factors of intellect, and a complex social organization which creates desire for social power, acclaim, and intercourse, which permits communion on a basis of understanding, complicate any impulse so that fleshly solutions are insufficiently perceptive," Dave told Woods, aware that he did not understand much of what was being said, and amused at both Woods' bafflement and his own grandiloquence.

"That's so; that's so; I've always said you can't know too much about sex. Now you take the flowers; even they smell sweetest at the moment of copulation—you know flowers copulate—that is, they do, don't they?" Woods started off, at first to inform Dave, then recalling that his information might be *passé*; of a generation forty years back, then turning in his mind to consult David.

However, instead of going into this theme, David went on with his. "It's probably society as a whole that needs to be psychoanalyzed rather than individuals, because there is certainly vicious suppression in any social organism which expresses itself consciously in such conventions and moralities as deny the cleanness of at least the presence of natural impulses, and place a premium upon ignorance and unvirility."

"You're quite a Bolshevik, ain't you?" Woods asked and went on, "That's the thing for the young generation to be."

"No, not a Bolshevist or a socialist or a communist, politically not much of anything but a spectator. Change occurs because of the strongest force, generally that of the aggressive minority rather than of either the majority or of the intelligent few. I'm sure that communism would oppress sensitive beings, artists, scientists, and people who want a morality higher than the economic, quite as much as the present system of government. There is more oppression in narrow moralities than there is in economic or political situation. I don't mind not eating now and then, but I do mind not being able to say what I sincerely feel and think because of conventional attitudes. Not having any assurance of intelligence amongst the greater portion of humanity, one man or group can never know how any ideal social system will work out—anyway I'm not one of the types of beings hopeful enough to devote my direct energies to battling for an ideal societary system."

Old Man Woods went off into a mood of abstraction that might have meant deep thought, but which David suspected was the dazed idealess reflection of a man given to apathetic trances. The day was too hot for continued speech and drowsy with late afternoon. After a time he looked alert again, and Dave was aware that he was looking him over.

"You have an intellect, my boy," he started.

"No, no, no, please! That remark would have pleased me once, and it may again, but for the time being, I'm sick of intellect, it doesn't mean sense. I know I'm strong on ideation, but that doesn't mean I'm intelligent enough to be mentally and emotionally adjusted."

Conversation stopped again, with old Woods going off into another dazed trance. After a time he stated that he'd have to start back to town and walked off absent-mindedly.

"Takes coke, doesn't he?" David asked Harry.

"I don't know. It ain't liquor that makes him that way. Mr. Somerland would have liked to hear you say that. Them two ain't friends at all," Harry said.

"I rather believe that the old man is the wiser of the two by nature but he probably isn't much of an engineer," David murmured, reflecting on the states of mankind and growing no wiser because of that reflection.

"He may be getting too much bumping from that Widow Brown he knows, Harry said, or just getting stupid from sitting around on his ass too much. That's the only thing I've ever seen him do."

It was quitting time, and the laborers came walking up the levee to get into the trucks and be driven to town. Harry and Dave sat in the seat of one truck and Harry's brother came in one behind them. In an hour they were all at Garna.

"Come on over to the shanty pool hall with me and have a

drink. Old Joe wouldn't give it to you alone. I'll introduce you so you can get it after this, by yourself," Harry said to Dave.

A fat, greasy-faced Mexican in sloppy trousers and a dirty shirt that was open all the way down the front, so that the tip of his belly-button showed, was sitting out in front, of the adobe-hut poolhall. With a grunt he led Dave and Harry into a back room and served them, then departed, leaving them sitting at a wood box for a table, but they soon finished their whiskys and left the pool hall and each other, David going to a Negro restaurant which he thought cleaner than Charlie Ling's.

The old mammy who ran the place recognized him and was vociferous in her greetings. "Us cullud folks in the valley has been getting religion this summer; and they ain't no more bawdy girls amongst us. Down whah we lives we holds evangelical meetings nights now instead of actin rowdy," she told David, but he wasn't sure she was as pleased about that as she might have been, because later remarks of hers about the cullud minister were disparaging.

"He's a God-fearing man, but he has his hungers. Lawdy land how that niggah can eat. He remarks to Sister Beachum that 'ah can't preach heah on earth and board in heaven: the word of God ain't dissembled gratis,' and she told him to eat at her place. Mah goodness, she didn't know how he can eat."

After Dave had eaten he went out into the street and saw Paul coming down the one street of the town, with several other men. Paul separated and joined David. He immediately began to talk about national politics.

"I've ceased to expect much from either political or social systems," Dave said, "realization of value is individual rather than group—O perhaps a little rope; the majority are tied to a stake —their material hungers—and they wind up their own tether rope, so that they have less space to circle about in some times than others."

"That's simply a lazy mental attitude," Paul responded.

"Hardly that: it doesn't say you don't work mentally in striving to understand, relate, and as an individual use what experience existence thrusts in your way."

100

"Selfish egoism."

"What's humanitarianism but the generalizing of your own self-pity. Nothing solved by sentimentality. One might as well try to have as hard an intelligence as the force which casts events is hard."

"What does one do?"

"Solve one's own difficulties, and the difficulties of such as around you as you can help. The application of an inclusive social, political, or religious ideal plays the hell in general, as bigoted morality now oppresses America and England—well—if it isn't puritan narrowness however, it's something else. All solutions of life are individual. That's not selfishness in any material sense; it's recognition of the limitations of human intelligence."

David felt a restless irritation in himself; a desire to be away from Paul and not discussing social theory. Soon he excused himself to "write letters" and went to his room in a shack that lay just on the edge of a stretch of desert, across which a quarter of a mile away lay the Negro village that two years before had been a redlight section.

The day was a coal ember from which the fire was departing in the cooler vapors of evening. Mist veiled the dry clarity and colored mist—pale lavender, dim prismatic—colors, curled around the bodies of the mountains that cut off a view of the horizon on a level. Already, voices, the strumming of banjos and other musical instruments came sounding from the Negro village. The mellow voice of some darky shouting at his horses as he was unharnessing them after a day's work; the friendly bark of dogs; the calling of a female voice across some backyard to a neighbor; curses, laughter, came across the stretch of sand intensifying the quietude and tranquillity that David felt about him. No sweeter odor than the odorlessness about him, no sweeter music than the punctuated silences—it seemed to David that his spirit, his mind, his body had been being racked and tormented for years, but that now, here, he could rest, and think thoughts that did not turn upon him to wound him with irritation, insistent upon the stupidities and oppressions that are everywhere in the world.

The sense that he had gotten in the morning of the structural solidity of the desert was increased, but with the increase came a feeling of the suavity of its structural simplicity; the plastic invisibility of the ozoneous sky, darkening now, erected upon this vastness of sand. Space is a monument carved with utmost simplicity.

Night decreased his world, and increased his comfort since he rested snugly in a cleanly dark portion of a valley enclosed in mountains. Memory was with him: yes, outside there were cities, throngs of people, a cosmopolitan world. They had always been hovering around the unreality for him; they were now dim, distant, completely without reality, even that of a dream. Ideas that were wont to taunt him—of achievement, of lust,—unrestful, self-accusing ideas—discontent with environment, with social systems—all had become so meaninglessly unreal. He stood for a time at the doorway of his shack, shirtless because much heat was still in the evening air. It rather surprised him when his hands touched the flesh of his own arms as he put them akimbo. Even his own body had partaken of unreality. Not a happy feeling within him; not an unhappy one; only one utterly quiescent.

Now the sound of many Negroes chanting, and praying, came intermittently to him; space, and tiny gusts of breeze acting like stop valves to shut off the echoes, then re-opening them to let the contralto, burnt-orange tones of melodious mournful voices come into his ear.

Velvet-clad hoofs, tiny and exquisitely wrought, were pacing on bronze stairways, making music as they loped on the ascending plains for moonbeams up the sky, startled antelope with slender necks and gracile erect antlers were lifting neat heads upon lithe undulant necks, as they listened with ruby-bright gleaming eyes, before darting upward and away through the veils of yellow gleaming in the musky glow of desert night; the desert an ember within which vermilion heat still burned inside the ashy exterior of darkness.

He put a shirt on, and stepped out into the sand to walk nearer to the Negro village so that he could hear them in their religious rites. Arriving outside the tumble down shack in which the ceremony was being held—a shack held together with poles, boards, and covered scantily with dirty canvas—he stood looking in through the doorless doorway.

A woman was talking. As she talked other voices, spoke reverently, in fatherly tones, in patronizingly motherly tones, saying, "O Lord" "Heah the woman Jesus" "She's yours God." Her words came to his ears:

"It ain't as if ah was advisin' you Lawd, ah's youah servant lawd, an what you see fitten for me to have ah has and is radiant wif joy; but ah's askin you to be wif me, caus the serpent of sin is around me lawd, urging me to be bad lik ah has always been befoah you glohaified me. And the way of the serpent is calculated to git around me and drag me back into sin. He ain't like de snakes out heah on dis heah desert. He's sociable and when he talks, he talks like he talked to dat woman Eve and his voice is sweeter dan honey—Ooooooooh Lawd, be wif me. It ain't like I hadn't been a wicked woman and knows de pleasures of de flesh; it ain't like dreams don't come to me, and when dey comes dat de serpent ain't dey askin' me to come and lie wif him in de shape of a man. O lawd; O blessed Jesus, you's mah man now; ah's all yoah's Jesus, all yoah's."

As the woman continued speaking her voice rose to shrillness and took on all the volume of which it was capable until her talking was an incoherent stream of hysterical shrieking, she beat her bosom and ran her hands through her hair. At last she stopped and after a deep male voice had said,

"O help her Jesus," there was silence for a moment or so, until all the darkies took up a spoken song that swung into a chant, beat with rhythm, and became fervorous. David walked away from the shack in which the black people were sitting towards that of his own room. Moonbeams were running in streams up the sky. Making the night to effervesce, electric with soft vitality; as champagne which is charged with a steady current as it bubbles.

The next day David was out at the levee with the laboring gang by seven thirty. Even days of unremarkable events followed each other, but hot, mistlessly clear days, which in the early morning were aggressive with clarity as though innumerable bright flowers were being thrown into the air, so that their petals were fluttering about, petal on petal of clarity, falling, floating, keeping the air bright and scentless of all scents but that of spaciousness. Later in the day, the heat brought a consciousness of intensity brooding somewhere in the infinity of sky, and of a red glow gleaming hotly through the opaque petals of clarity.

During the day sometimes Mexican and Indian laborers would strip, while waiting for a wagon of rocks to come along to be piled along the banks of the levee. Then they would jump into the silty, clay red-hued water from the Colorado River to cool off and splash about, their luminous-skinned bodies gleaming where portions of them showed above the satin rustiness of the flowing water.

Some days Old Man Woods, or Paul, would come out and spend an hour or so. David would exchange desultory conversation with Paul, habitually friendly. With Old Man Woods he would converse with seriousness upon problems of the universe, life, religion, sex, botany, or men.

"I tell you the flood's going to break that dam; them engineers won't stop it with rocks, and besides they didn't start piling rocks soon enough to have a bank sufficient before the flood hits the levee banks," Woods said one day.

David believed that he was right, simply because an instinct of inevitability was in him, not because of belief in the old man's judgment. The flood breaking would be an economic fatality for some in the valley; loss of property and of cotton and melon crops. It seemed to him hardly worth attempting to forestall fatalities, but that this was the way to do, go on working doggedly and expect what you wish but accept what comes.

Saturday nights Harry would take him to a dance in some Mexican hall, and they would stand around, drinking wine or beer, and conversing with other men. Generally Harry's wife would be there in a black velvet dress, cut low at the neck so that her orange-white flesh gleamed erectly above it. Other Mexican girls were there sitting along the sides of the walls wait-

104

ing to be asked to dance; but few of them were asked and would dance with each other. There were only two of nearly twenty of them who were good looking and they were so surrounded by Mexican swains that David despaired of dancing with them often and would take on Harry's wife or Harry's sister-in-law, a huge woman in a green plush and embroidered dress—of material like chair upholstery. She could not dance, so he would simply keep his feet out of her way and smile and talk; and lead her to her seat at the end of the dance thankful that it was over and feeling very generous within himself for his philanthropic nature. Harry's wife was a different story, but David suspected that Harry wasn't keen on having him dance too often with her, because he'd remark:

"My wife's some kid, ain't she? You like her, I guess. It's a fact, she's classier than I am. I ain't had much schooling."

One night there was a Negro barbecue and dance on in town, and David could get no one who would go with him. Paul was busy; Harry had to stay with his wife and children; others were afraid that the party would get too rough with some razor using; and perhaps resentment on the part of some of the Negroes towards white men. However David managed to get to the dance hall at about eleven o'clock at night after the barbecue feast had been held on the outskirts of town and the Negroes had left the remnants of food, cantaloupes, pieces of roast chicken, corn fritters, and half-empty beer bottles, strewn about where the central fire had been blazing. Many of the older colored people had retired to their homes, and only the gay bucks and maidens had come to the dance hall in numbers at all, though some old mammies and gray-headed males were sitting around with wistful shining black faces as they listened to the music, tapping their feet or shrugging their shoulders in rhythm.

David came to the door of the dance hall and looked on. After a time he stepped inside and stood near the door watching. There were no other white men about. One or two Mexicans, and over in a corner an Indian girl, a flabby, early matronized body she had, were watching proceedings with desiring yet apathetic eyes.

105

In the orchestra was a violinist who swayed and rocked and shouted out like a dog howling at the moon frequently, a pianist who bounced up and down on the piano stool as he played, doing dance steps with his feet, wiggling his shoulders; and a drummer who beat his drum madly, banging his bass and snare drums, and all their metal contraptions with inspirational bang and excited enthusiasm. Now and then he would grab a potato whistle and make yodeling, minor, shrieking, calliope noises. Shouts and half-started melodies came from all over the room, particularly from the young bucks dancing with the dusky-skinned charmers. The scene was too openly an intoxication of sensuousness to be lascivious or obscene.

After a time however David found the flesh-odor in the room, the smokiness, and closeness irritating and oppressing, so he went out, and back to his shack to sleep. As he was starting down the street a young Negress accosted him, saying: "Hey thah Honey, whah's you goin? Doan you want company?" He laughed, looking at her dubiously. "No, I think not, hardly worth the chances," he replied, thinking that if it weren't for the smallness of the town and the way stories spread he wouldn't be so sure.

The water had risen twelve inches during the night, and already for the last four days every rancher in the valley who could possibly get away from his work was working on the levee, bringing with him from home all the gunnysacks he could, to fill with sand and pile up along the banks to restrain the flood waters. During rest periods some of the ranchers could be heard complaining because this or that other rancher hadn't arrived. "He won't have any crop to work on if the flood breaks. This is a community matter, but you can trust that man to always let somebody else do his civic work for him," they'd complain.

Other men would boast that they hadn't slept for twenty-four, or thirty-six hours, but had piled sacks at leakholes, or had carried coffee around to the men. Everywhere was a great disregard for all the ordinary routines of living. Everywhere were men pumped full with excitement and consciousness of their own necessity in this crisis. Whenever any one of them stopped to talk, he always was just resting a bit and had to rush back to work immediately to direct the Mexicans, or the other ranchers who were less efficient and able to see just what spots to pile sandbags on, than was he. There wasn't a man on the job who did not know that if the flood was diverted, it would be because of something he had advised or supervised, and that if the flood broke that it was because somebody else had failed to follow his directions.

Back some ways from the levee banks, several thatch-roofed shacks stood, speedily erected to serve as kitchen roofs, under which cooking might be done, and men served meals. The ground about the place had begun, in the last few days, to be soggy with water that was coming up from underneath because of the flood water pressure. Not more than 50 feet from the kitchen all of the horses were fastened to a line of poles, and there they were fed. That same line of poles had served for years as the stable for horses hauling for laboring gangs who worked about the levee, in consequence of which all the ground about was covered with manure so that when the water had dampened it, ammoniacal odors arose in the air and permeated the whole atmosphere near the kitchen.

Several cooks were employed about the place. One horribly dirty Mexican with a screw fastened into a wooden stump serving as one arm; another, an old Scotchman with a cross dog disposition, the sort of man who has led a precarious life, isolated from ordinarily decent human contacts. Still others, waiters, kitchen boys, assistant cooks were about the place, cursing and reviling each other, the men at work for their carelessness and for their appetites, and the location for its uncleanness. The management of the water company came in for its curses too, for not being prepared in case of such emergencies, and for rushing out such stoves and such equipment as though it were possible to prepare food fit for humans to eat with such a layout.

If the Mexican cook ever washed his hands no one saw him. He would go about bare-armed, from kneading dough for pies or biscuits, to rolling lumps of ground meat into loaves. Stopping sometimes, he would stop not far to the side of the kitchen

107

to excrete his organs, which function being performed, he would return to work, stolidly and sullenly. To exaggerate the condition, millions of flies were about every pot on the stove, every can of fruit, bit of pastry, barrel of sugar, and during meal times were in swarms about the foods on the table. Many men could scarcely eat because of the flies in the cooking, and the flies swarming about their heads. Others ate on indifferently, remarking: "This ain't no time to be delicate."

David could not eat; before coming out in the morning he'd stop at a restaurant in town and eat; and have nothing more until the next morning. He'd discovered that a cook shack lay down the levee in which a crabbed old Irishman worked, placed there permanently, to have food on hand for any of the executives or engineers who were held on the job over meal times throughout the spring, summer, and fall months. However, he discovered also, after having eaten one meal there, that this old man's habits of cooking were as unclean as the Mexican's at the major kitchen. Now the shack that he was in was surrounded by water—it was built upon a foundation of driven piles and stood above the water generally, just off the levee banks. The old man had always thrown his food leavings out of the shackhouse door into the water, and it stayed in the vicinity of the shack, because of water brush that would not let it float away on the stagnant, almost motionless water. Occasionally now that the flood was on, the old man would jump into the water from the shacksteps and with a broom brush back the slops toward the open bay. Then he would climb out and let the sun dry his clothes, which were never changed. So David gave up the idea of eating through the day.

Through the twenty-four hours of night and day, automobiles, trucks, horse-dragged wagons were coming and going with loads of men, loads of cement lime, loads of gunny sacks. The heat was intense. The rising flood waters had put a humidity into the air so that it was stifling to breathe. Heat and humidity were circling, coiling, writhing, and laying oppressive vapors upon the lungs of everybody. Horses dropped in their harness, men felt sick at stomach, and rested in what shade they could find. But the water was still rising.

David had been up till two or three in the morning every day for the last week. He would retire at 3 A.M., and get up again at seven to go back on the job, rushing back and forth to keep the various gangs supplied with sacks and men more needed in one place than in another.

At about noon of this day the ranchers and the engineers began to feel that the crisis was past, and many of the ranchers departed for home so all gangs worked in a more desultory manner. On a corner, an intersection of a diverting levee channel, the main supply shack was situated; and David was sitting on a pile of gunnysacks chewing on a ham sandwich. Down the levee about an eighth of a mile away some twenty Mexicans were working without energy. Suddenly a shouting began. It increased and became hysterical and terrified. David jumped up. A moment later he heard a great rush of water. The levee had burst. In fifteen minutes acres about were being flooded, and the water kept pouring on. There was no way of stopping it now; only the subsiding of the flood would halt the continual pour of water down upon cotton crops, into stockfields, and around ranchhouses so that families would have to move back, taking their stock and carrying what machinery they could.

The rush of water, which would have sucked under any man attempting to swim across it, shut off all the twenty laborers who had been working down on a levee, so that they were stranded there as on an island. Some of them were shouting to be rescued, much afraid, but after a while others had assured them that they were safe as the levee ran for miles back. Only they were shut off from food and might have to sleep on the levee banks that night.

However, David knew that they were all being hysterical and were quite safe, only the sight of the rush of water, swirling in whirlpools through the break in the levee frightened them — all illiterate Indians and Mexicans; with perhaps one or two white men of a poor sort who liked the importance of being appealed to by the others. In fifteen minutes after the water had broken through the entire gang was standing about calmly, smoking cigarettes, talking, feeling at ease almost now because the flood waters had made a decision and the work of piling rock and sandbags along the levee was over for the summer, which would put them all out of a job.

Knowing that down the levee in the opposite direction on his side of the break was a cookhouse, near which a boat was moored, David went in that direction, and arriving there jumped into the boat and pushed off. He intended rowing through the backwater bay, under the cottonwood brush to get to the men. Then they could all row back and forth across the break, upon water that was gaining a level as it poured through the break, a torrenting falls at first.

He got well out into the backwater bay, and had to bend his head and back and propel his boat forward by pushing against the thin trunks of trees growing out of the water, because the brushwood leaning over him, and the cottonbrush trees about him did not permit his sitting upright, or his rowing. After five minutes of this, he was as wet with perspiration as if he had jumped into the water. Around him on all sides now, and overhead, was the crisp foliage of the cotton brush, the leaves of which were covered with cobwebs and with cotton wool caused by the bursting of the seed-pods of the trees. He could feel cobwebs in his lungs, they were tangled up in his tongue so that he must chew at them and gulp at them. The atmosphere was smothering under all this brushwood, and his breath was coming in ink-tasting gasps. He cursed himself as a damnfool for coming under swampy, sweating foliage, thought which he could not see to know what direction he was going, forward or backward, or out away from the levee. Waves of despair were going through him; the only thing that made him go on was the stifling oppressiveness of the atmosphere.

After what seemed to him an interminable time; he saw a clearing and headed towards it. Arriving at it, he saw the gang of men not far away and rowed to them. "Before I'd do that again you could sleep on the levee for three nights running," he commented as he came up. After resting for about a quarter of an hour to get to breathing naturally again he jumped into the levee water and let the current carry him down the stream. It sucked him under once, and held him sufficient time for him to think thoughts of drowning and of self-condemnation, and realization that he might as well have gone across in the boat, and have cooled off in the stiller waters on the other side of the break. However he came to the surface again, was whirled in several whirlpools of water for a minute or so and then thrown out by the current into water that he could direct himself in by swimming strokes. So he regained the levee bank on the other side and crawled out to shake the water off him a bit and dry a trifle before he climbed into an automobile to be driven back to town.

The next day men were standing around town talking about the flood, boasting of the work they'd done, each one saying his reasons why the thing had happened, and wouldn't have happened if.

Within a week a routine of existence more stale and oppressive than the breezeless weather had asserted itself. The streets of the town during the daytime were deserted, only an occasional woman would drive up in a buggy to the town grocery store, a cloud of silt dust subsiding behind her buggy. A man or woman would come out of the town bank, or the newspaper office, or the post office and disappear soon, into another door—to get a soda water or ice cream—or down the street towards home. Some dogs dragged heat-worn bodies from one shady spot to another, irritated at the sun's having disturbed their unrestful doze. David knew that now his job was only a pretense since most of the Mexican and Indian laborers had been discharged or had quit and all work was subsiding for the hottest months.

Soon, in the levee ditches, where the water had been sixteen feet high it had sunk to four feet, and the water lay stagnant and ill-smelling in the bottom of the ditch. So little water was there now that ranchers were continually howling about not having the water they needed for the irrigation of their crops, much fewer of which were destroyed by the flood than David had expected would be.

Through the drag of the days and nights David became

111

acquainted with most of the people in town, and heard them chewing and re-chewing old rags of conversation—exchange of criticism of the water company management; of the ineffi- ciency of such and such a person; the insinuation that another such and such a man was seen at the Negro section of town more than looked right. He was stifling with the same com- ments on the same flirtatious banker's daughter, the same uncareful Mrs. Goldie—who had no last name; fifty times in the course of the week he listened to Paul Somerland criticiz- ing the theories of Old Man Woods; sixty times a week he listened to other people criticizing Paul; and when aiming at amiability or graciousness the repertoire of entertaining con- versation of the goodly valley inhabitants was yet more limited.

One day Harry Gallego came up to David and told him that he was driving through the desert to Los Angeles, and that soon he'd drive to Fresno and contract some grape-picking jobs, as there would be nothing further doing in the valley till late fall. He wanted Dave to come along, rather afraid of doing the ninety miles of desert in which there was not an inhabitant alone. David agreed to go and upon telling Paul, found him rather relieved to have him quit the job though his manner was regretful. The situation in which Paul found himself after three years away from any life but the kind lived in the valley appalled David; he felt angry at himself for not being able to in some way halt the circumstances that were making a mere human animal of Paul. He could not, however, so he said goodbye and that night started off in an automobile across the desert. As they were leaving town they passed Old Man Woods, who, after some parley, decided to come with them, just as he was in a flannel shirt with his coat thrown over his arm. So he got into the car and on they drove.

They had been driving along, well away from town, and in sight only of desert stretches unplanted, before much talking was done. Harry drove the car, and he would chatter on a bit getting answers of abruptness. Old Man Woods was in one of his abstracted contemplative moods, and David's mind was filled with schemes and plans about his activities when he got

112

back to Los Angeles. Finally, perhaps because of the cooling evening air, and the sweet odorlessness of the space extending upward and out all ways from them, Old Man Woods began to liven up and then to speak.

"The older I get, the more of a pantheist I become; and it's bare places, or places away from men that make me feel the oneness of force in all nature. On the ocean too, as well as here on the desert—my mind struggles to think that infinity is really small, and that I'm puzzled about things in it only because my senses can't reach out enough to see, hear, and feel the edges of the universal complements of all my possible experience," he said to David.

David watched the old man's face whimsically, as he was speaking. "Does the idea of death disturb you; or have you always felt that way about the universe? There's a potential mysticism in us all but your processes had struck me as rational rather than as inspirational," he asked Woods.

"Worry me—death—I don't know. I don't know, boy, what I think or feel about it," Woods answered, then he chuckled. "You're meaning to suggest to me that I'm getting into my dotage aren't you?"

"No, no, not at all, I simply know that older people, men particularly, after the turmoil of 'succeeding in life' quite often relax, and decide because they as individuals can't govern events much," David commenced.

"As they can't when they're younger either," Wood interrupted.

"No, but one doesn't understand any better by believing because hungers in one make one desire to believe. Religions are so often but a rationalization of primitive fears; the savages with their animisms, fetishisms, and superstitions, aren't so very far behind many of us—there's mystery enough about us all right—our wills are limited in their ability to achieve—nevertheless there's no use in adding to universal mystery by a more finite variety easily explainable by psychology," David answered.

"What are you going to be after you're through college?" Woods inquired.

"There I'm more fatalistic than you, I guess. I'm going to be

113

as rational as possible, then what degree of understanding—intelligence—that I possess will discover for me what to be . . . Now, I don't know."

"Ah, but you're ambitious, aren't you?"

David laughed reflectively. "Ambitious—for what? I'm not past adolescence yet. The only ambition I have is to understand, to be able to accept reality instead of try to re-create the universe continually, because romantic impulses in me rebel against the type of experience it inflicts upon me . . . I'm afraid of ambition a little, I believe, because I've known too many men, commercial giants mostly, since this is America, who had ambition, for power. How utterly tired they leave me, and hopeless, these Napoleons of finance; the individual Napoleon strikes me as stupid and insensitive. If there's nothing finer than that, the whole process of life is a miserably futile one."

Harry broke into the conversation. "But say, that guy Napoleon was some man. He's the only person in that school thing, history, that I take my hat off to. That boy had a brain."

"Maybe a brain's not enough. I don't know which is the worst fanaticism, mental or emotional. Military genius feeds no spirit."

"You're one of these dreaming poetical fellows. The world's got to be fed, hasn't it?" Harry responded.

"Has it been any better fed or any happier because of Napoleon, or of various commercial geniuses, or do these 'brainy' men get much satisfaction out of existence themselves finally? Don't be sure I'm dreamy. The moon doesn't get too much attention from me; neither does sentimental romance nor love. If you were listening to Somerland and me the other day you'll remember that it wasn't I who was feverish about retaining the ideal of patriotism. Don't be so sure that your own admiration of Napoleon isn't a dreamy ideal. There's a harder, more inevitable force than any military force that ever he could assemble. Why rate human life and material as inventoried stock?"

Harry looked perplexed, and nothing more was said, as David was watching his face, and recalled what a ready-made sort of existence Harry had had to live, amongst mines, working at day labor from the time he was a boy. The night was as dark as it would be, for it was about ten o'clock by now. Still it was possible to see the desert ahead and around them for an indefinite distance since there were no distinguishing features to mark off the space. The grey sheen of desert night through which moonlight and starlight filtered was about them as they rode on. Complete quietness and tranquillity were everywhere. The heavy breathing of Old Man Woods emphasized the tranquillity. David wondered if he was dozing, or simply brooding in an apathetic wonderment of life.

They went along without speaking for almost an hour until Harry remarked that the car's radiator was about out of water. "We'll soon be at Skinner's well though and can get some water there."

When the car came along the roadside entry to a shack-house near which stood a well, placed in the desert by a man who'd lived there alone for a time, but who had now been gone for several years, Harry stopped the car, and he and David went over to the well. There was not a pail around and not a rope to cast into the well; only a barbed wire of great length, that was bent and twisted however, so that it was impossible to manipulate in a manner to sink a little pail they'd taken from the car into the water of the well.

The well was sunk some five hundred to a thousand feet into the sand. Looking down, it was possible to see a little glimmer, perhaps water, perhaps mud. The dim suggestion of star reflection looked up. Down the side of the well was a ladder that went all the way down to the water, it appeared so far as they could judge.

"We have to get water some way. Cars don't pass by this desert for days at a time, and when the heat comes on tomorrow we'll choke with thirst if we're stuck here. I guess we had better take a chance though on having one of us climb down that ladder for water. That's a long climb; the steps may not be solid now, and it'll be suffocating down there," Harry said.

David stood over the well looking down, and trying to make himself think that they were in a perilous predicament. He could not however. The night was too gentle, tranquil, and

115

unthreatening. He could look into the well, somewhat mystified in his senses, for it seemed strange that out here forty miles from any human settlement so well sunk and built a housing arrangement as this shack existed since there were no evidences about of mining or of agricultural opportunities.

"The man who had this dug and lived here must have been a queer sort," he commented.

After trying for a time to jerk the barbed wire about so that the pail fastened to the end of it would sink into the water far below, they concluded that if it did strike the water and sink the pail, the distance they'd have to draw it up with the unwieldy wire would prevent the pail getting to the top with any water in it.

"I tell you," Harry said. "I have to empty my bladder anyway. Do you?"

So they went back to the car, and told Old Man Woods that they'd have to drive on and take a chance on making the next thirty miles, to country where a few ranchers lived, and if the water in the radiator didn't last till then they were up against it. So after the three of them had urinated into the water tank of the car, they climbed in and drove on. Within half an hour they passed an intersecting road, and stopped. Dave went down it and after a ten-minute walk came to a house, which he discovered to be deserted after shouting about for some time. Off to the side of it, however, was a stock watering tank and in it was a little water covered with green stagnancy. Beneath the green stagnant mosses was sufficient water to fill the tank of the car, so he and Harry drove to the tank and after they had filled the car, and each drank a little of the water, they drove on and inside of another hour had come to a district where little towns lay from ten to twenty miles apart. Beyond the first town a range of rocky hills lay, and turning the corner beyond one hill they came to a rock over which spring water was falling into a rock basin. There they stopped and lying down in the sand, after drinking, they slept for some hours, until the morning sun woke them as it drove away the rock shadow that protected them.

By twelve o'clock noon, they were in Los Angeles and separated, David departing for home, after he'd made arrangements

116

with Harry to go down to a Mexican bar to sit around and drink beer in the evening. Old Man Woods was noncommittal, declaring that he'd have to go back to Garna the next day after he'd attended to a little business. "He probably has a woman in town, or has come to replenish his stock of dope, or of whisky," Harry suggested.

"Something like that, I suppose. It doesn't matter. I have no curiosity about how the old man will spend his time here, or his remaining years."

Arriving at home David greeted his mother, who remarked when she had kissed him: "Home again? They always come back sooner or later," and a little later was talking about what David had better take up in college the coming semester.

"Let the subject of college rest, mother. I'm not going back. There's nothing I could ever do with a degree because I shan't live the kind of life in which such letters signify."

"What then—you can't drift forever."

"No?—Well probably not. But I'll be leaving for New York or Mexico or China or South America—leaving for somewhere within the next week."

His mother looked unsatisfied, then resigned.

"You will go your own way; that's all right too. I guess everybody must be their own salvation, but you won't find what you're looking for in any of those out of the way places. You might just as well settle here."

"I might just as well not, too," David answered ironically. "So that's that. You just leave my generation's problems to be solved by the members of that generation."

"You want something to eat, I suppose. I'll see what I can fix up for you," his mother parried, and went out to the kitchen.

Mexican Interval

AWOKE FEELING PANIC swell through the room, and could not at once remember what city or country I was in. There was a beat and throb throughout, a thud against the wall, and the flutter of wings. The pigeon, flying at a velocity into the sunlit clarity of my high-ceilinged room, had struck the wall and now fell to the floor. It tottered dazedly; too stunned and stupid for panic. It would not guide easily, but finally I drove it towards the window and on the balcony it stood dazedly for a second before taking flight towards a group of pigeons wooing on the palazzo roof nearby. The event, with sleepless hours during the night because of innumerable bats entering the room, and circling endlessly with flutterings of blind imprisonment, increased a sense of ever-impending catastrophe that comes often upon abrupt awakening.

From the balcony I glanced towards the mountains. The light was ultra-violet upon the richly subdued colouring of arid country vegetation and silty soil. It was early, but already too hot for further sleeping. In the land of mañana, amid many tomorrows, there is always other time for slumber. The pigeons knew and were unfeverish in their love making. There are always other days for mating. The foolish dove had dispersed my dreams; and that was as well too. Mañana is time enough for dreams begot from childhood and other lands far removed, and times past for which there is no urge to recall.

The sun burned hotter across the room's bare spaces. Coming through the wide door-window to fall upon my nudity it distressed me to modesty. From the next room came the ever-crying baby's wail. When, I wondered, perplexed by life-birth-death irritation, would the señora depart and take her brood of giggling schoolgirls? Not speaking their language one could have no mood for coquetry with the half-grown girls who were wont to scramble, tittering, past my private balcony, adjoining that of their room. If they would indulge in such play they could take their chances of seeing me asleep, stripped, on the cot. Thompson, Johnson, I, and Salvador, the impoverished Hidalgo who dealt in bootleg tequila, were accustomed to having the hotel to ourselves, as a man's hotel, and these summer graduation girls were an intrusion on our privacy. Pretty some of them were, but well guarded by elderly and forbidding duennas. And to the girl children one could not respond with coyly impudent gestures, similar to their own. Indeed though, it was only I who was conscious of shyness. The mother left her room door open and flagrantly arranged that crowning glory, her hair, upon her flat back-head. She did not mind the bareness of our male chests as we sauntered indolently, pajama pants flapping, to wash away dawn sleepiness in the cooling shower bath. She hadn't alertness, awareness, and had she curiosity? Could she wonder at the ill-fated loves of the gentlemanly but *loco* British inventor, Thompson? Could she know why and for how many years Johnson had wandered, seeking continually that mine of gold or silver which was to enrich him fabulously? He trusted his beloved Mexico.

"The postman wasn't three days late. He'll never get here,"

Johnson said, coming into my room, rosy from a shower bath. "He was killed in the mountain pass. They found him with two knives between his ribs. Some bad hombres got word that he was carrying a thousand pesos. But here are some letters for both of us."

"Ecstasy and adventure have their place in youth, but they prove deceptive. Will you never achieve balance?" Olivia's letter teased me. And no, my conscious answered, but it is not so much ecstasy or adventure I want as that I don't want you. But you know; you are preparing yourself again against disillusion, so banal, but always to you, sudden and precocious. I won't return to your not-so-solacing common sense. What need have I for your quickly-forgotten decisions and wiles? Mañana I may write you that neither time nor your ponderings affect my hardly gained tranquillity. You are lonely and ask why I don't return? I am lonely too, but cleanly alone, uncorrupted by the loneliness your presence brings tormentedly into being.

"*No le hace in México*. No laughing in Mexico. No matter in Mexico." Thompson's morning formula of forced gaiety resounded through the patio as he came down the balcony. Which of his obsessions would be dominating him this morning? "They needn't tell me I'm crazy. I know it. I tell them first," he came booming into my room, wanting somebody to breakfast with. "You men don't mind my craziness. Twenty-five dollars for the man who isn't crazy, in Canada, England, or America. Twenty-five dollars. We're all crazy."

"Right, Tommy," Johnson said, grinning.

Thompson strives for gaiety but Johnson's glance admits that he too knows this will be one of Thompson's intricately loco days. Thompson helps himself to mescal, sighing, "I know you don't mind." He gulped the drink, and breathed heavily. "Yep, we're all crazy. I used to belong to the Scotch Greys. Their beautiful uniforms and swagger blinded what natural sense I had, if I had any. I believed in war and armies. My namesakes' bones lie in France. Gladiators, they're gladiators, like the Romans and Greeks. England, Japan, and America, gladiators! All crazy. Hey, parity, where is your purity, parity?

120

With all the fleets we could gather in a hundred years a college boy can fly overhead, drop poisoned powders, and kill the fleet in an hour. It took me sixty years not to be a damn fool. I belong to fighting stock. My ancestors' bones lie in the Crimea, India, Afghanistan, France. One was chucked overboard at Trafalgar. Ye-unh! *No le hace in México."*

Thompson, sedate, plumply dignified, drew designs on the floor with his cane. Helping himself to more mescal, he brooded, breathing heavily, more from reflection than from age. Why, since he had known Johnson but a few days, he made confidences which he had not made to me in six weeks, I don't know. Possibly he sensed that he irritated Johnson, while to me he was somewhat of a comic figure as I had no intention of brooding upon his pathos.

"Yes, I am crazy. My wife broke me. I was making good money, had inventions ready to go on the market to make us millionaires. She wouldn't wait. She said she had one god, money, and she would go to the streets for it if I didn't supply her. It cut me to the heart when she said that. Her voice was harder than flint. I gave her all I had and cleared out. I don't see even my daughters, and Clarie, the one I love most, the only one I love, may not be mine, I know now. *Si, no le hace in México.* That little girl loved sleeping with me until she was ten years old. No bed was as comfortable. Nobody understands the human heart, what love is or where it strikes and why. Ten men are rich on my inventions. They needn't tell me I'm crazy. I say so first. They haven't even paid me the $40,000 I was to get for my new water filtering system."

Standing by the balcony window I saw a string of cargador burros bearing brushwood down the mountain sides. They were followed by two lean, barefoot, unwashed arrieros, one of them Juan, who was crazy as well as constantly loco from mescal. Careless rags hung about their sinewy limbs, and apathy did not hide the grace or the animal-lithe strength of their bodies.

"Breakfast, Tommy, breakfast. We can't solve women on an empty stomach this time of the morning," Johnson said, knowing well Thompson couldn't be jollied out of any obsession

121

when he was really intense. He or I were in for having Thompson drop into our rooms continually during the course of the day. We sauntered from the hotel, across the plaza, down to the Alamos where Cuca's kitchen stood beneath the cotton trees. Cuca, years before a school teacher, pure Indian, and for years after the main woman of the town, had served many American and English men variously. She knew, at least, their tastes in food. She spoke to me, smilingly, when I was seated. I could not understand.

"That's it, is it?" Johnson joked. "You have been casting eyes on Merceditas, have you?"

"Mercedes," I said, glancing at the child who waited on the table. "She isn't over twelve."

Johnson was serious for a time. "No, she's fifteen or sixteen, not just an over-mature child. She came two months ago, from a rancho sixty miles back in the mountain. Some love affair made her run away, and parents don't bother hunting these girls out. Cuca is suggesting that if you have no little friend, here is Mercedes."

Merceditas was laughing at us. She didn't understand what was being said. I noticed that the healthy red, apple clear, was applied to her brown skin. She was pretty, childish, Indian, but lightmoving and alert. Cuca was not joking, I gathered. She felt sure that after three weeks in the town a young American would be lonely for a girl friend. I felt ill at ease, for Merceditas and Cuca had arranged things, and the child's eyes were direct and willing; not bold. What was suggested was natural to her. I squirmed to feel what Christian civilization and *morality* create in the way of immodest pudency. I didn't want Mercedes either; she might be sixteen but she struck me as a little girl.

We sauntered back to the hotel, Thompson stopping in the market place to buy figs, I, limes for a mescal-julep. Lemons, melons, papayas, beans, potatoes, and tomatoes rested in piles on the poorly arranged tables, behind which stood draggled, grimy, natives. Strings of sinewy black meat, jerked to preserve somewhat, hung along the market rafters. Innumerable flies hovered about, but if one is to travel, in the East or in Mexico, one must forget undue fastidiousness about sights and about what one eats.

As we loitered back to the hotel we noticed a flock of scraggly sheep scrambling about the mountain side, seeking meagre forage. It was dazzlingly hot now. The two orange cats, lean and wild, and the fat drooping dog moved agedly in the patio, to get out of the way of the cargador burros bringing firewood to Señora. An indolent sense of the town and market lived in me. The muchacha called to the Señora that los Americanos had used all the water in the shower bath, and Anatolio was not to be found. He *never was* about when the shower bath tank needed filling.

There came the sound of music, thin, wailing, Indian music, and the beat of drums. A group of Indians straggled by, going to some ceremonial dance. Johnson felt lazily talkative. "You should have seen this town before 1917, before the last revolution, when they played native music rather than this banal jazz the boys think they must try now. You will hardly believe it. There were bars, clubs, rich stores, and the nightly promenade around the plaza had aristocratic class. Peons never dared walk on the inside circle in those days. The train nearly made this town a mainline stop. Old General Orozco stopped all that in the 1917 revolution. He took two million pesos and 30,000 head of cattle from Alamos alone. The next year he was served arsenic in his soup. No one knows who got the money he stored away. And now there isn't even a drugstore here. The people don't value education. The teachers don't go above the fifth grade themselves. Their last governor absconded to the States, owing the teachers of this state five months' salary. They should have been paid monthly, but they didn't raise a row. No use having hope in these parts."

Johnson's guile did not keep Thompson's mind off his lonely complications. "*No le hace en México,*" Thompson boomed out the most maddening of his repeated phrases. "I expected a letter from my sweetheart today. Maybe she's angry at me. No matter. She's only one. I have others and more to be had by answering notices in the matrimonial journal. This one has me worried for her, though. I feel her grandfather. She writes that she's eighteen and in love with a married man. She's ill, and can't see him often. I told her to look before she leaps. If his wife won't divorce him for three years he will have done with her by then. No laughing in Mexico.

"If my man, Felix, gets back with the car I'm going to rancho San Bernardino," Johnson says. "Do you want to come along, Kit?" I saw that Thompson was getting on his nerves.

"Yes, Felix is probably downstairs chewing a straw and talking to Anatolio. I'll look him up. We need variety."

"That's all right boys," Thompson said, really kind. "I know I'm a dull old bore. I can't help it when my mind gets filled with problems. You go along. I'll look in on Señora Marcur. She may have some American magazines to give me."

Within half an hour we were in Johnson's Ford truck jogging across the desert. Innumerable longeared jackrabbits loped frantically across the sagebrush stretches on the approach of the car. In the luminous light, from a distance, they appeared magnified to deer size and looked amazingly deerlike. Felix and Johnson were silent for a spell, and I was wondering.

Yes, silver, copper, and gold were in the region; and fertile soil, and foraging land for millions of cattle. There was too the story of the hidalgo who paved the street from his casa to the church with silver slabs, for his daughter's wedding. Next year he was put against the carcel wall and riddled with bullets.

Now silver bullion prices were low. These people don't know when they are well off. When everything was going well, with people richly prospering, they had to have a revolution.

A neat native, surely an Indian peon, passed by and spoke greetings. His donkey was extra precious, deerlithe, neat, and sweet, with dainty feet prancing as though the mountain paths were intricate lace. Some Indians rode right pretty steeds these days, prancing, rearing, champing, but gentle too. Jacinto's Andalusian stallion was *brioso* but docile, and needed no mouth-breaking bit. He danced a pretty dance, coy with his dashing longtailed beauty. I wished we were headed towards

124

Jacinto's ranch rather than San Bernardino. Bad hombres loitered about the ranch.

"Gold in them hills," Johnson said breezily, to break the silence.

"Guarded by rattlesnakes, cactus, and the Mexican government," I said.

Johnson turned regretful. "They don't mine themselves, and won't do business with anyone who will."

"They have had experience with those who want to and do."

Johnson's mind deviated from desires which he had not fulfilled. "Once the Señoritas all wore black, and veils, and went every morning to say their prayers. They've left off their veils, but they're still cagey. Their short dresses are a sign though. Do you notice how you can always spot a girl with German blood? Thick ankles."

"The Spanish or the meztizo have the quality. At a ball for the Governor last week, you could have seen twenty girls dressed as though they were from a recent fashion show in Paris. How do they know?"

"They make their own dresses," Johnson mused. "They sew, stay indoors all day, do the plaza at night, and wait for mañana. Would our girls consent to that routine? Oh boy! You wouldn't sense, if you didn't know, how hard these people can be. Three days before my arrival, last year, they shot five bandits. They were still hanging on jail hill, as warning, when I got to town. They picked the prettiest spot in the country for their jail too. If they catch the Indian who killed the postman we'll have another killing."

From far away, from some ranch off any main or even minor trail, came the beat of drums. "Hey Felix," Johnson is boisterous, "are those Yaqui drums? What messages are they sending? Are they coming after us? Felix loves the Yaquis."

Felix looked perturbed, his Indian face less a mask than most because of seven years labour contracting with Johnson in Los Angeles. "Yaquis, me no like," he said with stolid automatic insistence.

"Why, Felix?" Johnson joked. "They're fine fellows once you

get to know them. You didn't make friends with them that time they captured you. Tell Kit about it."

Felix, subnormal anyway, pondered with deep fear an experience of his childhood. Johnson has teased him too much. He feels he must tell the story and does so haltingly. "One time father had fine haciendo, San Bernardo, where we go. Me just kid, with mother, brother, sister. Yaquis come, two, t'ree, hundred. Burn house, kill twenty people, sister, mother, father. Me and brother they take. One man they ham-string. We walk three days in mountain. No shoes. One man's leg, he break, leave me guard him. I see. He dying. I only twelve. I see him die and pretty much quick I run away. See brother dead, hanging to tree. I run quick, hide. Yaquis no find. Yaquis pretty much tough guys. Me no like."

"Felix nearly shook out of his pants as we rode across Yaqui country coming down," Johnson said, bothersomely teasing and jovial. "Why don't you get chummy with them, Felix? They're fine fellows once you know them."

"Yaquis, me no like" Felix insisted, dumbly, apparently unaware that he's being teased.

We arrived at San Bernardino to find a wedding fiesta going on, for the third day. The groom was drunk on mescal, and surely had been taking marihuana. Porfiria, the middle-aged woman who called herself Felix's wife on this ranch, said that one man had been killed the night of the wedding, in a drunken fight.

"You drink with us. In America we drink with you, we do as you. Here you drink mescal, Mexican drink." Alvaro, the bridegroom talked challengingly to Johnson. He had come from San Diego, with his father, to marry a true Mexican girl. Johnson hated mescal, but Alvaro was far gone and combative. We drank.

Our drinking pleased Alvaro and the other ranch Mexicans. We tried to join in their songs, as they repeated the melodies and words to us. They called us best friends, but Alvaro disappeared. Later he was on a rampage. Loco with mescal and mad with marihuana he wanted to fight everybody. His friends could not get his gun or knife and he brandished both, threatening murder. He ran down to the stream nearby and fell in, but when friends tried to rescue him he threw rocks at them. When the water had cooled him a bit he swaggered into the hall and up to his bride. There, in the center of the floor, he threw her down and raped her. Two Mexican children rushed up to Porfiria, who was in the kitchen. Alvaro had, they told her, plunged a knife into his bride. They had seen the blood spurting. Porfiria, already knowing the incident, nodded drily and glanced at a pair of ducks waddling about the kitchen. "Yes, Señor Drake murders Señor Duck so every day, many times."

"He'll kill his wife before the month's up." Johnson predicted. "That boy's a bad hombre. No good. His father is ashamed of him. His sisters have left the party ashamed of what he has done. They're American trained. The natives don't mind."

The wedding celebration goes on. The peon orchestras keeps twanging sad music, patient, but insistently wailing nostalgia and love desire. An owl hoots from the primitive church top. Dawn isn't far away. Bats are returning to the palm-tree they chose to nest in. In the hills nearby the dogs are at their barking which demands, perhaps, that something will happen that doesn't, never does, happen. Roosters, tricked by the brightness of the night, crow early dawn's oncoming. The descending moon sheds deep lavender on the hills. The cool atmosphere is an effervescent current. Still there is no feeling of peace or rest about this night.

"Let's clear out and drive back to town," Johnson talks sotto voce to me. "Porfiria and the Chink and a few of the drunk Indians are planning to snitch a lift in my car back to town. They're too drunk and hopped up. I'll get Felix."

San Bernardino ranch is too removed; Porfiria too embedded in dirt whch has collected upon her through the years. Her food is impossible. The memory of the murder and the rape make the place sinister. There are no decent houses, or rooms, to retire into. The ranch is only a group of uncared for buildings. We would not feel safe sleeping on the ground or in the midst of this crew of drunk, doped Indians. No telling how they might resent us. Johnson found Felix, who drove away from the ranch. There we joined him, to depart, undetected by any of the wedding party proper.

"A sweet honeymoon for the bride," Johnson grunted. "But believe it or not, away from these parts I always feel its romance dragging me back. It's in my blood."

II

Señora Marcur, the town taleswoman, is talking. She has decided that I am near enough her class to be considered. She does not know how like a vulture's her eyes and expressions are when she tells of the misdoings of others. Now she is being nobly generous. "Poor Señor Thompson is touched, but we all see he is a gentleman," she concedes, and I note how amazingly thick are her ankles in her shoes. Has she dropsy? "Some day he will be really mad and they will turn the lock on him. That will be the last of Mr. Thompson."

"Yes, poor Tommy. He always has some new invention. I broke his heart today. He was grieved because various governments do not answer his letters. He would have them sell butter and cream in tubes, like toothpaste. Today he is disgusted with England, and has written to the Irish Free State, about interior rubber heels to save soldiers' feet from shocks. He was going to write to Spain about his portable shower bath for use in the deserts of Algiers and Morocco. 'A child can use it in the dark,' he said. When I asked him where they would get water on the desert, he looked pained. That he had not thought of."

Señora Marcur nodded, grimly sympathetic. "His own people do not look after him. He spends much money on postage stamps, forever answering advertisements in cheap magazines. It is not well that he should live so, touched in the head, in this land, where no one knows when we may have a revolution. We had revolutions when we were well off, and now there is no rain, no corn, no sale for silver, no mines working—" she hesitates, gracious now, but I know she wishes to talk again about her ancestral birthright, her culture. Nevertheless she talks on,

128

about Mexico and her people, generally. She leads up to her main theme carefully, wishing me to understand that she is an educated, thoughtful, woman.

"The resignation of these Mexicans does not mean they have no slyness. They also have pulque, tequila, mescal, and marihuana."

"And mañana."

"But mañana is not enough, Mr. Downley."

"No, a fury at time can accumulate in the breasts of many, to coagulate into a horde frenzy. There is need for variation and revolutions break the routine of dull time. They seem resigned to death and failure and oppression. A revolution, to them, is little more than a passionate day of fiesta, warm with blood."

"You are ironic, but we have need for a sense of humour," Señora Marcur remarks, and takes up her old refrain, sung to me the three previous times I have encountered her. "But the history of this town for two hundred years would be an interesting study. My ancestors came shortly after the conquistadors, with the Jesuit fathers. My grandfather owned the casa you are now in as a hotel. My uncle owned the block where the Japanese make their silk. We still own this block, with eighteen rooms for the three of us. Before the revolution, until five years ago, I spent my winters yearly in San Francisco. There I was educated as a girl, and before, I had spent my childhood in France. Though you see me here in this decaying town where I was born, I am a cosmopolitan, a woman of breeding, without a country, virtually. I have a vital interest in culture, in cosmopolitan literature. I keep in touch with the outside. There are few of our class here, few with whom we can associate. There is Indian in most of the best families now, or degeneracy. The sons are worthless, of weak minds, given to drink, and to carrying on with the native girls. That I do not object to, but they weakly marry the girls, at times. There are children, the young men are lonely and become fond of these children."

Señora Marcur recites her tale as though she were a history teacher repeating her points to impress them upon the mind of a slow-minded child. I try to convey the idea that I know she is educated, well read, an aristocrat. She is soured, and delights in macabre details, and claims to believe I, as an American, feel myself superior not only to the peons but to the Marcurs. We talk of the ancient civilization of the Aztecs, which she grudgingly admits, but there is a barrier at once when I suggest that fanatical priests destroyed records which were best not destroyed, for history and for art.

Señora Marcur is, one discovers, Catholic before she is cultured. A bigoted gleam flames intensely in her penetrating blue eyes because I have doubted the wisdom of her ancestral priests. She changes the subject and talks of her townsmen, as viciously as a buzzard tearing at dead meat. She speaks truth, one does not doubt, she was not meant for so narrow a world, and festers, but I wonder if Señora Marcur is not too aristocratic, cultured, and superior, even for heaven. I plead an excuse and get away to saunter about the plaza. Here things are gaily casual. By sitting with Thompson I can chat fleetingly with groups of passing señoritas. He is loco, and calls to them that they are *locos tambien*. They laugh gaily and twit him, coquettishly, flashing quick glances at me. They are willing; it is only their training and tradition which is obstinate. If I spoke Spanish but a little, I believe I could contrive to know Elena, at least. She looks and acts rebellious.

It is nine o'clock in the evening. The first class señoritas begin to walk around the plaza, walking arm in arm, showing no awareness of the young men. Many of them are getting on in years and are overblown. There are few young men to marry about. Only because Don Fernando's three other daughters have made good marriages and make good wives does it look hopeful for plump, flirtatiously tomboyish Elena. She uses her eyes and her sex appeal far too much for modesty, but that is the younger generation's way.

Señorita Marcur, who teaches English in the Catholic school, and who was also educated in San Francisco, consents to sit and talk with Thompson for a time. I understand, she feels that townspeople will say she's looking for a husband if she shows too much interest in me. Thomspon calls Elena

his sweetheart, excited gallantly by her pretty violet-eyed cud-
dlableness.

"But she thought to be engaged," Señorita Marcur said, "to
Señor Seron. I told Elena he was married, with two children. It
was no use. She claimed to believe that I wanted him for myself.
I am not like these town girls. I have been educated in San Francisco and do not think about marriage as they do. I have my
music. Señora Seron lived in Guaymas, but she heard news.
One day she came, took her husband's hotel key, went to his
room, tore up Elena's photograph which was on his table. That
night she walked on the plaza with her husband. Elena and
Señor Seron were both furious because I had warned her he
was married. He must be mad, in the government service and
a Catholic, to say he is not married, and flirt with the girls in this
town."

Obviously Señorita Marcur is pent up, and wants to get away.
Since the last revolution, when her father spent two weeks in
the carcel, where he contracted rheumatism, at seventy, she
has not been away from the town. The family fortune is gone,
except for their casa and a miserable income. The girls to
whom she gives English lessons do not learn and are interested
in nothing but clothes, she claims. One detects that she frets
at the stronger will and the insistences of her mother, Señorita
Marcur is soft and gently perplexed.

"Yes, the girls here dress beautifully. They get fashion journals and make their own gowns. That they know. It is their one
way of attracting men, but there are no young men. The bright
ones leave by the time they are fifteen, and when they come
back to visit, they usually have girls elsewhere. Would the world
believe that such dullness and decay exists in the midst of scen-
ery and natural wealth such as this! You love it, as an outsider.
I hate it as a wall I can't get beyond."

Señorita is wailing the wail about dullness and monotony
which is immemorial, to towns, cities, and all countries, among
people of imagination. I watch groups and couples passing our
bench. Looking on is so much of life, the chief entertainment
of the day, here.

The boys circle in twos, threes, or groups, their arms entwined or thrown about each others' shoulders. Those under eighteen have little heed of class lines. They walk with their arms about the shoulders of peon lads whose fathers are becoming wealthy, or who have learned cleanliness. The older boys, however, have an air of aloofness to those not of their group.

The younger boys, or the older in fact, show little sign of sex interest. It looks as though they accepted things in direct simplicity, for in their casual stoppings and chattings with girls there is a town-companionable attitude and little coquetry.

Augustín Dossier, sixteen, typist for his father, and town banker, has trouble keeping his shirttail in, so squirmy is his walk. He is ticklish, and Andrés Salazar likes to goose and tickle him to make him start nervously. Augustín is the only one of the Dossier boys who is not a bit off. Carlos is comic, a fine violinist, witty, irresponsible, and wily at slipping away from his brother, the redheaded Alexandro, who should watch over him. Carlos is apt to get very drunk, stay drunk, and disappear. Alexandro understands, but is it not good for the Dossier name and fortune, and the family is poor. In the older generation there are three unmarried sisters, and two irresponsible brothers to take care of. The Dossiers don't make much now of having aristocratic English blood, the blood of people who do things in the world. Carlos twits the idea too much, and talks heedlessly of the degeneracy and decay which goes on among the blue-blooded. He visits me frequently, because there is mescal in my room, and also he is sincerely pleased to see a white man wearing Indian huaraches about the town. The bankish formalities of his banker brother and other town tradesmen bore him. He needs much mescal to forget his boredom.

Jesús, Alfredo, Juan Edmondo, and Pepé are a bit loco on tequila; they have been at a dance on the outskirts of the town. Dons Loreto, Ramón, Ignacio, and Manuel are all fat enough to belong to that ideal navy; Don Moreno has Buddha sagging eyes, jowls, belly, and buttocks, to make up his three-hundred-odd pounds. He is the town telegraph operator, amiable, and proud of his few words of English. His ponderous procession about the plaza is a spectacle, but one waits for him to sit down,to see if his trousers split. Hernando is *flojo,* even more *flojo* than Francisco or Pepé, and in a town where one has to be a genius of laziness to be called *flojo.* Conchita, the town's haughty belle, does not care for Francisco, but his father has wealth, and there are no other men in town to marry who seek her. As yet Conchita's green eyes smoulder promises, but still she resembles her mother markedly. It may not be long before she too will have extra chins and stomachs as has her placid parent.

Miguel and Nacho are good boys, fondly and gay, but they are *muy loco* tonight. Music sounds from the outskirts of town. An Indian dance may be going on. Tonight, surely, there is some extra impulse in the air to make the boys drink. Miguel and Nacho go about the plaza with their arms around each other, steadyingly. It is difficult. They sit on the curbstone and look dazed. The moon is coming up. They gaze at each other, and take each a sip of mescal. Miguel mumbles understandingly to Nacho, who begins to calf-moo a minor-harmonied lovesong. Miguel joins in, and bleating and braying, they harmonize. These tender animal sounds touch their heart chords and instincts. The boys, full of lonely, beautiful, feelings, get up and totter off for more mescal. Señor Marcur and Jew Khrem sit on their corner bench, criticizing them and other town boys and girls. These two old men buzz like rusty rip-saws. Of Ignacio they say, "The only time he speaks the truth is by mistake." They laugh at this joke, as they have laughed before, for the one who said it first that night about somebody. They look at me askance, implying that, even if my feet are clean it is not fitting for a gringo to wear huaraches.

Upon my arrival in town, after being introduced to them by Thompson, Jew Khrem and Señor Marcur implied that I was acceptable as honorary member to their spit, argue, and scandalize club. Now they are puzzled. Jew Khrem understands that he is no new type to me, and has stopped trying to impress me by what he fancies his position. A German Jew, he has in forty years of selling dry goods and canned goods to the natives become a rich man. He doubtelssly had other ways of picking up money too. Señor Marcur is puzzled that his wife, who is particular and exclusive, seems to approve of a gringo with democratic tendencies, who wears huaraches and talks readily with the Indians, getting noisily drunk with them, it is rumored. He does not know that Señora Marcur is puzzled too, but likes the French, German, and American magazines and books I let her take. Mainly though, Señor Marcur and Jew Khrem are sour. Too few people sit with them generally, and they need more audience than each other. They want new ears to hear them talk of the indiscretions of various señoritas, the worthlessness of young men, the disgraces in the Almada family. They should know too that Señora Marcur tells all these tales well, much more quickly and with surer aim. She is a pure Castillian aristocrat, a traveled woman, a cosmopolitan, and cultured. When she wants to gossip, she has volocity. Señor Marcur has French blood, once was interested in Mexican and local politics, and in money making. He has not the specialized training of his wife.

Johnson joins me to suanter about the plaza for a few rounds. The señoritas are disappearing; the older boys disperse; only Roberto, who fancies me as a foreigner, Andrés, Jesús, and Anatolio, of my hotel, linger.

"A peon coming from his ranch with fifty litres of *brincadores* (Mexican jumping beans) was found dead five miles from town," Johnson informed me. "He was knifed in the back. What those Indians will chance for a little money is nobody's business. His slayer can't sell that quantity of jumping beans without being caught or at least suspected. The fear of death doesn't exist in them. They're ready for it, I suppose. In the mountains they'll kill for enough to buy a bottle of mescal."

"Which suggests to me, I'm restless," I said. "Let's get a bottle of mescal and do a little drinking."

"I hate the stuff. I'm going to bed soon. I'll take a sip with you though," Johnson conceded sociably, but soon left me sitting with Roberto, Andrés, and five other boys not desiring to go to

134

bed. The willingness of the young men of this removed town to stay up was proof that neither the twentieth century nor cities invented nightlife.

Slowly rain started. It was but eleven o'clock, but the feeling of oncoming rain had emptied the plaza early. I drank mescal, waiting for midnight so that I could go to Duba's thatch-covered kitchen for menudo.

The bats were still coming from their palm trees, but in small numbers now. Two hours before, they had disentangled themselves layer by layer to flutter, windblown leaves, from the palms. Circling interminably, they foraged for insects.

The rain became heavier, the night darker. Against the lamps about the plaza, rain was a blacksilver downpour, whispering commiseration through the palm leaves. León, the crazy cargador, staggered by, his upper body completely bare, rags hanging about his limbs barely covering his parts. He was madly intent upon another drink. Young Andrés, seeing that he was headed for trouble with the policia again, called him. León was persuaded to subside in a corner of the hotel hallway, a small bottle of mescal in his hand.

Anatolio left, suggesting that I return to my room too, and saying, what I knew was untrue, he would have to lock up the hotel. The hotel door was never closed. Nevertheless after a time I became aware that Andrés, Jesús, and even the faithful Roberto were hinting that I had better go to bed. Was I then very drunk and rowdy; did they think me loco, as were Thompson and León? The idea tickled me that they should be protecting me because of my simple mind, and I wanted menudo at Duba's kitchen. The downcoming rain did not bother me, so scant were the clothes I wore.

We trudged down the road through rivulets of muddy water. Duba was in her shack, dignified, gracious as a worldly salon hostess, and conversational. A dim light burned in the thatch-covered shack, and rain dripped steadily through the roof leaves. We seated ourselves at the bare-board table. Over the charcoal fire a huge pot steamed. Some older Mexicans sat eating menudo, but this night they were not drunk or quarrelsome, though all of us had bottles of the inevitable mescal.

Duba served our group large bowls of menudo, a soup made of the tripe and unnameable innards of a cow. It was thick with grease, and the only part I could eat was the soup, and the corn. Duba removed the thicker grease from the top of my bowl, and, hearing the rain's downpour, feeling drops on my neck and back, I felt comforted by the hot comfort and rich nutriment of the concoction.

Arturo Ortiz, who spoke English, having been a salesman in America, came in. He had a passion for menudo and some pretenses to interest in reading. Soon his face was buried in a first, then second, and a third bowl of menudo. Periodically he looked at me, not quite comprehending. His face shown with grease, he belched, and uttered grunts of satisfaction. "Um, menudo good, you no like, I like." He patted his sizeable stomach. Arturo was goodnatured, mildly intelligent, and gross only as most Mexicans are about their eating and table manners. His lack of nicety did not distress me. "You no eat the menudo," he said, disdainful of my delicacy when he observed that I did not eat the sinew, cords, and gristle in the soup.

"No, if after a lifetime of having all this in her stomach the cow hasn't digested it, I don't plan trying," I answered.

"Um, menudo good," Arturo grunted and handed his bottle of mescal to me, to pass on. A tow-headed youngster of fourteen had a bottle of mescal, and an empty one which he had finished. It was nothing, I knew, for boys to start drinking mescal here by the time they were seven or eight, and this boy, Hernando, was already a confirmed mescal fiend.

"We go some night to Navajoa, see girls there. I take my car," Arturo invited. "You get lonely here, no?"

I laughed. "But Cuca offers me Merceditas." I was not keen on the sixty-mile drive across the sand in Arturo's bucking car, with him a wild driver.

"No bueno, not for you," Roberto said, shaking his finger, and speaking some of the few words of English I had taught him. I had let him use my camera and taught him what I knew about light and effects; and he was intent on doing woodcarvings. Since seeing the crowds of dirty-footed peons doing art exhibitions in Guadalajara, I had become very hopeful about the sense of color, design, and of plastic quality existent in the native. Roberto was alert, a handsome boy-Indian, with lithe beautiful movements.

"You don't think she is a virgin then," I asked.

"Yo creo que no," Andrés, the fifteen-year-old son of my hotel patron said. Jesús, his fourteen-year-old brother nodded, and all of the boys talked with Duba laughing. She glanced at me, much as an ironic woman of the world would look at any innocent youth. I did not understand what she said, but Arturo explained that Duba said she would find me a young girl who was absolutely pure. It tickled me that they should all, without the suggestion of an appeal from me, be so anxious that I should not be lonely for a girl.

Andrés, particularly, was handsome, delicately so, as a brooding flower-faced child; Jesús looked more studious and boydreaming,but both of them were fine types of Spanish youth with a suggestion of Indian on their face. It interested me to note how like sage old men of the world these boys talked, concerning the matters of sex, venereal disease, and at times local and national politics. They were, had been born, actually natural before natural facts.

The rain had ceased and I had finished my second bowl of menudo before we got up to go. Now I had a sheepish feeling that Roberto, Andrés, and Jesús had merely stayed up to look after me. They thought me drunk, and Roberto feared I might wander off towards the edge of town if I heard music. There, if some of the rougher natives were drunk, or resentful of gringos, I might get injured. Roberto took my arm, but finding that I did not stagger except as the dark made me unsure, he let Andrés and Jesús take me back to the hotel when we came to the road leading towards his home.

A violet throb of calm was cool upon the night. Insect voices threaded themselves though the silence, and frogs croaked bass symphonies, happy after rain. From somewhere a pigeon coo thrust warmly into the velvet silence. On the edge of the town

Indian music sounded thinly, tinkling on the soothing tranquillity. A sense of germination was in the atmosphere, for there
had not been rain before for months. As the moon came out
hugely and mounted the sky all the night was murmurous.

Though the light was lavender-grey and luminous deep summer night was on, I was too warmed with menudo, too swirling
in the head from mescal, to stand long reflecting. But I was
happy. I crawled upon my cot and let another night flow into
mañana. A sense of companionability, of being protected,
dwelt in me. This town, these people, had something beyond
the usual Mexican type and place. They took pleasure in their
town, and had few resentments against gringos, as the patronizing type of Anglo-Saxon or American had lived here little. The
town was primitive and modern too, but mainly I felt myself in
a place where time didn't matter, and relativity had so arranged
affairs that I was getting some quality of an archaic town's communal life, with the contemporary world and all its neurotic,
noisy, nerve-driving, civilization of go-getters easily accessible.

Here, in Alamos, for three hundred years, removed by one
hundred miles at least from modern and contemporary
influences, life has gone on. They know of the radio, the phonograph, the moving picture, but these things are little of their
lives; and few of them are actively aware of even newspapers.
They are not primitive, or provincial; not medieval, naive,
unsophisticated; they have the sophistication of a people and
race which knows that life has gone on a long time and will go
on. Unlike moral and cultured and civilized peoples, they know
and accept simply, with kind sympathy, variations, economic,
psychologic, and physical. They need no psychoanalysts, no
sociologists, and no fervid advertisements about cleanliness.
They are not obsessed by sex or sensuality. Nature is nature to
them. Birth, life, and death continue. At moments I think them
the only balanced and sophisticated people I have ever encountered, for there is nothing they will not speak of or discuss
directly, without refined posturings or protest. Their problems
are the real, tormenting ones of poverty, when it is there, politics, or revolution. Passionally they are not moved to dramatic

posings by romantic-tragic literary legendizings. Fondliness and companionability they have, and love, but I have seen no evidence of that decadent emotion, jealousy, come from egotism and vanity and the possessive desires. They are not Latin or Spanish in that way; they are Indian and communal, removed perhaps from the main Mexican tendencies; inhabitants of a town that might well be an island where people have had little contact with the outside, but still retain an awareness of life's implications which is timelessly primal.

"Kit, come here and see what's on the plaza," Johnson's voice calls from his room, directly on the plaza. Going to him I look below. There, beneath the already hot sun, lies a peon, a deep gash in his head. He does not move. We wonder if he has been stabbed or struck with a rock.

An elderly peon comes along and strives to help him up. With a jerk he arises and is loco—fighting mad. It is not safe to go near these natives when they are mescal or marihuana crazed. They are as apt to bash a friend as an enemy in the face with a rock. We learn that the policia, having taken the peon so far, let him lie. The night before he had fought with another peon over some political argument. Neither were trustful; both fought sober friends who wished to separate them. For four hundred years, under Spaniards, under many governments, in revolution, robbed and abused by foreigners and countrymen alike, they have learned to trust nobody.

A feeling of relief sank into me. Probably Roberto, Andrés, and Jesús had known of the drunken party going on at the bar on the outskirts of town. That was why they had stayed with me, and tried to get me to bed.

Thompson booms into the room to help himself to a glass of Johnson's sherry, though he prefers mescal. Today he is being ironic, very British and full of scorn. His own problems do not obsess him. "Snowden!" he scoffs. "Chancellor of the exchequer for England! Did you read his article bragging of his achievements in spite of being a cripple? For a cheap American magazine. I have written him telling him he is a disgrace to England. Once we had men who didn't need to brag, especially

139

of their defects. It's brains we want, and action. His article isn't even well written. Such as he can't beat sense into the gladiators. I have just written too to Hoover, to all the senators. Why don't they use what brains they have seeking to prevent disease and unemployment? It's a disgrace. I write to the various governments offering them inventions, for nothing; inventions that will insure peace. They don't answer my letter when I pay postage and write on questions of national, of international, importance."

"Tommy," I said, "Here are the snapshots I took of you; not bad."

Thompson looks at them, and his reddish, grey-mustached face falls. "Good? Do I look like that. I suppose I am a fat, pompous old duffer. They tell me I don't look more than forty of my sixty-four years. I can't send these to my sweethearts."

"You're a handsome old codger, Tommy," Johnson claims. "You don't want to look a strip of a lad. The girls want men of experience who have done things."

"Never mind," Thompson made himself forget his disappointment in the snapshots. "You don't mind my nuttiness. I don't often ask it, but lend me a stamp and an envelope? I want to get this letter off to my sweetheart. She thinks she's hooked a rich and lonely old boy. I had my day, and it slipped by, all for the bloody war and a wife mad for money. Once there was no engineer who could beat me. Today I may sell some self-threading needles to some señora. A needle a blind man can thread in the dark. Ignacio Salazar bought six buttons a child could put on blindfolded yesterday, but he can't get them on his trousers. Too dumb. Never mind, Ignatz doesn't care if his pants are buttoned or not, and he's not dangerous."

The day was very hot, with a dry heat that however smoldered into the heart to make it sweat. From the window the mountains made sculpturesque lines against the sky, but Johnson is fretful, wanting activity, to be locating new mine possibilities. He transmits his restlessness to me, and I regret that he is staying in the hotel. Otherwise I might remain calm and write. We await our mail. When the papers arrived they informed us that Carol has become King of Roumania, but Thompson doesn't

140

think that will get us anywhere. Right now Thompson had a moment of wondering if some of the señoritas did not cut him on the plaza. Generally he is sure that every one of them considers the possibilities of hooking him into a marriage. The rich widow he admires he would not marry, he claims, for she has money and they would say he married her for her money. Thompson has moments of knowing, but he brushes them aside. His calls and greetings and fooleries on the plaza do not anger the Señoritas, but they embarrass them, particularly Señorita Marcur, who is reserved and who, knowing herself neither pretty, graceful, nor well-dressed, does not wish attention fixed upon her by teasings.

A sharp rain comes down suddenly, but the sun is still out and clear. It protests its fire-rose rays against the dark silver of the downpour, particularly among the palms on carcel hill. We stand looking at the view, surmising how many rebels, bandits, and politicians have been shot against that shell-battered wall. Alive today some of them might be governors. Outlaws today, the just tomorrow; dead bandits, with sons who are lawmakers and the righteous.

"I'm going down to Señora Marcur," I say. "Have some magazines for her, and may borrow a book to read. Do you want to come along, Tommy?"

"No, as you say, she's a buzzard. I'm nervous today," Thompson answers.

"So you will stay on through the summer," the town taleswoman began when I was seated in her reception room. She had been long in coming, and her daughter, busy with housework, had been shy of remaining to make conversation. She feared, evidently, that I did not think she had the intellectual and cultural interests of her mother. She perhaps felt herself plain and uninteresting, too much so, for she had charm, fair looks, and goodwill. She gathers too, possibly, that I understand her mother is so long in coming to greet me to make her arrival more important. Drably dressed, her long skirts however did not cover the hugeness of her ankles, and doubtlessly her calves, as she walks. Her grandly social and gracious manner is too intense.

141

"Yes, Cuca's food is monotonous, but a young friend, Roberto, brings me aguacates, apples, grapefruit, plums, limes, and melons."

"Ah, you eat with Cuca. Refugio Soto is her name," Señora Marcur's voice suggests deep and subtle intrigue. "She is pure Indian, but educated. She taught school before she went wrong. I scold her whenever I see her. She could have married a man of her own class, one who had also been to school for a time. Instead she lived with various men far above her station. They could never marry her. Living alone they were tempted, and there was Cuca. Before the revolution we did her a service."

Señora waited for me to become anxious about the secret she was to reveal. "They wished to make her take her restaurant to the edge of town. Señor Marcur was then influential. He said that she had only a restaurant, was over fifty, and had not for five years lived with a man. Why should she not remain in town? Cuca was grateful, and returned Señor Marcur's aid."

Now Señora's voice took on deeper significance. She did not lower her voice, but she made it deeper, and dramatic. I wondered, had she not once yearned to be an actress?

"In her restaurant she heard various political men discuss plans over coffee and drinks. They came to think that Señor Marcur was in league with the devil, for a few hours after any discussion he knew all that they had said. Cuca could not go to him. Being what she is she thought I and others might misconstrue if she was seen talking to Señor Marcur." Señora's tone was grave and very moral now. "She came to me and told what she had heard, and I told Señor Marcur. So Cuca expressed her gratitude. But she has no business head. She is always wanting to borrow pesos. With her restaurant and rooms she could do very well, with management, but she has Indian indifference and does not value money. But Cuca can write a literate letter as few other women in the town can. Living with wellbred gentlemen has educated her. She can serve a meal most elegantly, if she wishes. It won't do, this mingling of the classes. I scold her for not having married a man of her class."

Señora Marcur looked very intense, and worn by the failure

of townspeople to appreciate her efforts to keep class strains pure. "Once it looked," she continued, "as though Alfredo Dossier intended to marry her. She would supply him the mescal he demands. He does play the violin very well. Fortunately his brother was able to stop the marriage. Ah yes, the Dossiers are a study in degeneration, as are the Llaberdesques. None of the sons of either family amount to anything. There is idiocy or disease in most of this last generation, though we don't speak of it so outrightly among ourselves." Señora spoke subduedly now, confiding to a near stranger what she would not speak of outrightly among her own.

From the schoolhouse, where teachers of the region are having a convention that lasts six weeks, comes the sound of children's voices, singing in hard onrushing tones, hurdling the high notes lithely. Accelerating an eager intentness, their tones are youngly resistant or unaware of resignation and nostalgia, but the promise of sensuality is there, starkly revealed. Is this the new generation, created anew, by a wiser educational programme?

Señor Marcur goes through the room, looking much the old French dandy, in decay. He potters past us agedly, after a courteous nod. He is going to join Jew Khrem for a before-luncheon talk. Señora Marcur informs me so, and sensing somehow that I don't care for Jew Khrem she makes a humble confession which surprises me. I think, perhaps only the narrowness of life has embittered her; surely she has human and cultural hungers, and her bitterness against the townspeople is only because they emprison her.

"I know, as Mr. Thompson tells me you say, when Mister Khrem is scornful of the lower classes, one does not think of Jerusalem and of ghettoes. He is no fine type of Jew, but he has wealth. Once Señor Marcur could be independent, but since the revolution—" Señora's voice fades away. I understand. The Marcurs hope to sell some of the arid and valueless thousands of acres they possess; and wish at least to procure loans.

Her voice takes up the refrain. "I can't respect a man who turns on his own race, and Mr. Khrem's pretension, here, where

143

we have the blood of ancient aristocracy within us, is much to bear" Señora Marcur was actually, warmly, helpless and sad. I knew the young Jew Khrem thought he might marry Señorita Marcur, for her family connections and the position he could have as her husband, in Mexico City. He too plays the piano. But yes, Señora Marcur has had a difficult existence. For a woman brought up in wealth, and educated abroad, her present circumstances are humiliating, but I thought of France, Austria, Germany, Turkey, and Russia, after the war. How the postwar times dry the heart which sentimentally begins to have sympathy? Before the Señora tells me again of her still rich uncles in Hermosilla, I depart, without a book to read. The only book she had to offer me was one in French, about a girl of English blood, brought up in Italy, Germany, France, and later America. Her life is wrecked; she is eternally condemned to loneliness; to liking and understanding the common people of her various hometowns, while never being understood by them. Señora's heart saw too much of her own sad life in that book, I fear, and as she told me its story, I believed a self-pitying woman had written it. Señora is too intent upon telling me, subtly, how truly she despises Mr. Khrem while forced to accept him, to notice that I forget the book which rests upon the hall table. Señora would wonder more about me if she knew I thought Cuca had done about right to get the most out of her life; and that many of the Indian boys or young men were better stock than her degenerating best families. She hadn't heard my remarks about high classes needing class, I judged.

Roberto was in front of the hotel when I got back. So were eight other youths between the ages of fourteen and eighteen, and I grieved that I could not understand Spanish, for they were gravely discussing Mexican and world politics with two older men, and from the laughter it appeared that Anatolio, plump-seventeen, lazy, droll owl-faced, and generally reticent, was gaining most points.

Not understanding however, and observing that Roberto had an expectant air when telling me he had left something in my room, I went upstairs. He had brought me quantities of limes, three huge grapefruit, a tremendous sized aguacate (alligator pear), papayas, melons, and a quantity of tomatoes. There was too a quart bottle of pure olive oil. It surprised and pleased me how quickly he had noticed my love for aguacate salad and fresh fruits, but he was holding something back. Finally he went and took something from beneath my cot. It was a carved wood container for typewriting paper, envelopes, and manuscript, very elaborately done. As I was looking at it I realized he had tried to copy Mayan designs he had seen in a French art magazine I had given him.

"Roberto," I said, "these are nice, but you mustn't bring me so many things. Keep the carved piece yourself. I can't pack it when I go away."

My Spanish was so inadequate as to be naive, undoubtedly. Roberto's face, Egyptian-boy rather than Indian, broke into smiles. "No, for you, you have the blue eyes."

"Haven't you ever seen blue eyes before?"

"Not blue-blue. You come to our orchard and I'll show you where I live."

It was but eleven o'clock and I was ready for a walk and not anxious to have lunch before one. As we went down a path leading into the country, past the graveyard, Roberto said, "A brother of Andrés and Jesús," indicating a two-year-old baby playing on a doorstep.

"But Señor Hermantes doesn't live here. He lives with his wife at the hotel."

"Si, si," Roberto agreed easily. "She is not the mother of Andrés and Jesús. They each have different mothers. And this baby is of a different mother. Señor Hermantes has twelve children, all different mothers. His wife he married late and she can't have children, but he likes Jesús and Andrés most."

My understanding of Spanish came to me belatedly, and I understood that Andrés had informed me Roberto was the fourth son of a woman who had a different father for each son, and that every one of the fathers had been a man of position, two of them governors of the state at some time. Thompson also said that Roberto had a touch of Chinese blood. In any case he was an interesting study, for he certainly had no sense of there being anything wrong in his background, and he was proudly conducting me to his aunts for presentation. His mother was in Mexico City.

On the edge of town we came to a dry-goods grocery store, for the peons, and there Roberto entered. Behind the counter was a pretty woman of middle-age, but a youthful middle age. Soon, hearing laughter, two other women came in. Roberto was full of glee, teasing them about being 49, 52, and 55 years old. Certainly none of them looked it, and sisters, they looked alike, and were filled with mirth whenever Roberto said "Yaqui, yaqui." Evidently to accuse someone of being a Yaqui was the height of joyful comedy.

Having shown me off as an exotic exhibition, Roberto led me to the garden where he insisted upon presenting me with more aguacates, and pointing out a marvelous tree in which the trunk of a smaller tree grew through the hollow, decayed part of a tree two hundred years old. "You stay till September, for the fiesta," Roberto chattered. "We will make the—." He used a word I did not catch, and did not catch the second time. "This," Roberto said, and glided across the ground at an amazing speed, effortlessly, as though sliding, with a fleetness of grace which startled me. I recalled tales of Indians who can run 100 miles without stopping. His movement evoked lithe beauty as few dance gestures of great dancers do, and it had not their conscious effect. It was rather pure wild animal, as Roberto was completely an alert and curious faun. His existence was a state of being in which one need not think of the mental, of intelligence, of self-consciousnes, or of any emotion or attitude which inhibits and frustrates so-called civilized beings.

We walked on to his aunt's orchard, two kilometers from town. There was a swimming pool, the water filled with branches and weeds now. Roberto informed me that a year before a twenty-year-old youth had drowned there, because he couldn't swim. Since then they'd neglected it. The orchard was full of lemon, orange, grapefruit, papaya, aguacate, apple, and pear trees, and well taken care of. At my remark that it was too bad the swim-

146

ming pool wasn't clean, so that we could take a swim, Roberto said, "If you like, we will clean it, and you come out here to swim."

Roberto's amiable and spontaneous generosity was delightful, and surely had no other motive than an alert curiosity about the outside world of which I could inform him. He intended to go to Mexico City the following year, to become an aviator. He wished too to go to the United States, and Europe, to anywhere on the map, so soon as he knew of the place's existence. Roberto was surely one of the bright young boys who went away; while other lads in the town were amiable and lively enough, they had little restless imagination or curiosity.

Roberto puzzled me. Was he a peon whose family had improved itself, or was he just alertly curious and friendly? On the way back to town he revealed that he would go next year to Mexico City. He wished to be an aviator, to go to America, and now since I had talked of them, to the countries of Europe. Roberto then was to be one of the bright young men who went away. Most of the boys his age were lively enough, but had no curiosity about the outside.

"Me you like?" Roberto essayed English.

"I certainly do, Roberto."

"My mother tells me I'm old race," Roberto talked and I understood his Spanish as I could. "I saw you one night look away because the pimply faced Pedro spits all the time and is dirty. He hasn't a clean home, and doesn't cure his diseases. I like being clean too."

I had noticed that Roberto was, as were Andrés and Jesús, always clean, fingernails, teeth, and clothing. "Don't you like Augustín Dossier?" I asked, thinking ahead of Roberto's comments to wonder if perhaps the Señora Marcur idea of class lines had not affected his life.

"Yes, I like him, he likes me, but we get older. We are not the same, and he does not want to learn things." The Dossier family fortune was solely in the town, but Roberto knew. Class snobbism would keep them unimaginatively bourgeois, unless they became Alfredo-Dossier drunks and decadent.

147

Once in town, as we were passing a casa, a very pretty girl of about sixteen spoke to Roberto. He answered, smiling gaily, but came on. "Don't you want to stop and talk with her? I'm going to eat," I said.

"No, last month she was my girl, but I have changed."

"Don't you like her any more, or is it that you like the new one better?"

Roberto was very sagely cheerful. "But no, it isn't discreet to have the same one too long. She, her family, and other people, think then of the marriage. I will be an aviator and know the world more before that." As he left he bowed in a military manner, saying he would have his aunt have me to dinner some night. The alert, attentive, courtesy of his manner, first struck me as unusual, until I reflected that primitive and country people, except the oafs, are generally the most truly well-mannered if not the most sophisticated.

Through the months I came to know that Roberto and his family were different; they had not Spanish-Mexican, mestizo, or Indian attitudes. When his three older brothers arrived they too were different. They had not the nonchalant arrogance of the "aristocrat" young men of the town; and they had not the tendency, when drinking, to become violent. They were amiable friends, more than brothers; of a family, yes, but more of a tribe or a clan. The aunts, and the other unrelated women who were constantly about the household, and usually around or over fifty years old, were all amazingly young, lithe, and good-looking. A mixture of bloods, Chinese, Indian (Apache), Spanish, and perhaps a touch of French or English blood, had filtered into their stock for the last three hundred years. Nevertheless they were still regarded as Indian peons by Señora Marcur's sort. It did not matter. Roberto's family was self-sufficient, removed, and amiably merry about the town. The boys all were away, or planned, when age sufficient arrived, to go away, to Mexico City, Guadalajara, or the States, but they loved the caressing tranquillity of this removed mountain town. It came to be nothing for me to go to meals with them, on a moment's invitation from Roberto. They served me what they had, without apology.

Señora Marcur, at one time, overdoing herself, had Thompson and myself to dinner. It was to her an occasion and we were made to feel it so. How much more casually and graciously Roberto's folks handled the matter of hospitality! One felt not an outsider, not an intruder, even without a language in common with the others. One understood and was understood by a common wish of goodwill. The need for a spoken language was not present. All topics of conversation were simply discussion or merriment about the routine of town and family life. There was not straining for ideas, no sense of problems.

Pablo Gills sits drinking mescal with Felix and Johnson when Johnson calls to me. Pablo has brought him a small box full of white-gold ore, and he is excited. Perhaps at last he has found his mine, but the thought of Mexican prohibitory laws depresses him too.

Pablo looks English, or New England Yankee, except there is dejection and despair on his face, and surely no tendency to puritanism in his nature. Before the revolution he had a hacienda and 50,000 cattle. There is a slash from his left eye to his lip, given him in some bandit-rebel political fray. Recently his aged aunt has died, leaving him two ranchos, and supposedly twenty thousand pesos. The pesos however are banked with the Dossiers and it would bankrupt them to pay Pablo his inheritance. Instead they have bargained with him, and Pablo has accepted 100,000 acres of land.

Pablo has a most energetic son, who buys gold ore, sells corn, and is unhappy when not active. He paces the floor constantly, and while a dutiful family man, pays scant attention to his wife and children once his quickly eaten meals are over. Pablo thinks possibly his son's energy is good. With rain there are good corn crops, gold to buy it, money to make selling it, but — Pablo, having been broken three times by revolution, does not now over-value enterprise or possessions. Possessions particularly are often dangerous to the life of their owner.

Pablo does not care to bother with mining, but he is ready to help Johnson locate a mine and to talk, over mescal, of how Johnson may cope with Mexican law as an American prospector. The mescal does not remove the burned-out look in Pablo's eyes, except for flickering moments. Blond, blue-eyed, Pablo speaks only Mexican and does not respond when Johnson asks him what other race blood he might have. Johnson should know better. Pablo is not the kind of Mexican who has kept his family background outlined. He may not know who or what nationality his father, or grandfathers, were. Only because he loves to fondle the bits of ore which he has brought Johnson, only because he is solicitous about Johnson's passion for mining, does he reveal a quality which is not entirely mañana-resigned.

At Johnson's suggestion that we drive to Pablo's new property, where there is a stream and a huge pool, Pablo acquiesces, and feels proud perhaps to think the land might ultimately have value. Felix and Johnson are boyishly sure that we can catch fish in the pool; that we might shoot a deer, or a wild cat; and at least break the monotony of the very hot day. Stopping at the Chink's restuarant we have sandwiches made up, procure three bottles of mescal, and start down the bumpy road which leads to an even worse road that will beat us the eight miles to Pablo's new land. On the way a blacktailed deer lopes gently across our path, unfrightened, and the day is too hot for energy. It is gone however before any of us think to chance a shot. The atmosphere is so dry and hot, the landscape so arid, that we are all thinking it rather a silly idea to have left the small comfort of our rooms for a muggy swim and the Chink's sandwiches eaten beneath a ruthless sun. No possible shade trees are about, and all vegetation is ashen dry, giving no sensation of water having ever caressed their roots.

Small brush and trees, however, made it necessary to leave the car inside the stone fence enclosing Pablo's newly acquired acres. We walked through the heat for half an hour, to be rewarded by coming to a stone-bottomed pool. Standing upon the rock cliff above it was possible to see that the pool was twenty to forty feet deep. Quantities of sizeable fish swam through the clear water, but we had no lines or hooks. Felix, however, had some sticks of dynamite in his knapsack. These he carried for possible blasting in veins where Johnson might believe there was ore. He fixed a fuse, to blow dynamite into the water, and a minute after the explosion the surface of the pool was covered with a quantity of fish, most of them too small for use. Johnson and I stopped his fixing another fuse; the destruction of the fish was futile and brutal, for they weren't nicely edible. The water was too lukewarm. Instead the lot of us undressed and dived into the pool. The water was too warm to be refreshing, but outside the heat was penetrating and the sun dangerous upon our bare skins. We loitered in the pool, talking of the fertility of Pablo's land, and the wealth that it could bring him, if irrigated and managed properly. Pablo's interest flickered for a moment only. He hadn't the money to develop the land, and he had been burned too often. What few cattle he had, which straggled about this property and came to the stream and pond for water, he would keep to let breed for a few years, but Pablo's hopes were too seared for energetic planning any longer. This land could lie fallow. It was only because he had despaired of getting money from the Dossiers that he had bothered to accept it as substitute. His sons or grandsons, in a more developed Mexico, might utilize it.

Back in the hotel, as it is a Sunday afernoon, it is even more necessary to spend hours at a siesta than usual. We may not nap, but if we linger in one room, as a group, neither conversation nor drinking is necessary. Hayes, a newcomer since three days, has come in from the backlands and we are ready to see what sort he is. Perhaps he is *loco tambien*, Thompson hopes, singing, "For I am crazy, and you are crazy too." Thompson is upset. He can't get his song copyrighted because the patent office does not answer his letters, and he is sure the song would be a great popular sensation and make him rich.

"*No le hace in México*," Thompson is cheery as he helps himself to mescal. Johnson has flopped on my cot, and I stretch out on a canvas chair. "My new sweetheart wants to marry me. She doesn't *sabe*. I answered her advertisement because she said she was a literary woman. I want her to re-write and market my stories, and patent my inventions. A man gets nowhere with a woman set on wedlock. I wrote her that I won't make any more children."

151

From Hayes' room come wild animal odors. He has been looking for the winged snake, which he is sure is still existent in Mexico. He insists upon discovering the real significence of the serpent in religions. He swears he loves and understands animals, and that they respond to him. Nevertheless his mapache, a monkeylike fox, will not tame, was meant for wildness. The iguana is friendly when I bring it bugs; as friendly to me as to Hayes. The boa constrictor, Lulu, is not afraid of me. She twines her length about my waist, seeking to hide her head beneath my shirt. Sure that her strength is not great enough to constrict me I wear her about my neck. I, who do not care for snakes, think Hayes talks nonsense.

"You have that something extra of people who understand snakes," he tells me. "She knows you now. Her tongue serves her as eyes, and she's affectionate, recognizing affinity."

Johnson, who will not handle Lulu, winks at me behind Hayes' back. We both know that Hayes has come into the room to head for a bottle, of mescal or of sherry, whichever there is. Johnson has warned me, and I him, that Hayes will be telling a sob story before long and wanting to borrow money. Neither of us believe his tale that he is writing an article for a well-known geographic magazine. Van Dyke beard, and appearance of rundown aristocrat, he has, but underneath Johnson and I smell the ineffectual dreamer eternally on his uppers.

Lulu amuses my lazy sense. She is dry and glistering and scentless. She appears to like twining about my body, but going to a chair I see she wishes to escape. Twining through my palm she undulates to go rhythmically up the chair-rungs. She ripples grace and lovely movement. When Hayes drags in his mapache she is disturbed by the odour. She and the mapache are instinctively antagonistic. He perhaps belongs to the rodent species and she feeds on rats. The odour of drugs about Hayes annoys her too, possibly. From downstairs we collect a playful kitten. Towards Lulu it is at first playful, but suspicious. Lulu reaches out a darting tongue to scent the species. The kitten makes playful gestures, and then becomes angry, spits and scratches at Lulu. The snake retreats, somehow shamed, to

152

twine her coils up the legs of the table. All of this disturbs Thompson. He does not like the snake, the mapache, or Hayes. Going to his room he takes his accordion and sits on his own balcony playing snatches of music.

"Call the poor old crutch in here," Johnson said. "Something's bothering him, and I feel lazy enough today not to let anything bother me. Give the old boy some drink."

Thompson's pompous form comes into the room in agitation. His accordion music is not calming him as usual. After starting to play "Annie Laurie" he stops and bitterly complains that this morning they brought him water for his tea that was no more than lukewarm. It started his day off wrong.

"And they have written me a letter from Washington saying my caricature on Hoover and parity on the sea was in bad taste. It could not be shown to Hoover, had been filed, and they will investigate my activities. *No le hace en México.* The newspapers carry worse cartoons. Who's Hoover? Leader of gladiators! I'll write the senators he's a numbskull," Thomspon grew careless and cheerful with more mescal.

"All right, Tommy. Some righteous-minded clerk wrote you that letter," Johnson joked. You don't think the real important boys ever see what you write. If they did they'd send for you to help them think."

We are all lazily restless because of threatening rain which does not come. Señor Roy, a Scotchman, married to a wealthy Mexican woman, comes to call. It is too hot for the long drive to Navajoa for a beer bust. Señor Roy suggests that we get ice from the Chinks and make a tequila punch. He has given up thoughts of gold or silver mining and has gone in definitely for agriculture. The profits are surer.

There is a childlike or boyish quality about Roy, and he tells confidences very naively, but one wonders if his manner is not deceptive. He is one of the wealthiest men about. "This spring I found five acres cleared in my desert land," he relates, "planted to poppies. They milk the poppies and ship opium to the states with carloads of pineapples. It would be dangerous to let that go on in land I owned. I wrote the government and

153

they destroyed the poppy field, but we never found out who had planted and cultivated those acres. That's a gamble I won't take on, and everything's a gamble. I lost 21,000 pesos on peas and melons. It is as much a gamble dealing with vegetables and fruits as with mines. With new laws we might get somewhere. Now we lose, the government loses."

Suddenly the rain breaks, in a cloudburst. It is so sensational that it is but a few minutes before the town streets are rivers, and the months-dry river bed is torrenting rapids. Huge tree trunks are swept down the stream in the torrent.

After the first cloudburst the rain subsides and the sun appears for a short period. The mist still causes the mountains to recede in grandeur, though where sunlight breaks through the peaks glisten. Fog rolls over them again, however. The rain starts slowly dribbling again, but from nooks, alleys, from the plains, barefoot figures appear, splashingly joyful because of rain. The vegetation seems brightened on the hills. Peon huts look cleansed. Bright figures move in tropical huts and yards. As at the governor's ball the town gave forth señoritas of beauty and elegance, now the town reveals a population of gaily attired natives in quantities a usual day would never permit one to imagine. They all have a gay, helpful, communal, sense; ready to splash into the newmade rivers to help dislodge autos from water holes. Many of the town's young bloods feel now like attempting to get to Navajoa, for a visit to the ladies in the cabaret there. At least it is a lark getting their balky cars across the torrenting river bed, if only to turn back two miles on because of washed out roadways.

Wanting to be in action I went to the plaza. The sun appears for a few moments, fiery between two black clouds. On the distant hillsides the rain's black satin downpour glistened. On the plaza the town's idot cripple falls and lies helpless until someone comes who will lift him to his feet. Alfredo Dossier sees me from his casa portales and by asking me where he can get Scotch reveals that he has already been drinking. Discreetly I do not hear except absent-mindedly. Scotch is very expensive at the cantina, and Alfredo lovingly does not leave one for hours once he is drinking.

Grande Dame Dossier is distributing coins from her portales to her favourite three of the town beggars. Most of her off-spring are eccentric, but she is too old to mind. She wishes only to end her years viewing herself as a powerful and benevolent aristocrat. Of Señora Marcur she is disdainful. Never was Señora Marcur beautiful, and her ankles were always fat. Her husband was bought her. Grand Dame Dossier is arrogant, witty, and outspoken; to be caustic about her children and grandchildren. "I worried once for my children; for my grandchildren I will not," she tells Alfredo, who is deaf to her suggestion that he does not go to the cantina for drink. She once knew London and Paris, but over fifty years ago. The one time I spoke to her she was momentarily curious about the outside, but ended by saying, "Yes, my English is gone. I have forgotten those other years. I am old. My last years I will have in peace, escaping mis-ery as I can. I will not try to remember."

In the market Elena coquettes with me. I see she actually hesitates and realize she dares to be more indiscreet with me, a foreigner, than with her townsmen. She sees that I feel flighty with drink, and laughs when I offer her a soft drink at the mar-ket stand. She and Conchita look at each other and giggle. They wish they dared accept my invitation. Yes, they know, American girls could accept, but Elena looks around warningly, wishing me to understand. She manages to confide that she has heard I am a good dancer. Yes, and it is too bad that tonight there is no dance. The lapse of cool after rain, the germinal atmosphere, has made the Señoritas wish to be indiscreet. They are young, and I am foreign, but everybody knows every-body else too well in this town. Conchita acts as though she might linger to chat, but she is annoyed because she does not understand my Spanish, and I do not understand her English. There is nothing for me to do. I will go to the cantina, and do as the Mexican young men do, drink with other men.

At the Cantina Ambrosio, the townhall clerk and English translator, is drunk, as he always is when anyone will buy him beer. With his first glass of beer Ambrosio starts peeing his pants. Every beer he pees off quickly, staining his white duck trousers. The smell near him is necessarily urinal. He does not gather that others do not love to have him stand affectionately near them, in the hope of being offered another beer. He goes to tables. By taking him to the bar and buying him a beer men at the tables rid themselves of Ambrosio, who is too Ambrosio to be *flojo* or *loco*. He is Ambrosio who can't drink beer without peeing his pants.

Salvador is very gay. Evidently he has recently made a sum of money off mescal which has escaped the government tax. He drinks and dances, bearing himself with military elegance. He is graciously amiable when I tell him he dances well. We dance together, and he admits I am good, almost as good as himself. Salvador has, for fifteen years, been wooing Carmelita Almada, but they quarrel and delay the day of their marriage. Each is waiting for a wealthy aunt to die. Then they will marry. But Salvador joyfully fancies himself enough not to grow wan with love for Carmelita. They do not charge him for his room at the hotel, as the building is rented from his Aunt, with whom he eats. Life is simple, and Salvador is ready for mañana to solve all things.

Arturo Ortiz, more restless and active from American training, is drinking too. He wants to drive into Navajoa to visit the girl houses. He explains, that like all Mexicans, he doesn't give a damn about anything. There is no use. His car springs are broken; the car plunges, wheezes, and charges through the sand and puddles of water. It has gout, epilepsy, and a hacking cough; but we get to Navajoa, drunk, abandoned, and to hell with the rain. I in the backseat, have been bounced against the auto top to scrape a strip of skin from my forehead. Arturo's driving is mad, and the car viciously bucky. It doesn't matter. Where we get to is where we're going. For five of the younger boys who have come into the girl cabarets in other cars this night's trip will make conversation for months. The arid desolation of Navajoa has to them the qualities of a metropolis.

V

A letter from Olivia has arrived, and therein she reveals her-

156

self in one of her phases of staunch simplicity. Rather wistfully she compliments me and envies my tranquillity amongst really simple people, and she would be, is simple, but I refuse to accept her thus.

Well, well, Olivia, tranquillity isn't so placid or simple as to make one unaware of confusion. These people are just more people and it won't be from me that you will hear of the deep enigmas in their eyes. What simplicity there is might be in ourselves alone, but I don't think these people are simple. They know revolution, sudden death, dancing, color, music, resignation, — but boredom, or ennui — no, they are not endangered by the philosophy of defeat and too great a sense of futility. They don't soulprobe; aren't spiritual. Olivia, I believe simple is a word to apply to people obsessed with ideas, and should I write that to you will you find me deteriorating not to value either ideas of your precious simplicity, much?

Roberto comes into my room bringing figs, grapefruits, and three quails, which Cuca will cook for me. He is happy that I am pleased, and by the way he looks at me and laughs I know that he doesn't think that such animals as me really exist. It tickles him that I want to make wine out of pomegranates, but why, he wonders, when I seem so ready to be happy on mescal or tequila. Like Señor Thompson and the idiot cripple and José, the half-wit, I am *loco,* and Roberto has an Indian-gallant sense of protectiveness towards me. My silly lemon yellow hair and blankishly blue-blue eyes somehow fascinate him. His serene belief that a two mile walk is more than I can do makes me realize that he looks upon me as fragile, if not as an invalid.

Having a quantity of American papers to bring to Señora Marcur, I take them to leave for her on my way to the post-office. In her way she is my contact with a world I understand, and don't like, but familiarity holds one in its way. She scandalmongs in a way one has known in village and group life, always.

Señora Marcur is puzzled. My entrance into her patio caught her unaware, reading, so that she had not time to stage-set an entry. She cannot place Roberto, she, a Marcur, who has known all of her Alamos townspeople for years. He is courteous, with a manner; he is clean, alert, and not shy before her. Still she sees that he is not of pure Spanish stock; not of a best family, or she would know him. She does not know that his mother, who was a woman, evidently, of character enough, has taught Roberto to be proud of his Indian blood and rather disdainful of his Spanish. She doesn't and wouldn't know, as a Catholic, a pure, and moral woman, that Roberto has never known the idea that it is shameful to be the child of a man and woman out of wedlock.

As Roberto speaks no English, Señora Marcur talks of him to me, in front of him. She is bothered that he does not show peon awe before her. She is resentful that he does not realize that she is an Aramaza, the original owners of most of Alamos, an aristocrat to whom his ancestors bowed before her ancestors had brought Christian knowledge to save them. She is curt when I say that Roberto has grace, with a Chaldean youth beauty which recalls the best quality in archaic sculpturing. Some sign of respect which she desires is lacking from both Roberto and myself.

"You Americans," Señora Marcur reprimands me, "think no Mexican has a cultural background. You make me speak your language. That means I'm your inferior." There is a flash of malice in her eyes.

"No, no," I quickly explain, "that means merely that you have superior linguistic talents. You speak French, German,Spanish, Italian, and English, and I speak even English not too well."

Señora is placated, but, not quite directly, she implies that only because I am a foreigner who does not understand would I accept Roberto as a personal friend. She has placed him, and knows that his mother was unmarried. At cross purposes with her high ideals she starts talking of "the best families," and I gather that there has been much intermarriage, with the usual result of degeneration. Heredity tells. Blood will out. The Dossiers and the Almadas are upstarts, and it does not do to exaggerate their weaknesses by intermarrying. Señora Marcur has a grimly joyful period of discussing the decay which happens in old families. She talks of Russian, German, French, and

Dutch novels, which have depicted such decay. Particularly she remembers the "Little Souls" novels of Couperus.

Roberto, not understanding the language and too lower class to cope with Senora's intellect had he understood, recalls that he has promised to get pomegranates for me. He departs, leaving Señora Marcur to puzzle that he, a bastard, of native stock, should have poise and well-bred boy courtesy, but no inferior's shyness before her.

"No, no," Señora is soon setting me right. "The Almadas have never been one of our best families. Four generations ago one of the boys, Spanish, yes, and of good family, lived with an Indian girl. He married her when they had four children, and it is from him and his children that the Almadas are descended. Naturally we have never quite accepted them. Señor Almada went to live in Los Angeles, but he had no wealth according to American Standards. One of his girls eloped with what she thought was a Frenchman. He thought she had more money than the family has. She went abroad with him for a year. When she returned she had so little education or taste that she talked. Her husband, we found, had been Egyptian. He took her into the depths of Egypt. Had she been intelligent she would have known she had lived virtually in a harem. He has been back for three years now. I believe there has been a divorce, but of course, the Almadas have no culture. We do not associate with them, except to be kind when necessary."

Since the revolution, one reflects, Señora Marcur's impaired fortune has caused townspeople to be less impressed by her great culture. Her family name does not create the atmosphere of awe she claims it once did. She has retained ideas about the divine right of kings, one gathers, and feels possibly sad for her that she is not viewed with some fearsome respect for being a Marcur. In this town they respect neither age nor culture, she sighs, somehow accusing me of failing to understand the superiority of old age. She has, she claims, no desire to go abroad, though she could afford the trip now. In Alamos they do not understand culture, but abroad they would not understand that she is an Aramaza-Marcur.

Señorita Marcur comes into the room. Somehow she is meek and self-effacing, not seeming to realize that she is of her mother's blood. She has, however, some of her mother's, or is it of woman's, or of mere human's, tendencies. Or had Señor Serón attracted her. He was, at first glance, a romantic type. His brooding violet eyes; his matinee idol good looks; his sad, lost air; his manner of chivalry; had attracted Elena and other town girls. Señorita Marcur, over thirty, balanced, sensible, not as the other town girls, she claims, is driven to telling me of the scandal of his life.

"It was for Luz Torreón he nearly made tragedy," she talked. "Luz is over thirty. For a time he saw her every day, several times. Every day she made herself a new dress. She was deeply in love, planning marriage. She was furious when I told her Señor Serón was married. When she found out the truth she sent him away, but the silly Elena would not believe her or me. Now neither of the girls nor their parents dare show indignation. As Señor Serón is the tax collector they are all afraid. It disgusts me the way people fuss over that nasty little boy of his. He is defective I am sure. His wife is a rich woman, too. For that reason they fuss over her."

Visions of Señora Serón floated through my mind. Poor Señora Serón. It was said that his wife, when he married her, had been slender and beautiful. Now she was tremendous; short, dwarfish, and certainly weighed 250 pounds. Señorita Marcur continues discussing him.

"Señor Serón must be mad. At Pancho's the Chinaman's, restaurant, he got a fourteen-year-old girl drunk. As she became sick he did not have his way with her, but nobody would have reprimanded him if he had. It is disgusting how men in politics are immune, when in power. Now that Señora Serón is here she guards her husband well. He is afraid of her. She is a sensible woman, but I think there is little doubt that her husband is mad. Mad about love. She knows and understands. He has a look in his eyes I do not like. It is not difficult to be a Don Juan in a little town where the girls believe the tax assessor a great man."

The day is quiet, so calm, that a burro's bray, birds' notes, the

160

cooing of doves, a dog bark, are cameos of sound against the blue, dry, silence. At the church the ceremony for Grandfather Goyceola is being held. He had died some days before, well beyond eighty, and upon the plaza for the last few nights none of his numerous descendants were seen. From the States and from other parts of Mexico, surely, descendants come, faithful to their father's or grandfather's or uncle's memory. Old Goyceola had too much wealth, as had his many relatives, for this funeral not to be a ponderous family affair. In the afternoon the fat fifteen year old, Pepé, loiters past the hotel and speaks to Andrés and myself. He is brooding, but he is acting sadness somewhat too. He sheds a few tears, saying "I loved my grandpapa," in infantile tones.

A dirty, minute boy is playing in the plaza, a desolate baby. Pepé as he goes on speaks to the child and comes back to Andrés, leading the child. "He has no papa, no mamma," Pepé explains to me. "He rode in on a cargador burro, because he has no home and at Rancho Francisco the woman told him his papa and mamma would never come again."

Pepé, whose father is school superintendent for the district, led the child away, saying that his father would find a home for him, and his mother would feed the child. "We always got the place for the little boy with no papa, no mamma," Pepé lisped, giving the impression of being proudly patriarchal and also communal. Surely there were several children in town who had no papa, no mamma, and no set home, but they were taken care of in some manner, as were the beggars, idiots, and helpless cripples of the town. Being a strayling did not necessarily mean cruel times here. Pepé's orphan was not frightened, was full of play and spirits, in fact.

Late in the afternoon Johnson comes into my room to advise that we go to the cantina. "Big doings there," he said. "All of old man Goyceola's men relatives are there drinking beer, wishing they could be back at their own homes, since they've dutifully attended his funeral. Let's get in on the wake."

The evening was sweetly soothing; the landscape so soaked with beauty that mañana-drifting should be the attitude towards living here. Through the clean cobblestone streets two cargadors with five burros were hawking their last loads of fire-wood. Barefoot, lithe, indifferent now, beneath their apparent apathy dwelt the will to have mescal and be loco this night. The town lamplighters are out, and we observe that they do not lay down their guns even when they mount posts to light the lamps. They have been ordered not to, as some Indian might grab the gun and run away. The days have been going on with such peaceful tranquillity that one forgets tales of brutality and violence; that the natives, when fighting drunk, often have to be killed or knocked unconscious, to be made to give up fight-ing. There is desperate, uncaring, violence beneath their appar-ent whipped resignation.

VI

At the cantina there are seven of grandfather Goyceola's male descendants, and how like a gathering of Rotarians, drummers, or Deacons-on-a-tear they are! One, a grandson-in-law, has a luxurious undertaking parlor in Hermosilla, and he is gaily buy-ing whisky. Accustomed to funerals, declaring himself modern-minded and American of ideas, he has dared suggest that per-haps old Goyceola had lived his proper day. He, and a dapper looking grandson of the old man, mildly suggest that this funeral has taken them away from their businesses at inopportune times. Johnson and I know, however, that they are saying this only because their other relatives, with them, cannot understand En-glish. The dapper El Paso broker, grandson, assures me that in America we are viewing family and relationships in a proper light. I wonder if, in the States, he does not belittle his Mexican blood. He is too proud of having attended an American private school, as the only Mexican boy at the school.

It is so that these Goyceola males, who have not seen each other for years, and who have varying degrees of wealth, do not know what to say to each other. They are glad to play poker and to drink with Johnson, myself, Arturo, and other Mexicans who are not relations. The brewer grandson invites us to visit his brew-

162

ery in Juárez; the undertaker is proud too of his establishment, but invites us rather to stop off at Hermosilla someday, and he will show us what a promising town it is. The lawyer grandson finally admits that old an Goyceola has left much less money than had been expected, and with so many heirs—it was hardly worth while for any of them to have taken time away from their business to come to this out of the way town for the funeral. He catches himself being indiscreet, however, and decides to drink no more beer or mescal.

This gathering is not Mexican; it is timeless, raceless. It is a group of descendants little interested in each other going in for the convention of mourning, while wondering what money each is to inherit. Unrest, ever ready to breed, gains force in my heart. I have imagined much that is primitive, archaic, communal into this town and its inhabitants. The peons and Indians are nearer to a state of nature than are most people I know. They have both the kindliness and the ruthlessness and the lack of conscience of nature, but these only as uneducated beings have, elsewhere. Romantic history and literature has been causing me to see this town and its people in the light of ancient Sumerian, Italian, Greek, or Egyptian towns, but coldly the business men descendants of old Goyceola reveal themselves as Babbitts, but harder Babbitts than the American type. They are distinctly suspicious of and on their guard towards each other. Suddenly I realize that my stay here has been a vacation of variation only; it has not been release, and I don't want to escape from the world I knew before.

I am not anti-social; I do want my own kind and familiar qualities. I want cities and traffic and turmoil, which is not turmoil when one is habituated. Too often have these Mexicans questioned and wondered why I am staying in their town, since I am not as is Johnson, a prospective miner, nor as Thompson, a loco, antiquated engineer, striving to find intermittent employment on irrigation and electric light projects. Mine is not a mañana nature; there is for me no Mayan-masked enigma about tomorrows for one has aggressiveness and makes plans and decisions. This has been a nerve-soothing rest, but to Arturo I now confess, after the Goyceola males depart, that I am keen to get to the States.

163

"Me too," Arturo says. "This month I have made good money selling the jumping beans. Now I go to the States and see if I can get a job, with a canning company, to travel between here and the States. For you, you laugh at Señores Khrem and Marcur, the buzzards, you call them. For me, I can't hear more their telling what once this town was. To hell with what was, with them or in the town. They are old cocks trying to crow who never crowed well. Tonight I drive us into Navajoa, if you like. You get you the morning train for Nogales, if you like. We get us a bottle of mescal, and go to your room while you pack."

Arturo too is restless and depressed. The funeral group depressed him, for he is married into a Mexican family similar to the Goyceola, and Arturo confides that marriage and family does not solve life for him. Forty is a bad age when one remembers how little one has accomplished and how little satisfaction the past has given one, or so it seems. Mexicans do not give a damn, do not hope or plan much; it is no use giving a damn, but Arturo is thinking romantically or two successful years in Philadelphia. Then he felt himself very American. Here, ambition is rather futile, and it mars tranquillity. Arturo is not resigned to letting fate manipulate his situations. Mañana may not have all imagination for him, for Arturo has an idea of making himself good money by operating perhaps illegally between the States and Mexico. I do not ask indiscreet questions about mescal, opium, or marihuana.

Roberto joins us in my room. He too has become restless during the weeks. Señora Marcur has been irritated because he forgot to bring her fruit she hoped to have from him for little money. She has become too cosmopolitan, no doubt, to understand that Roberto is another boy become restless. To him she is an old woman who talks unimportantly of her class and family background, and such talk solves none of his desires. His imagination is opening to receive new ideas. He too has doubts about waiting for tomorrows and wonders, could he not get into the States, rather than go to Mexico City. A mixture of race-bloods is torrenting in him, and soon he will be another young man who has gone away. Is there not good money to be made in the

States? He doubts my warning that he might be deported, and if not, be forced to work as a mere day laborer. Two days ago I could have advised him more strongly to stay here, where life moves easily among the charcoal stoves; in the market where women pat tortillas; where nights he can eat menudo with Duba. There have been warming nights in Duba's hut, where steam from her pots add greasy shine to already glowing faces. There, menudo-eaters have seen each other darkly, comfortable in their bellies, feeling night develop into another casual day when worry will not be more needful than on this night.

Roberto, for the first time in his seventeen years, will go to the cabaret in Navajoa with Arturo, Andrés, Jesús, and me. The younger boys do not know; they will dance with the girls, but they admit frankly that they are shy. With boys their own age they would abandon themselves to young bravado, but neither Arturo nor I are anxious to drive them into Navajoa. We will forget, but we have no wish to sponsor their first crop of wild oats.

As Arturo's rheumatic car drove up to the hotel two barefoot Indians were being led by the policia to the carcel. They were drunk, as ancestors for centuries had been drunk. One's eye was cut deeply by, the policia informed Arturo, a sharp stone. The other's face is battered beyond having features. It is seldom worth while asking what caused these fights. They are dirty by ancestral tradition too; and have, sadly I admit it, more trust in mescal than in mañana.

As we drive into the desert buzzards are circling against the primitive blue above a mountain. Where scavengers float there has been death, and has death a mañana? The little Mexican town has already retreated from my active conscious as I strain forward to an American tomorrow. Because of this the experiences of the last five months have become a keenly sketched painting of warm colors. Reluctance has me; reluctance to turn back, and reluctance to go on. I am leaving something peacefully sociable, and protective, beneath the sinister brooding quality of nature grown strange upon a temperament too little primitive. I feel Alamos and its people as an entity; for it I have a fondness, as it has fondliness for me. Like all entities it has its

limitations as well as its beautiful qualities. Still, it is not my
tempo. I am of the machine and scientific age, and time does
not go backward.

It was dark before we came into Navajoa. On the way in we
thought we saw a car approaching. The lights were however
merely the luminous glare in the eyes of a wildcat, mountain
lion, or puma, who gazed fascinated at our approaching car
lights. As it leaped from the roadway into the brush, the darkness and magnifying quality of our lights made it appear
tremendous. Further on a deer sprang across the roadway.

The slow moon was coming up, and the mountains were
more clear of outline. Nostalgia possessed me, but I rejected it.
Beyond the mountains and mist mañanas persisted, mystic-
masked, concealing the future with their original enigmatic
smiles. I wondered if a little of mañana-feeling might not stay
with me in more active countries to make existence less flurried
and nerve-driven.

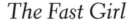

The Fast Girl

ERRY JENKINS WAS NOT at all like his brother, Deacon Samuel Jenkins; he was a "rake," a "roué," a "cheap sport" who would stand on the pool hall corner and make comments about women's ankles as they went by. My sisters always became frigid with hauteur when passing him. But, not to let my sisters know about it, I found him much more tolerable than the Deacon. He slipped me a nickel about every time he saw me; the Deacon always looked at me as though his austere sense of the righteous was shocked.

Jerry wore patent leather shoes, and a sporty vest; his keen brown eyes didn't miss much attractive in the way of woman-flesh that struck town; but his sharp-featured brown face didn't have so ferret-like a look as the Deacon's. He at least was liberal with his money, and it was he who'd given Sue Gallagher money enough to get out of town when she was going to have a baby, which he was not responsible for either.

Yet every respectable woman in town disapproved of him; and the men in town, even if they didn't dislike him, had enough things to explain to their wives generally without getting the name of being the same kind of man that Jerry was by being seen with him. No one could blame Mrs. Jenkins for having divorced him; maybe no one could blame Jerry for having let her, after seeing the lady, but when a man and wife are the parents of two nearly grown children it's supposed that a man's old enough to settle down.

Louise Dutton was as striking looking girl. The fellows in town, also the ladies, were divided into two parties regarding their opinions about her. One party said that Louise rouged, screwed like a mink, and only got away with it because she was clever; the other side said that her color was naturally vivid, and that simply because her mother was poor and had to take in sewing, people gossiped about Louise, who wasn't nearly as careless in her manners and actions as other girls whose families were well fixed.

The first time Jerry noticed her and said, "Who's that pippin," and was told, he added "For Christ's sake, it doesn't seem yesterday that she was tearing around the town in knee dresses, and with a running nose. She's learned how to keep her face clean and dress like a million-dollar race horse, hasn't she?"

What happened to Louise would not have occurred had it not been for Jake Murray and Dave Thomson. They worked at the roundhouse and were a wild sort of lowbrow. After coming back from the city, where he'd had a job as a travelling salesman for a men's notion house, Dave'd taken to being flashier than ever. Jake was another of the same kind except that he'd get converted about every three years when an evangelist came to town, and instead of strutting around town showing off his bullying strength he'd take on the job of Sunday School superintendent for a time—til his backsliding. He'd be given the job in the hope that responsibility would bolster him up.

It was on Halloween night when gangs of boys, youths, and men—one man as old as fifty, and several well towards thirty—had collected all over town. At about ten thirty the gangs had all marched down a back street of town and there were so many marching that the procession was four blocks long, marching in such a straggling manner as they did. The special policemen in town couldn't do much. The various gangs turned over out- houses, dumped hayracks into the town pond, poured tar on the main high school building steps, stole bell clappers, and piled privies, wagons, and barrels of ashes before schoolhouse doors, churches, and county buildings.

It was one o'clock and most of the boys and youths had gone home. At any rate the various gangs had separated, but Jake Murray, Dave Thomson, and about eighteen men were stand- ing around planning some new devilment to get into. Several of the men were nearly drunk. All were noisy, profane, and "to hell with everything" in their attitudes.

Louise Dutton had been dancing at the town dance hall until twelve, and had stayed talking to various fellows and girls who'd come into the ice-cream parlor that she'd stopped at to drink soda water on her way home. Just as she was turning the corner leading from Main Street to her home, an avenue that ran past the town theatre, some of the men in Jake's gang recognized her. It didn't take more than a remark or so, and a suggestion, for them to decide to hold her and make her talk to them.

It was Jake who grasped her wrist as she came along and chucked her under the chin.

"You cowardly brute," she said, and tried to jerk away. That angered him, and he grabbed her to him and placed his face so near to her that she could feel his breath.

"Don't you kiss me, you animal," she exclaimed.

"Oh it ain't kissing I'll do to you," he said. "What about it, fel- lows. She's too good with her airs, and we all know what she is. Let's have a good time."

It did Louise no good to protest, or to appeal to the group in the hope that someone would protect her. There were some harmless enough fellows in the crowd; Dutch Simmons, who drove a grocery delivery wagon; Bill Peters, a haberdashery clerk in the town's one men's furnishing store. But these harmless

169

fellows didn't have the guts to go up against Jake Murray and Dave Thomson.

No one knows whether all the men in the crowd actually did "have a good time" with Louise or not, but she had to be carried home. Some of the fellows carried her, saying that if she was found laying out on the street by the policeman there'd be an investigation and trouble for them all.

There was no investigation. Louise was sick for several days. When finally she came out again and was seen on the street many girls refused to speak to her. Men, particularly the men who'd been in that gang, treated her with familiar contempt. One day as she was going by Jake Murray he made some slurring remark to her. She turned a blazing gaze on him, lifted her head, and walked on.

She did not appear often on the streets any more, and when she did she would not look at anybody, or speak to anybody, but walked erect looking through all people. So many people she knew had cut her that she burned with anger at everybody. One day she was going by the pool hall corner, towards the post office, when she heard a voice:

"Miss Dutton."

She turned and saw that it was Jerry Jenkins speaking to her. Her first impulse was to jerk her head up and walk on, but she concluded that now her reputation was such that to talk to him could not make it worse. Furthermore his tone, at least, was respectful. So she stopped, saying, "Yes?"

"I guess you'd like to be able to get out of town and never see this place again wouldn't you?" Jerry asked her.

"Like to, yes—that takes money. I will get out of town soon, but can't right now," she answered.

"Let me help you. I'm going to Minneapolis myself in a few days," he hesitated, watching her face, which expressed little of what she might be feeling. After a moment he went on. "Of course it wouldn't be a good idea for us to leave town together, but—you could meet me in Minneapolis."

"Yes, I could," she emphasized the *could* a trifle. "Yes," she smiled, "if you want to arrange that, I am willing."

Jerry walked down towards the post office with her, and while doing so, took his wallet out of his pocket, and extracted ten twenty dollar bills, which he gave to her, under cover of his hand, being careful that no one should see him.

"I'll be at the Hôtel H . . . in Minneapolis next Monday. You can register there under the name of Mrs. Jenkins if you wish," he told Louise.

She took the money and soon after left Jerry.

Two weeks later Jerry came back to town after a trip to Minneapolis. He had not seen Louise Dutton. She had left the home town ten days before. Neither Jerry nor the town ever saw her again.

Sometime later Jerry commented on the fact that he'd made an arrangement with Louise to meet him in Minneapolis.

"I'm for that girl; damned sorry I didn't give her a thousand dollars while I was at it; if I'd known she wouldn't show up I would have."

People joshed Jerry about the trick Louise had played on him for several years. "The old rake, that's the time he got fooled," they would say.

The Psychoanalyzed Girl

D ANIA WASN'T IN THE room for five minutes
before she was telling whoever it was that sat
near her that "I am all tangled up psychologically. I have the mother and brother complex."
She was a strange girl, Dania, that is to a person not used to
strange girls, and people who live in "Bohemian quarters." In
Paris she could be seen walking about the Montparnasse district with a paisley shawl thrown over her shoulders, a many-
colored beribboned hat, mauve stockings, or pale green—some
exotic color always—and the skirt that showed beneath her
coat made of paisley shawl was generally a corded silk one with
red, white, and green, broad and thread, stripes.

Needless to say people noticed her as she went by. They might
have noticed her anyway, had she dressed quietly, because her
eyes were soft brown, shaded with impossibly long eyelashes;
her skin was bronze olive, and days when it might look sallow,
Dania knew just how much rouge to put on to give her cheeks

a warm glowing appearance. Very narrow shoulders, she had drawn up within herself usually. She contradicted her own manner, giving alternately a quiet, mouselike impression, a hard embitteredly sophisticated one, and again an impression of confused, wounded naive childlishness.

"I don't know how to be happy, that's me; don't know how to have a good time, and when all these Americans here want me to go around I can't find any pleasure in the noisy things they do," she said, one day as I walked down the Boulevard Raspail with her. "There! that's me. Analyzing myself again. Why can't I leave myself alone?"

"You are suffering from life rather than from sickness, Dania," I commented. "Don't look so hard for happiness, and stay away from the Bohemians at the Rotonde who are neither laborers, artists, nor intelligent—only moping incompetents, scavengers of the art world."

One day Dania hailed me from across the street, so we joined each other and went walking down the street together. It wasn't till afterwards that I remembered how artfully Dania managed to stop and ask a directions of a young Frenchman, who was a helper about a piano van-wagon.

After talking about where a certain street was for five minutes, very conscious that his eyes were admiring her with open curiosity and desire in them, she came on saying: "Ain't he the handsome devil though."

"There you are Dania; you say you want experience. He'll take you on. Look back. His eyes are following you yet."

The young Frenchman was a swarthy, black-eyed being with lithe energy. He was wearing a red shirt, and had a red scarf bound about his waist making a corsage for him. Except for Dania he'd simply have been part of the local color of the quarter for me. Now I wondered whether he was from the south of France, or of Spanish or Italian descent. There'd been boldness, respect too, in his attitude towards Dania. He must have been Paris bred not to have had some shyness in him.

Another day I ran into Dania, and we passed the young Frenchman again, loading furniture into a van. He looked at Dania,

173

and an expectant look came into his eyes. Dania was returning his glance from under her long eyelashes, and flickered a tiny smile at him, whereupon his entire set of straight teeth showed in a smile.

"He always smiles at me now," Dania said.

"You pass him often, do you?"

"O yes, I usually manage to come down this street at about the same time every day, when he's coming in on the van to the storage house to put up the truck. . . Isn't it ridiculous, though. He catches my fancy, but of course I couldn't."

"Rats, Dania, take a chance. Start something with him, if he doesn't with you; and he will if you'll bat your eye the right way. Why stand on the threshold of 'experience' eternally saying that you don't live, but merely exist? You must set Rome afire if you're going to sit watching the flames with enjoyment."

It was useless for me to remark however. The last time I saw Dania, two months after that day, she said "I'll have to go back to New York and get psychoanalyzed. I must find out why I can't have average emotions, and enjoy life just a little bit."

"Tut, tut, woman. Some of them there will be telling you again that you're setting out to hurt yourself because of perverse instinct in you when you slip on a wet floor because of new shoes."

If one could be sure that Dania enjoyed her unhappiness as the only thing she dared permit to give importance to her egotism. . . But there she is—in Paris—Dania.

The Little Ninny

CAT MAY LOOK at a king," Goldie
said, and made one realize that even
if she was a rattle-brained person, or
perhaps because she was so entirely
pinheaded, her sentiments made a grand ideal of Tom Gladden, who had once queened her, and who now after several
years' absence was revisiting the old home town. He had had
many notices in the paper as a star football player since Goldie
last saw him.

Goldie had changed in the intervening years too. It would be
hard to conceive of her wearing a flashing purple suit, made
sheath fashion with a slit to her knees, now. The change was
natural of course, because it is always the younger girls in town,
the ones in high school, who giggle most exuberantly and desire
to attract all people's, particularly all men's attention, that are
remarked upon. After a time the townspeople get used to the
fact that they've become young ladies and are pretty, or grace-

ful, or chic, or witty, and begin to wonder what kind of marriage they'll manage to make or if they'll manage a marriage at all, and if not whether they'll teach school or drift to the city.

"Tommie certainly used to know how to make love, didn't he Marj?" Goldie asked Madge Rensch, mooningly reminiscent. Madge smiled. Her dignity of carriage and hauteur were surface qualities only, because on a sleigh-ride party or a picnic she could cuddle and hug and be as free with her loving as any of them. Of course people didn't really believe that either she or Goldie would really—well, of course, they both were gay and liked a good time, but they never lost their—social position.

Strange, that in these few years Goldie had faded so amazingly. Her yellow hair was yellow as ever, and her cheeks as pink. The doll-blue stare was still in her eyes, but a sparkle that once played about her was about her no longer. The fellows in town paid little attention to her now, not because she wouldn't fuss and cuddle as much as she ever did, but they rather felt she expected something to come of fussing and cuddling now. Goldie wanted a husband, and, not Madge—because she wanted a husband too—but some of the other girls would say that she wasn't going to be very particular either. She didn't go in much now for walking up and down the street with other girls in the town, in a new dress or hat as often as she could get one, stopping to chatter with the young men who loitered around. Oh, on vacations, when the older men got back from college or came to visit from various cities Goldie still navigated forth, but she was an old story to the older men. Madge interested them more; she at least had an Irish wit, and an independent mind of a sort to carry on an "interesting" conversation which wasn't all soft regretful sighing for the old young days.

Then too, no fellow cares to be seen talking too much with a girl who is willing to go around with a grocery delivery clerk, who quite openly swaggers around town drunk a good share of the time, noisily talking about poker games, and the way the various waitresses in town screw. It wasn't quite good taste on Goldie's part to go to dances with Tim Donaldson, even if there were so few men she wouldn't get taken otherwise.

But when Tom Gladden struck town, he seemed exuberantly glad to see Goldie. "She's a little mushhead all right, but. . ."; he didn't quite know what to say to justify her, since his initiation into loving had been conducted by Goldie in the days of their not-so-far-away past. Besides, Tom saw the look in Goldie's eyes, knew it to be reverential towards him, and wondered.

So he made an appointment to call on her in the evening and then strolled off to talk about the various football conquests of the old days when he was captain of the town high school team, and it was the champion team of the state. How well he, and the other fellows too, remembered this or that play—a run across eighty yards of the field, a trick shift and punt, or a great tackle. At last that conversation gave out, however, because Len O'Brien, and Jerry Porter, who'd been figures themselves in the town as football players, didn't care to sit around worshipping at Tom's shrine. Others than he would have made names for themselves if they'd had a chance to go away to college. So Tom began to tell them of other things he'd done in the city—of women.

And when he left the bunch to go to dinner he remarked: "Anything doing with Goldie? She seems to have relaxed a little, doesn't she?"

The next day Tom said nothing about Goldie, and paid little attention to her for the rest of his stay in town. When anybody mentioned Tom to Goldie a struck look came into her eyes and she hesitated, waiting for the conversation to shift without quite the ability to change the subject herself.

"Goldie's a silly little idiot," Madge commented. "If Tom had any brains what does she think she could mean to him, and did she think that newspaper notice had made a Sir Galahad out of him. I never thought though she'd have sense enough to see through Tom enough to realize she'd been heroizing a dub."

Madge, however, did not know that Goldie had not realized anything about Tom, except that after years, and her idealization of him, he could ask her, casually, what he had asked.

But Goldie married Tim Donaldson, now has five children, and as to her social status, the degree of her happiness, how are these things judged? Madge's husband was a hardware store owner; Gertrude's husband a barber; several other husbands were travelling salesmen, some were bank clerks, grain dealers and the conversation of them all . . . ?

Because Tom died a year or so after Goldie married, and because she grew—not less silly perhaps—more used to real motives than to ideal in men, and in women, she manages to extract much that is sweet in remembering Tom, and in re-reading the vast sheath of letters which he once wrote to her.

Green Grow The Grasses

HEY USED TO SIT on the lawn weaving flower chains or looking for four-leaf clovers. He often put his head on her lap and she would weave grass into his wavy black hair, bright with healthy oil. My *stupid* sister and I were quite as apt as other children to titter and mock at mushiness on the part of lovers, but we did not at them. Probably we sensed bravado. Sister Liz was given to moods and sulking, because my older sister was inclined to tell all of us we were ill bred or silly. Liz sulked and wept quietly to herself when alone sometimes, because she wasn't school-bright. However she could blurt out savagely, and generally struck Rhoda's weaker spots when her amiable nature turned momentarily savage. She was nevertheless aloof, and permitted no one to become fresh with her. Knowing that, it didn't surprise me when Liz didn't register indignant dignity one day when he greeted her. "Hello sister, has your schoolmarm sister been razzing you again? Give us a smile."

179

Liz instead gave him a smile, and explained to me sheepishly that he was just an easy-going fellow who'd always be getting himself in messes. Liz and I understood then that each of us liked him very much. When Rhoda scoffed at his tiresome mush with "that girl," Liz retored, "You needn't talk. Watch yourself in a mirror when you're acting skittish with some of the fool men you have at parties. You just can't stand seeing that they like each other."

I wasn't without haughtiness either, and didn't know him, but one day after a quarrel with Rhoda I sulked down the street. He was in his oil truck and gaily jumped out, and flipped me a dime. "Here son, sneak off to the movies. That sister of yours likes to ride you kids. She's too healthy and has to take her heat out on somebody."

I understood what he meant very well, and though I scrapped with Rhoda she represented to me elegance, and the outside city world. Whenever she returned for a vacation I adored her with awestruck wonder. Nobody else, certainly none of the usual sort of town male, could have made such an insinuation without my flaring up. His manner and gesture however were spontaneous; and he took me by surprise, understanding so well what I was brooding about. He made me shy, but he made me adore him and feel that he felt as I did, that there was some understanding between him and me.

At first I thought him merely nice and clean looking, for a working man, but soon I was thinking him the most beautiful person I had ever seen, and beauty wasn't a word I thought could be used in mentioning a man. He was supple, with a nonchalant swagger of amiability. While his manner didn't take away my shyness it let me act similarly towards him. His smile flashed brilliantly out of his dark face. I knew nothing of sculpturing but one day as he passed and spoke absent-mindedly, I noted the contours about his dark eyes, and their beauty struck me. I know now that my first awareness of how the loveliness of a sculpturesque line can cut into one sharply occurred at that moment. My sympathy went out to him with a pained leap, because he looked sad and worried. It tormented me that

180

I couldn't ask why, or help. I noticed that she was not waiting at the door for him, and generally she ran out to embrace and kiss him. I missed that for him as much as he missed it; possibly more, because he knew why she wasn't there this evening. For two or three days I missed and brooded over not seeing them on the lawn. Yet the picture of them playing on the lawn's green grasses persists in my mind. Paintings by Watteau, Renoir, Cézanne have recalled their scene, but none of the paintings have the essential naïve sweetness their picture left in my conscious. I am not saying innocence or purity, because I was always an aware child, and anything that innocence can mean, meant then that various interests were not awakened in me, or were not inherent, and so I failed to question various things I observed. Things between them were sweetly all right. I knew, as young animals know, and I knew as children know what one does not say or do around certain people, older, or with attitudes which bring out the actor in children.

I was reserved, but was not by nature timid, however shy I might be before older people whom I knew had reproving or patronizing manners. Now it strikes me as strange that I did not know they were unmarried. My mother didn't indicate disapproval of them, however, but remarked that "she is a flighty girl, though there's no harm in her." As mother was given to austerity, and was for me a model of correctness, I knew they must be all right. In any case mother could not know that Liz and I adored them, him particularly. He was only the driver of an oil wagon and mother could have no way of knowing how vividly aware we were of them, wishing that we could join them evenings as they sat on the lawn. Poor Liz was sixteen, and impulsive, and had a shamed fear that she must never let anyone see how she adored him. Intuitively she knew I wouldn't tease her about him, particularly, and Liz and I seldom teased each other about our "crushes." We were both given to them. Before we had always picked much older people to look at worshipfully, and people of "our" class.

Walking in from the country one day I saw his truck and he offered to give me a lift back to my house. Had it been anyone but him I would have said no, because I was looking for birds' eggs and had no desire to be at home as it was early afternoon. There was an oil can on the seat and I crowded in. Not wanting to be in the way of his steering I shrunk against the can. He saw and put his arm about my shoulder, patting me. "Sit close, bucko. You're not in the way. You're a nice looking kid. How old are you?"

"Fourteen," I said.

"You have the prettiest eyes I ever saw, except for my girl. I noticed you the first day we moved in. That younger sister of yours is a cute one, and I'll tell the world she isn't dumb if your old sister does ride her. She tickles me when she imitates the old hens in the neighborhood. I saw how you felt the other day when your sister caught you talking baby-talk to your kitten. She ought to be married. She's a fine woman, too, but if she was married she wouldn't tease a kid like you for being affectionate with his pets. She doesn't think much of us though. Your mother's not bothering to treat us chilly. She gave my girl a little talk, but Enid didn't mind. She knows your mother's a fine woman."

I didn't know what to say. Something was not as people thought it should be in their lives. That Rhoda was scornful about their mushiness meant nothing, as she was given to grand disdain. However I felt happy to be with him, and he was carefree and spontaneous. As the auto swerved around the corner I was thrown closer to him. He put his hand on my leg and patted it. "You're a well set up kid. Have you got the lead in your pencil yet?" he said lightly. "I tell you I'm nuts about that girl of mine."

I didn't feel uncomfortable or teased in an unclean way. I remarked that I knew from seeing them on the lawn that they thought much of each other. It seemed to me strange that I didn't feel uneasy. He actually was the first older person who had spoken to me without seeming objectionable about a subject which I was accustomed to think must be spoken of secretly. He went further to suggest that the lawn scenes were but preliminaries to joys later, and told me I'd understand soon. There was no innuendo, no indication in his manner that had a thought of saying anything I should not hear freely. I listened with animal curious alertness.

While he didn't tease me, he was older about my being yet a child. I was drawn to him when he said I was a well set up kid, and talked about the innocence of a boy my age. I thought him naïve to think I didn't understand. There was nothing strained in either his feeling or mine. It was mere human sympathy, and a deep satisfaction in regarding somebody likeable, capable of feeling or of later to feel the benefits of being a healthy, unafraid, physical being.

"I'll be a pop before long," he boasted as he helped me down from the truck seat. He patted my back, gently. His tone was youngly vain and he regarded me young-paternally. "Your mother can know things will be all right between the girl and me, as she sees things. To a kid like you what kind of pop do you think I'll make?"

His dark eyes glistened in his olive skin, and the flash of his teeth charmed me so that I wished to embrace him. I did stand to let his hand rest on my shoulder, when with most people I would have moved away. I felt older than he. His black hair gleamed about his shapely head which sat beautifully upon a clear neck. I say I adored him. I couldn't say how marvelous a pop I thought he would be, because I thought of fathers in terms of my own, and he was an elderly man, fussily officious, much as small town professional men often are. I did not then so analyze it, but I knew my father would never have tousled me to comment with satisfaction upon my being well set up.

Rhoda had a friend from Columbia University, and towards her, Hortense, Rhoda was almost humble. At first the glory of Hortense did not strike me. She had carrot-colored hair, a clear pale skin, a large mouth, and an awkwardly-graceful, free-moving body. It took me several days to think her beautiful, and by then I was awestruck by her "intellect." One Sunday, as Rhoda did not care for her long hikes, I went with Hortense. We struck across the fields and walked five miles, Her stride was long for me, but I felt her vitality and the rhythm of her easy swing. Sometimes our bodies touched. I was in a daze of sensual happiness. She told me of New York, the theatre, and talked of books, and as if I was completely an equal. It tormented me later when she talked with Rhoda, and they laughed, agreeing I was a bright child, with promise. Their implication that I was acting old and pretending to understand books we had talked of put resentment into my awed infatuation of Hortense. I hadn't pretended; I had admitted what I didn't understand or know, and had asked questions, trustingly letting Hortense know the extent of my ignorance. Now she was betraying me, and to Rhoda, who delighted in tantalizing children.

Rhoda, given to social research work, gave me the Chicago Vice Commission Report and it fascinated me, with horror, but more with incredulous curiosity. She had me read *Damaged Goods*. I heard her talk to Hortense of putting a "wholesome fear" into me. I heard often when they didn't know. My adoration of Hortense was sullied because she pretended, and was different when talking to me alone than when speaking to me before Rhoda. With me alone she had admitted confusion and wonder, and had told me of her own childhood.

My feeling about "them" was clear, however, and now the girl spoke to me whenever I passed. One evening he, Antoine, called me. I went to sit on the grass with them. "Take a look at this boy, Enid," Antoine said. "He has eyes, hasn't he? And eyelashes. His skin is as nice as yours, honey."

Enid laughed a chortling contralto. I blushed. Antoine caught me to him and patted my head, running his fingers through my hair. Then he leaned and held his face against mine. "This boy and I savez each other. Maybe someday we'll have a bright kid like this, and I'll sure like being his daddy."

I didn't ordinarily like being handled, but I did not draw away from Antoine. He kept his arm about my shoulder, and felt of my arm muscles. Looking at Enid with a smile he said. "Do you think the kid feels anything yet? How about it, son?" and patted me intimately.

"Antoine, you embarrass him. You are a tease," Enid said.

Enid was wrong. Antoine didn't embarrass me, and neither did her presence. No sense of modesty in me was upset, and I knew clearly his impulse towards me was nice. I merely felt sheepish and little boy, and happy. They were accepting me

184

as one of them, who understood, and life had much free affectionateness.

Soon they were gone from the neighborhood, and I heard at last that they were married, because a neighbor woman commented that at last they'd gone decently through with marriage. Liz told me, defiantly defending them, when I questioned. Enid had been married at sixteen to a much older man, and later had simply gone to live with Antoine. Only one faint rumor that Antoine was in trouble over money came back to me. I adored him, but adoration is a passing emotion. His presence delighted me. When he was no longer there I forgot him.

A few months later my father died, leaving no money. My family moved to the city, and there was little enough so that I got work afternoons to help support myself. Such work as a boy my age could get was that of being an errand boy, a collector, and later a news-office cub. I came to know the Salvation Army, the Civic Flops for unemployed floaters, the Three Sisters, tenements where were housed the inmates of the redlight district, and sometimes copy of mine was used by the yellow journal for which I worked. It was horrible or excellent sob stuff, wrung from my boy-agonies. There was now in me, powerfully, with the force of a highstrung organism, my adolescence. I knew bowery dancehalls, the lake resorts where if I were older I could pick up girls, but I was still small and looked a complete child. It need not be said that the "wholesome fear" lessons taught me by Hortense and Rhoda did not lessen the torments of those years, for I could not see a scarred face without recoiling.

Interwoven with wanderings about town was the experience of reading much, for I was lonely. Unused to a big city I didn't know how to become chums with young people in the huge high school which I attended. I discovered Chehkov and Dostoevsky. It was the nostalgia, revolt, and ennui in Turgenev's *Fathers and Sons* which started me, but soon I was reading till all hours of the night, and generally about tormented, epileptic, frustrated characters and emotions. This increased my shyness, and my tendency to feel different than other boys my age. It would have been easy to remain a more or less unawakened boy, healthily

185

consorting with other boys, but not after I had discovered Dostoevsky. He was to me then a passion, what I now think a disease, for the characters' emotions are over-imaged.

The year the war broke out I was past fifteen and had visions of getting overseas to enlist, but I was too small, and knew no way to get over. It blasted something in me. Both my feeling of helplessness and the instinct that the war would last made my adventurous impulses despair. I was seared with despondent cynicism and morbidity, and I was carnal. No despair broods more than the romantic cynicism of pubescent boyhood. I imagined wracked and tortured bodies of young men in battle, but this did not have the effect of making me hate or want to avoid war. Rather I thought I might as well be in it, taking chances with the others. If I was killed, I didn't then treasure life as a precious fluid to be preserved; and I was sure that, crippled, I would kill myself. In the midst of the war was where the excitement was, and I felt imprisoned by dullness and poverty. That hatred of the bourgeois insistencies in life is no rare emotion, much as biographers make of it in writing of "artists." One forgets or ceases to brood in older years, but then, much of the time, my conscious was an inflamed plate registering horror-impressions quiveringly.

The next summer mother wisely let me go back to Lansing to do farm work. Soon after arriving there I found an easy job with Mr. Grayson, whose wife was a friend of Rhoda's. He was almost a bright men, rosy, hardy, with a manner of jovial cheer. I trusted him with youth, but not implicitly. It pleased me when he let me hear him tell his wife that I was bright steel. I was willing to get up at five mornings and work till eight nights, since he made a great point of calling me himself when the older men had to be Johnnies-on-the-spot by their own efforts. He liked it that I always sang or whistled at my work. I was such a happy boy, and he understood well how flattery made me work.

He was not bright however in giving me a cot in the corn-crib with two other farmhands. Soon I found that they were underpaid. They advised me to go at my work less zealously, because he complained that I did more work than they. That made me observe. I did, and they got $35 a month, to my $20, and they assured me that other farmers paid their hands $40 or $45 a month, with day wages during harvest season.

I heard the other men speak of Dandalo, the jailbird, and knew that a man and his wife occupied the room above the cow stable. Never having heard Antoine's last name I did not realize it was him. Having seen him across the farmyard I had not recognized him. Two years had passed, and the man looked thin and worn, and his wife was dragged out with apathy from overwork. They cared entirely for twenty cows, doing the milking, barn cleaning, feeding, and the wife also took care of the chicken coops. Dandalo and his wife, the men told me, got $40 a month and the room they had to live in for their work.

The story aroused my curiosity. I learned that Dandalo had served a year in prison for stealing money from the company he worked for. At the time his wife had been with child and he needed money, so the sentence had been light. When released he had trouble getting work, even day labor. Why, I wondered, since a man would have little chance to steal while digging ditches. Mr. Grayson had liberally employed the man and his wife, and now they did the work of several people for $40 a month. The other hired men thought I was crazy to resent the imposition on the couple who, Mrs. Grayson told me, had been most honest with them and were making an effort to reclaim themselves.

"How much did he steal?" I asked.

"Something over a hundred dollars which he had collected. Antoine says he intended to pay it back at the end of the month when he got his salary, but it was more than his salary, and the company wanted to make an example of him. Poor Antoine, he works very hard, and Enid was such a pretty girl. They are very young. He is not twenty-five."

"Antoine?" I said, but I knew. That night I went to the cowshed where they were milking. He didn't recall me at once. He looked tired, and I had grown. His dark eyes were dull. I had no adoration for him then. I was simply thwarted with a wonder at life, overwhelmingly. My memory would visualize them as they looked sitting on the soft grasses of their lawn, playing with carefree spontaneity. How could such a change take place in less than three years? They now had two children and it was obvious that Enid was to have another. Why had they not been careful? Didn't they realize that life can't be let to drift? People would say they were paying for their sin, but they merely had not been careful.

Antoine's face regained some of its luminance when he recalled me. The debonair swagger and spontaneity of manner weren't much there though, and I was no longer just a pretty kid. I wasn't a gangly adolescent; I was still small for my sixteen years, but his attitude was more man to man now. He agreed that he and Enid worked pretty hard for little pay, but he shrugged his shoulders.

"Why don't you go away, Antoine? Why don't you go to the city or to another town, far away from here?" I asked. I knew I was being uselessly full of advice.

He looked apathetic and shrugged his shoulders. None of the adoring feeling I had for him would have flamed within me, but he smiled rakishly and his eyes glistened. His teeth shone evenly, brilliant, white. The dark beauty about his eyes was there, and I felt a clutch within me for the brooding tenderness of grace which his expression evoked.

"You're a game kid, with fight in you. You get that from your mother. She didn't disapprove of Enid, and you don't think a fellow not fit to talk to because he's been in trouble. Well, the wife and I can't get away with the bambinos. Where's the money? We're waiting. I'm not finished, but the girl. . ." He shrugged his shoulders, tired now. I thought he meant more than that she was finished. Her prettiness was gone. She looked miserable. With a flood of panicky pain I thought Antoine meant they didn't have joy in each other anymore. They had only duty. Yes, John Barrymore was playing in *Justice* in New York, and I remembered drab stories: Gogol's "The Mantle," of fugitives, and outcasts. No, no, they should remain indifferent or become reckless. They shouldn't let themselves be made examples for people more sordid. I almost said "Why don't you steal on a large scale, Antoine? To hell with the sacredness of money." Crook plays, particularly *Within the Law*, had given me romantic ideas about intelligent crooksters.

"Don't ever do anything you hadn't ought," Antoine said. "Not unless you're well covered. I'm not a crooked bozo, but I didn't think quick what money means to those who have it. The girl had to be in a hospital and doctors charge money."

I wanted powerfully to put my arms about him, to make him understand that he need not explain to me, ever. He got up from the stool with a full pail of foaming milk. It was white-steamingly lovely. He poured it into the container of the separator, and I offered to turn the crank. "Today's been light work for me."

"It won't be next week when the threshing crew gets here," Antoine said dryly, and patted my side. "You're the one I hear singing around here nights. You keep some of those songs in you for later, when you'll need them. You're going to be as good-looking a man as you were a kid. I hadn't forgotten you, but you've grown."

I thrilled with a warm emotion at the fondling caress of his hand, but the thrill was pained with a devastating pity. "There won't be any hard work for me on this farm next week." I boasted. "I'm quitting and going to work by the day with threshing crews. Old Grayson can't kid me. Ike Nelson, down the road, says he'll pay me $4 a day if only to be water-boy, and he's sure he can let me drive teams to the elevator. Then I'll get $5. That Swede is not so goddamned afraid he'll over-pay a kid, or give a living wage."

"That's it," Antoine was cheerier now. "Keep your pecker up." Later, as he was milking another cow I asked how much money he needed to go to the city with his family, and would he go if he knew there was a job waiting for him.

"You think you could get me a job?" he said with a flash of happy grateful emotion. "You'd lend me the money out of what you earned?" He shrugged his shoulders, ironically resigned now. "What about the girl? We are caught here till the new one comes."

I left Mr. Grayson the next day and he blustered at me, scold-ingly, saying I had a vacillating nature. I'd never get anywhere if I did not learn to stick by what I started. I was too shy to say what I felt, but later wished I had been able to curse at him violently for trying to bully me into retracting my resignation. I'd earn more in a week with Nelson than I got from him in a month, and he knew I was only doing farm work for the summer. Going to town I was full of plans to make as much money as possible, quickly. I might be able to lend Antoine as much as $50 in a month, and I could get work in the city about as soon as I returned. He'd pay me back, I knew. I might tell some employer of a good man who wanted to move to the city if he knew a job awaited him. Surely I would remember Antoine's plight and write him a letter containing good news.

I worked six weeks in the harvest fields and saved up one hundred dollars. About were many Germans who were going back to the old country to get into the war as soon as harvest season was over. Some of them had been sent for. There were a variety of types among the floating workers, and I, trained to be sociologic-minded, was alertly interested. The world was full of interesting problems when one felt lively, and in the country I had little memory of the drugged despondency of being lonely in the city. Had I seen Antoine I'd have loaned him the money, but I didn't see him. Going back on the train I had a copy of Barbusse's *Under Fire*. It fascinated me. It hypnotized my rebellious emotions and my morbidity to read what the *poilus* were up against, and to realize what they had been up against in peace times.

I didn't mean to forget Antoine, but I never wrote him about a job waiting for him. There is much chaos, and every man has his problems. Mrs. Grayson wrote Rhoda that I'd be sorry to hear Enid had died in childbirth; the two babies had been adopted by a farmer's wife, and Antoine had disappeared. Possibly he had gone to Italy to be in the war, although he had come to America as a baby.

Anyway there was the war, my future, and no money in the family, so I had to work. Of course I was ambitious. I thought sometimes I'd be a journalist, an advertising man, a dramatist, an author, but also I was most restless and had the usual adolescent despair of life as a process worth enduring.

Years later in Eleusis the remnant torso of a boy sculpted by an archaic Greek struck a pang into me, but what it evoked was elusive. One knows that the quality of beauty in sculpturing is even more undefinable than that in music, or in human beings, still I persisted in recalling that forgotten flowing-image which was dormant in the subconscious.

I thought of a dance scene in which the ballet swept forward stooping to sweep their white draped garments in a movement suggesting the sea waves' rise and fall; of a possible scene when an actress has intoned an intellectual thought at the heat of passion, while poised to catch form at a moment of abstract beauty which is held static for a pained interval. It perplexed me that I thought too of pretty, weak, but loveable, young people making a mess of life because of spontaneous joy. The gracious qualities of tenderness and beauty were confused with those of disillusion and beaten disintegration. Suddenly Antoine was clear in my memory, as I had first adored him, as I last saw him, and then as he probably became. I had not thought of him for ten years, but the young-boy torso evoked some quality he had aroused in my emotions. Having located the sought-for image I forgot him, knowing he had been to my awakening adolescence a symbol of faun-spontaneity with the clean sweetness of human relationships. The thought of him as another of the used joy-beings which society breaks and throws into the discard was distressing.

I knew resignation would never be complete in my nature. A wish to encourage him and what he stood for leaped hotly within, and I wanted to know what had become of him. My rebellion asked why are not such as he given just enough calculation to be careful. Society has little trust. Why should he have been naïvely generous-willed? One can't let one's arrested-development emotions dominate however, so I forgot Antoine.

Potato Picking

"I F I LET YOU GO to Mr. Schultz's farm you must be back for Sunday. He would let you pick potatoes that day I am sure, and four days of such food as he gives his workmen will make one of your mother's meals look good to you," Bessie Donley told Grant.

Grant felt impatient with his mother. She knew he was janitor of the Episcopalian church and had to clean it Sundays as well as ring the church bell. He had been selling papers and magazines for the last year to make money; he had done many odd jobs. She might know he understood that if he was to have proper clothes and spending money he must make it himself. Why, when he "loaned" her money, must she take the attitude that she was granting his boyish whim when he went to work for the money involved? If she didn't know that picking potatoes gave a fellow a backache and was no fun she might better learn so. He had no patience with her attitude that he must go to Sunday School and Christian Endeavor either, since many of his playmates never bothered. She refused to realize that at twelve years old a boy knows more about what having to make a living means than she wanted to admit. Not bothering to promise her to be back for Sunday, he went to the front yard.

Who was that woman at the front gate? It looked like one of those gypsy women, of the lot camping across the road under the willows. Going to the front door, Grant called, "Ma, there's a woman coming up to the house. A gypsy."

She was blowsy skinned and her hair was coarse and disheveled. Grant stood as she was talking to his mother.

"Yes, Missus, I had to run away. You will help me, lady, won't you? He's threatening to kill me, and the bairn, and it's only six months," the woman explained. She had a strange accent. Scotch, she said to Mrs. Donley, and Grant pretended not to be listening. She had married in Scotland and come with the man and his mother to travel in a camp wagon through America. Her husband took to beating her when they were only a week married. He drank and was uncontrollable when drunk. Would the lady let her stay in her house that night? Yes, and have something stolen from her, Grant thought. No good came of believing gypsy women like that one. He had better go and see that his pet, club-footed pig wasn't rooting around near their wagons. The woman wanted to get out to her sister in California, nearly two thousand miles away. Mother was saying that of course she would put her up for the night, and call the sheriff if any ruffianly husband came storming at her gate to demand that a terrified wife be given back for him to have his drunken brutal will with. The woman was kissing mother's hand.

"It's a bonnie lad you have," the woman said, and her accent made Grant think she meant he was skinny. She ought to have sense enough not to say that when she was asking a favor of his mother.

"Don't be silly," Bessie told her son. "The woman is no gypsy, I know. She comes from the Scotch highlands near where my father was born. She's frightened and sick. It is those ruffianly men, and her mother-in-law is a reprobate, too, I'm sure. The

193

girl would be terrified, naturally, coming from a simple, godly home, to traipse all over America with such a crew. *Bony* is the Scotch pronunciation of *bonnie*. She was being nice about you."

Nevertheless Grant did not like the woman and her wild windblown look, black hair, dark eyes. She was a scold and probably pestered the life out of her husband so he drank. Why didn't she get on the train and just go to California and leave him? Then he thought and was sorry for her, because of course she had no money for railway fare. Scotland must have taken a long time to come from, across the sea, and everbody would think she was a gypsy and a thief because she went around in a covered wagon.

Grant went to bed early to be up early and join the other boys going to Schultz's farm for potato picking.

2

Grumpy with sleep, Grant met Gould Lamar and Ellsworth Cummings in the Schultz backyard. The wagon was leaving at once, to be at the farm before seven o'clock. By the time it was half a mile out of town, the boys felt fine and bragged about how many potatoes they would pick. No one of the three boys paid any attention to Sloppy May, who was the high school superintendent's son, but nobody liked him. He picked his nose and chewed his fingernails and told dirty stories.

"I hope the potato hills are full," Grant said, "except he's paying us kids by the row rather than by the bushel. I know he's paying the older men by the bushel and we pick just as fast. They think they can get by with anything on us because we're young and I bet we do more work than most of the hoboes he gets."

They passed the hobo jungle soon. About twenty men were hanging about, sitting on ties thrown by the railroad track. Heaps of cans, some new, others rusted with last or several seasons' rust upon them, were off to the side. A big tin of coffee was boiling over the fire built in a hole in the ground. The men looked without interest at the boys and the Schultz wagon. It was well known that Schultz furnished lousy grub, and hired kids when he could get them more by making them think he was doing them a favor to employ them at all.

"It'd be swell being a hobo," Ellsworth commented. "Just nothing to do but loll around and go wherever you want to and when it's the best season to be there. You can always pick up meals somewhere and sleep in haystacks or barns."

Grant reflected that Ellsworth was a putty-nosed mamma's boy, never knowing much about anything and always getting caught if he did anything his mamma had told him not to. "You and I'll take rows next to each other," Grant whispered to Gould, "and if one is quicker than the other let's wait for the other to catch up. Potato picking isn't a fire we got to put out right away, I guess."

Later Grant was disgusted. Gould could not pick potatoes for sour apples and a fellow can't earn anything waiting for him to catch up. Sloppy May made a fellow work hard to keep up with him so he couldn't think himself too damned smart for being the quickest. Why couldn't he take a row other than one just next to Grant? He bet Sloppy pretended to know a lot more than he did, because kids don't know for sure all the rot that Sloppy was talking. Grant fretted in the heat and dust, not being able to think his own ideas so long as Sloppy picked potatoes alongside of him, and kept talking. His back ached. The sun was scorching on his dust-grimed, sweating body. His neck was sunburned. It wasn't fun picking potatoes, but he could stick it if the others could.

Sloppy May would have to grab the wash basin first and not even throw away his dirty water after using. Grant did not want to use the same basin right after Sloppy, and the towel was black with dirt, because you get covered with dust picking potatoes when the wind is blowing. Later the food tasted good, though. "I guess he can afford to feed us well," even Ellsworth agreed. "He makes a pile of money every year with his produce and he's got two hundred acres of onions planted, too. We can have a job picking onions after this job, if we want to. We ought to make him pay us a man's wage though. It's the work we do and not

195

our ages that should bring the pay. We shouldn't let him kid us, because maybe too our working so hard stunts our growth for life. You never get a chance till you're grown up."

Grant saw that Gould Lamar looked pale, and Gould wasn't strong since that fool doctor cut out his appendix six months back. He wished Sloppy May would wipe his nose and not eat as though he were at a trough. He wasn't the only one who had been doing a little work and had a backache.

It was going to be good to have some sleep this night, Gould, Ellsworth, and Grant agreed. They climbed up to the haymow with their horse blankets, and hid behind a pile of hay, hoping that Sloppy May would not find them. They talked in whispers until they knew he had located himself, and maybe he would go to sleep quickly. It was a sure bet he snored something terrible, along with his other bad habits.

The city, what would the city mean? Would Gould someday be an attorney like his father, and go into politics? Grant guessed Gould would stay in this one-horse burg and go into his father's office, because Gould didn't have any ambition or desire to change his life. Ellsworth said he wanted to live in the city. What was the matter with Gould that he could stand to think of living all his life in this town?

"Are you asleep?" Gould whispered, lying nearby in the hay.

"I'm not," Ellsworth answered. "I don't feel a bit sleepy like you'd have thought the way our backs ached from picking those damned potatoes. Let's take it light tomorrow. My shirt's as wet as if I'd swum in it."

"I can't sleep either," Grant answered. "Listen to Sloppy snore. He's like a pig anyway."

"It's kind of chilly. You wouldn't have thought it, hot as it was today," Gould said. "And dusty. I felt sick in the morning, but we'll get toughened up. The third day's the worst, they say, and after that you just kind of go along."

"Let's put our blankets together and cuddle up to keep each other warm," Ellsworth suggested. "We don't want to let no draft in and the hay is down a guy's neck too. Let's put one blanket under us, and the three of us can crawl under the other two."

"There is going to be all the hoboes in the country about this burg soon, if they aren't starting now," Grant said. "Those guys never stay more'n half a day on a job. Us kids stay longer and work more. We ought to make old man Schultz pay us more than he does. Being kids doesn't mean we do less work."

They were cuddled together. Grant was in the middle and felt no draft coming from the sides but his feet were chilly and a draft came from below. Wisps of hay worked their way down his neck and back. He felt itchy and wanted to toss about, but maybe the other fellows were sleepy and he didn't want to toss and have them cranky. He felt Gould's breath on his face and Ellsworth's on his back and neck. A warmth from the other two made him feel too smotherily warm, if only his feet were not in a draft. But he began to feel drowsy.

"Damn draft. Wish I had the middle place," Ellsworth muttered, putting his arm over Grant's shoulder and snuggling closer, Gould snuggled closer from the other side too, whispering, "You got all the luck. This is heaps of fun though, ain't it? Wished that Sloppy was a decent guy and I'd get him to sleep on the other side of me to keep the draft out."

It was eight o'clock Saturday night when Grant came up the path to his house. He knew he was all tanned but he felt a millionaire with six dollars on him. He would beat it down to the drugstore as soon as he had kissed his mother and could get away. He didn't want her to catch him charging things —ice cream and soda pops—on her account. He whistled, and whistled again. Then he called, "Porkie, Porkie," but his pet club-footed pig did not come squealing. Grant's heart sank. Those Scotch gypsies. He looked across the road. They were still there.

"Mother, mother," he said excitedly as he went into the house, 'Where's Porkie? He doesn't come when I call. Them damn gypsies have stolen him, I bet, and maybe they have butchered him already." He was trying not to cry but he blamed his mother very much. She had promised to look after Porkie and see that he wasn't stolen or didn't wander off while Grant was away. He wished you could take pet pigs on jobs with you the way you can dogs, and Porkie was funnier than a dog. He didn't like mud, either.

"He was rooting around the yard not long ago," Bessie said, feeling guilty. "He must be around. I'll help you look for him."

Grant, hot with excitement, ran out into the barn, the chicken coop, and back to the cow pasture, but there was no answer to his call. He went running to the gypsy wagons.

"Have you seen a small pig around?" he asked a red-faced old woman who sat darning socks in one of the wagons, and he noticed that the wagons were packed, ready to drive on elsewhere. He was frightened. He could not say he must look into their wagon and see if Porkie was there. "Nae, laddie," the old woman answered. "You're a bonnie laddie. We wouldn't be taking a piggie on ye."

Grant ran down the road calling, and suddenly stopped in an eagerness of expectancy. He heard squealing, and it came from the empty barn belonging to the house next his. He ran to its door and opened it. There was Porkie, tied by his hind clubfoot, and squealing with delight at seeing Grant, who ran to hug, pet, and release him quickly. Porkie was too heavy for him to carry now, but he came hobbling at a great pace, to keep up with Grant, who ran quickly, happy now, but not wanting that damned old drunken Scotch wife-beater to come along and pretend that Porkie was his pig.

"There you are," Mrs. Donley said later. "I told you the man was a reprobate. It's the young husband who tried to steal Porkie on you. The womenfolk are good honest Scotch women, but he hasn't a scruple in his lowdown nature. If I only had the money I would give the poor girl fare out to California, though she is foolish enough to say she wants to stay with the man even if he does beat her. It's men like that who seem to get the strongest hold on some women."

"I'm not going potato picking Monday if those people are still camping anywhere in this neighborhood," Grant said with morose decision, wondering if Porkie would really be safe locked up in the grain bin in the barn. He wondered if he might not smuggle Porkie to his bedroom for just this one or two

198

nights. It was a sure thing, and Grant knew it, that Porkie would have to go to the butchers or be butchered by his older brothers before long, certainly before winter. But Porkie was still his pet and he didn't want no Scotch gypsies stealing him. If there was any money to be made from Porkie it should be his, except of course if Porkie was butchered at home and eaten by the family there wouldn't be any money paid. But anyway, he didn't want Porkie stolen by no-good people he didn't know and who never did any work so far as anybody knew.

The Jack Rabbit Drive

T WAS AGREED UPON by members of the community that the thousands of jack rabbits throughout the countryside must be exterminated, in part at least. Their burrowings and nibblings destroyed too much grain and property. So for two weeks the day set for a drive was given wide publicity.

Horace slipped out of the house through the kitchen, stopping there to sneak cookies from under Linda's eyes. At the moment, however, she was feeling in good humor, and her black face, already gleaming with perspiration, gleamed more with a tender smiling at his six-year-old guile, and she gave him six cookies, whereupon he went joyfully into the back yard to look hopefully about. Maybe Freddie was around to be played with. He didn't like Freddie much but he was better than nobody. Horace felt uncomfortable because his mother had put a new suit on him, and made him wear an overcoat, and if Billie Anderson saw him with his yellow hair slicked back Billie might call him "mamma's boy" and that would mean another fight, because he and Billie were supposed to have a great scrap someday to show which was the best fighter in town of their age.

It was somewhat sheepishly that he began to play with Sally Porter a few minutes later. She was more fun to be with than Freddie, if she only weren't a girl. She dared do anything, and wasn't nearly so scared of going blocks from home if she could without her mother seeing and calling her back to play on the Porter's front lawn. Horace didn't want to play there because every boy in the neighborhood could see, and Sally might want to play doll-house, which Horace didn't mind if Billie Anderson wasn't apt to know about it. The Porter horse, that was to run in the County Fair races, was picketed on the lawn too, and he'd stepped on Horace's bare foot one day when Horace was petting him. That was no fun, you can bet. The horse didn't mean to maybe, but Horace didn't want that to happen again.

As playing on the lawn was no fun at all Horace and Sally were out in back of the barn, almost without thinking to get there. It was the alley they were supposed not to play in too, because the nigger washerwoman's kids played there, since their ma's shack sat on top of the alley. Mrs. Darian told Horace there wasn't any harm in his playing with the colored children, but Mrs. Porter wouldn't let Sally. They had not been there long, however, before Horace got scared, remembering that he'd killed one of those niggers' chickens by hitting it on the head with a stone he'd thrown; except he hadn't really killed it. He had only stunned it, because when he and the nigger kids, all scared of what their mas would say, buried the rooster in the manure pile, it began to flop and finally got up and ran away, dizzy in the head. Maybe Mrs. Lincoln, the nigger woman, wasn't mad at him though, because she had sent him an egg no bigger than a robin's that one of her hens had laid, but he didn't know. Maybe she'd just sent it to please his mother for whom she did the washing.

"We gotta go somewhere else and play because I'm not going to have them darkie kids butting in on us. I have an idea anyway. Billie Anderson says you can get a cent a bottle

201

for beer bottles from the bartender at the saloon."

"Why you awful boy, Horace. If we did that we'd just get the hide licked off us and you know it," Sally said, pretending great horror. "Why mamma is always giving it to papa because he goes in there and if she heard I did that! And she would because someone would tell her."

"Aw rats, don't be a fraidy cat."

"You know I ain't no fraidy cat."

"Maybe you ain't, but Freddie is. I ast him yesterday to look for beer bottles with me and he wouldn't, and he cried and ran home and we scrapped, and he was going to tell on me, but I didn't care. I told him

> Tattle-tale, tattle-tale,
> Hanging to the bull's tail—' "

"You are the naughtiest boy," Sally said with triumphant righteousness, and so daring Horace, encouraged him to the scandalous conclusion of the ditty. Sally believed it her duty to act shocked and refuse to speak to Horace for a few seconds, but the strain of that soon told on her, and being sure that no older person had heard Horace, she relaxed to curiosity.

"Where do you suppose we can find some beer bottles?" she asked. "We could hide them and collect a lot and then maybe get in the back door of the saloon and Mr. Murphy wouldn't tell on us."

After an hour's search in the alleys Sally had found one bottle that might be a beer bottle, or even a whisky bottle, and Horace had found three bottles that he was sure were beer bottles, as he was sure Sally's was only a pop bottle. So the two went around to the alley behind the main street until they came to the backshed entrance to the saloon. They were afraid to go in, but after a consultation decided they'd better go in together and both get lickings if they were caught.

"The men will take it more like a joke if you're there," Horace sagely informed Sally. "They always think girls don't know nothing."

Sidling up to the bar inside Sally looked discreetly wide-eyed and innocent as she piped up, "I'se got some beer bottles, Mr.

Man. P'ease give me some pennies for them." Horace was too scared to notice much that Sally was putting on baby accents.

"Well, I'll be—" Murphy, the bartender, started to say, but checked his profanity. "You kids will get paddled if your families hear you're coming in here. You'd better beat it quick. You'll get me in trouble too if they hear I let you in."

"We want candy." Horace broke in, feeling more at ease as he sensed that Murphy was a companion in guilt. "Just this once, buy these bottles." His heart was going at a terrific pace and he felt uncomfortable because of many strange men about the bar who had laughed raucously at him and Sally.

"Here's a nickel. Now quick and beat it, kiddies," Murphy said and handed Horace the money.

"Don't I get none too?" lisped Sally.

"Divide that, you two kids. You'll founder yourself on all day suckers or cheap chocolates if I give you more," Murphy explained good naturedly, leaning over to pat Sally's tow head, and to tweak at one of her braids. He relented, however, and slipped her a nickel too, so she and Horace went happily out of the saloon, in their glee carelessly going through the front door, when they quickly remembered and were scared.

"O golly, Sally. I'll bet yer pa can see us because his office is right across the street."

"It ain't papa I care about knowing. He wouldn't lick me and he wouldn't dare tell mamma on me either, because she'd say that was his blood coming out in me. That's what she always says when she licks me."

The children now felt completely involved in guilt and decided it wasn't any use resisting temptation anymore that afternoon, so they bought some all day suckers, and gum, and chocolates. They walked down the main street and soon came to the edge of the town where Daly's pasture was. It was a warm autumn afternoon, but too chilly to sit on the bank of the pond long, and few minnows were to be seen in the muddy water. A few cows were grazing on the dry grass in the pasture, but the children saw that they didn't come too near.

"I wonder which gives the most milk, the papa or the mamma

203

cow," Horace queried, remembering the cow his father had sold because she went dry.

"It ought to be the papa cow because that's how cows support themselves, and the papa ought to always support the family, but mamma says it ain't so with us, cause papa drinks up everything he makes. I like pap better though. He isn't cranky every minute of the day."

This problem did not interest Horace much. He was full of candy, and drowsy in the sun except that it was cold on his pants when he sat on the ground. As his mind wandered he remembered that his brother Ralph had spoken of a jack-rabbit drive at the breakfast table. That had excited Horace, but his mother told him of course he couldn't watch anything so brutal.

"I tell you, Sally," Horace said, "there's a jack-rabbit drive to end up at the corner down the road. Let's run down there and see if there's any sign of it."

Since ten o'clock in the morning groups of men and boys had been occupied with the jack-rabbit drive. On every side for miles from town, farmers, farm boys, and all the countless dogs of the country side had been scouring the land to scare up rabbits. The clamor of guns firing, dogs barking, men shouting and beating with clubs, and horses trampling about was calculated to terrify all the rabbits who came within range of the two semi-circles of inclosing rabbit hunters.

It was by now four o'clock in the afternoon and evening chill was coming into the air. Going to the corner fence Horace knew of, Sally and he soon began to discern noises of the drive off in the distance. Now and then there was an echo or re-echo of a gunshot. Faintly, as though imagined, the resonance of a shot would sound, though neither Sally or Horace could verify any one report as the noises were becoming more clear and decisive, or their expectant senses made them alert.

"I saw Dingo, pa's half-breed hunter dog, tear up a rabbit's burrow once, and he just ripped that rabbit all to pieces," Sally said. "That made pa mad because it showed that Dingo was no good as a hunter to tear game to pieces. That rabbit squealed once when Dingo grabbed it but it just squealed once."

"Ralph said he bet all the rabbit burrows in the country would be dug open, there are so many dogs," Horace volunteered. "I've never seen a jack rabbit. Only them pet rabbits I had when I was a baby two years ago. Gosh, I was mad at mamma for making me wear skirts a whole year after Billie had been wearing pants, but it wasn't as bad as Freddie having to wear long hair up till just last month. His mamma wants to make a girlboy out of him."

Fifteen minutes passed, with sounds of the drive coming clearly to them, and again seeming to grow dimmer, until finally the resonance of noises became continually louder. The distinguishable bark of dogs could be heard: the baying of hounds, the yipe of fox terriers, the excited joyful bark of mongrels, and the general hysteria of all the dogs' excitement. It was infrequently that a gun was fired.

Suddenly there was a rush of men from across the fields on every side, and they were shouting at each other.

"Here you are, boys; here you are." "Get in on every side." "Get your clubs ready. Knock them out as fast as they come hurtling against the fence." "They'll be here in thousands inside of three minutes." "Kill 'em at one blow."

From the village men, women, and children too had begun to arrive for the end-up of the drive, the sounds of which had echoed through the town for the last half-hour. A share of even the women from the village carried clubs, or limbs of trees, and all the men and boys in the drive were so armed. The hullabaloo grew greater, with cursings, leaping about, and rabbit-threatening gesticulations in mock display of what they'd do to the rabbits.

The rabbits began coming. Tearing along, panic-struck huge white jack rabbits catapulted across the prairie towards the fence corner. Men on horses, men on foot, and dogs with lapping slobbery tongues circled in on them. The rabbits hurled themselves on at leaps of twenty, thirty, or even forty feet in the case of the huge-sized jacks. Shrilly, above the pandemonium a shriek of rabbit pain sounded now and then as some dog captured a jack and ripped it to bits.

Horace and Sally, standing near the front of the spectators, watched feverishly. Rabbits smashed into the impenetrable fence to be beaten on the head by men or boys jumping about. Before struck, terror was making the rabbits squeal. A continuous ripping, tearing sound, punctuated by the thump, thump, thump of clubs against the light-boned heads of the rabbits, went on.

At one moment Horace saw a rabbit caught by a great lean greyhound. Within a second another dog had caught the same rabbit by another portion of its body. Horace heard the squeal of that rabbit, saw the look of rodent terror in its eyes; and—dizzy within himself—heard the rip of the body. A stunned feeling held him, watching as though hypnotized. He was biting his lips and twitching his face nervously, unaware of himself or of his reactions to what he was seeing. It didn't seem that what he was seeing was actual. The jack rabbits looked so powerful and electric as they came across the prairie, and so limp, like damp besmudged cotton, as they lay torn upon the ground with the yellow of their hides, and the red of their interiors, showing.

Shortly the thing was done with. Heaped in piles against the fence were more than a thousand rabbit bodies. Their dull, glazed, half-open eyes, Horace noticed. He lingered, half wondering if they might not move again. Surely something more was going to happen after all this excitement.

"What happens to rabbits when they're dead?" Horace wondered, dazedly curious, to Sally, having heard of death before, but never having realized what it might mean.

"Huh, listen to the kid. Say sonny, them jacks is dead, and dead they'll stay and not be destroying crops on us farmers," a heavy-set man said with rough good nature to Horace, who shrank within himself from the obscenity, to him, of the man's manner. Yet his wonder made him speak in mechanical bewilderment.

"But they were alive just a few minutes ago."

"Sure kid, but they ain't now. We saw to that."

Horace didn't know how to think, and maybe he was afraid

206

but not in a way he could cry about, or he could ask his mother about. What if something began chasing people like the rabbits had been chased?

Sally was ready to go home, though she was still looking fascinatedly at the pile of rabbits. Horace had a moment of aversion to her because she leaned over and touched one, and didn't seem to feel sorry for it. A farm boy picked up a little mutilated rabbit and handed it to her. "Here, girlie," he told her, patting her head, "take this home to your mamma and have her cook it for you. It's nicer than chicken."

Sally took the rabbit and started to follow Horace, who had walked ahead of her. She caught up with him.

"Your aren't going to take that rabbit home, are you? You couldn't eat it, could you?"

"Why not? Mamma feeds us rabbits lots of times."

"But it's dead," Horace explained.

"Every meat you eat is. That's what happens to all the cows that get shipped out of the stock yard every week."

Horace's mind was stalled. He couldn't think. He changed the topic. "I'll bet them rabbits were stronger than you or me. I'll bet we couldn't have held one without its kicking away because a man I saw grab a live one could hardly hold it."

Sally, becoming conscious that Horace walked away from her because she was carrying the rabbit, threw it aside with a quick gesture and said, "Nasty dead thing."

"It isn't its fault it's nasty," Horace said.

"I think it's awful. The poor rabbits."

"I don't know whether it's awful or not. People said it was a good thing to get rid of them."

When Horace and Sally got back to their houses they separated. Horace went through the kitchen, not even noticing Linda. In the sitting room he avoided speaking to his mother and, taking up a picture book, buried himself in the big easy chair. There was much he wanted to know but he didn't want his mother to know he had seen the jack-rabbit drive.

Continually his mind reverted to the rabbits, how their white furry flesh had been torn, their squeals, the fear in their eyes.

As he sat trying to think his mind was filled, not with definite pictures of rabbits, but with a flood of nervous images of rabbit carnage that made him shudder and want to shut the thought out. But he didn't try to look at his book. He even felt impatient with his mother when she began talking to him and so prevented him from thinking about the rabbits. He liked to think that as he shuddered he was trying to shut out the white ripping and squealing image.

Through dinnertime Horace was very quiet, and his mother asked him if he didn't feel very well.

"Rats, sick," his brother Ralph said. "Don't baby him. He's probably been up to something and keeps quiet not to give himself away."

"Nonsense, Ralph," his mother answered. "I can see that the boy is pale, and his eyes have a feverish look. Don't think I don't know children better than my own son knows them. Think of your wanting to let him see the rabbit drive. At his age what would you have thought? He's been hearing about that brutal affair I'm sure."

Soon after dinner Horace was sent up to bed, where, after saying his prayers, he was left, and ducked his head under the covers as soon as his mother was out of the room and he was alone in darkness. He began to tell himself a long story about a rabbit drive, except that the rabbit drive would come later on in the story. He kept delaying it, wanting a very exciting situation to work up to. Gradually, however, sleep overtook him, in spite of his fear in the dark, out of which anything might come. Suppose a great jack rabbit leaped right on him through the open window. He wouldn't know what to do then. He lay still, except that at imagined sounds he peeked from under the covers. At one moment he was sure there was something standing at the foot of his bed, but he knew he'd get scolded and teased if he called out, or ran downstairs, and he would have to say of course he didn't believe in boogie mans. He wondered if Sally was scared in the dark too, if she really was, but maybe she wouldn't say so any more than he would.

He was standing way out in the dark fields, and everywhere

rabbits were nibbling about him, so many that he could not walk without stepping on them. They nibbled at his feet too, trying to eat him up. And one came running terrifically to leap at him; and after him many others came, running straight at him to knock him down and cover his face and body with their cottony bodies. They would smother him like the two princes smothered by their uncle. He couldn't move and they kept coming. Awaking, he moaned, and then, knowing it was a dream, kept quiet with his fear. Looking out from under his covers he saw the moon shining through the window, so that he could see there was no one, only his coat, at the foot of his bed. Half of his room was almost in day lightness, but back there in the corner, or in the closet—

He wanted to cry, almost, but nobody he wanted would hear him, and if there was somebody back in the corner and they heard him they'd know he was afraid. He must not cry, so as to be able to speak if they came over to get him. He must tell them that they dare not touch him; that he wasn't scared.

At last he went to sleep again.

The Laughing Funeral

DAD O'BRIEN WAS DEAD. At the fire stable they would miss his coming to sit, leaning his chair against the building while he ruminated, smoked, dozed, talked gossip, told funny stories, and knew the life stories of every person in town. Once the town mayor, he wasn't comic for everybody. Some still addressed him as Judge or as Mayor long after his sole occupations were doddering about his home and strolling to the firebarn. When Horace Darian went by his house and saw crepe on the door the place took on dignity and mystery in his mind, as did the departed.

Once, at graduation exercises, Horace had sat watching. The superintendent spoke in introduction and then the students marched up the aisle, slowly, each attempting to keep just three feet behind the one preceding. Some were consciously awkward, others vain, in their new clothes, the girls all in white dresses, which home-made, were not too well fitted. After marching in awful solemnity up the aisle they looked at the superintendent as he spoke, behind masses of carnations piled at the edge of the platform. He was speaking to them, loud enough for the audience to hear. These young people were not finishing school. They were beginning life. He said *life* with reverent emphasis, as though it was a mystery just to be revealed to them as it was already known to him and parents. Watching lumpish Pete Maitland fidgit, and others looking grotesquely intent, Horace felt a desire to snicker coming up in him. The idea of some of those going earnestly with exalted expressions into "life" could but strike the comic sense. Lizzie Potts was by name ridiculous, and so made as to stumble and knock into everybody and everything her ungainly form encountered. It was only when the class valedictorian, a girl as usual, began to deliver her address, that Horace could contain his snickers no longer. Awkwardly sprawling in an attempt to be dramatic she lifted her arms grotesquely and squawked about "living one's ideals." The occasion and the rendition were taut, unreal, mocking grandeur and sincere feeling, he felt. He held his nose, stuffed his handkerchief in his mouth, and thought of trying to pass people seated in the row to escape down the aisle and out the building. Finally his laughter broke and caught. Carrie giggled more readily, not shy, and Horace hadn't for the last year had a crush on Carrie. Now he was adoring Miss Ramsay, the orange-haired history teacher. Carrie was a rough and ready comic with whom he chummed and to see her laughing made him know that she too thought things screamingly funny. Choking sounds came from about the hall, even some of the older people catching the infectious desire to laugh.

Old man O'Brien was dead, and on Thursday morning his funeral would be held in the chapel which was rotund and inlaid inside with mosaics. It was a beautiful little chapel that should purge a person entering it of all thoughts, for reverence is not a thought but an emotion.

The Rev. Davidson was to officiate. He was young, not three years out of college. His brow was high, white, still clear with youth, as were his eyes. His sermons were always lofty, as though written as poetry is presumed to be written, blinded by fervor.

211

Because Dad O'Brien had been a Mason as well as town mayor, many people came to his funeral. People do not die or marry often in towns the size of Lansing, and have ceremonies such as ex-mayor O'Brien was to have. Others could not afford to miss his funeral. The chapel was so full of flowers that it looked as if there would scarcely be room for the chief mourners in the front row seats. There were calla lilies, white and red carnations, roses, and innumerable violets, not only because they are fitting at a funeral but because Dad liked violets. There were wreaths, baskets of flowers, and potted plants. The atmosphere was laden with fresh blossoms and heavy with the mystic silences of death and the reverence which the little chapel imposed upon people. Horace had a seat because Mrs. O'Brien remembered that her husband had always favored Horace among the town's small boys. He had whittled freakish boats, man figures, and said "You'll hear from that boy later," while assuring Horace that of course he was not to stay in Lansing and become another town loafer. Dad had wanted a son, but his wife had borne him instead six daughters.

Horace sat quietly, his wondering eyes turned towards the coffin which was submerged with flowers. He felt important for having a somewhat special seat when the chief mourners came in. They were Mrs. O'Brien, her four married daughters and their husbands, and the other two girls. All of them were in black, hats, veils, dresses, all newly bought. Mrs. Terwilliger, the oldest daughter, had a veil so long that it touched the floor, and so voluminous that it fell in misty folds along the sides of her face to bring her clear profile into sharp relief. Horace believed, with a sense of shame, that she knew this.

Both Rennie and Maggie O'Brien looked funny and self-conscious. Maggie was generally acting the clown, and Rennie was skinny and twitchily nervous, giggling constantly. They looked funnier than ever in their black clothes, which did not fit. Queerly shaped black hats roosted on their heads as though placed there in just such comedy as Maggie liked to act. The appalling thought struck Horace that he must snicker, here, while the ceremony was going on. Maggie made him think of comedy, and Carrie was sitting two rows back of him.

212

Rev. Davidson arose as soon as the chief mourners were seated. The silence was complete. One could hear the breathing of people, particularly those who breathed heavily as did old Mrs. Ford. Rev. Davidson stood erect, grave-faced, for effect. Then his voice spoke, prophetically.

"Think ye not that death is the end. It is but the regermination of the soul to be born into the everlasting."

For another suspended moment there was complete silence as Rev. Davidson waited. Only the movement of feet could be heard. "Rise up, rise up," Rev. Davidson spoke again.

Horace was horrified because Maggie O'Brien stood up, and as Rev. Davidson continued, realized that he had not meant for them to get up. Scarlet in the face she re-seated herself. Everybody saw, and the other chief mourners looked uncomfortable.

In slow, profound, tones the minister's voice went on inevitably. "Think not alone of the passing of that earthly thing, flesh. There is a power which overrides all, a power reaching down to the earth to pluck from the clay of flesh that spirit which is the flower, and the end, of life. The solitary reaper has been among us this day to gather his harvest, but that harvest is not the end. It is rather the beginning of life. As in the spring the fields are planted with barley seeds, which take from the soil their sustenance, to be harvested in the fall multiplied seven times over, aye more, man is planted into eternity to blossom refulgently in the spirit."

Horace listened to the minister's chanting voice. "Not the end but the beginning" reminded him of the commencement exercise at which he had laughed. The end is always the beginning. A flood of memory, always of ludicrous circumstances, poured into his mind. He remembered funny stories Dad had used to tell, each time with droll gestures, mimicking the person and evoking the unique circumstance of which he told. Dad had talked politics and discussed theological problems with the Rev. Davidson, winking at Horace or grimacing through the tobacco cud in his mouth to show that he was teasing the young parson. Horace found it impossible to conceive of Dad's spirit as a flower plucked. Rev. Davidson had mentioned barley, and everybody in town knew that dad had been over fond of whisky.

Both the mention of "barley" and of "spirit" made Horace see things comically rather than seriously.

A sense of the grandiloquent absurdity of these obsequies was overcoming Horace. Dad had always chuckled at the Masons for their love of pomp. About, however, was awe, the tension of reverence before death. Horace wished to hide his face, not to weep, but to shut out from his sight and hearing what was going on. His eyes wandered to Maggie O'Brien. She sat with her mouth wide open, gaping at Rev. Robinson. Her face looked foolish and she was always taking off people who look ridiculous. A snicker came up in Horace, a catch of breath between an impulse to cry for not being able to understand death and that Dad was dead, and a desire to laugh. A lady near frowned at him, but her severe expression struck him as funny. He recalled too how drolly Dad had talked about old Jake Miller's funeral.

"Why the old soak's preserved in whisky for eternity. That's it, when a man dies, give him wings. I can't see old Jake fluttering lightly heavenwards with that bay window of his, but give him wings."

Dad O'Brien's funeral was on now. Dad, who had never had respect for anything, who joked about all things sacred, jollied every parson in town, and made no pretense of having honor for the dead, was to be buried, and funeral services were being held for him. The affair was too unreal.

Horace gasped to hold his breath, put his hand into his mouth, and choked at his throat. He tried to squirm past people on his way to the aisle. Mrs. Harper looked fiercely at him, always having thought him in impudent boy. At last he reached the aisle. Just as he reached the door an explosive sound broke from him, and he bolted out, but everybody had heard the giggle. A feeling of hysterical laughter was in the air, for Carrie Farmer was trying to repress her giggles too and didn't have control to get out of her seat and out of the chapel. From various places in the chapel came repressed chokes of laughter. Kate Love rose and went to the door; Bill Cook followed soon. Outside Horace was sitting on the sidewalk, doubled up with

214

laughter so that tears streamed down his face. Kate Love was laughing too, in tears of mortification that she could not stop herself on such an occasion. Bill Cook laughed and stopped to swear at Horace. "You damn rattle-brained kid, I feel like walloping you. Stop giggling, for God's sake, stop giggling." Bill's remark only served to start them all laughing anew.

By the time the services were over, Horace, Bill, and Kate had disappeared. The next day Mrs. Harper came up the Darians' walk, and Horace was sure she was coming to tell his mother about his having laughed at Dad O'Brien's funeral. He didn't like her, and neither did his mother. She spoke severely to Mrs. Darian, and as Horace was near, started to scold him. Mrs. Darian said with fair sharpness that what reprimands Horace needed she could attend to, but Mrs. Harper kept insisting upon Horace's disgraceful conduct. Horace, recalling that Mrs. Harper was not a friend of any of the O'Briens, and that her husband had once run for Mayor against Dad O'Brien, chanced his mother's anger and answered back. He was highly indignant at her because he had no grounds whatever upon which to defend his silliness.

"Why were you at Mr. O'Brien's funeral anyway? You always gossiped about him and said he was disgraceful. As long as people like you attend funerals for something to talk about you ought to be glad I laughed to give you a chance to spread more scandal. You were running short, but I suppose you could invent gossip enough to go on. Anyway I told mother about it and don't have to listen to old dames like you scold me. You aren't a friend of mother's, and she disapproves of your butting in on other people as much as you disapprove of my laughing at the funeral."

Saying this Horace left the room. He had made a mistake however. His mother had not threshed him for laughing at the funeral, and he believed she wouldn't have threshed him for talking back to Mrs. Harper. It was, Mrs. Darian explained, his telling Mrs. Harper that she disliked her when the woman was a guest in their own home.

215

A Boy's Discovery

ARRY WRIGHT WAS A delicate boy; even more delicate than the rest of his family. In spite of the fact that his sister Nellie was pale—O pale, pale—there was the promise of a glow beneath the eggshell smoothness of her cheeks, and her wistful eyes could sparkle, so that her pallor and delicacy simply made her beauty more precious. Possibly if Harry had lived past ten years old he would have become stronger, but at nine, just six months before he caught lockjaw and died in agony, he was a frail, slender-limbed lad, with grey eyes that seemed never able to open wider in wonderment at things in life, so great was the wonder in them at all times. There was a quality too withdrawn about him, however, for him to be lovable in the way of ordinary affection.

Mr. Wright had come to South Dakota, years before because he had only one lung left, and doctors said he'd be fortunate if he lived six months more, though it's hard to understand why doctors will insist upon it being so much more fortunate to live than to die. The country air, and the climate, apparently cured him, for after twenty years he was alive, and with no noticeable trace of tuberculosis in him. A year after he had arrived he had married, and much worry about himself and about managing his affairs in general was taken off his hands, for Mrs. Wright was a grand and capable woman, out of Chicago. She rented out farms he had come to own, managed their little department store in the small village of Lansing. Every Sunday she would go to church, always in a much finer black dress than other mothers wore, and they all wore black silk or satin dresses to church, believing it not seemly for mothers of families to appear in giddy colors. Mrs. Wright's dresses, though, were criticized somewhat, but quietly, because she was haughty and indifferent to people, anyone could judge, though her manner was courteous even if it was aloof. But her dresses were usually of fine black lace, and she wore a bustle that made the folds of material in her gown stand out around her hips, long after bustles had passed out of style. Her hats too were modish, not in the style of the day, but in a distinctive way, and upon her hands she wore fine lace gloves. The train of her dress was generally long enough to sweep the church floor and soil itself on the dust there.

Mr. Wright, following her absentmindedly, with his weak eyes trying to strain ahead through very thick glasses, was like a trusting, utterly helpless dog, blind with old age. If Harry had been left to Mr. Wright's care alone, the boy would have poisoned himself at once eating candy from the stock kept in their stores, and gorging on fruit all of the time, so that he never would eat at mealtimes, which Mrs. Wright found it hard to compel him to do anyway. Harry had always been a frail child, and not disobedient, but not happy. Everything that could be done for him was done. He read much, didn't care for toys, and didn't know how to play with other children in town, who were always a little rowdy, and mischievous as though they believed that it is necessary to be that so people will remark "boys will be boys." Harry didn't like wetting his clothes, or muddying his shoes, because these things felt uncomfortable and he knew they might make him sick. He didn't like to tie cans to the tails of dogs, because that didn't make him split with laughter; it only made him sorry for the dogs.

All in all Mrs. Wright was delighted when Harold Morris came to town, and Harry seemed able to get on capitally with him, for Harold, while delicate looking too, was able to take care of himself with other boys in town, and wouldn't stand for being called "sissy." After a while he wouldn't stand for having Harry called that either, because he realized how much sickness Harry had had all his life. Strangers seeing the two of them together mistook them for brothers, perhaps twins, for Harry was usually flushed and excited and nervously happy when he was with Harold, since he was at these times always learning things he hadn't known before, and playing games such as doctor, or lawyer, or minister, or some game that Harold would invent so they wouldn't have to run about too much since Harry always tired when he tried to climb to the top of the town elevator to get young pigeons, and one time had nearly fainted halfway up the town watering pipe which stood over a hundred feet high in the air. By the time Harold had held him up and helped him down from that he never again would lead him into anything that took much daring or strength.

Summer was on, and vacation. Through the days all the boys in town would play about Main Street, catching rides on farm wagons and buggies coming and going from town, or performing stunts on the iron bars that ran between hitching posts in front of the village grocery stores. There weren't more than ten boys of their age in town since the whole population of Lansing was but two hundred people. Sometimes they'd roll their pants up as far as possible and wade in the pond down by the mill, or straddle a log and row; again they'd go out into the country and of course by the time they'd gotten out a ways some of them would tire, or would be afraid they'd get a licking from their mothers and would turn back. So often Harold and Harry were left to go on alone, which Harry could never have done by himself, but Mrs. Wright had decided that Harold could take care

218

of both of them. Naturally Harry looked to Harold for information, and asked him questions he'd always been shy of asking older poeple, and wouldn't, because of boyish contempt, ask other boys—Tuffy Thomas, Gordon Rensch, Wallace Spear.

About a quarter of a mile out of town was a farm where they could stop and get milk to drink—sweet milk or buttermilk. The daughter of the family was a "Mrs." Richardson, who had a boy three years old, and who worked for Harold's mother sometimes, sewing, or washing. Harold rather understood why his mother said of her that "she shouldn't have to pay forever for an error made when she was so young a girl as sixteen," but he had little curiosity. He liked Mrs. Richardson, and she would always give him cake, and buttermilk, whenever he came out to the farm to see her. Her father and mother were kind to him too, rather liking to have him call on them, because that indicated that his folks did not disapprove of their daughter overmuch, they thought.

As summer deepened, and there had been no rain for weeks, almost every day would find Harold and Harry at this farm, because the village streets were a foot deep in dust so that it was no fun catching rides, or playing on the bars between hitchingposts. Mrs. Wright, and Harold's folks came to know that if the boys weren't home at noon, and weren't home till seven o'clock at night, they were safe, and would get their meals at the farm.

The grain fields were ripening about the farm. The boys would sit and dream stories of their future to each other. A pulsation and vibration of clear life and light was about in the clover-scented air; even about the barns was a clean odor, a mixture of fresh hay and of fresh manure.

"I like the odor of horse manure, and it isn't dirty, it's only made up of grainseed husks and hay. You just think it's dirty because of how it comes about," Harold would say sometimes.

For an hour at a time they would rest in the shade of a haystack without speaking, still widely awake, and alertly conscious of each other, of nature, of life. The silence seemed potent with great significance. Out in the pasture they could see cattle browsing, or resting as they chewed their cuds complacently—

arrogantly disdainful some of them. On the other side of a fence dusty sheep were pastured, and bleated, as they strolled about nipping on dry, hooftrod grass that they'd nipped close to the earth; in an individual pasture was a bronze-colored bull, that at times would paw the earth sullenly, lowing ominously. Off the side of his pasture was another in which a bay stallion was kept, and at times it would stand with its head lifted high up, its eyes dilated, as it snorted and neighed, and its mane was blowing as it stood in the wind. In the farm yard were many trees, all green with foliage. The umbrella trees seemed a green eruption like a spring that spurted a thick green spray which fell in equal arches on all sides. Across the road, as a background to the farm house, was a forest which ran for a quarter of a mile, and was for that space a green avalanche which flooded the landscape. If the boys went into that woods they saw many birds, and would follow some of the flamingly beautiful ones. A golden oriole would flit, flame-bosomed, through the dark green foliage; a goldfinch would cheep and flutter about; rose grosbeaks, scarlet tanagers, olive kinglets, brown thrushes came fleetingly, and some of them would hop and flutter about on the spongy mosslike soil in the woods for a time. Pungent odor and life all fresh were about everywhere.

The wheat fields were ripening, caressed to sleek maturity by the sun as a calf is licked by the tongue of its fond mother, and upon its bosom the sunlight poured and rippled so that across its gold expanse was continual gentle breathing. Young turkeys went hopping and fluttering over fences into pastures, searching for bugs, and worms.

"You and I will have to be together always, won't we, Harold?" Harry would comment sometimes, and looking at Harry's face in answer a feeling of sorrow would be in Harold, because he didn't know that he even liked Harry, or was anything but sorry for him. He felt that Harry was somebody that needed to be taken care of, and that next time the family moved—Harold's family was always moving—he'd remember him as he remembered Lloyd of a year ago, dimly, as though he were hardly a real person.

220

"I have never loved anybody like I do you. I don't like people," Harry would say again.

"How do you know? How could you love people—your mother and father who always give you medicine, and those kids in town who tear around—you never are with them to know them like you have been with me," Harold would answer him, and would often wish to be alone, or with some other boy who would climb about, and adventure more than Harry. Still, every morning, when a bunch of the boys were out on the street, he and Harry naturally joined each other, and separated from the others to go out to this farm.

One day the two of them watched while a mare that had been brought out to the farm was bred, and saw the excitement of the stallion, heard him neigh and whisper groaningly.

"What does he do that for?" Harry asked while the act of breeding was going on.

"So there will be a colt. That's how young things are always made," Harold explained.

"Not babies—not us—the doctor brings babies," Harry said, shocked.

"Rats, that's a fairy story like Santa Claus. Men and women do that same thing,—only a man's thing isn't quite as big as a stallion's," Harold declared a little impatiently.

Harry was silent. A feeling of nausea and horror was numbing him inside himself.

"Don't you remember the afternoon that Tuffy Thomas came out of Casserly's barn and told you and I to go away, that he and Hazel were going to have a good time together. . . I knew they couldn't really—too young. You have to be grown up to be able. But Tuffy swore that he got his thing in. I don't believe him though. He likes to brag."

Harry did not speak for some time, until at last: "But it isn't really that way—not my mother and father, I know—they couldn't do that—I tell you what I think—they just pray and God sends a baby to them."

"O don't be foolish. You ask Mrs. Richardson. A man puts his thing in a woman somewhere, I don't know where, and then

221

after nine months she has a baby. You ask Tuffy, or Hazel Casserly, or any of the older fellows. It's no use asking your father and mother. They tell you fairy tales. You don't suppose it happens one way with animals and another with people, do you?"

For days Harry could do nothing but ask questions about how babies are made. The other boys about town had their curiosity too. Whenever a group of them were together and sitting down where they could talk the conversation would turn to that subject, and each would have a theory about the act.

"I tell you I know how it's done; I've done it with Hazel," Tuffy would delcare. "I'll get her and show you."

One day,—it had rained the night before and the roads were too muddy to walk out to the farm—Harry, Tuffy, Gordon, and Harold were playing about the barn in back of the grocery store. A rack full of hay stood beneath the loft door, and they were turning somersets in the hay as they jumped out of the barn-loft door to hay in the rack, ten feet below. After they'd been doing this for a time they all sat along the edges of the rack to get their breath, and to talk. When they had been seated there for a while Tuffy Thomas saw Hazel Casserly and Ruthie Jenkins. "Hey girls, come on over, I want to ask you something," he called to them. The girls came over, and climbed up into the rack.

"These fellows don't believe that you and I did—you know what, Hazel," Tuffy said.

"Why you awful boy. I never did, and you know you said you wouldn't tell. Anyway you couldn't when you did try. Nothing happened at all,"Hazel said.

"You liar!" Tuffy responded.

After some talk Hazel's indignation subsided, and Ruthie, who declared she thought they were all being nasty, also began to talk, and wonder if babies really come about the way they thought they did.

"I'll tell you, let's go inside the loft, and you girls show us what you have, and we'll show you and maybe try and see if we can make anything happen," Tuffy said at last.

"There's no use trying that. Nothing does happen until

you're at least fourteen, and you don't get any feeling till then anyway. I've heard older fellows talk," Harold broke in.

Hazel and Ruthie said they wouldn't think of it, and that the boys were dirty things to mention that, but after a time they weren't so sure, and finally Hazel said she would let each boy look, but one at a time, and the others would have to stand away while he was looking. So Ruthie agreed to this also.

"If I let any one of you try to do anything with me it will be Harold—or Harry—they aren't so nasty as the rest of you, but Harry's too nice a boy to want to, aren't you Harry?" Ruthie said.

Harry could say nothing. His heart was beating at a terrific rate. He was—not afraid—terrified rather with shame.

After they had all looked at the girls, and tried to understand how things were done, Tuffy said he could demonstrate. Hazel refused, saying that she wouldn't, not with anybody but Harold, and he said he wouldn't, not with everybody looking on, but he would try if they'd all go away and leave him and Hazel alone together, and if Harry would go on one side of the loft with Ruthie, while he and Hazel were on the other side. After Harold, Hazel, Ruthie, and Harry, had all sworn that they would tell just what happened and how it felt, the others went out, and after much exclamations and accusations, to the rest that they were peeking, Harold and Harry tried.

"I couldn't feel anything but a feeling like when your hands have gone to sleep and there's a tingle in them," Harold explained.

"We couldn't do anything at all—how can a thing go in when it's soft I don't understand," Ruthie assured the others, and a little later, after explanation, asked Harold in a whisper if he'd try with her sometime, when nobody knew.

From that time on Harry seemed to care less for Harold, and wouldn't play much with him or any of the boys, but it may not have been his discovery, or the actions of that day. School had started a few days after, and his mother, saying that he'd had a free time all summer, kept him around home much, and told Harold that he'd better come up and play inside with Harry so they could get their lessons together, but Harold, not liking to be indoors and never studying anyway, would not go very often. About two weeks after school had started it rained hard one day, and Harry got his feet wet, so that a bad cold attacked him, and his throat became inflamed. He was out of school for a week. When he returned he was pale, and for the next two months coughed much, was always sickly and tired, without an interest in anything. Harold was sorry for him, and for Mrs. Wright, but he couldn't make Harry happy even by being with him because the cough and sore throat kept him miserable all the time whether someone was with him or not.

It was three months after school started before Harry was really well again, and even then he was apathetic and lifeless. Then very suddenly he died. A case of lockjaw developed within a day, he could not speak, or move his mouth; he was in agony, and when Harold went to see him his eyes had nothing but the light of torture in them. It was a great relief when he died. It is horrible to watch somebody suffer and be able to do nothing.

"No, I'm not sorry he's dead. He never would have been wild about life if he had lived, any more than I ever will be," Harold told Tuffy Thomas, and Tuffy was shocked, saying that was no way to talk about a dead person.

Machine-Age Romance

S A MODERN I naturally am fascinated by turbines, glistening pistons thrusting, motors, and all things mechanical which shine. I have stood watching the thrust of steel carrying a funicular to a mountain top. I stood several times in the engine room loft looking down at motors and rods which propelled our ships towards, first, the Panama Canal, and then Los Angeles.

"Are those things pumping water for the ship?" Miss Forbes asked me, and I knew she was gaining courage to venture speaking. She was tiny, shriveled, and bewildered looking as a worried monkey. Her cheeks were ruddier for having been two days at sea, and her tiny figure sagged less than it had.

"They are what make the ship go," I told her. "Aren't they wonderful?"

"Oh yes," she sighed, and dared further. "You're a great lover of music, aren't you? I hear you playing that machine, but I didn't come in because I thought then you wouldn't play the pieces you like best. You have an ear for pretty things."

"You can play the phonograph, but there are only a few records."

"Oh I couldn't play that machine. I've never heard one before. What is it you call it?"

"A phonograph. It's easy to start and stop," I answered, curious of a person her age who had never heard one before and who was in awe of it.

You know how rotogravure sections carry photographs of skyscrapers and mechanical devices: smoke stacks, metal carriers and dumpers, glistening pistons, etc. They write of glass or steel skyscrapers to be, and painters even use machinery to make abstract designs. It's the machine age, you understand. various European magazines have talked of it for some years, and now American periodicals are taking it up. The British are slower, but they are a conservative race anyway. Even among them, though, Wyndham Lewis discovered some years back that forms made by engineers can have an "art" significance, forced upon them by sheer structural necessity, mind you. A modern like myself would know about that sort of thing, and might even have thought that humanity and his or her emotions became standardized so long ago that machinery might invent a new kind of standardization which for a time would not be banal. What was I to think, confronted by Miss Forbes?

I walked down the deck towards the bow, and Miss Forbes knew she and I had struck it off. She followed and we stood at the bow. The sun which will sink every day was still shedding bright colors on the horizon, and porpoises plunged beside the ship, racing it until they found this a silly pastime. Flying fish shot into the air and flew various distances, blue and shimmery as glass hummingbirds in the spray of water about their iridescent wings. It was our bad luck that the ship was too high for any of them to fly on board. The ship cat was only a kitten, so wouldn't have known how to devour them anyway, no doubt.

"It's lovely, isn't it?" Miss Forbes asked. "I love pretty things."

I asked her if she had ever been at sea before, or out of England. "I was in Australia and New Zealand with my mother, and I remember as if it was yesterday. I'm going to Vancouver. I have a friend who wrote me a year ago to come and stay with her, but mother just left me three months ago, so I couldn't get away till now. Do you suppose I could go to Australia for a visit after I've been in Vancouver for a time? My sister is in Australia, but she might not want me and I'd not want to be too far from Vancouver."

"It's over a month from Vancouver, I'm sure. You might ask the Captain. How long since you were there last?"

"Fifty years. I was twenty-seven when mother took me. But I can't go now. I could if it took only eight days. I like to travel by sea. How long before we will be in Vancouver?"

"It will be about thirty-five days more for you. I get off at Los Angeles," I said, wondering at her simplicity.

"Oh," she sighed. "But time does pass quickly. We've been on the sea three days now. There is so much to think about. I was frightened the first day and didn't dare come down to meals. Mother was ailing the last twenty years and I couldn't leave her, but to buy groceries, for a few minutes a day."

What could eight or thirty days mean to Miss Forbes, I wondered, visualizing her fifty years of tranquil life in an English village where she had never heard a phonograph. She was a playmate for me. There were ten other passengers besides her and me on the cargo boat which took passengers. One was an English Lily boy who shared my cabin. He was up on Proust, Cocteau, Gide, Brancusi, Picasso, modern art that is, but it would take more than thirty days at sea for his chatter to interest me. His sort of thing was what I was rather seeking to escape. The retired army captain talked of what France, America, England, or somebody should have done during the war, and his wasn't an interesting line either. The captain wrote poetry, he confided to me wistfully. He gladly showed it to me, disclaiming greatness. It was about unrest, longing for home, far places, dream loves, the sea, with mysticism and a legendary note now and then. Some of it had appeared in shipping journals. His stories had a brave tone and a manly moral, but he didn't find *The Nigger of the Narcissus* a good portrayal of sea life. He had books

227

to lend me, some of which I had always planned to read when I could get thoroughly into them: Doughty's *Arabia Deserta*, *Confessions of an English Opium Eater*, Herodotus, Thucydides, Browning's poems, and these, with travel books and memoirs in the ship library, would last a few days, and after that I might try reading the Bible as a literary production. I was skeptical however. Too many of my bereaved father's friends had used to say that any man who had read the Bible and Shakespeare was a cultured man, and I supposed that meant they had. They weren't my idea of culture, not that I over-rate that either.

It was no help to my machine-age soul that sixtyish-year old Mrs. Brisbane talked of reincarnation and was sure that I had lived before. Her husband mildly agreed with whatever she said, and they were an ideal old couple who had loved each other throughout the years, but their cabin was next mine and I heard her tell him that people aboard would think him illiterate. He never talked and if he did, said nothing. I had no feeling of having lived before, either. I was a victim of modern ennui of a temporal sort. In bars, cabarets, and other joints, I drank and led a strenuous life whenever in a city of the size which permitted it. Reflection, contemplation, resignation, were ideas I knew of, and had even tried, but I was still a vulgar young soul seeking life as action. Her messages gave me no solution. The other people aboard were elderly ladies that an unkinder generation called old-maids, though one of them was male. Just the same a spinster is a spinster, and surely none of these had experienced the revelation. They looked askance at me when I tried to address a cheery word of greeting to them. They had no conception of gregariousness as I have. Plainly I'd have no one to drink with except the Captain and he disapproved mildly of intoxication. I hate solitary drinking.

I naturally was pleased to find Miss Forbes a comfey soul, who took to me. I won't get photographic on her because soon some camera will photograph psychologies down to the last gelatinous quiver of the hyper-neurasthenic sensibility sensitizing itself before the lens to display, enlarged, every dementia,

228

mania, inhibition, and aberration, and then where will Dostoevsky, Joyce, and Lawrence be, let alone the mere two-dimensional recorders of life?

Miss Forbes hadn't a complex I could detect but possibly I'm so modern complexes are old-fashioned for me, and maybe I'm mechanical myself which means I operate to the pattern. Complexes can't turn out anything standardized and she wasn't that. The word *frustration* puzzled her though, when the English Lily used it, but Mrs. Brisbane looked very bright indeed about it, wanting us all to realize that one does encounter informed and interesting people in strange places.

"The sky is so pretty," Miss Forbes told me. "I never knew if there were flying fish or not. Are all those things we see all the time sharks or whales? I wanted to ask somebody?"

"They are porpoises, seapigs, and quite harmless," I said, feeling grand about being right there with information. "Are you finding it restful on the sea? I wish there were more books aboard to read. I read fast."

"I have a book I will lend you," Miss Forbes quavered, with eager timidity. "It's a sweet book. About a poor old lady who is left without money. She begins to wander the streets and forgets everything. She is so hungry, and the city is big and nobody knows her. But some nice people find her and the book is happy at the end. I liked the book. Would you like to read it?"

"Yes, do lend it to me," I said, feeling that Miss Forbes was revealing too much of her life and inner emotions to me. She surely was talking more than her wont, because her voice bled, and she was pathetically, sweetly tender and concerned about the plight of the story book old lady. "Your mother must have been rather old when she died." I suggested.

"She was one-hundred-and-three, but she always told me how to manage until the end. Till just three days before she went away. She wasn't conscious then." Miss Forbes' voice was simple, but not sad. I suggested going in to play the phonograph, but she said, "It's so sweet watching the pretty sunset. I love the water. I haven't talked to anybody since I came aboard. You are nice to talk to me."

I couldn't look too closely at her, but I did see she was not hump-backed or a dwarf. She was tiny and withered, but well proportioned. Did she know there had been a war? I asked by saying that times must have been hard during the war.

"But our town was so quiet, and I hadn't ever been outside much, but mother did miss her sugar. We never ate much," Miss Forbes said. A vision of her seventy-seven years of limpidly tranquil life passed through my mind, and fifty years of it in one small house, with an aged mother. Yes, the machine age. Jazz and excitement and sensation seeking, and the world of science and new intellectual worlds to conquer in a universe of new dimensions in variable relativities all at a speedier velocity.

We went into the ship parlour to play the Gramophone. It was nicely companionable to have Miss Forbes growing rosy with delight and restraining herself from moving in rhythmic joy. She found Galli-Curci, when rendering *Caro Nomé*, sweet and pretty. I adored it as burlesque, remembering the falsetto wailings of female interpreters who render the Flower Song ecstatically. The voice trilled its gymnastics, twirled, walked the tight wire, and ended in a glory of brilliantissimo contortions. Miss Forbes didn't care anymore than did I for the sweet Irish voice of diseased tenor with which McCormack sang "Mother Machree." She liked the "Blue Danube." That was sweet. She grew flushed with joy, and because she had trusted me when I assured her that one port wine would do her no harm. Dardenella excited her more, though, and "On the Beach at Miami" was her favourite record throughout the trip. Yes, indeed, Miss Forbes and the machine-age myself got on very well together. She had the instincts of a jazz baby for music.

The ship docked at San Pedro and I stood impatiently waiting to be allowed to descend. It would have been pathetic, I might then have thought, if in my rush I forgot Miss Forbes, but there she was at my elbow, to quaver a goodbye. She was sorry I was going because she didn't know who would play the machine for her now. She knew she couldn't learn to run it. I believe she thought me a great musician, but she was skeptical of the Captain's talent, and Mrs. Brisbane would talk of "fine music" and sigh regretfully that there were not better records on the ship. Miss Forbes told me she would always remember me, and if she lived to be as old as her mother had lived, that would be some years for anybody to remember a runabout like myself. She hadn't know many people ever. I had a panicky thought for her. What if her friend did not meet her in Vancouver? Something may have happened in the year since she had written.

I landed and was in a taxi towards Los Angeles, however, seeing any variety of hot dog stands, an aviation field, and soon skyscrapers. I would not have to know my own machine-age land through rotogravure sections any more. It's strange, but I felt something "hick" in the atmosphere, when I was headed towards Hollywood, which many bright people claim now gives the world her fashions. Why that feel of hick when it was all machinery, modern, and stylish about me?

Miss Forbes would get on, I mechanically concluded. I had had a moment before leaving her of thinking I'd kiss her good-bye, but decided it wouldn't be delicate as she might be fussed. She didn't feel herself a pathetic little old lady, and I, instead of pitying her lostness, might envy her simplicity. Anyway, the romance with her was finished. In Los Angeles, New York, wherever I headed, I would want the latest model romance, geared up to seven or twelve speeds.

Light Woven into Wavespray

**E**VERYTHING IS JOY ON this beach, I can tell you. The girls are ready to laugh with you, and sunshine is free, very free," the Spanish boy remarked, after he'd told me that Paris was the only city that made him as happy as Mexico City. He rubbed his brown legs in the sand, running his hand up and down his thigh, perhaps because the sunshine and the salt sting of the air made him like the feel of his own body. It was evident he was proud of his body's beauty.

"In Paris they know too well when they are happy; here they are just happy. I have known lightheartedness like this but a few times—in Tampico when I was a little boy, in Mexico City when things were gay, and on this beach in other years."

Jaredo Musice, he called himself. He had told me his name with a lingering intonation upon its syllables. I listened to him casually, because of a lack of interest I have in strangers, and

232

also because of phrases he used such as "these people," "the crowds here," used in such a way as to give the impression that he was not one of the many, but was always an onlooker. I was tired of sophistication, and of "onlookers." It isn't enough to look on at life and detect its unique gestures, and succeed but poorly at feeling its emotions. I hadn't come to the beach to talk to somebody with an intellect, not while the sunshine was full of capricious caresses, and the ocean breezes came in bearing peace and vigor in its arms to lay next to my heart.

It was enough to rest on the sand desiring nothing, knowing nobody. Many children in tiny bathing suits that sagged round their skinny or plump limbs dabbled in the sand, thrust timid feet into the waves that tossed up as though playfully trying to frighten them. Some of them would cry out to their mothers occasionally, but even in the fretting and scolding of their mothers was a quality of contentment.

Then there were the young girls with modestly scant bathing suits upon them, modest enough so that there was no pretense of concealing the fact that they had nice limbs and knew it. Some of them had laughed at me; I had talked to some of them, and knew that when I felt like it, I could run out into the water and splash and be splashed by them. I didn't know but what a nice one of them would have dinner with me, and dance with me. One never knows what girls on a beach may do, until one explores.

"It was but yesterday that I have saved a woman's life— young and beautiful. She has told me I was a brave man; that I should come and see her." Jaredo spoke, and it flitted across my mind that I was too tired to be skeptical. "You will see her?" I asked, since it's not hard to be gracious and one desires graciousness oneself so often. Anyway there was the sand to lie on and the sunshine to abstract oneself into.

"No, no I shall not see her. That is done with. One should never attempt to complete such experience with intimacy. I have learned that in life. The fancy serves much better than the fact," he answered. "My God, the voice of all the tired culture in the world is speaking to me," I thought. I was weary, before coming down to the beach, of realizing how little satisfaction there is in facing actuality, so was not ready to take up the conversation on that strain. Consequently I said nothing.

A slow wave of apathy, akin to nausea, submerged my consciousness. It occurs to me at times that there is a pathologic quality in my aversion to people at some times, and particularly to the unknown person who makes himself an individual out of a crowd by speaking to me. Here, with the sunlight flickering in sprays of gold sandust around me I should have been of the texture of that irresponsible brightness. But one mood, sea mood, one sheen, sun sheen, and one fibre—that of the light alchemized breeze patting the brine of the ocean's rhythmic tranquillity upon the beach, fitted the place, and I had fitted the place because of naïveté in me, until this person—who had naïveté in him too for that matter—had estranged me from its quality. Like figures in a kaleidoscopic design people in colored garments, in bathing suits, resting under huge beach parasols; expectant, air-sniffing, inquisitive canines, seaside candy and refreshment booths, wove themselves into the atmosphere. The occasion should have been taken for joy of light and movement, of the tint of flesh on young people exuberant with vanity about their own symmetry; for my own moment-ago buoyant conceit of being... Then it struck me that I was caught at a moment of Philistinism, ready to battle with the doggedness of mediocrity not to have my little moment of contentment annihilated by the travail of thought. Indeed there is more than sheep willingness to conform in the ordinary insistence upon convention; there is terror, in a manner, that facing life more barely means the loss of much personal security, and—also of happiness. It is not amongst the conformers of life that combat is most vicious.

He had me. I was forced to converse with him, to tell him that there is such a thing as will; that one might as well complete any experience that seems desirable and take the pain of discovering its futility if there is the tedious tragedy of disillusionment in its acceptance. Fearsome inaction is a bitterer experience than any other.

234

The conversation was uninforming. I had known that he was an embittered adolescent, with an intellect that justified his unhappy emotions on the ground of spirituality. Probably I could more than compete with him at the little game of soul-tormenting, but there he was, inflicted upon me because of sympathetic understanding in me, making me disgusted with him, with myself, while I came back with emphasis to a disgust at life. It was such as he that drove me away from youth my own age to people double that age, and irritating they were to me too because of "maturity," which is quite generally a complacent sinking into "I used to think that too" sort of attitude. Having, in an attempt to bolster up his spirit, thrown myself into the morbid agonies, I then took command saying: "We'll forget such talk for a while. There's two likely looking girls, let's ask them if they'll dance with us," and suited the action to the idea. It was necessary to go about the matter with some subtlety — about that of an elephant's tramp through the forest — and the girls said they would like to dance, and were direct and un-kittenish about their acceptance. When we had all gone into the bathhouse and dressed, and Jaredo and I saw them again, there was in me the self-congratulatory feeling that I always did have a good eye when it came to judgments of some sorts. Very trim, slender, and good class were both of the girls, and the one I chose to walk with had misty grey eyes and ashed pepper-red hair. A better humor had by now returned.

A waltz was being played at the dancehall as we entered; a heavy cadenced, deep-colored waltz, which beat into the rhythm of my emotions at once, drowning my mental will. One needs never be bothered by intellectual ideas in dancing, not when Leona—the name of the girl with me—will dance as though she, I, and the music are one, and that one a langorous rhythm. And the odor of her hair was cleanly scentless; the touch of her cheek as—as smooth as only the touch of a Leona's cheek can be. She knew how to laugh as though there is nothing but laughter. Leona is the only girl to love—Leona who one meets on a beach in California, dances and laughs with, and never sees again, because Leona is leaving for somewhere tomorrow. . . and it's too bad if she isn't leaving and one does see her again after having told so many friends what a beautiful girl one picked up casually.

The sun went down, but we being in the dancehall did not see it; there was for us the music, the moment of shuffling feet and light bodies that danced delightfully, because who but good dancers would be at the beach on a weekday, and presume to get on that floor to dance to that melancholy swaying undercurrent-sobbing music of minor ecstacy?. . . So we danced. . . and later as we said goodbye to Leona, and Daisy, the sulphurous illumination that plays out over the ocean waves some nights, only some nights, was out there this night. Goodbye to Leona, as the mystic lights hover above the brine and the satin swish of waves sends water up sand on the beach to run down again, quicksilver mirroring yellow sparkling moon and star reflections at the sky.

So Jaredo and I were left together, and when we had walked a ways and talked some he said: "That was a lighthearted time, wasn't it; but then such times accomplish nothing."

An insistent irritation swole within me against Jaredo; and I knew that much of the irritation was against him because he echoed my own thoughts. "What is accomplishing something?" I asked him impatiently, and my intellect was condemning my own brooding emotions for not taking a situation and extracting all the joyous gaiety there is in it, and accepting it for the moment's satisfaction.

From the ocean came the muted sound of a passing ship's whistle; the lap of waves softly tossing; from the city came the dim clangor of streetcars banging on their rails, the whisper of voices of many people that made an irregular insistent murmur. A few beach booth sellers still called out their wares. Sadness lay itself upon my spirit; I knew it had lain itself upon Jaredo's spirit; but beneath the melancholy in us both was driving unrest and bitterness. I could feel in his voice that a rasp of detesting discontent with life, a harsh sense of frustration, would not let his moods be gentle inwardly. And condemnation of him arose within me, since it is so futile to storm and fret inside oneself, so stupid, and little able to change conditions. To evade riding in the streetcar with him back to the city I explained that I would go and stay with a friend I knew in the beachtown, and I knew no one.

Going back to town on a later car, I moped, alternately blaming myself for foolish romantic yearnings; saying to myself that I, detesting sentimentality, was more sentimental about myself—always myself—than anybody ever had been about anything else, and then I would protest to defend myself that life is wrong, oppressive—people are dull, mercenary, and selfish—but so was I, as Jaredo had been. Together had either of our groping individual desires accepted the plight of the other to help make the passing friendliness of the moment one of sympathetic response.

I was a fool—with hungry blood, hungry spirit, and a mean narrow mind—why couldn't I understand that all people are caught, and try to give in a way I desired to get—my heart seemed running to liquid that poured through me diffusing across my chest, sinking into my stomach, a thick warm sickening liquid of sadness, that made me feel incompetent to go on—and my mind has a virulent detestation for melancholy and incompetence.

Some moments at the swelling urge of a violent protest against—against what?—only a driving protest, it seemed that blood vessels in me would have to burst, the cords and veins of my neck taut—would I ever be reasonable about life?

The wind coming through the window of the streetcar was clean, and sometimes brought sweet odors to my nostrils; the night was lovely grey flesh with an amber glow about it; the night was peaceful—and I was riding through it, hopeless with vanities, and ambitions that I could not even locate to myself. But gradually the clear air made me feel a little happy.

237

Evening on the Riviera

T BEING SIX O'CLOCK EVENING, two hours before dinner, Toodles had already begun to talk about how she would not serve cocktails, to herself, or to the other people about her, that night.

"I'm through; not another cocktail does anyone get from me for three weeks, so unless you all love me for myself—and you do love your Toodles, don't you?—you needn't come around. The General tells me I've run into my next quarter's allowance. Think of it, my bill for drinks last month was over three thousand francs, and that doesn't include things I sneaked through on the General by paying for them on the spot," Toodles, otherwise Mrs. Dawson, chortled.

To see Toodles one had best think back forty, or even forty-five years, when she was a girl of between fifteen and twenty. She must then have been a cuddling, elfish creature, full of high spirits, and confiding, neverending prattle. She still saw herself as a joybird, claimed to be but forty-five years old, and explained that the photograph of her three sons, the youngest of whom could not be less than thirty-three, must make her seem aged, but she'd married so young, at seventeen. About the question of age, however, her own, or anybody's, she was shy, and inclined to halt for a moment in her prattle, distrustfully.

"I'm sure she's still a beautiful woman, and that men are as wild about her as ever," she was inclined to comment if some friend of her earlier days was mentioned. Toodles bore no one ill will, except at moments when they stood in the way of her desire to bubble on, irresistibly seeking to be the center of attention.

"I must dress for dinner now," she told Allen Cowles, who was thrumming out jazz on her piano after others had left the room. "And of course you'll stay, and play music for me. And listen," she whispered, "I'll make you just one wee little cocktail, but don't you tell the General. You know, there's nobody can make cocktails like your Toodles, is there?"

Tonight, Toodles, always high-spirited in action, was feeling more than usually high spirited as she'd rested much in the last few days. Her right eye, that became decidedly crooked at moments of fatigue, looked almost direct, and a flush was on her cheeks so that her face flesh looked firmer and younger too. It could not actually matter how old Toodles became; she'd remain somewhat elfish, exuberant, and primitively childlike to the end.

Because she could not abide living with her sons and their wives, not to mention the places they'd chosen to live in— South Africa, and two other out of the way places—Toodles had for the last two years been a paying guest in the home of an ex-Russian general and his wife. What other paying guests stayed were generally friends of Toodles who liked staying with her because of the constant stream of people around her. Toodles did not want to be alone much more than five minutes at a time, during daytime, and not at all during the evening until she retired. For this reason, the General and his wife, Madame Cavallera, found her at moments wearing because she'd be at them during busy hours to chat with her.

Remaining at the piano Allen Cowles began playing Puccini, which he and Toodles adored. As soon as he started an aria from *Tosca* an exclamation of delight came from Toodles' room, and she appeared at the doorway loosening her day dress at the shoulder. Standing, posed dramatically, she raised her hand and began to sing with mighty fervor. That section finished she said.

"Did I tell you the joke on the General? He heard me singing while he was working in the garden and asked his wife who was the woman with the wonderful voice. I could have made a go of it when I was younger, but Fred wouldn't have it. No sir, he wanted his little Toodles in his own home, and I must say never a moment's worry did he ever give me because of his attentions to other women. That's why I've remained single these ten years he's been gone, though many a chance I've had; and the Princess Gurn tells me I'm foolish not to take a lover."

Allen went on playing, as Toodles slipped back to her room. He was a young American she'd picked up weeks back when he was playing jazz music at a casino dance, and Toodles said she could see at once he was more of a gentleman than jazz players are usually. At any rate it was quite the thing at the moment to be enthusiastic about jazz, and to entertain jazz players.

"You're my boy, aren't you, Allen?" Toodles commented, coming out of her room, dressed now in a black dinner dress that fell in loose folds about her short, rotund, figure. "See, I'm wearing this string of pearls for you tonight. The General makes me keep them in the vault in Paris for fear I'll be tempted to pawn them sometime, and he's right too. I always need a man to look after my money affairs for me. Smell me. Isn't that wonderful perfume? Now I tell you, there'd be less unhappiness in marriage if all women know how to handle and please men the way I did Fred. I always dressed so he'd be proud of me; kept the house cheerful, full of flowers, and fresh odors, and he never ceased being my lover."

There was a shout to Toodles from outside, so she slipped to the balcony which overlooked a mountain and seascape outside her room.

240

"Ha, ha, there's another one of my boys. And your Juliet speaks to you from the balcony. Come on up Eddie; you'll stay for dinner. And just one cocktail, no more, remember, but don't say anything to the General. He's been frowning at me for the last three days because of my drink bills, and declares he doesn't know how he can manage to make my allowance meet everything if I go on."

Eddie Campbell, Toodles declared, looked on the dark side of things, but not when he was around her. "I give you a cocktail, dance with you while Allen plays, and you feel better, don't you? What you're needing is a woman with the right disposition to keep you cheered up," she informed him some minutes after he'd come up. They were standing together on the balcony looking at twilight come over the mountains and ocean, as Allen was playing the love music from *Tristan and Isolde*. As he played Toodles chanted a phrase, and gestured with her hand over her heart to Allen, and then to Eddie. When the music ceased, she stopped her fervent gesturings and came back to the balcony, waving in her right hand a long ivory cigarette holder.

"Now I'm a woman of the world, and you mustn't think that I don't have profound thoughts. As Fred's wife, when he was Ambassador to Munich, and in circles that I've always been drawn into, I had to know how to parry a point and how to conduct myself. It's a matter of philosophy for me to be cheerful. I say, keep the bluebird in your house, and in your heart. Now look at nature, that sea beneath the colorings in the sky, and the mountains. You Eddie, you should certainly be able to write poems of ecstasy on that. Ah, ah, ah,—well, but let's stop mooning, and I'll slip into my little kitchen and make my boys one of Toodles' cocktails, you know them. But just one."

"Not tonight for me Toodles, I think," Edward said. "I don't want to get buffy tonight; have to work tomorrow."

"Now, now, you want cheering up, and Allen there's looking thirsty."

Edward chuckled. "Neither of us would insist on one, Toodles; I'm afraid you have the taste for alcohol."

241

"I, bosh, go on with you. As if I ever took too much. I know how to conduct myself," Toodles asserted, prone to be offended upon this point. She retired, and soon returned with a full cocktail shaker.

"One of Toodles' own cocktails; she knows how to make them, doesn't she, my boys?" she bubbled, setting one cocktail upon the piano before Allen, and handing one to Eddie.

The cocktails downed, Toodles wanted Allen to play dance music, so that she and Eddie could dance. "There's no debutante that can dance better than your Toodles, is there Eddie? I am light as a feather to dance with, aren't I; get the rhythm of jazz steps? That's all there is to it, but I have such a feeling for music. My soul just sings and dances." Toodles prattled and danced closely to Eddie. "If only you could play so dear Allen would have a chance to dance too."

Ceasing to dance Toodles went to stand back of Allen. "You do love your Toodles, don't you Allen? We two understand each other; both of us are just children in our hearts, and music is such a bond. We aren't serious and gloomy like Eddie, are we?"

At a quarter to eight Madame Cavallera came into the room, and after her a slender young woman who was introduced as Mrs. York and who looked Javanese. Her slight figure was dressed in a long, clinging, apricot-white dress that fell in Grecian lines from her shoulders to her ankles.

"Well, Toodles," Madame Cavallera said suggestively.

"I know, I know—well maybe—the General won't be up, will he? Look and see. All right then, we'll all just slip out into the kitchen and have one tiny cocktail before dinner. But don't you tell on me."

"Yes," Madame Cavallera argued, "I've been working hard all day, and a little drink lets one talk so much more freely at dinner. Now that the boys are staying, and that we'll have dancing after dinner, we might as well do what we can to be gay."

Mrs. Green, a blond woman with intelligent blue eyes, and a sensual mouth, came into Toodles' room, and slumped her well-made body into a chair in a way that emphasized the animal quality of her being. "Hoh," she exclaimed resentfully, "this beastly climate. I *am* so bored," accenting her words with middle class English intonations. "I *do* so want some excitement. It's extraordinary how dull days can be."

Soon Toodles had six cocktails prepared, and saw to it that the two young men got double sized ones; whereupon, after the cocktails were drunk, it was time to descend to the dining room to eat, which was done in a gay procession, with Toodles confiding to Madame Cavallera what a noble woman she thought her. She diverted her remarks then to Edward, saying:

"Such a brave woman as Madame Cavallera is—and if you only knew who she is the daughter of—but she manages all this house, and has to keep the General in spirits besides, as he becomes depressed so easily. There's not littleness in her, I can tell you, and," she lowered her voice to a whisper, "let me tell you, she's very attractive to men, even if she is a plain woman, and I'm sure she has her affairs on the side. She's no prude."

The General sat at the head of the table, a tall, slender man, with a well-made head, and fine features that betrayed, however, a tendency to neuroticism. He apparently was worried this evening, because he talked little, except to parry Toodles' patter. Mrs. York sat with precise dignity, like a Javanese statuette; Mrs. Green ate silently, evidently annoyed by Toodles' constant prattle. Madame Cavallera, at the foot of the table, helped carry on the general conversation, or talked aside to either Allen Cowles or Eddie Campbell, who sat on either side of her, the former next to Toodles. It was difficult for there to be any conversation except that of, or directed by, Toodles, who was persistently playful, and who indubitably possessed the greatest facile energy and vivacity, to pun, prattle, coquette, and essay childish paradoxes.

"Of course she's never touched life," Madame Cavallera said in a low voice to Eddie, "and one must hide one's impatience at her eternal need to be amused however inopportune the moment may be to oneself. Certainly she doesn't possess enough imagination to understand that, dear and kind as she can be, she's obtuse about other people's suffering."

"That's not a bad thing at times, is it, because it might make

243

the other person less intent upon his or her emotion. But she can wear a being down. How you must want rest from Toodles at moments!" he responded.

Mrs. York spoke in a lowtoned voice of strange timbre and vibrance, coming from so slight a being. The quality of her voice carried with it a significance that her words had nothing to do with. "I ran into Mrs. Rice this afternoon, Toodles, and she said she and her husband would drop in on you after dinner, so it is nice that Mr. Cowles is here to play music for us all."

"Isn't that lovely? You boys will just adore Mrs. Rice. She's a famous beauty—and Thomas Rice too—how I love both of them, and they think the world of their Toodles too. But everybody likes Toodles. She's never done harm to anyone, and she so likes making people happy, doesn't she?" Toodles chattered.

"You say how we all love you so often for us, Toodles, that we have no need to tell you," Mrs. York commented.

"How nasty of you," Toodles exclaimed, woundedly pouting.

"No, no, Toodles, you really know I did not mean it that way," Mrs. York responded with direct naïveness.

Dinner over, Toodles went to her drawing room with the two young men, inviting all of the others who wished to come with her. There she gaily rolled up the rugs so there could be easier dancing, while Allen played. Her maid brought in two liqueur bottles, one of cognac, one of benedictine, and Toodles sympathetically saw that Allen, at least, had a liqueur.

"If he's to play we must reward him, mustn't we? I see that my boys aren't neglected."

Mrs. Green came into the room, and seated herself on a double seat with Edward Campbell. Observing Toodles she commented acidly, "She's too obvious, really you know. Did you notice how she looked at me? She likes me in the daytime when she wants companionship, but not at night when any men are about. She must have all the attention."

"Yes, but there's no far reaching design in any of her dislikes. She's made by each moment's emotion."

"So I am too, for that matter. I'm so pent up in this atmosphere of old women, and with worry about money to keep up appearances. Of course if it weren't for Toodles and her money, and the people she brings here, the General and Madame Cavallera would be completely on the rocks, and it all bears down upon Madame because the General is a fussy old maid, pinpicking at everything. I help run things you know, to pay for part of my keep. I do wish my husband would get his leave—he's in the army—and we would get off to Egypt where we intend to settle."

Mr. and Mrs. Rice arrived, and soon Mr. Rice was leading arguments into the conversation. Irritatedly Madame Cavallera moved away from him and came to sit near Mrs. Green and Edward.

"How cross Mr. Rice can make me! He deliberately chooses his subjects to antagonize one. I will not listen to him when he scoffs at patriotism, decries England, and praises the spectacle which the German Kaiser made of imperialism. Mrs. Rice too, whom I so like for herself, and who is lovely to look at, is a nuisance with her assents to his pretentious triteness. I had thought she was an intelligent woman, but she's lived with him for eight years and still thinks 'Thomas is so original.' Utter rot, that," Madame Cavallera asserted.

Mrs. Rice sat languidly in an easy chair. Her long body was clad in a blue Chinese-fashioned robe. Upon her ears she wore large-sized blue earrings; these and her blue gown emphasized the blueness of her eyes, and possibly accented the perfection of her profile. Viewed full face she was not so perfect, as her lips were overheavy, and there was not sufficient firmness to the oval of her face.

"Aristocracy seems to be a past concept in this age," she was drawling at one moment. "It puts me out, when I remember a state parade I saw in Berlin under the Kaiser's regime—when Thomas and I had just been married. It was magnificently stageset. The common people should certainly have been happy to have someone ruling them who had such a sense of statecraft and stagecraft.

"This modern generation!" Mr. Rice exploded vehemently. "As if all the vulgarity, the modern improvements, and the cheapness of democracy were anything new to the world! What is most disgusting too is talk about science, the degradation of a civilization. What we need are a few emotional geniuses who illuminate the subconscious, and know what the throes of inspiration mean. I'm a snob. We're all snobs. Healthy snobbisms are good for the world. Some men are made to serve, and some are made aristocratic. I don't want my servants becoming chummy with me."

"All one asks," Eddie Campbell broke in, feeling that he was of the generation Mr. Rice deemed modern, "is that aristocrats be aristocratic. Too many imbeciles, degenerates, and obtuse individuals come in the wake of old families and wealth to think that either of them form a good basis by which to judge aristocracy. I can't think of a way in which the lines between classes can be so strictly marked as you wish to make them. After all, it's only a matter of what's interesting, and neither class nor wealth are that in themselves, while intelligence, and ability to produce, are. And perhaps beings who possess intelligence don't emerge solely, or even often, from what you call the aristocratic classes."

"But it takes the aristocrats to subsidize and patronize them; to recognize them."

"That's it; they don't want to be patronized, and resent needing to depend upon patronizing subsidies. And also the willingness to subsidize doesn't often occur. Aristocrats devote their attentions to themselves, and to getting acclaim for themselves that they haven't earned."

"The proofs are earlier civilizations, where class lines were distinctly drawn, and which produced great works of art—"

"That's an involved discussion, isn't it, and doesn't take into account modern and scientific improvements, which, whether we like them or not, have occurred, and which we don't eradicate by disapproving of."

"You say then you like this present social order; this revolting, money-grabbing, psychoanalyzing, disrespecting of our wives and mothers, system. I tell you this is the vilest age that has ever existed on the face of the earth."

246

"I wouldn't be surprised; still there was Sodom and Gomorrah, Rome under Nero, and others we don't know too much about. The Aztec race lived through a civilization about as flagrant and barbaric. I can't judge social orders, but can feel that one has to do what's possible in the time one happens to be born. Emotion doesn't turn the clock back to the hour we want it; it's more apt to turn it only to fanaticism."

Mr. Rice was getting redder in the face where it could be seen around his sideburns, and above his whiskers. His smokey-blue eyes concentrated into intense gleams; he moved his chair nearer, and then away, nearer and then away, from the man he was speaking to, in a nervous anxiety of antagonzied vanity. The discussion went on for a few minutes, and Mr. Rice condemned names which he obviously had never heard before, painters, musicians, writers, brought into the discussion by Edward in trying to indicate that even this age could let one hope a little.

"I tell you, all the times do to me is drive me into my country home, and make me wish to see nobody but my lovely wife—and my children—my son, who, I tell you, I'm bringing up to be the president of the United States so that this damnable, filthy, democratic idea will be done away with."

"You are driven? Perhaps if you're driven enough you'll be driven to meditation, even the kind that produced the sort of cryptic wisdom you say you find in old Chinese art; or the enigmatic quality of removal from temporal experience that the Egyptians possessed. Perhaps that's the answer; if one is driven enough one quits storming about today and the things in it that change overnight, and becomes either a producer or a philosopher."

Toodles had listened to this argument all she could. She feared that her younger guest, one of her boys, was being rude to Mr. Rice, but she was unable for several minutes to break in, so ferociously had the two talked in each other's faces. Toodles did not understand what was being said, but she did understand that it was not about her, and that it was not the sort of thing that was socially gracious and easy. Finally, at loss to know what to do, she whispered to Allen to start playing.

247

"Now, now, we've had enough of profound talk, and little Toodles is going to sing you a song and then we'll dance."

The evening had begun to tire Toodles. Her bad eye took on a more crooked expression than it had had earlier in the evening. It could even have been thought that Toodles had drunk too many cocktails, and perhaps a liqueur or so, unnoticed during the discussion. Standing by the piano she waited till Allen began to play *La Bohème*, whereupon, she assumed an operatic pose, hand over heart, other hand uplifted, feet sprawled a little apart, and started to sing, rolling her eyes, she believed, seductively, and swaying her plump torso for the same effect. The first moment or so Mr. Rice was fidgety in his seat. However his emotions began to quell; his courtesy re-asserted itself, and he listened politely as Mrs. Dawson—he never called her Toodles—sang. When she had finished there was applause and exclamations of approval.

"Bravo, Toodles. There's nothing Toodles can't do, is there?" the General commented, facetiously.

"You're in such wonderful spirits tonight, Toodles," Madame Cavallera stated. "It's a joy seeing one who can be so eternally young and irrepressible as you. Such energy, you dear thing."

"Dance music, Allen, your little Toodles wants to dance," Mrs. Dawson requested. "And Mr. Rice is going to dance with me. Give us something soulful. You do like to dance with me, don't you Thomas?" with an amorous gesture.

Mr. Rice arose gravely as the music began, and circled with slow steps about Toodles who was cavorting around the room tossing her arms, and swaying in a way meant to be willowy. No one could accuse Toodles of self-consciousness. Mainly she danced alone, but at times she would face Mr. Rice, and lean towards him sirenly, lifting her plump, birdlike, face, with its crooked eye. As she thrust out arms in invitation she turned, upon his response, immediately coy, as Toodles again danced the dance of the pursued nymph. Long before she, Mr. Rice was exhausted as well as ill at ease, commenting in a whisper to his wife that, "Mrs. Dawson is making a display of herself, and she's a grandmother, but she puts all the sen-

248

sual desire of her nature into her wriggles."

Ten o'clock came and Mr. and Mrs. Rice made their departure. The General retired; Madame Cavallera took herself off having first had a whisky and soda; Mrs. York too, bid a quiet goodnight to the others. No sooner had she left the room than Toodles said.

"Did you notice that somebody looks—don't say I said so— as though she had nigger blood."

"Do you mean Mrs. York?" Allen asked.

"Don't repeat it; but nothing much is known about her. She came from New Orleans, and doesn't seem to want to to talk about her family. The poor little thing married a man much older than herself. She mentions her mother, but never her father. When that old man, her husband, died, and left her hardly anything, she came over here. My son almost married her, but he stopped that when I suggested to him that she might have—of course it may not be true—she's a dear little thing too. And she seems to love being about me, but everybody loves Toodles."

Edward, sitting with Mrs. Green, having heard this, asked her about it, and she answered.

"It may be the case but she obviously is well bred."

"Certainly that, and lovely in a porcelain statuette way. She must sense that people believe that Negro blood story, or probably she thinks it is true herself. There's a restrained tragic quality about her. As I talked to her a few minutes this evening her attitudes struck me like those of a quaintly romantic boarding school girl. Toodles hadn't ought to start that story. She might let people discern it and think it for themselves."

"Not Toodles. Mrs. York is too attractive for that. Several men have been quite taken with her, and she needs marriage as she has almost no money, and there's nothing she can do."

"Many men who'd marry her wouldn't want children either, but the snobs in this part of the world wouldn't pass up a thought like that. It's too bad."

Toodles was leaning on the piano whispering to Allen in an affectionate manner. "We'd better go out on the balcony and let Toodles and Allen have the room to themselves," Mrs. Green suggested. "She ought to be told not to show so clearly what she wants."

On the balcony Mrs. Green stood looking into the night beside Edward, whom she finally leaned against. He put his arm about her, asking her if she was cold.

"Oh no, not that, not that. But—Oh, I'm going to make a bloody fool of myself—but—I want you—I must control myself," in speaking she bit her lip, and turned her head desirously to be kissed. He kissed her.

"Have me then," he answered. "Should we go for a walk, or can you take me to your room?"

"I wouldn't dare; everybody in the house would know about it. Oh I am a bloody fool. I hate my husband. I hate my life. Why am I here, wanting money, and that woman in there has so much she can tear it up? I want you. I'll throw myself over rock-end if I can't have an experience soon."

"Nonsense; you can have me, for tonight, if that is enough. Walk back to my room with me. You can be back here and in through your window by five, or six, if that's before anybody else gets up."

"I can't. I can't. I'm a fool. I can't make you understand why I can't. I hate my husband. Why did I ever marry him?" As she spoke she twisted herself about writhingly in his arms, and brushed her hand nervously across her forehead and through her hair, loosening it.

"Yes, you are being foolish. You're perhaps right not to have me because I have no particular passion for you, and wouldn't want to make things difficult if you'd try to make more of me than a passing episode."

"O I wouldn't; I wouldn't. I could make you care, I know I could make you happy for a few minutes anyway; for several times. But—I can't—I can't."

"If you can't then—"

"But you had not ought to listen to me. You should go right ahead, you know."

"Come on; we'll go out for a walk."

As they went through the room Edward noticed that Toodles and Allen were not there. He concluded that they'd gone to the kitchenette to have a drink. Standing for a moment before the fireplace he heard Toodles whispering huskily.

"Don't go, Allen. Don't go home tonight. My boy. My boy. Stay with Toodles."

"No, no, I can't," Allen answered in a pettish voice. "You don't mean that to me."

"Don't go, Allen. Don't go."

Allen's answer was in a weakening voice, pettish yet.

Mrs. Green came to the door, and she and Edward went downstairs together. "The age is never by I take it," Edward said to her. "I suppose you heard what I did."

"I wonder—do I strike men like that?"

"Um—Oh no—well, what if you do if you get what you want?"

Going to her room Mrs. Green got a shawl to throw over her shoulders, and reappeared, tiptoeing. She put her fingers to her lips, and indicated that Edward should come through her room.

"We can step out of the window and go out. I daren't let you stay there because the General's and Madame's room is next."

"Would they mind?"

"No, not she anyway, but he—one can't judge. He'd disapprove, and I can't stand his prying into my affairs."

The Highly Prized Pajamas

GIRLS SUCH AS YOLAND USED to be called of the half-world, though it can not be explained why their world is more half than the world of aristocrats, workers, or the bourgeois, few of whom take so much into the range of their experience as Yoland did.

She was about the Latin and Montparnasse quarters for two years before people commented upon her archaic Greek beauty. I associated her with a type of low-class *poule*, who without mind and abandoned, soon grows bloated and ugly and disappears. One may hear of them as dying of consumption back in little villages, on farms; or one may forget to remember if they are mentioned. Integral a part as they are of the French social organism, no one, or one year's crop of them, is essential. Each season brings its new recruits.

Yoland went about with Andra, of young pig-faced charms, and Arlette, who, darkly striking, soon disintegrated into bovine aspects and was soddenly drunk nightly until she became consumptive and disappeared. Any of the three was apt to be in some bar at any time of day, from noon till five in the morning. There was little outward evidence that they were plying their trade. However, they had money to drink on, dressed well, and rather than gold-dig off foreigners they were inclined to gather in flocks with others of their kind. Their laughter taunted like that of so many hyenas as they sat before their drinks, jeering and laughing at the strange habits of foreigners.

Seated in the Parnasse bar, which was empty but for Jimmie, the barman, I was having a sandwich and a beer when I noticed a copy of Proust's *Sodome et Gomorrhe* on the table next to mine. I picked it up to scan and Yoland came from the ladies' room to stand waiting for me to hand her the book. I was surprised that a girl of her sort should be reading that, so I asked her to have a drink. She would, and sat down. When I asked if she liked to read she crackled a dry, inhuman laugh, unlubricatedly metallic. Mechanically the laugh had cuteness.

"I don't like sentimental things. Sometimes I read. This," she indicated the book, "is of things we all know if we aren't stupid. The author I wouldn't like," her rusty crackle of laughter sounded, "but he wouldn't like me. He liked only men. His heroine is a man he has made a woman in the book, but I like his manner."

It occurred to me that I'd underrated Yoland's perceptions considerably. We chatted, but she had no intention of telling much about herself to a stranger. Thoughts of her past apparently irritated her. She did say that until she was thirty or no longer good-looking she would live a life of freedom, abandon, if people wanted to call it that. She didn't want marriage, or family life, and why should she give up freedom to become settled or a woman of the home? She knew when young more than she wanted to know of these things.

As we sat, a photographer who liked doing studies of unusual looking people came into the place. I asked him to sit with us, and said, as Yoland did not understand English, "Have you ever noticed how beautiful Yoland is? A more perfect and delicate profile doesn't exist, and her eyelashes are really long and black. It isn't *maquillage*."

Her teeth too were straight, not too small, and glistening white, and her eyes large, and softly grey if one didn't detect that their softness was no evidence of a tender nature. The photographer, as we sat analyzing her perfections, agreed, and asked her if she would pose for him.

"My body is not good," she said finally, assuming at once that he meant for her to pose in the nude. "I have more than enough breast, and my waist is not subtle."

When assured that he wanted to photograph her face, three-quarters or profile, she agreed, and said she often made money posing for romance photographs one can buy in postcard shops. The idea amused her; she mimicked sweet young love poses she had taken for these pictures. Incidentally she appraised the photographer with her soft gaze, not assuming that he wished too to make love with her, but she informed me later, to judge whether she was willing if it came to that, and whether he was another man who pretended he wanted her as a model when he had other intentions. With such, she declared, she was ruthless.

The photographer left and Yoland's cute, unhuman laugh creaked after him. It struck her as droll that he should want to photograph her when she had posed for so many sentimental postcards which sell as a joke or to simple-minded people. "You know his friend, that dirty old man with white hair who would be droll if he was a Negro?" she asked, chortling, menacingly this time. "He asked me to pose for him, and they say he is famous. I believed he wanted a model. He showed me screens and pictures," she shrugged her shoulders. "I didn't care for them. He was to pay me two hundred francs for the afternoon. But the foolish old man thought he could make love to me too. I was cold and said 'no' and meant no, but he battled with me. Then I showed him my nails, on this hand." The nails on her hands were long and sharply pointed. "I can handle them when they get difficult. I would have torn the skin off his face, and then I said, 'You give me two thousand francs, and I will go. I won't pose for you. Without the two thousand francs, now I will tear your face, and call the police.' Never before have I done that. I don't like that sort of thing, but if he thought he could be brutal to me I would show him."

Yoland didn't need to inform me that she was hard. She wasn't apache class, but she had many of the tricks. I'd seen her break a glass and threaten to thrust its broken rim into the face of a man who annoyed her; and had heard her quarrelling with some girl she did not like. Then she had been aflame with cold menace.

Yoland evidently decided that she liked me, as a comrade, though she didn't like Americans generally. She wasn't flattered by my remarking on her beauty; she rather wondered why I commented on it now, when we had seen each other about for over a year. Just now she had the idea that she was making me think her cruel, and said, "I am *sensible* with those having emotions and sensibility, but usually I find little use for sentiment in this life."

"Independence of spirit is a quality I like too," I told her.

Her unlubricated rusty laugh chortled and she looked at me mockingly. "Ah, yes, you are independent, but as a passion."

Her remark struck home, and I hoped that one more clear realization of needless lack of detachment had functioned into my emotions.

After this she and I were comrades whenever we met and hadn't more intimate friends with us; we sat together and chatted pleasantly, without inquiring into each other intimately. Yoland drank copiously, and stayed up most nights till five o'clock. Her laughter mingled with that of other girls to make hyena noises. She threw glasses, cursed out the *patrons* and *patronnes* of bars and restaurants, and she was not unique in doing these things. However, she began to dress better, and people were soon commenting on her beauty. It was when she came forth in a pepper-red coat and dress, wearing a hat made of shiny black cock feathers that curled above her forehead and about her ears, that her profile stood out luminously white and perfect. Her teeth, when she smiled, were the perfection of dentifrice and glistening beauty; and her deep grey eyes glowed, but were aware people knew that their glow came from the dilation of drugs rather than from emotion stirring within her. In the emotion of anger they flashed hatred as she glared through her narrowed lids.

Yoland had, as had many others, fought with so many of the *gerantes* in the various cafés and bars in Montparnasse that she was a well known figure to the police. When a small and stuffily cozy bar opened near the Jardin du Luxembourg she changed her rendezvous spot; so did many old-time Quarterites, to follow Jimmie the barman, who went to work there. Jimmie, a Liverpool Irishman, and an ex-prizefighter, was genial, tittered readily at the careless habits of his clients, was openhearted, and informed of the open-secret lives, amorous and financial, of about everyone in the Quarter. Eight years before this time he had arrived, naïf to Paris and full of alive curiosity. His first night he got drunk too, and seeing a fire-signalling box, banged it, and stood. Not then understanding French he didn't know what he had done. But the firemen arrived and wanted to know where the fire was. Jimmie didn't understand, but the police understood Jimmy, and he spent three weeks in the Prison de la Santé. When liquored up he was apt to remember his fighting days, and insist upon "protecting" friends he drank with. Sometimes his protection resulted in a night in jail for both Jimmie and his friend, but as the police took him with an ironic sense of comedy his sojourn with them was seldom overnight. When his blood pressure was too high from overeating and drinking, Jimmie had a habit of going to his room, banging his own nose so that it would bleed, and thereby reducing his blood pressure. Sometimes he would slit the lobes of his ears to lose more blood. In all, Jimmie suffered the pangs of loving and losing, and was a barman prone to understand the habits and attitudes of his clients in all their various types of drunk-ons.

In the New Bar Yoland collected an Argentinian lover. She wasn't attracted to him, but he persisted; he was wealthy; he gave her expensive clothes and jewelry; he gave her money, paid her apartment rent, and submitted to her tempers, so she accepted him for a time. He, José, was a thin, fidgety man, given to drinking vast quantities of pernod, but he seldom ate. When intoxicated he wanted to dance, and humped epileptically about the room, singing. The song was always the same. "Toreador, Toreador." His rendition was one apt to irritate anybody, let alone a nervous person. It surely irritated Yoland and one night José found himself sitting on the floor with a sore jaw. He'd sung one "Toreador" too many and Yoland slammed him. From then on she was apt to beat him up nightly, until it was a bar joke and comic even to Yoland. As fist-hits from her seemed only to please José, she took to scratching his face with her lengthy fingernails. The Madame of the bar would take him upstairs, put plasters on his face, and José came down ready for more punishment from his ladylove.

It became too much for Yoland, however, He bored her; he drove her wild; she crashed a broken glass into his face one night, tore from her neck an expensive pearl necklace he had given her, threw it at him, and departed. José was disconsolate, but as Yoland was not to be located for several weeks he moved elsewhere, and was out of her life. She, hearing of this, began again to make the bar her nightly rendezvous. She stayed in the hotel above. Madame Camille, thinking that Yoland would find José when she needed money badly, permitted her bill to mount, but when she argued that some amount of the bill should be paid, there was a violent quarrel. Madame Camille indiscreetly suggested that it was like stealing not to pay one's bill.

"You dirty cow," Yoland spit at her. "I am not a thief. That remark you will pay for," and a series of glasses flew in Madame Camille's direction. She hid behind the counter, too afraid to say she would call the police. Yoland, highly insulted, stopped her when she tried to make a placatory remark, for Madame Camille knew she'd never get money if she stayed enraged.

"Madame Camille," Yoland said frozen with hauteur, "I will not dispute further with you. You are a woman without education or breeding." At this she went out and took a taxi to haunts in another part of town. She was not seen about the Quarter for several months, and when she returned it appeared that she was amply provided for from the elegant clothes she sported.

Seated at the Dome bar one afternoon Yoland chatted amiably, when Madame Camille appeared with a look of insecure triumph on her face. At last she had found Yoland and might collect what was owing her. Yoland was frigidly courteous, but Madame Camille got nowhere with her. She did finally get an address, however, and went away, saying that she would call on Yoland to collect.

Yoland's eyes were stony black with rage. "She calls me a thief. Ha, ha, ha, ha," her menacing laugh rattled deathbones. "I did not give her my address. I gave her the address of my friend, and he will break her face in if she comes."

Yoland passed through a period of being *"une femme sérieuse"* while she lived with a wealthy Egyptian for several months, and she confided that at last she had found the race which knows how to make love. Before, love-making had been more or less of a bore to her. However, the Egyptian left, and she then lived with a forty-year-old Polish man, who, to my amazement, Yoland permitted to strike her in the face without her using either fingernails or broken glasses on him. Later she said that he was irrational. He was very gentle, but when he drank much he went crazy because of shell shock. "It is not me he hits at. It is a crazy something he sees," she said, and shrugged her shoulder, thinking me foolish to suppose she'd mind being beaten up under such circumstances. Could one fight back at a crazy man? He gave her a squirrel coat and various pieces of jewelry; and their romance was either successful or not, in that Yoland never got to the point of doing him physical damage. He, however, departed after some months, and Yoland was again about the Quarter daily. She now did only the better-class bars, and came into them generally alone. Andra, her pig-faced ex-friend, was about, and a very successful bourgeoise *poule*, but to none of her two-year-ago girl friends did Yoland pay any attention. She wasn't curt. She had decided that what amused them in life didn't amuse her, and she, instead of having lost her looks, was more elegantly and glisten-

ingly beautiful than ever. Her pallor glowed; her teeth had a diamond sparkle, and she had learned what a hat and a color could
do to give her beauty a setting. Nevertheless before long she
was hard up. She'd grown more definite and positive in her
tastes. I wondered if she was calming down and yearning for a
settled and secure circumstance.

2

I found one day waiting for me a letter from Arthur Stout,
who had been given my address by a friend. He had no reason
to look me up except that he did not know Paris and I might tell
him what to see and what to avoid. Also he understood that I
was the friend of a psychoanalyst and interested in the subject
myself, and as he had a deep affection (platonic, of course) for
a woman who did not care for men he would like to talk to
somebody more worldy than himself. A book-lover and scien-
tist, he hadn't sampled any variety of life.

One gets used, in Paris, to having acquaintances and friends
of friends think of residents as convenient guides and hosts,
and I felt no inclination to conduct this unknown Mr. Stout to
sights and other places I'd seen or didn't care to bother about.
However, liking the man who'd given him my address, I
dropped a note saying that he would be apt to locate me at the
Coupole bar at aperitif hour almost any night. My morning letter reached him that day, for when I went into the Coupole the
barman told me that the gentleman in the corner had inquired
for me.

Stout presented himself and offered me a drink. He was
quiet-looking, and I understood at once that it is hard for a man
not speaking French to get around in Paris at first, and Stout
confessed that he had only one week before sailing back to
America. "And I have three thousand dollars with me and don't
care if I spend it all. There's more where it came from. I rather
gathered from Morris (our friend) that you'd be the chap to
locate an attractive sort of girl to keep me company when I'm
at loose ends. In any case, whenever you or any of your friends

are with me, all the bills for eating or drinking are mine."

I didn't jump off the barstool and run outside to blow the fire whistle, but certainly during the course of the evening I let various regulars of the always-broke quota know what had come upon us. It seemed cruel on Mr. Stout, but Morris should too have informed him that Montparnasse, where deadbeating is an art, is no place where he need make an offer such as the foregoing.

Mr. Stout said that he'd just come from the Riviera where he had read Frank Harris' *Life and Loves*. As I'd never more than glanced at the book, and then not to be interested, excited, or amused, we couldn't go far into that subject. Next Stout spoke of a cellar where Verlaine, Baudelaire, and others had once sat in discussion while drinking absinthe. He spoke of Dr. Hirschfield of Berlin, of sexual variants, and asked, reticently, what curious places there were to visit in Paris. Not too decisively I concluded that he was in search of subtle, aromatic vice, as imagined through literary gleanings. He obviously was a small-town product, and showing me his notebook of addresses such as college boys, Legionnaires, and businessmen collect, he wanted me to tell him about the various places. As most of them were of *bourdelles* where people go to see poses, or for mass promiscuity—mainly for tourists—his interest lapsed, so I told him of more exotic places. He looked only mildly physical and sensuous, and his manner was slowly kind. It was probable, I thought, that he was merely sentimental and afraid that he was missing experience in life. Again he spoke of wanting a girl, and an aware, worldly girl, with intelligence.

Yoland came into the Coupole and spoke to me as she seated herself at the end of the bar. She smiled enigmatically. I concluded she had been taking heroin or opium, because though her smile seemed directed at me I knew she wasn't even looking at me. But her gleaming teeth glistened blue-white between her lips incarnadine, and as she turned to arrange her jet locks beneath her hat her clear profile gleamed white against the shiny shadow on the mirror.

"Who is that girl?" Stout asked, and there was tensity in his curiosity now, where before he had been merely casual.

260

I concluded that Yoland was a good answer for him.

At my suggestion Yoland came over to drink with us, and Stout admired the crystal clarity of her skin, and the modelled perfection of her facial contours. He couldn't speak much French, and I had to translate between them. Yoland noted Stout's admiration and looked at me to chortle a low metallic crackle. I told her that he found her grey eyes lovely, faunlike, and tender, that he was sure she had a sweet and tender nature. She chortled cutely again, and her long eyelashes swept down over her drug-dilated eyes which had such liquid beauty. I suggested to Stout that he'd better not be too moved by Yoland, to listen to her laugh as much as he believed the mysterious glow in her eyes. He was appearing altogether too much the small-town man in middling years wanting to break loose, and if Yoland had been taking drugs, she might get him into some row that he couldn't handle. I had no intention of spending the evening with them. Every warning I might give Stout, however, but further interested him in Yoland.

"I know by her face that she has an old soul," Stout said. "I don't go in for reincarnation, but I knew when you came into the bar that you have an old soul too. I knew it was you before you spoke though nobody had ever described you."

His talk would sometimes have made me uncomfortable, but I felt easy, knowing that soon the night aperitif crowds would be filling the place. I told Yoland that Stout wanted me to tell her that she was beautiful, and she merely rattled her machine laugh, knowing that she was so, and that I knew the matter didn't much interest her since so many people who liked her beauty irritated her.

"He likes you very much," I translated.

She asked, "He is rich?"

"Enough. He's ready to spend quite a sum of money while he's in Paris. He wants you to have dinner with him."

"Very well. I need a new coat, and dresses. I'm disgusted with the clothes that dirty pig José bought me. If he would see me in them he might still think he could come and speak to me." She observed Stout with a sidewise glance. He was charmed.

"He is nice. He is sentimental, but that does no harm for a few days, since he goes in a week," she concluded.

Stout took her hand to kiss, and wanted me to tell her that it was an aristocrat's hand, that he knew she had lived before. She leaned towards him and straightened his coat collar with a caressing pat, and looked at me again to chortle dry rattling laughter.

"I love her laugh," Stout said. "You say she is Basque? They are a race thousands of years old. She has lived many times before. Her laugh is cleared of emotions."

"Go careful on her temper though. See her fingernails. She keeps those on the right hand long and pointed to tear strips off a person's face when she's in a fight. Well-kept hands and nails are fairly general with French girls."

"Ask her why she has never married, if she intends to marry. Say she is too beautiful to live this kind of life."

"She might resent it. She is not given to thinking of herself as a lost soul. But I'll ask her about the marriage part."

"I want liberty," Yoland said curtly, and relaxed a little. "I don't love love if it binds me. What would there be for me to do if I was married?" She left us for a few minutes and when she returned the pupils of her eyes were huge black; she had put on more *maquillage* too, and looked smarter because her black hair was sleekly peeping from under the rim of black cock feathers on her hat. Quickly she saw that I noticed this, and crackled a laugh that came out in sharp hard spurts of metallic sound. Her glance agreed that it was funny that she should be acting coquettish because she saw that the simple, sentimental Stout expected that of her. She wondered at me too, that I asked her questions about her life, her family, and her first experience in love. Although she knew I was merely translating for Stout she didn't connect that type of question with me. She, however, answered, since she knew me well enough for two years past.

"He thinks that he will be serious with me," she jeered, cutely taunting. "When I was fourteen, I was seduced by a woman. Women didn't and don't interest me, but no matter. Soon after I seduced my seventeen-year-old boy cousin. And before either—" she hesitated before she decided to say the last, "I had known my father that way since I was twelve. In every case I was willing."

"And your mother?" I asked, having translated her remarks to Stout.

"My mother? I don't know. A country woman. She was not a wife. My father's family took me. He said I was mature and beautiful at twelve. At fifteen I was disgusted with my town and my father's home. He was old; he handled me. I didn't hate him, but I didn't want him, so I went away with an older woman and she wanted me to become a coiffeuse." Yoland laughed, harshly disdainful. "Me, a coiffeuse! I did not like small villages and I do not like people enough to fuss over old women's hair. Always I intended to come to Paris, to be free, and abandoned if I liked. You may tell him I am sufficiently well educated. My father has money and would send it to me but I want nothing more to do with that old man. I know life is nothing. Never have I expected anything of life. For me it is amusing only to be in bars and cabarets and with people who pretend no class."

"Let me read your hand?" I said, lightly curious.

"No, no," she answered, with a quick hardness, drawing her hand away. It was the first evidence of anything noncynical or superstitious I had detected in her. "Why should I be curious about my future? I take what comes and will always do so." Again she said that at thirty, or if she lost her looks or health, she might consider marriage, but that was eight years to wait yet.

"She is damned quick," Stout admired her. "The old race knowledge. She has lived before. It's my luck to fall for girls who like their own sex, I guess." His mild Teutonish face had a pleased expression. "She likes me, though. I don't know why." Yoland responded easily as he stroked her arms, and she smiled her glistening, mechanically glamorous smile, into his eyes, he thought, but she was looking at Andra too, with whom she had taken up anew in the last few days while she had been in financial difficulties. If she drank she might get rid of Stout and go away with Andra who had some attraction for her. Possibly the young pig-faced Andra took drugs with her.

Stout was evidently hoping that he was the man to awaken a soul in this girl, and as that is a hope aged with tradition I was glad that Yoland and Stout were holding hands and no longer asked me to translate back and forth. Other poeple came into the bar, among them four men I knew well, and with them I was wandering off to dine when Stout reminded me that I and all my friends were to be his guests if we wished. We waited, and had more drinks. Sporty, the hearty, hardy, and more generally used girl of the Quarter, came in, and she too joined us, and we all went to L'Avenue for dinner.

As Stout and Yoland kept gazing at each other Sporty engrossed the interest of the other five men. She told Groen-lun that she would pose for him for nothing, but her face, he could see, was battered. She had been drunk three nights before and had fallen downstairs onto her face. But her body was not cut. No, no lover had beaten her this time. Later she confided to the party's youngest man that she knew a very rich man who liked boys, and who liked her too. "We will sleep three, non?" she asked the boy with generous hope.

The boy looked shy and indicated that he was not interested. "You no like?" Sporty accepted his rebuff with three of her ten words of English. "No go. Hello, goodbye then." She had as usual done her best to arrange things so that as many people as possible could enjoy themselves in this human world of ours, but with her sweet peasant sympathy for all desires, she understood not wanting everybody too. She decided to leave us, and as she was Sporty, with catholic tastes, she was sure to find company for the evening.

With her departure we others left Yoland and Stout together, as Yoland wanted to go to La Cloche. by eleven o'clock they came back to La Coupole, however, and came up to me. Yoland was laughing her unlubricated laugh, steadily now as she was intoxicated. The jeer and taunt in her weird laugh wasn't at anybody in particular so much as it was at everybody, at fate, at the world.

"My little girl nearly got me into a jam," Stout told me proudly. "As we were leaving La Cloche in a taxi a girl tried to take her. I was afraid she would go, but the three of us went to a small bar. An Argentinian was there. I didn't understand the quarrel, but Yoland smashed a glass in his face. The Madame fought with her too, but she started to scratch the Madame's face. She just came away at the sight of the police. We slipped out a side door."

"It's good you slipped away. That Madame is after her. Probably the police have a silent sympathy for her though, and weren't as bright-eyed as they might be," I said, and asked Yoland her version of the story.

"That dirty cow, Madame Camille, calls me a thief. I decided to show her I wasn't afraid of visiting her place. She was sweet to me, saying that José would pay my bill. I told her José could do it, he meant nothing to me. And he tried to talk to me. When he sang 'Toreador' I told him to shut up, but he didn't. *Toreador*," she made her voice nasal and mimicked José's jerky way of singing. "He gave me disgust. He tried to kiss my hand when I was not in the mood, so I struck him with a glass. He bled. He will have scars for weeks."

"She'll kill that Argentinian some day," I said. "He is awful. He gave her syphilis, I think, but he did pay for her treatments afterwards. But she damned near killed him the night she discovered she was sick."

Stout was more sentimental about Yoland than ever now. She confided that he had given her five thousand francs and promised to give her more in the morning when he'd been at the bank. She laughed a warmer rusty chortle now and her clear face was carved above the blue-grey fur on her coat collar. She smiled sphinxly. "He is foolish. He nearly weeps that I don't talk love to him seriously."

When Stout disappeared into the washroom for a few minutes Yoland told another girl of his generosity, and they shrilly shrieked laughter. He was unbelievable to them. Yoland, however, was gentle to Stout when he returned, and they soon left for his hotel.

For six days they were about together. Each day Yoland arrived with a new outfit, a jewelled cigarette case, jewelled vanity box, bracelets, shoes, etc. And Stout continued not only willing but anxious to pay bills for people. Several times when I asked the barman what I owed he told me that Mr. Stout had paid.

At the end of the week Stout departed for America, and I didn't see Yoland for several days. Coming one night into the Dome bar I saw her at the end, seated with Andra, Sporty, and two other *poules*. They were having a hilarious time, and Yoland's voice was higher and more abandoned than usual. It shrieked, but rustily mechanical rather than human. Their jokes could not be heard because of the laughter, in spite of their being loudly spoken.

"Hello Yoland," I greeted her.

Her long lashes went over her grey eyes lizard fashion, and her head swayed towards me, brightly staring, and then it registered in her brain who I was. Whether only drunk, or both doped and drunk, I couldn't judge. She gave an inebriated rasp of laughter, and gasped out, "He wanted my photograph, but see," and showed me a cabinet-sized picture of herself. "He paid two thousand francs for a face that sells on postcards for five sous. He said he would send me money from Canada, whenever I need it. He wants me to write him and he'll have my letters translated. Ha, ha, ha, ha." There was no unkindness in her voice. It was simply ruthlessly unhuman, ironic, unbelieving.

"And he cried at the station, that man. He wished me to marry him but said he understood I wanted freedom. He would wait and if I ever wished I should write him and he would come for me. He is droll. A really sentimental man."

"I guess he finds small town life doesn't furnish enough exotic excitement," I said.

Andra made a remark that caused the other girls to shriek their shrill hyena laughter again. Yoland's cute crackling ripple sounded more subdued now, because she had laughed too much before at Andra's joke, or because she felt that I might resent their laughing so at a man I'd introduced.

"His pajamas," Andra sputtered, "his beautiful blue

pajamas!" She was overcome with mirth and held her hand over her heart.

"They were magnificent, they were blue, but he would not give them to me," Yoland explained, crackling. "I had worn them when I stayed with him. Instead he would give me a necklace, a bracelet, whatever I wished. But the pajamas he would keep, always, without washing, because I had worn them. He liked it that I cared for women. He was droll. What a *type*!"

ED LORUSSO *lives in Albuquerque, where he is a doctoral candidate at the University of New Mexico. He edited and introduced the UNM Press 1990 reprint of Robert McAlmon's* Village *and wrote the afterword for the facsimile reprint of* The One Who Is Legion *by Natalie Barney, reprinted in 1987 by the National Poetry Foundation, University of Maine. He plans to edit a second collection of short fiction by Robert McAlmon and is currently working on a novel based on McAlmon's life.*